The Good Provider

Young Kirsty and Craig – her childhood sweetheart – leave the remote hills of Ayrshire to seek their fortune in Glasgow. Their first home is a bleak boarding house and their 'marriage' a pretence. Struggling to make a living, Craig drifts into crime and Kirsty seeks solace with another man.

In *The Asking Price* – the second volume of Jessica Stirling's quartet – Craig and Kirsty's tenuous relationship is put still further to the test, despite their mutual love for their son Bobby.

Jessica Stirling was born in Glasgow, and has enjoyed a highly successful career as a writer. Her previous novels include those in the best-selling Stalker trilogy – *The Spoiled Earth*, *The Hiring Fair* and *The Dark Pasture*, and in the Beckman trilogy – *The Deep Well at Noon*, *The Blue Evening Gone* and *The Gates of Midnight*. In her recent novels, *Treasures on Earth*, *Creature Comforts* and *Hearts of Gold*, she returns to the starkly dramatic Scottish setting which made her earlier novels such a success.

*Also in Pan Books
by Jessica Stirling*

The Spoiled Earth
The Hiring Fair
The Dark Pasture

The Deep Well at Noon
The Blue Evening Gone
The Gates of Midnight

Treasures on Earth
Creature Comforts
Hearts of Gold

The Asking Price

Jessica Stirling

The Good Provider

Pan Books
London, Sydney and Auckland

First published 1988 by Hodder & Stoughton Ltd

This edition published 1989 by Pan Books Ltd,
Cavaye Place, London SW10 9PG

9 8

© Jessica Stirling 1988

ISBN 0 330 30182 9

Contents

ONE

The Promise

Nine sorts of weather, one for each parish, had whipped over Ayrshire in the course of that mad March day. Now, towards evening, the wind had backed northerly and great skirts of cloud hid the Carrick grazings and the autocratic hills of Galloway. Hail came hopping over the brow of the Straitons and swiftly engulfed the track that straggled up to Hawkhead farm at the head of the vale. Sheep turned tails to the stinging grains and moved to find shelter among broken dykes or in muddy scrapes under the lip of the hill. But the cattle, all lean and thrawn, roared defiance and stood their ground, refusing to be chased from the burn bank where new growth, mainly weed, gave them bite to supplement the mouldy hay that Clegg had flung out for them that morning.

For Kirsty Barnes there was no shelter. She trudged by the side of a huge Clydesdale horse with nothing but an old potato sack cowled over her head to give her protection. Winter, it seemed, was reluctant to yield to spring and Kirsty was ill-clad for such a changeable season. She had left Hawkhead bare-headed and had been soaked by a rain squall on the trail downhill to Bankhead Mains. Mr Sanderson had found her a towel to dry her hair and the potato sack to serve as a shawl on the long road home. Mrs Sanderson had filled her up with a bowl of mutton broth and hot buttered scones. For Kirsty there was always a kindly welcome at Bankhead; yet the Sandersons' generosity made her uneasy for usually the purpose of her visit was to scrounge a piece of tackle or the loan of a plough on behalf of her boss, Duncan Clegg.

Not for the first time Mr Sanderson had said, "Tell Clegg I'll expect a hire fee for the beast in future. If his horse is sick it's his own blessed fault. If he fed the poor brute it'd thrive and do the job for him. Will you tell him what I say, Kirsty?"

"I will, Mr Sanderson."

"By the look o' you, you could do wi' some fattenin' yourself, lassie."

"I'm fat enough as it is."

"Aye, you've a shape t' you now, right enough." Mr Sanderson had grinned. "I can understand why you've turned young Nicholson's head."

"Who says I have?"

"The lad told me hisself."

"Craig Nicholson's a daft loon."

Mr Sanderson had laughed, his warm brown eyes crinkling at the corners. "Ach, I'll spare your blushes, Kirsty. I was young m'self once, though you'd never think it to look at me now. Will I have to brush my lum hat for a weddin' soon?"

"Weddin'? Never."

"Would Craig Nicholson not be a good catch?"

"Craig will not be for me."

Mr Sanderson might have teased her further, but the reason why Craig would never be for her had dawned on the farmer at that moment. Tactfully he changed the subject. It was not that Kirsty would not have had Craig for a husband, but that the Nicholsons would not permit their first-born to court, let alone marry, a girl who had come from the Baird Home, a girl without a shred of pedigree or standing, though the Nicholsons themselves lived in a rented cottage that was only marginally better than Duncan Clegg's run-down dwelling.

Bankhead Mains was different. At the Mains there was an air of prosperity and endeavour. The *chug-chug-chug* of new steam-powered machinery from the long shed was the heartbeat of the place. If only she had been given out to the Sandersons and not to the Cleggs, how different her life might have been. But in 1889, when Kirsty, at ten, had been old enough for fostering, the Sandersons had a legion of sons and daughters about the Mains and had no room for a child-hand. Without a family, the Cleggs had room in plenty and, on the surface, a better claim.

At first Kirsty had been pleased to leave the Baird, a bleak, institutional building on the outskirts of Maybole. She had imagined that the Cleggs had picked her because they liked her, and might in time come to care for her as if she was their own. But Duncan and Mavis Clegg had not wanted a surrogate daughter, only a pair of hands to labour about the house and farm. For seven years grindingly hard work had been Kirsty's lot. Only her schooling, insisted upon by the district truant officer, had given her relief from the isolation of Hawkhead. At Dunnet school she had come into contact with children of her own age, Craig Nicholson among them. The day after her thirteenth birthday, however, as soon as she had earned her Elementary Merit Certificate, the Cleggs had pulled her out of school and

Hawkhead's dismal hills had closed about her like the walls of a prison.

There had been other drastic changes in the course of that year too. Mavis Clegg had fallen ill of a stomach disorder and had been dead before Doctor Pollock could come to a proper decision about treatment. Soon after Mrs Clegg's funeral there had been an enquiry into Kirsty's 'moral welfare' at Hawkhead. Duncan Clegg had foreseen the authorities' concern and had lugged Kirsty's mattress from the cottage loft into the bothy which he had freshened up with a lick of whitewash and a dab of paint. He had even hammered together a box-bed for her and purchased new blankets and sheets to impress the inspectors and had thus managed to convince the delegation from the Baird Home that he thought of Kirsty as his own child and that it would be a cruel stroke to separate her from her 'home' so soon after the loss of the only 'real' mother she had ever known. Kirsty had not had enough gumption to refute the farmer's lies. Shyness had been taken for adolescent ingratitude. She had been given a solemn lecture by Mrs Ashton-Clarke on the blessedness of charity and left to slave for old widower Clegg.

Hail riddled down on Kirsty's shoulders. Even Nero, the muscular Clydesdale, felt the nip through his hairy hide. He halted abruptly in his tracks. Nero was a docile giant, well used to handling. Kirsty had borrowed him so often from Bankhead that she had learned to speak his language. Heavy horses responded best to cajoling though control rested in the short line between bit ring and the handler's fingers.

Kirsty held the rope with a light grip and stepped forward to show herself in front of Nero's leather blinkers. "G'ay on, lad, g'ay on wi' ye."

The Clydesdale shook his head, not petulantly, but to loose the cold sticky little grains that adhered to his muzzle hairs. Grumbling his tongue over the bit, he snuffled in discomfort.

"Wheesht, y' great lump," said Kirsty gently.

Nero regarded the girl dolefully. He dwarfed her completely and might, if he wished, tug the line from her grasp without effort and slap away down the hill to his clean warm stable. But he had been trained by Hinchcliffe, the Sanderson's wily old horseman, and was too well placed in Bankhead's comfort stakes to have rebellious tendencies.

"A touch o' hail'll not melt you," Kirsty told him. "If you'll stir those muckle great hoofs we'll be home in five minutes."

She tightened the line. Nero gave an enormous nod and started again up the track towards the outline of the farm that showed like a charcoal tracing through thin grey cloud.

Hawkhead was hardly the vision Kirsty had had of a home when she had lain in her iron cot in the dormitory at the Baird. She had imagined carpets and gas-lamps and a plump woman in a pinafore setting a table with china plates; laughter and kisses before sleep. There had been none of that from the Cleggs. Even Mavis had been severe and undemonstrative, more like a twin to her husband than a wife.

The bare wind-swept hill was a stupid place to build a farmhouse, but common sense had never been all that common in the farming community and the farmstead's high situation had been useful sixty years ago for catching the first and last light, so Mrs Dwyer, Kirsty's teacher, had told her. But not even Mrs Dwyer could explain why Duncan and Mavis Clegg hated everything about them, as if life was, and always had been, an insupportable burden. It could not be poverty; the Cleggs were not on the crumbling cliff of penury. Though Hawkhead was a small holding and rough, other farms in the district of similar substance managed to provide a decent living for the tenants. Dimly Kirsty realised that Duncan Clegg enjoyed his hardship and was freed by it from responsibility. She felt only a watery pity for the man, and, these past months, a growing distrust.

On reaching the barn Kirsty found Clegg waiting for her at the door of the byre. There was no milking-herd now. After Mavis's death Duncan had disposed of the cows and based his meagre economy on raising and selling cattle and sheep, an activity which, as he practised it, took very little effort.

He wore a filthy tweed vest under a calico jacket whose best parts were the patches that Kirsty had stitched over the tears. His trousers were greasy and stiff with dirt. A cloth cap was tugged half over his face and his hands, as usual, were stuffed deep in his pockets. Kirsty thought of him as an old man, but he was not much above fifty, fifteen years or so younger than Mr Sanderson. His grey hair was thick and matted and stubble merged with an untrimmed moustache. He was sober – he seldom touched strong drink – and he watched Kirsty with a sly squint as she steered the horse to the stable. This past year Kirsty had had the prickly feeling that Duncan Clegg was spying on her not as a master might spy on a servant to keep the work up to the mark but for reasons more secret and sinister. Slowing the Clydesdale to a walk, she hesitated.

"Where the hell have you been, missie?" Clegg demanded, his words measured and accusatory.

"To Bankhead, Mr Clegg, where I was sent."

"Aye, an' where else?"

"No place else."

"You went to the Nicholsons', did ye not?"

"It's three miles from Bankhead to the Nicholsons'," Kirsty protested.

"Three miles is only a skip for a young lout wi' nastiness on his mind."

"I – I don't know what you mean, Mr Clegg," Kirsty said.

"Did you not contrive t' meet *him* then?"

"I – I saw Mr Sanderson, if that's what you mean."

"Damned well you know what I mean. I mean yon Nicholson tyke."

Duncan Clegg had slandered Craig before. How the farmer had found out that Craig and she had been school sweethearts was beyond her. Mr Clegg was seldom in village company, except at market. Certainly she had given him no hint of her feelings for Craig Nicholson. And Craig knew better than to show his face within a mile of Hawkhead. Mr Clegg was afraid that she would one day marry Craig and he would lose his unpaid servant. He would be hard pushed to wheedle another orphan from Baird Home since he was a widower now and single men were not trusted to make good masters.

Kirsty said, "Mr Sanderson told me t' tell you that you canna have the plough horse again unless you pay a hire fee. I think he means it this time."

"Damn an' blast the greedy bastard," Clegg said. "Is he not rich enough? An' me wi' a poor sick beast an' no ploughin' done."

"It's cold," said Kirsty, who did not like to hear the Sandersons maligned. "I'd best dry Nero and give him his feed."

Nero was not the only creature in the yard who was damp and miserable. Though the hail shower had dwindled away, twilight shimmered with the promise of frost and the dark blue wind was wintry. Kirsty shivered. She turned to draw Nero into the stable to find him a stall and brush him down. She would have to check on poor Mustard who lay weary and wheezing and on Trimmer, a raddled old horse who would be teamed with Nero tomorrow on the heavy plough to break hard ground west of the hill.

Clegg jerked his hands from his pockets.

"Give it here, the rope. I'll see him in."

11

Startled by the man's sudden movement Nero shied and it was all Kirsty could do to hold the horse.

She stiffened when Duncan Clegg's thick fingers touched her neck and squeezed her hair.

He said, "Aye, you're wet too. I'm not wantin' you keelin' over on me. You'd better dry off. Down to the skin."

She had been strapped by him when she was younger, skirts up and drawers down to her ankles, but she had not been forced through the humiliating ritual of punishment since Mavis died. He clouted her with his fist now and then or stabbed a kick at her backside but he had never before laid a fondling hand on her.

She stepped back.

Clegg's hand remained in mid-air, floating and uncertain.

Thickly, he said, "I'll be needin' my supper soon, so be bloody quick doin' what you have t' do."

She handed him the rope at once, turned around the butt of the hay barn and entered the bothy that clung to the barn's gable end. She closed the door and rattled the latch so that Mr Clegg might hear it. The latch was not a lock, of course, but it provided an illusion of privacy and, with the room's only chair propped against the door, she felt secure enough in the bothy.

At seventeen Kirsty was not ignorant about sexual matters. She had heard precocious gossip in the Infant Girls' playground at Dunnet school, stories of lassies who had teased ploughmen and had been flung on their backs and had had their skirts knotted over their heads and been given more than they had bargained for; had heard of farmers on outlying steadings who took servant-girls as 'extra' wives, and slept three to a bed. On one of her infrequent visits to the mart at Cawl she had encountered a young girl of fourteen, a farm servant like herself, waddling fat with child and had been shocked to see the girl's master, a respectable man and a kirk elder, smirk and swagger when his brethren congratulated him on his virility and prodded at the poor lass as if she was no better than a dumb brute come into season for the pleasure of the bull. The sight had turned Kirsty cold with fear and anger and sne had snapped at Mr Clegg on the road home and had had her ear slapped for her impudence.

At least the girl had known the name of the father of her bairn. Kirsty did not know which of the wild lads of Girvan harbour had spawned her.

It was said that bastards bred bastards and Kirsty Barnes's lineage seemed to bear out that cynical adage. She was the bastard daughter of a bastard mother who had been, in her day, a ward of the parish too, put out to serve a fish-curer at the age of nine. But Kirsty's mother, who had had a thrawn red-headed streak in her, had evaded monotonous servitude and drifted into night trade about pubs and taverns of Carrick until she died in a tinkers' camp on the low shore south of Girvan when Kirsty was less than a year old. In storybooks virtue inevitably triumphed over circumstances. But in the real world, Kirsty had already learned, victory usually went the other way. All she knew of her mother had been imparted in righteous tones by Mrs Bream, wife of the warden of the Baird Home for Orphans, before Kirsty was of an age to be boarded.

She propped the chair against the door and breathed a little sigh of relief.

The bothy was an improvement on the loft of the cottage, though it could hardly be called comfortable. There was no stove, only a grate inset into the wall. Kindling and coals were doled out on strict ration by Duncan Clegg who expected Kirsty to spend her evenings in the farm kitchen, sharing his hearth, while she did his sewing, mending and ironing. She hated the winter, shut up from dusk to bedtime in Mr Clegg's company. She went to bed early, even for a country girl, crossing to the bothy about eight or half past, though she would not find sleep until ten or eleven o'clock and would lie in the darkness listening to the rats skiffing and scratching along the hay barn's rafters or, distantly, old Mustard wheezing in his stall.

The only item of furniture that Kirsty could call her own was a small pinewood chest that the Baird had gifted her on her departure. The chest contained her clothes, such as they were, two lengths of hair-ribbon that Craig had given her last Christmas and ten hand-drawn cards that marked various festivals, including St Valentine's Day. Clegg did not know about the ribbons and cards which she hid from his prying eyes not in but under the chest, wrapped in a sheet of clean newspaper. Sometimes on dreary winter nights she would take out the ribbons and tie her hair in a fancy style and stare at the cards and think of Craig and how it might have been if she had not been a product of the Baird or if she had been fostered to a decent family like the Sandersons and not stuck with the Cleggs.

She opened the lid of the chest and took out stockings and a pair of flannel drawers. There was only a faint glint of twilight in the bothy's tiny window now and she fumbled for matches and lit the stump of candle that stood in a dish by a jagged triangle of mirror on the shelf above the hearth. She had found the broken mirror on the Dunnet dump four or five years ago and, with a young girl's natural vanity, had brought it home and cherished it ever since. She studied her reflection soberly. She was, she supposed, pretty enough, though her nose was too flat for her liking. She had light brown hair tinted with auburn and eyes that Craig said were green, though she did not believe him, and a tiny bridge of permanent freckles across her cheeks. In heavy skirt and bodice, however, she looked as old and dumpy as one of the peasant figures carved into the lintel of the *Star of Robbie Burns*, a public house on the Maybole Road.

Bracing herself, Kirsty stripped off her damp garments. She seated herself on the side of the cot and rubbed her bare legs with a rough towel. Standing again, she rubbed her shoulders, stomach and breasts until her skin tingled and glowed. By candlelight she glimpsed herself in the broken mirror. For once her hair seemed almost lustrous. She flung back her head and worked the towel, arched her back and let her loosened hair fly thick about her face then, before the cold could reach for her again, swiftly turned and picked up her stockings.

The sudden movement caught him out. For an instant his features were visible in the window. Kirsty gasped. She clasped the stockings to her body and gaped at the square of glass. But he had ducked out of sight and vanished. She had recognised him, though; Mr Clegg had been spying on her, ogling her nakedness. She shuddered as if a cockroach had crawled upon her, and without hesitation flung herself into her clothes.

She was seething with so much anger that she lost perspective on her position at Hawkhead, and her common sense. She stamped out of the bothy, crossed the yard, flung open the door of the cottage and stalked inside to confront the farmer.

"How dare you!" she shouted. "D'you take me for a peepshow? How could you be so wicked?"

"Shut your damned mouth," Clegg told her, without a trace of contrition.

"I will not. God, if you ever try that again I – I'll tell — "

Kirsty's threat was smothered, her anger changed to fear.

He stood by the fire, jacket and vest removed, three buttons of his trouser front unfastened. He had not run from her window out of shame, Kirsty realised, but out of necessity.

Duncan Clegg believed that she belonged to him. He believed that he could take her by right and that the age-old excuse would stand up if she ever dared open her mouth and accuse him; he would claim that she had led him on.

He said as much now. "Struttin' before me like a bloody trollop. Night after bloody night, flauntin' yourself. I'll say it was you came an' begged me. My word against yours. Everybody in these parts knows fine what sort o' stock you come from. A whore's bastard."

It would indeed be Kirsty's word against Clegg's if she made a public complaint against him. Mr Sanderson might take her side in the matter but most folk would believe the man. Doubt would be cast, dirt would cling. Craig would despise her. Duncan Clegg had her in a vice. Once she had been demeaned, he could treat her as he wished, do anything to her and she would be powerless to prevent it.

Rage at the injustice of it flowed within her. She would not surrender to him, not give him what he wanted no matter what it cost her or what folk thought.

She turned on her heel.

"I'm goin'," she said. "Leavin'."

Clegg was too quick for her. He grabbed her hair and the stuff of her dress and dragged her back.

Screaming, Kirsty struggled against his strength. She had supposed that her boss was feeble, but years of labour had left him with a wiry strength that far exceeded hers. She could not send him off. She struggled ineffectually, appalled at the sudden attack, knowing that if he wished he might take her here and now, throw her to the floor and enter her as easily as he might drive a stake into soft turf. The man's casual brutality sickened her. He thrust an arm between her legs. Kirsty screamed again.

"*Shut your damned mouth.*"

She continued to scream.

He struck her with his fist, dazing her.

She sagged against the table. Once more he struck her, flat-handed, and pushed her down on to the stone.

Instinctively Kirsty sought to protect her stomach with her forearms but she had been weakened by the blow and could not fend him off.

Clegg dropped to his knees. He snared her wrists, stretched her arms above her head. He nuzzled his face against her throat, dragged his lips to her mouth. She tasted stale sweat and smelled his foul breath. She gagged. Amused by her reactions, Clegg chuckled. His eyes glinted and seemed to have a spark in them as if her helplessness had awakened forgotten emotions. Struggling, Kirsty stared up at him, then went limp.

She let him paw and fondle her breasts, trail his tongue across her lips. She did not even resist when he bundled her skirts over her hips and exposed thighs and belly. She lay still as a leaf on a pond, yielding to his wishes.

Clegg did not recognise danger in her passivity. He sat back on his heels and impatiently fumbled with his trouser buttons. He was stupidly self-assured and, when exposed, glanced down at himself smugly. In that moment of inattention Kirsty saw her chance. She drove her foot like a piston into the pit of his stomach.

The farmer let out a strangled cry. He doubled over. He had no mind for her now, no desire. Everything was wiped away by the waves of pain that radiated from his groin. Kirsty had hit the mark fair and square.

She shouldered him aside, scrambled from under him and ran from the cottage into the yard. She stumbled, rose, shook down her skirts, ran on. She expected pursuit and glanced behind her. To her surprise she saw that Clegg was still as she had left him, doubled over on the stone floor of the kitchen. Kirsty's control evaporated. She wept. She ran, and wept, turned the corner of the byre and sped down the path that ribboned down the vale under a big cold luminous sky.

She was still weeping when she reached the field gate that gave access to the grazings of Dalnavert and the path to the Nicholsons' house.

Coals cracked in the polished grate. Their flames, reflected in brass and copper ornaments, masked the kitchen with cosy contentment akin to one of the depictions of domestic bliss on the cover of *Leisure Hour*, a journal to which Mrs Nicholson regularly subscribed and whose general philosophy was her gospel and her ideal. Sometimes, especially on raw spring evenings, Craig shared his mother's simple faith in warmth and companionship as the bedrock of family life. Seated on the old 'nursing-chair', a low straw-bottomed object, sharing the light of fire and oil-lamp with his mother, Craig rotated a little boot on his fist and snipped at the twist of wire by which he had fixed the torn eyelet to the leather. He put the card of wire and pliers to one side and with a gentleness that amounted almost to stealth, surveyed his handiwork from several angles.

Lorna's feet were growing at an alarming rate. The boots would not last her much longer. Money would have to be found to buy her a new pair. They were ugly things anyway, not right for such a dainty creature. Soon Lorna would rebel against them, would girn for footwear that was grown-up and fashionable. Craig crushed the prickle of wire with the ball of his thumb and dropped a dab of spit on to a scuff mark on the boot's broad toe. He dabbed polish on to a duster and smoothed it into the worn leather. Behind him the click of the knitting-needles ceased.

Craig heard the mutter of his mother's voice counting off stitches. He did not turn, but, like Gordon and Lorna at the table, crouched just that wee bit lower over his task in the hope that Mam might respect the quiet hour and choose to prolong it.

At any moment, though, Mam would say, "You pair, off to your beds."

Lorna would whine and Gordon would begin a long harangue about being treated like a bairn, and Dad would say, "Ach, Madge, let them bide up a while longer," and the nightly contest of wills would begin.

Craig sympathised with his sister and brother. At twenty, he was not too old to remember the impatience that once possessed him, a hunger to be grown up, to be responsible for your own comings and goings. He would not take sides tonight, however, even if the argument developed into a howling match and Mam shouted at him, "Take that boy," meaning Gordon, "out of my sight." Gordon would turn defiant and there would be a scuffle and he, Craig, would have to put a headlock on his brother and drag him through the long hall and into the icy bedroom at the back of the cottage while Mam cornered Lorna and marched her to the tub for a cold scrub that would be more like a punishment than an ablution. All the while Bob Nicholson would sit in his chair by the fire smiling through the clean sweet reek of whisky, distanced from petty squabbles not by his position as paterfamilias but by meekness and by drink.

Bob Nicholson, was a secret drinker *par excellence*. Except at funerals, weddings and on Hogmanay, when he would allow himself to be pressed into taking a wee dram, Craig had never seen him lip so much as a mouthful of any alcoholic beverage. It had not occurred to Craig until a couple of years ago that, while he had never seen his father ranting drunk, no more had he ever seen him totally sober. It was Gordon, quick-witted and wise in the ways of the world, who had first interpreted Mam's endless recriminations, coded to keep the awful truth from the children. Not even Gordon, however, had ever unearthed one of the caches of whisky that Dad had planted about the cottage, and, it was assumed, about the fields from here to Bankhead. If Madge Nicholson knew where her husband kept his stock of bottles, she gave no indication of it. She certainly never asked him out loud within earshot of her offspring.

Mr Sanderson would know of it – Mr Sanderson knew everything – but Bob Nicholson still ploughed as straight a furrow as any day-labourer at Bankhead. Bankhead earnings, as much as the income from the smallholding, kept the Nicholsons afloat, and Bob in whisky. Dalnavert was not, strictly speaking, a 'small' holding at all. Indeed, the farm was too large for Bob and his sons to cope with and many of its acres lay virtually untended and understocked. It was Mam's ambition – Gordon said – that had prompted Dad into taking on Dalnavert in the first place. Mam wanted to be the lady of a Mains the size of Bankhead one day, since she had been a house-servant there when she was a girl and fancied the life.

Dalnavert was demanding, would be even more demanding if Bob had let it take hold upon him. Craig found himself working all hours of the day and night just to shore up his Dad's neglect. Gordon had already announced his intention to shake the dust of Dalnavert from his feet as soon as he turned eighteen, to head for Glasgow or Edinburgh. Even Lorna was not enamoured of farm life and vowed that she would never marry a farmer, not for all the tea in China.

Craig, though, had no plan or notion in his head as to what would become of him or what he would do with himself. When he dreamed he dreamed only of Kirsty Barnes, of holding her in his arms, of being alone with her in a warm bed in a warm room. The fact that he saw little of Kirsty these days only intensified his longing and desire. But when Craig mentioned Kirsty's name, however casually, his mother would sniff her disapproval and give him a lecture about 'wasting himself' – whatever that meant. Any sort of regular courtship was unthinkable at this stage.

The tapping needles were silent. Craig tensed. Bob's chair creaked as he reached up to the shelf for his tobacco pouch and fumbled his pipe from his waistcoat pocket.

Dark, slender and small, and looking far younger than sixteen, Gordon spread his elbows about the book that lay open on the table before him and pretended to be absolutely engrossed in it. Lifting her shoulders like a gull before flight, Lorna shifted in her chair.

"*You pair, off to your beds.*"

Gordon feigned deafness. Lorna, less adept, gave a little moan and settled her bottom stubbornly on the seat of the chair. The knitting-needles clashed like swords as Mam thrust them into the pattern bag by her side. Her shadow cut off the lamplight. Craig swung his legs to allow her to pass.

"*Bed, I say, and bed I mean.*"

Aye, there would be a scene again tonight. Such petty crises had become the core of family relationships. Craig hated them. He could see no reason for them and tended to blame his dad's lack of authority for causing them to occur.

"*Did you hear me?*" Mam shouted.

Nobody answered her question.

Straightening his shoulders Bob Nicholson took his thumb from the bowl of his pipe and the stem from his mouth, cocked his head to one side and, to Craig's astonishment, said, "Hold your tongue a minute, Madge."

"*What did you say?*"

"Ssshh, Madge," Bob told her mildly.

Lorna had heard it too. Timid at the best of times she rushed from her seat and crowded against her father as if she expected a ghost to materialise through the kitchen door or robbers to break it down.

"What the hell sort o' noise is that?" Bob asked.

The faint plaintive sound was utterly unfamiliar.

"It's just a damned cat," said Madge.

"No, yon's no cat," said Craig.

"Burglars?" Gordon suggested.

The latch of the outside door rattled.

Since his father showed no signs of extricating himself from his chair, Craig took the initiative. "I'll see what it is."

Swiftly he crossed the room, yanked open the door and vanished into the hallway.

He let out an exclamation, asked a question.

The answer was a sob.

"Who is it?" Madge demanded, then raised a hand to her mouth as Craig ushered in the girl, Kirsty Barnes.

"Well, well, it's just Clegg's lassie." Bob Nicholson settled back, pipe stuck in his mouth again as if the whole of the mystery had been suddenly and completely solved.

Craig guided the girl to his mother's chair by the fire and gently pressed her down. She was in a dreadful state, hair plastered against her cheeks, dress and shoes spattered with mud. She was sobbing as if her heart would break.

"Tell me what happened," Craig said.

He was on his knees by the girl's side, Madge and the family forgotten in his concern for Kirsty. He touched her shivering shoulder with a tenderness that pricked Madge Nicholson's heart like a pin.

"What d'you want here?" Madge snapped.

"Gi'e the lassie time to catch her breath, Madge," Bob said.

"She's been up to somethin'," Madge declared.

"Come on, Kirsty, tell me what's wrong," Craig said.

Kirsty laid her forehead against Craig's chest. He hugged her awkwardly while she whispered to him in a voice so low that not even Gordon could make it out. Madge Nicholson observed the display of intimacy, heard the whispering and began to have an inkling of the girl's purpose here. When Craig's gentleness turned to sudden fury she knew that her guess was correct.

"Damn him, damn the bastard," Craig raged.

"Clegg?" said Bob, nodding.

"Damn the filthy swine. He tried, the old bastard."

"Tried?" said Gordon from the corner. "Tried what?"

"Never you mind," said Madge.

"I'll – I'll kill him, so I will," Craig cried.

Madge put a hand on her son's shoulder, offering what seemed at that moment like comfort and understanding. She pushed him away from the girl and leaned forward.

"You led him on, I suppose," she said.

"Mother, for Christ's sake!" Craig exploded.

"He just – just came," said Kirsty. "I'd been down to Bankhead to borrow the horse. I was soaked so I went into the bothy to change into somethin' dry. He – he was at the window. Starin' at me. At the bothy window."

"You knew he was there?"

"No, no, I swear."

"Madge, leave her alone, for God's sake," Bob said.

"Keep out of it, you," Madge said, without turning. "Did he *touch* you?"

"Aye, he threw me – threw me down on the floor."

"Where?"

"In the kitchen, in the cottage."

"Jesus, I'll kill him," Craig hissed.

"Did he do it?"

"What?"

"Do not play coy wi' me. You know fine what I mean."

"No," said Kirsty. "No, he didn't – didn't manage."

"When you went into the kitchen after he'd ogled you, what were you wearin'?"

"What's that got to do – ?" Craig began.

Madge ignored him.

20

"This, what I'm wearin' now," Kirsty said.

"Sunday best." said Madge Nicholson, vindicated.

"I've nothin' else, Mrs Nicholson. It's all I had dry."

"You led him on."

"Enough, Madge." Bob heaved himself out of his chair.

The unexpected movement provoked Madge to withdraw a little.

"We'll see what Mr Clegg has to say in respect of your accusations," she declared.

Craig, a little calmer now, scowled. Mr Clegg! He had never before heard his mother refer to their neighbour with such formality. She had always been scathing about the tenant of Hawkhead.

"Please, please, don't send me back," Kirsty begged.

"Where else are you to go, may I ask?" said Madge. "Besides, you're Mr Clegg's servant."

"Aye, but he canna do what he likes wi' me."

Bob Nicholson, who had slipped away without anyone in the kitchen noticing, returned at that moment with a glass in his hand. He offered it to Kirsty who, with a questioning glance at Craig, accepted.

"What's that you're givin' her?" Madge enquired.

"Medicine," Bob said. "Knock it back, lass. It'll steady your nerves."

Kirsty closed her eyes and obediently tipped the small quantity of liquor into her mouth, swallowed. She gasped, coughed and handed the empty glass back to Mr Nicholson.

The man said, "Is that no' better?"

"Aye, Mr Nicholson."

The effect of the whisky was startling. It seemed to loosen a knot of shame and embarrassment in Kirsty. She put her head into her hands to hide her face and began, once more, to weep.

The sight of the girl's distress stirred Craig's temper once more. He strode out into the hallway, whisked his jacket from the cupboard and snatched his boots from the rack and carried them back into the kitchen.

"Where do you think you're goin'?" his mother asked.

"Up the hill to wring the truth out o' that dirty bastard."

"Easy, son." Bob put a hand on his son's shoulder. "No point courting trouble because of the likes o' Duncan Clegg."

"Do *you* not believe what Kirsty told us?"

"Och, aye, I believe her. She's got no reason to lie. But throttlin' Duncan Clegg's no' the answer."

"Don't go there, Craig, please," Kirsty sobbed.

Craig hesitated, then dropped his boots to the floor.

"What *can* we do, then?"

"Sleep on it," Bob Nicholson advised.

"What about Kirsty?"

"She can bide here the night," Bob said.

"No, she cannot," Madge said. "Let her go back where she belongs."

Craig said, "If Kirsty goes, I go too."

Madge Nicholson's eyes were full of suspicion. "What's been goin' on between you two that I don't know about?"

It was Kirsty who blurted out, "Nothin' like that, Mrs Nicholson, I swear."

"Am I expected to take the word of a Baird Home brat?"

Craig shouted, "Believe what you bloody like, Mother. Either Kirsty stays or we both go."

"You're upset, Craig. You don't know what you're sayin'."

"I know fine what I'm sayin'," Craig retorted. "I'm sayin' straight out that I intend to marry Kirsty just as soon as I'm able."

Madge Nicholson swayed and sat down hard on her husband's chair. Her heart-shaped face seemed puffed up and her plump cheeks turned a fiery red.

"God! Oh, God! You can't marry *her*!"

Like the Nicholson children Kirsty said nothing. She did not dare intrude upon the crisis which had flared between mother and son, even if she was the cause of it. Even Bob was rendered speechless by his son's announcement, the empty whisky glass in his fingers like a talisman that had lost its power to protect.

Quietly Craig said, "I mean it, Mother. I mean what I say."

For over a minute Madge Nicholson sat motionless, spine straight, hands in her lap. The lick of coal flames sounded loud and the whirring of the clock, prior to striking the hour, made Kirsty start. At length Madge drew in a breath, clapped her hands to her knees and pushed herself upright. She did not so much as glance at Bob or Craig or at the intruder who had thrust her way into her life.

She said, "We'll discuss it tomorrow in a calmer frame of mind."

"What about Kirsty?" said Craig.

"Oh, she'd better stay, I suppose. Find her a place in the barn."

"Not the barn," Craig said. "Lorna's room."

A strange dry glance passed between mother and son. The

woman almost smiled but it was not a sign of amusement or of capitulation.

She said, "I'll fetch blankets," and without another word left the kitchen.

Craig sighed. He took off his jacket and draped it on the back of a chair while Bob Nicholson, still with the empty whisky glass in his hand, seated himself in his chair by the fire as if he had weathered the full term of the latest little storm. He scratched his ear-lobe then, without a trace of humour, said, "Did it not occur t' you, Craig, that maybe the lass doesn't want you for a husband?"

Craig swung round belligerently, challenging Kirsty.

"Well, do you?"

She answered softly, "Aye, I do."

"Are ye sure you mean it, lass?" Bob Nicholson said.

"With all my heart," Kirsty answered.

Wrapped in a blanket on boards in the slot by Lorna Nicholson's bed, Kirsty listened to the soft shallow breathing of the child. Lorna had been eager to chat, to put all manner of questions after the door had been closed and they were left alone. But Kirsty's mind whirled with too many questions of her own to indulge the young girl and she had pretended that she was very sleepy, too sleepy to talk.

Some time about eleven Mrs Nicholson had entered the tiny back bedroom and had stooped over her daughter to kiss her and tuck her in. Kirsty had kept her eyes closed until the woman had gone off again and then she had come awake once more, shiningly awake, lit by all that had happened that day and, most of all, by Craig's astonishing promise.

Marriage had never been mentioned between them, not even as a remote possibility. Their courtship had been restrained but not dour. They had been to each other whimsical and teasing by turns in the short hours of meeting, not serious at all. School seemed far back into the past. There they had been chums, as close as a boy and girl could be without incurring the opprobrium of classmates to whom male and female were still natural enemies, like dogs and cats. Kirsty could not bring herself to accept that Craig meant what he said, that the promise he had made was other than a display of anger. She tried to be sensible, to tell herself that she could not hope to escape so easily from Hawkhead and that this night spent under the same roof as her sweetheart would soon be no more than a memory.

She had no idea what time it was when the bedroom door creaked and, out of the darkness, Craig whispered her name.

Blinking, she sat up.

He had brought a lamp with him. He lighted it now and left it by the doorpost where its quivering rays would be too low to disturb his sister.

"Kirsty, are you asleep?"

"No."

"Are you cold?"

"No."

Over his nightshirt Craig had pulled on a threadbare coat. He knelt by the made-up bed on the floor, one arm bridging her legs, his face close to hers. Blanket held to her breasts, Kirsty sat upright. She felt wicked being here with him, wicked but not guilty.

"Pay no heed to Mam," Craig whispered. "She'll come round in due course."

"I doubt that, Craig."

"It's her hard luck, then."

"Did you mean what you said – about marriage?"

"Aye, every word. Unless you'd prefer to stay with old man Clegg."

"Please don't make a joke of it."

"Kirsty, I'm sorry it had to happen like this."

Locks of dark hair, soft and curled, bobbed on his brow. It was all Kirsty could do not to stretch out her hand and touch them. There was nothing girlish in the set of his mouth, though, or in the squareness of his jaw and when he clasped her hands in his she could feel the strength in him.

She said, "What'll happen to me, Craig?"

"I mean it, damn it. I will marry you."

"But – when?"

"You can stay with us for a while. Mr Sanderson'll find you day work at the Mains, I'm sure. Come autumn, we'll be wed, I promise."

Kirsty said nothing. In delay she saw a risk of losing him. She could not play tug-of-war with Craig's loyalty to his family.

"If I hadn't come here tonight," Kirsty said, "would you have courted me?"

"I've always wanted you, Kirsty. That's the truth."

He was trembling. She longed to put her arms about him and draw him down under the blankets with her, to hold his strong muscular body against hers. She drew back a little, pressing her shoulders against the side of the bed.

"I want you too," she whispered.

Craig sat back on his heels, widening the gap between them. He was tense and formal all of a sudden. "I'd better go. It's late and I've a hard day's work ahead of me."

"Craig, wait."

She crossed a forearm over her breasts and leaned forward, upward, offered him her pursed lips.

He hesitated then kissed her on the mouth, swiftly, and then left.

Bob Nicholson and his sons were late out of bed, late to the breakfast table and, by a good half hour, late starting along the road that would lead them to the cross gates where their ways would part. From there Craig would head up to the high acres and Gordon and his father would cut across the pasture to Bankhead. Craig would be planting grain seed all that day if the milky frost melted from the ground and if not he would be mending fences. For Gordon and Bob Nicholson it would be byre work since Jim Fry, the cattleman, was sick with a quinsy throat.

Kirsty and Lorna had been dead to the world when Craig peeped in at them. Lorna did not have to be up till a quarter to eight and Mam assured her son that she would not 'fling Kirsty out', not until the matter had been properly settled, though neither Craig nor his father had had the temerity to enquire what properly settled might mean. Craig assumed that Duncan Clegg would have to be told of Kirsty's whereabouts, the Baird Home too. He was unclear about legal obligations now that Kirsty was over the age of sixteen. In the meantime he was delighted that she was to stay on at Dalnavert. With the optimism of youth, he believed that his mother would come around to liking Kirsty, would soften, relent and bless a marriage between them.

It was almost half past seven before the Nicholsons emerged from the door of the cottage. The sky was light with the promise of sunshine and the cloudscape away over the Straiton hills might have been painted with a fox brush, russet tipped with cream.

No sooner had the boys passed out of the yard than Gordon said to his brother, "Hoi! Where were you last night, eh?"

"In bed, of course."

"Whose bed?"

"My own bed."

"Aye, for ten minutes, before ye slipped away. I heard you, you dirty sod."

"One more word, sonnie, an' I'll punch your ear."

"You were in the back bedroom, weren't you?"

"What of it?"

"Did ye get what you went for, Craig, eh?"

"I went to see if Kirsty was warm enough, that's all."

"Warm enough? That's a good one." Gordon skipped away as Craig lunged at him. "Was she *waarrrm* enough for *looooove*?"

Bob Nicholson walked with an unhurried gait just ahead of his sons. He seemed oblivious to their horseplay. Already he had a pale odour of whisky about him and a glowing spot on each cheek which gave the impression of rude health. The pipe in his mouth sparked like the chimney of a new-lit fire. But Bob was more alert than he appeared to be and when he drew to an abrupt halt at the roadside his sons piled into him like dazed bullocks.

Bob pointed the wet pipe stem. "See what I see?"

Craig followed the direction and saw at once the figure of a man waddling down the sheep track from the west.

"Bloody Clegg!"

"Wonder what he wants," said Gordon.

"Can you not guess?" said Craig grimly. "Wants his slave back, I expect."

"He's got gall, I'll say that for him," Bob Nicholson remarked and then, to his sons' surprise, climbed the fence and set off across the grassland to meet the farmer from Hawkhead.

"Well, I'd love to linger an' watch the fireworks," said Gordon, "but we're damned late as it is. I'll report to Mr Sanderson while you go up there an' give Dad moral support."

"I'll kill the wee pig, that's what I'll do."

"Keep your fists in your pockets, Craig. Let Dad do all the talkin'."

Gordon slapped his brother fraternally upon the shoulder and went on his way down the road towards the Mains, while Craig, simmering, hopped over the fence and loped across the grazings after his father.

Clegg made no move to avoid the Nicholsons. On the contrary, he changed tack and came to a meeting with them in the middle of the pasture. He wasted no time at all on explanations or apologies.

"My lass, where is she?" he snarled.

"She's not your lass, Mr Clegg," Craig answered, his brother's advice forgotten at the sight of the man who had dared to lay hands on Kirsty.

"She is mine. Damned if she's not." From his jacket pocket Clegg dragged out a wad of papers which he waved above his head. "I've got written proof of it."

"Articles!" said Bob scathingly.

Clegg cried, "Mine until she's eighteen. Months yet. Near a bloody six-month, in fact. Send her back or I'll have the constabulary on you all."

"What exactly do you want wi' her?" Bob asked. "You've hardly enough doin' at Hawkhead to justify a servant."

Duncan Clegg did not seem to hear. He shouted, "Whatever she told you's a bloody lie. I never touched her. I never laid a bloody hand on her."

"Nobody said you did, Mr Clegg," said Bob Nicholson.

"Did she not—?"

"I don't doubt the validity of the documents you're waggin' about," said Bob Nicholson.

"Give her back, then."

"Can't give what I don't have," Bob Nicholson said.

Craig bit his lip. His father's guile, and the lie, took the wind out of Clegg's sails. He stopped waving his arms and stuck the documents into his jacket again, puffed and huffed for a moment, then said, "Where else would she go but your place?"

Craig said, "Has she run away, then?"

"Aye, is that what you're tryin' to tell us, Mr Clegg?"

"She's a wilful, spiteful, ungrateful *bitch*."

"Perhaps she went back to the Baird Home," said Craig.

"Or if she felt she had a grievance against you, for some daft reason or another, perhaps she went to the constable," said Bob Nicholson.

"The constable?"

"At Dunnet."

Clegg cocked his head, scowled. "I think you've got her hid."

"Are you callin' me a liar, Mr Clegg?"

"I think – well, she might be hidin' at your place."

"Craig, walk back to Dalnavert wi' Mr Clegg," said Bob. "Let him look through the barns an' the sheds."

Clegg's mouth opened, closed.

Craig said, "Aye, come on wi' me, Mr Clegg. You can ask my mam if we're tellin' lies."

"Your mam?"

"Search the cottage too, if you feel you must."

"Nah, nah. That'll not be necessary."

Bob Nicholson nodded. "Very well, Mr Clegg. If I were you I'd bide at home for a day or two. If your lass has run off she'll not get far on her own."

"Aye, perhaps you're right."

"Did she steal from you?" Bob asked.

"Nah, nah."

"Did she take her belongin's?"

"Nah."

"When did she go missin'?"

"Last night."

"Oh, so you saw her go, did you?"

"I – I found her gone," said Clegg.

"I see, so you found her bed empty this mornin', is that it?"

"It's none o' your damned business, Bob Nicholson."

"It was yourself made it my business, Mr Clegg."

Clegg huffed and puffed again, then he capitulated. "I'll wait a day or two, as you suggest, then I'll consult the folk at the Baird Home."

"Wise," Bob Nicholson agreed.

Craig said, "Perhaps she's down at Bankhead, Mr Clegg. She's a favourite wi' the Sandersons, after all."

"Aye, well, I'll just wait." Obviously Duncan Clegg did not want to confront Mr Sanderson and have to explain why it was that Kirsty had run off. "I'll away home now. I've got ploughin' to do."

"Lassies can be flighty," said Bob Nicholson. "She'll come back when she's hungry, you'll see."

Clegg scowled. His outrage had been replaced by guilt, however, and undermined by Bob Nicholson's questions. He turned and, without bidding his neighbours farewell, trudged off uphill towards the crown of the ridge.

Craig and his father watched his departure.

"Nasty wee bugger," Bob murmured.

"Will those papers really allow him to take Kirsty back?"

"Who can say?" Bob shrugged. "But I'd take no chances if I were you, son."

"What's that supposed to mean?"

Bob took the pipe from his mouth and cradled it in his palm. He rubbed the side of his nose with a knuckle. "Look, I'd best get down to Bankhead. Mr Sanderson'll—"

"Take no chances?" Craig gripped his father's arm. "What the hell d'you mean?"

"I mean," Bob Nicholson said, "you should marry Kirsty Barnes just as soon as you bloody well can."

She felt awkward at breakfast. It might have been different if Craig had been there but she had been so late asleep that she had

28

not wakened at her usual early hour and was obliged to share the table with Lorna and Mrs Nicholson.

There was porridge, bacon and fried bread; bannocks too, fresh butter, even a pot of jam, a symbol of luxury as far as Kirsty was concerned. Whatever fate was in store for her she certainly would not starve while she was a 'guest' in Madge Nicholson's house. She did not eat her fill, however, in case the woman thought her scrounging and greedy. She was quick to help clear the table and carry dishes into the little kitchenette where a stone sink and cold-water tap were and where Madge Nicholson, wrapped in a canvas apron, was busy scrubbing pots.

Mrs Nicholson said not a word and Kirsty returned to the kitchen to chat to Lorna about the happenings at the school she had left four years ago. She found it easier to relate to Craig's sister than to his mother. She dreaded the moment when Lorna would leave for school and she would be alone with Madge Nicholson.

She felt lost in Dalnavert's unfamiliar routines. She did not know what would become of her if Duncan Clegg should come rapping at the door and demand her return. She had signed articles which bound her to him for a given period of time. She had not read the crabbed script carefully and could not remember any of the official jargon. She was determined, however, not to return to Hawkhead farm. Intuitively she knew that his desire for her had not been a weak and impulsive thing but a slow smouldering hunger which her resistance had not extinguished.

The thought of Duncan Clegg upon her, touching her, filled her with loathing. If Lorna and Madge Nicholson had not been there she might have wept at memory of the incident, from fear that she would be callously handed back to Clegg and spoiled for other men, for Craig. Kirsty had learned control, however. It kept her stable during the twenty minutes of breakfast-time. While Lorna went off to pack her dinner into her schoolbag, she occupied herself by sweeping the hearth and filling the brass coal-hod from the pile in the shed by the yard door.

It was a fine dry sort of morning and she wondered if Clegg had, perhaps, decided to plough and to let her take her own time in returning to him. Another kind of man, another kind of farmer, would have done so, for dry spring days were precious and Mr Clegg was far behind in his planting, so far behind that he might again miss the seed crop completely.

When she returned to the kitchen, lugging the upright hod, she found to her surprise that Lorna was not the only one dressed for outdoors. Madge Nicholson too had put on her coat and hat. They were not the sort of garments that Kirsty would have imagined for Bob Nicholson's wife. They were expensive and fashionable, with a hint of practicality in the choice of material. The tailor-made, windproof garment with its tight-fitting back and pouched front made Madge look years younger. The hat sported a bow of brown velvet and two small artificial roses, one of which was spiked through by the long pin that held it fast to Madge's hair. She was tugging on a pair of brown kidskin gloves, and seemed to have performed a miracle of transformation in no time at all, as if shedding the worn apron had brought her out like a butterfly from its chrysalis.

"Are – are you going out, Mrs Nicholson?" Kirsty, rather stupidly, asked.

"Shoppin'."

"Oh!"

"Aye, shoppin'."

It was on the tip of Kirsty's tongue to enquire what sort of shopping required such elegant attire but she said nothing. She put down the coal-hod by the grate and, for something to do, blew gently along the brass bevels to remove the thin layers of dust that had accumulated there.

"Will you be here when I get back?" said Madge Nicholson.

"If – if that's all right, aye," said Kirsty.

"I take it you'll not be goin' back to Hawkhead?"

"No, Mrs Nicholson."

"Well, there are potatoes in the sack below the kitchen board. They'll need scrubbed and washed. Enough for six. Can you manage that?"

"Aye. Is there anything else I can do?"

"I'll be back in time to see to the rest. Nobody's home much before six, except Lorna."

"Does Craig not come in for his dinner?"

"No, he does not."

"Will I take him out somethin'?"

"No, you will not." Madge Nicholson held out a hand to her daughter who had been waiting by the door. "Keep the fire up, though, if you can be bothered."

"I will, Mrs Nicholson," Kirsty said.

"Cheerio, Kirsty."

"Cheerio, Lorna."

And they were gone. And she was alone in the Nicholsons' house with virtually nothing to do and all day to do it, nothing, that is, except worry about Madge Nicholson's destination and what tricks the woman intended to employ to be rid of her.

Kirsty had not been deceived. Madge Nicholson had not dressed herself to the nines to visit the provision merchant in Dunnet. She had gone, Kirsty suspected, to the Baird Home to report the situation and lay blame for the occurrence where, in Mrs Nicholson's opinion, it properly belonged, with the servant and not the master. Kirsty went down the corridor, opened the back door and looked out into the yard. It was tidy enough, not like the dirty pen at Hawkhead with its slops and weeds and dung-spatters. Hens clucked and pecked contentedly about the barn and a dog, locked in one of the long sheds, barked at the unfamiliar smell of her.

Why, she wondered, had she sought refuge here? Why had she not gone straight to Bankhead? In all likelihood Mr Sanderson would have taken her part against Duncan Clegg. It was not too late. She could walk to the Mains in half an hour, tell Mr Sanderson what had happened, throw herself on his mercy and thus spike Mrs Nicholson's guns. But she could not bring herself to quit Dalnavert, even if it was unsafe. She was bound by the fragile hope that had brought her here, the hope that Craig would protect her, would take her in his arms and keep her safe from harm. She saw now, all too clearly, that a marriage between them would be difficult if not impossible, that Madge Nicholson would fight to keep her son.

Uncertainty and self-pity took hold of Kirsty again. Tears welled in her eyes at the realisation that she might lose him. He was, after all, all that she had in life.

The breaking up of Dalnavert's old grassland had been undertaken at Mr Sanderson's suggestion and with his support.

Craig was not shy when it came to hard field work. He had enjoyed the days stolen from the late autumn season and from the winter months when he had harnessed the two big plough horses from Bankhead and made a high cut that had opened up the matted sward to air and weathering. He was no expert with the plough, but he had been guided by his father's advice as well as Mr Sanderson's and had assiduously prepared a fine tilth for the seed-bed. But Craig's mind was not on grassland husbandry or cereal production that morning, or even on the job of fencing that he had set himself to do until the earth warmed enough to begin sowing.

An old dry-stone wall marked the northern boundary of the

field. Over the years cattle had rubbed it down in places and the hedges that had been planted in the gaps had been bruised and battered too. Craig's task was to stretch new wire to make the boundary secure. He had fetched up posts and wire by cart and dug out the post holes one cold day last week. Now he stood the posts into the holes and with a heavy hammer drove them in deep and firm.

The long swinging blows relaxed him. The shaft vibrated in his fists and his muscles stretched and sweat started down his spine. It was beneficial work for a day like today. Being with Kirsty last night had frustrated him and brought out a strain of discontent that had been in him all this year and most of last. He whanged away with the hammer on the stobs, grunting, releasing his sullen anger at the realisation that Clegg, that evil wee tyke from Hawkhead, might have spoiled Kirsty, his Kirsty, and nobody would have been any the wiser.

She was not, strictly speaking, his Kirsty at all. But when he thought of other girls – May Sanderson from the Mains or Helen Mackenzie from the mill at Dunnet, he found that the visions became unpleasant and did not give him the sort of feelings that thinking of Kirsty Barnes engendered. He did not know why every girl he met, even casually, should be instantly compared with her. Being a man was not easy, Craig had come to realise, and he often wished that he might be a young boy again, untroubled by confusions of the blood. Whanging away on a fence post with an iron-headed hammer was one way to cast out devils and Craig worked rapidly from section to section, setting the posts and leaving the stringing of wire until he ran out of stobs or of energy.

By dinner-time, when the sun had grown almost hot, Craig felt better. He had worked up a thirst for the cold tea in his bottle and hunger for the bread and cheese that Mam had packed into his sack. He had come a long way, though, from his jacket. He had skirted full half the field, lugging and planting and hammering, and he walked slowly back around the perimeter with the hammer over his shoulder, thinking, calmly and pleasantly, how good it would be to go home tonight and find Kirsty there, to have her at the supper-table along with folk he cared about and who cared for him.

It surprised him to discover his father seated against the dry-stone wall, tea-bottle uncorked and pipe smoking like a little lum. Bob Nicholson offered the bottle to his son.

"You could do with a swig o' this, I fancy."

The bottle had been in the shadow of the wall all morning and was cold to the fingers, the weak astringent liquid cold on the tongue.

Craig drank, wiped his mouth on the back of his hand. He reached for his jacket and draped it over his shoulders for, now that he had stopped, he realised that the day might be bright but was not warm after all. He studied his father curiously.

"What might you be doin' here?" he asked.

Bob Nicholson shrugged. "Visitin'. See how you're gettin' on with the fence."

"I'm gettin' on fine with the fence."

"Sit yourself down, son."

Craig did not obey. "Have you been at the pub?"

"Been at the pub? Me!" Bob said in an injured tone. "Hell, I've been puttin' in my hours at Bankhead, tendin' spring calves."

Craig seated himself on the grass, unwrapped his bread and cheese and bit into the sandwich. He did not glance at his father but sniffed, trying to catch the whiff of spirits, the old man's musk. The faint sharpness was there, as usual. Craig sighed and watched a pair of buzzards away above the hill turn slow, soft and heavy on the pale currents of air. Something had brought his father here, something more than companionability or the desire to inspect the fence. Craig munched bread and cheese, sucked tea from the bottle, kept silent.

At length Bob said, "I think she's gone to the Baird."

Craig said, "What would she have gone there for? She's safer with us, is she not?"

"Not Kirsty; your mother."

"Mam?"

"Aye. I saw her best coat laid out, an' her Sunday hat. She's headed for somewhere special. My guess is she's catchin' the train to Maybole to seek 'official advice'." Bob paused. "I'm not inebriated, son."

"I never said you were."

"I haven't lost my reason, either."

"Just what *are* you drivin' at?"

"She'll have the lass back with Clegg before the day's out."

"I'll not allow it."

"When her mind's made up you – not even you – can stop her."

"Christ! Do you know what Clegg'll do if he gets Kirsty back?"

"I can well imagine," said Bob.

"I'll throttle the bastard before I'll see that happen."

The movement was small. Bob dipped two fingers into his breast pocket and plucked out what appeared to be a spill of paper. He offered it casually to Craig.

"What's that?"

"Money. Four five-pound notes."

Craig stopped chewing and, hands on knees, leaned forward and peered at the spill suspiciously. "What in God's name are you doin' with twenty quid?"

"It's for you."

"What for?"

"Take the lass an' get out of here," Bob Nicholson said. "Go before your mam gets back."

"Ach, Dad. I could never—"

"Heed my advice, Craig. If you love this girl—"

"I'm not sure I – Look, let's wait an' see what happens."

"If you wait, son, you'll be done for – like me."

"You haven't done so bad."

"Aye, but I haven't done so well, have I?"

Craig watched the banknotes wag before him.

Bob Nicholson said, "Take them, damn it."

"Where did you get such a sum?"

"From Mr Sanderson."

"He loaned you twenty pounds?"

"It's the burial fund, if you must know."

"You cashed your burial fund! Mam'll go mad when she finds out."

Bob Nicholson shrugged again as if his wife's temper was a bagatelle, her anger of no consequence at all.

Craig drew closer to his father. Squatting on his heels, the bottle and the heel of bread tossed aside, he peered into the man's watery blue eyes. He could not be sure how seriously he was supposed to take the offer and the advice. He had been given bibulous nonsense in lieu of parental help in the past but this time he felt a deep underlying urgency that the old man's diffident manner could not quite hide.

"You mean it, don't you?" he said.

"Sure as death, I mean it."

"But why?"

"To get you out of Dalnavert. To get you away from here," Bob Nicholson said. "You'll not have a better chance, a better motive. If you even *think* you're in love wi' that pretty lassie from Hawkhead now's the time to act on it. If you stay, it'll be killed."

"What'll be killed?"

34

"Happiness. Opportunity. How the hell do I know? Look, take the money, pack a grip, grab the lassie and get on a train."

"Mr Sanderson – the plantin'—"

"Bankhead's been here for five generations. The field was here ten thousand bloody years ago. It'll survive without your supervision for ten thousand more." Bob Nicholson's diffidence collapsed into a show of temper. He scrambled to his feet, thrust the banknotes into Craig's face. "Take them, damn you. Take them an' use them. Go to Glasgow. Make a decent life for yourself."

Craig stared at his father in disbelief. Never before had he heard his father speak so forcefully. It was a kind of defiance, an authority that Craig associated with his mother and not the man. He was astonished by it, dismayed too. He did not know how to respond.

"Stand up, son."

Craig got to his feet.

"Here," Bob Nicholson said.

Craig closed his fist on the spill of paper money. It felt strange, new, refined in his dirty fingers.

"What can I do in Glasgow? My job's here."

"Do you want to condemn Kirsty Barnes, as well as yourself?" Bob said.

"Condemn?"

"*Think, for God's sake.*"

Craig nodded. Without being able to put it into words he understood what his father meant. It was not just Dalnavert's poor acres or the menial work at Bankhead from which his dad sought to free him, but the woman too, from his mam.

He felt a fierce hollow sadness inside him, a sinking, a fear of his ability to cope without the woman behind him.

"But Kirsty might not—"

"We'll go back to Dalnavert right now and ask her."

"Well—"

"If she's in agreement, will you go?"

If he'd had leisure to consider the proposal then Craig would have refused. But he churned with need of Kirsty Barnes and wove his desires into belief that he was doing it for her, to save her. He felt noble, like a martyr, and, with the quick responses of youth, switched himself to the new track, accepting the adventure of it. The twenty-pound stake made all the difference. He would not have had the gumption to break away from Dalnavert on his own account or the urge to scrimp and save a travelling fund. In a flash he saw how shrewd his father had been and felt a wary sort of gratitude towards the man.

"If Kirsty is willin'," Craig said, "I'll do it."

"Without hesitation, without turnin' back?"

"Aye."

"Before your mam gets home?"

Craig paused before he answered. "I could never face her wi' that sort of news, Dad."

Bob Nicholson said, "There's a train from Dunnet station at twenty minutes past three o'clock."

"If Kirsty agrees, we'll be on it."

"Good man," Bob Nicholson said.

Reaction to the events of the previous evening had made her weary, Kirsty decided. She did not feel comfortable in the Nicholsons' cottage and, after she had done the chores, she seated herself in a chair by the fire and tried to relax. She was certainly tired. She ached as if she had had an influenza and jumped nervously at every small sound outside.

She took the liberty of making herself a pot of tea and ate a slice of bread and butter but denied herself jam, in case Mrs Nicholson thought it 'an imposition' upon her hospitality. About one o'clock, or shortly after, sitting upright in the chair, her fingers clenched about the wooden arms, Kirsty fell into a light sleep. When, an hour later, the kitchen door crashed open she almost died of fright. She threw herself out of sleep and out of the chair with a cry.

"It's me, only me," Craig said, alarmed at the distress his entry had caused her. "Did you think it was Clegg?"

"Yes, yes, I did."

She felt weepy again but the sight of Craig gave her relief and when he took her hands in his and drew her to him she calmed at once and laid her head against his shoulder to be soothed. It was only then that she noticed Mr Nicholson in the doorway. He did not seem to disapprove of the show of affection, but to be pleased by it.

"Ask her, son," he said quietly.

Craig separated himself from her.

Kirsty felt a peculiar apprehension come over her at his frown and the manner in which he pursed his lips. He did not seem to know what to do with his hands. He did not speak a word until he had finally folded his forearms under his armpits and found a spot on the floor that suited him. He was, she noticed, still dressed for field work, damp with sweat, his jacket draped about his shoulders like a little cloak.

"Go on, Craig," Mr Nicholson urged. "Ask her."

"Dad's given me money, enough for us to go to Glasgow," Craig said. "If you want to leave here. I mean, we'll be properly married as soon as we can. In the meantime, I mean – Look, I'll marry you, Kirsty, as soon as we're settled in the city. I mean, I'm not just—"

"You'll be safer in Glasgow, lass," Bob Nicholson told her.

Craig stumbled on. "We would be goin' without prospects," he said, "but it would be safer, Kirsty, than remainin' here."

"But Mr Clegg – I'm articled to him, am I not?"

"Damn Clegg!" Craig exploded. "It's me or it's Clegg. Make up your mind."

"Son, son, have you no savvy?" said Bob Nicholson. "Never mind the long story. Ask her nicely. That'll do it."

"Aye, right." Craig unfolded his arms, wiped his hands on his thighs and then pressed them together as if he was praying. He did not meet her eye. "Eh, Kirsty, will you have me for a husband?"

She heard herself say, "*Yes.*" Before she could even think of it, she said again, "*Yes.*"

"See," Bob Nicholson said. "Now, son, away an' pack a few belongin's. Take the big canvas grip from under my bed. I'll never use it again."

Craig nodded. It had become perfunctory all of a sudden. Kirsty longed for more, for a kiss, for his arms about her, for a lingering moment alone with him. It was not how she had envisaged it, curt and sharp-toned and hurried.

She said, "I've nothin' but what I stand in."

Bob Nicholson brushed that complaint aside. "You can buy a new dress, stockin's, shoes, whatever you need, in Glasgow. Craig has money enough for that."

She glanced round and found that Craig had already gone into the bedroom. She could hear him rummaging about, drawers opening and closing, as he packed his belongings.

To Bob Nicholson Kirsty said, "Why are you doin' this, Mr Nicholson? You hardly know me."

The man answered, "Hardly know you? Why, lass, I've watched you grow up, though you might not have guessed it. Besides, Craig's hardly stopped talkin' about you for the past ten years. Nah, nah, I'm not sendin' the boy off with a stranger." He grinned. "Anyway, you're far too bonnie to do him much harm."

"But Mrs Nicholson—"

"Leave Mrs Nicholson to me."

Looking down she realised just how ill-clad she was for the trip. Glasgow, she had heard, was a seat of fashion and smartness. She would look like a scarecrow in its streets.

She hesitated. "Mr Nicholson, I—"

Bob Nicholson shook his head, amused, perhaps, by her vanity.

She realised with a start that the man had offered all that she had ever wanted without the arduous process of a courtship, with its formal rituals, its frustrations and dangers. All she had wanted for the past five years was to be with Craig.

Hesitantly, Bob Nicholson put an arm around her shoulder. She could smell that antiseptic odour, his whisky aura, though she could not imagine when he had found time to take drink. He seemed perfectly sober and serious as he gave her a brief reassuring pat and, for a moment, drew her to him for a cuddle.

"Thank you," Kirsty whispered.

At that instant Craig entered the kitchen. He lugged a grip of thick brown canvas with a leather binding. It appeared almost new. Kirsty wondered if it belonged to Mr Nicholson, had been purchased in hope, for journeys which had never been made.

"Got everythin' you need, son?"

"Aye. All I can carry."

"Get out of here, then," Bob Nicholson said.

"Are you not comin' to the station?"

"Nah, nah. I think I'll put my feet up for half an hour."

"I'll write you letters, Dad."

An expression of alarm crossed Mr Nicholson's face. He held up his hand. "Don't write," he said. "Not till you're settled."

"Will you come up to Glasgow for the weddin'?"

"Don't write, not a word," was Bob Nicholson's answer.

There was an awkward pause. Kirsty waited, a little apart from the men. She sensed their reserve, the shyness between them, saw, in the very corner of Bob Nicholson's eye, the glitter of a tear.

The man did not take his son into his arms. Bob Nicholson was a true-born Scot, an odd mixture of the undemonstrative and the sentimental. He stuck out his hand.

Tense with embarrassment, Craig pumped it and let it go again.

"Take — take care o' yourself, Dad."

"Never mind me. You be sure to take good care of this wee lass, you hear me?"

"I will, I promise."

Craig turned, hoisted up the grip, circled Kirsty's waist and, sweeping her imperiously before him, left the kitchen of Dalnavert for the last time. He did not, not once, look back.

Dunnet railway station, like all the local halts between the waters of the Girvan and the Doon, was no more than a ticket office and a brace of platforms linked by an iron bridge. Kirsty had been on the platform only once before, years ago, when Mrs Ashton-Clarke had brought her from the Baird Home to Hawkhead. She had been so petrified then that the journey seemed like a half-remembered nightmare. Today, however, with Craig's arm about her, clear at last of the oppression of the rugged hills, Kirsty's detachment was supplanted by an anxious anticipation of what was to come.

The iron tracks, glinting in the wan sunlight, converged away to the south. She could just see the engine, a spot of colour with a thread of smoke attached to it. A signal clanked and nodded, making her start. The railway clerk – father of Netta Deans with whom she had once shared a desk at Dunnet school – emerged from his cubbyhole and, hands on hips, looked up and down the track, checked his watch, put on his hat and took his stance at the foot of the bridge by the little green gate that led out into the lane.

Craig had set down the canvas grip and had taken his arm from about her waist, had left her alone while he went into the cubicle to buy the tickets. He did not appear to be excited. His expression was grave, a tiny furrow creasing his brow as he watched the train approach. He had not put on his Sunday-best suit but had changed his trousers and had replaced his working-boots with shoes. He might have been travelling no further than the cattle mart at Cawl or the seedsman's store in Maybole except that she was with him, the lass from Hawkhead, a fact that made it strange and remarkable.

Suddenly Craig said, "He asked where we were goin'."

"Who did?" said Kirsty.

"Mr Deans, when I bought the tickets."

"What did you tell him?"

"I told him we were just goin' to Ayr an' had met by accident on the road."

"But are the tickets not for Glasgow, Craig?"

Confused, Craig took the two billets from his pocket and squinted at them. "God, so they are! I asked him for two to Glasgow, no return. At the same time, in the same breath, I told him we were goin' to Ayr. He must think me a right damned fool."

"It doesn't matter what he thinks, does it?" said Kirsty. "We're not likely to be seein' him again."

"I suppose we're not." Craig paused. "Aye, damn him! Let him spread what tales he likes. We'll be safe out o' harm's way in Glasgow."

Silent again, Craig watched smoke thicken and plume across the fields. The vibration of the engine's wheels was audible now and its whistle screamed in the distance.

Craig said, "Comes up from Stranraer, this train. I've never been to Stranraer, have you?"

"I've never even been in Ayr."

"I wonder what Glasgow's like."

"I've heard it's big."

"Aye," said Craig. "It'll be big all right."

As it came closer it seemed to Kirsty that the train would not fit between the platforms, that it would grind its way up the ramp and fall upon her. Steam hissed and, even before the train halted, a carriage door slammed like a gunshot. She clung to Craig's arm, trying not to flinch, clung tightly to him as if she feared that he would vanish in the smoke and steam and she would be left alone there, foolish and abandoned, when the train pulled away again.

Craig propelled her forward. She glimpsed glass and painted wood. She smelled the choking cindery smell of smoke and the hot smell of grease. She saw a brass handle, heard Craig say, "Open it, daftie. Open it quick." She pushed down the handle. The door swung out towards her. The canvas grip nudged her from the rear. She climbed up and into the carriage, into the odour of stale tobacco smoke and dirty plush stuff. The compartment was empty, no larger, she thought, than a pony stall at Bankhead. Craig heaved the grip on to one of the netted shelves. He peeled off his jacket, unstrapped the window, let it rattle wide open and leaned out.

Seated, breathless, Kirsty stared from the window at Mr Deans who seemed oblivious to the drama that was taking place only yards from him, who would be there when the train pulled out, when they were gone, who would be there again tomorrow and the next day and for ever.

"Nobody else got on," said Craig. "Just us."

The engine jerked. Kirsty was thrown forward as if a hand had shoved her. Couplings clanked and clinked, stiffening. There was a great bellow of steam and, unexpectedly, the train was slipping slowly forwards, Dunnet station sliding neatly away from her, not she from it. Craig continued to lean out of the window.

Kirsty's anxiety congealed around the fact that she had read of terrible accidents on railway trains. She tugged at his jacket and begged him to come inside before his head got knocked off. He grinned, rattled up the window and threw himself down on the seat by her side, sending up a whirl of stale dust that hung like chaff in the streaky sunlight.

"God, you're bonnie," Craig said.

Kirsty was both frightened and flattered by his sudden change of mood. She had never been alone with Craig before, not indoors, not in a close and intimate place like this. Now she had committed herself to him. She was his. He could do what he liked with her. But his compliments soothed her. He had never seemed more handsome for spring weather had tanned his face and hands, long brown hands, not squat and gnarled like Mr Clegg's.

"Are you blushin', love?" he asked.

The carriage rattled and rocked. Green landscapes streamed past the windows. Kirsty had a vague impression of loamy fields, of trees, a steep bank of charred grass that duly obliterated the long view and carried the compartment into shadow.

"Come here," said Craig.

He put both arms about her and lifted her bodily on to his knee. Kirsty uttered a gasp just before his mouth pressed down on hers. Leaning back against the dirty plush, he cradled her. He put his hand upon her breast. He kissed her with more urgency than tenderness and, when he pulled away, left her gasping.

Once more he came down upon her, pushing her along the seat, almost smothering her. He brought up his leg and crooked it about her ankles and stroked and fondled her breasts through her bodice.

She had been kissed by Craig before, had been touched by him in the green lanes about Bankhead but then it had seemed daring and childish. For an instant she felt shut off from him, separate and alone. She put her fist against his shoulder. She did not quite punch him but the gesture was sufficient to tell him that she did not want to be taken roughly.

"Wait, Craig. Please wait."

He gave a growling sort of sigh and released her, let her sit up.

Craig was no bully, no brute. He realised that he had hurt her and said, "I – I don't know what came over me."

"It'll be all right between us, dearest," Kirsty told him. "But later, not now."

Once more he apologised. He looked so sad and solemn that Kirsty lifted herself against him and kissed him upon the lips, then

41

she laid her head against his shoulder and let him stroke her hair while they stared, together, at the changing vistas that lay between the railway and the sea.

Gloomy old Saint Andrew, leaning over an X-shaped cross, peered grimly down the staircase at Kirsty and Craig.

At first Kirsty had thought that the saint was part of a tall window and had been amazed to find such a thing inside an ordinary house. Soon, though, she realised that it could not be a window for it had grown dark outside and the painting was lit, albeit dimly, from behind.

She remained fascinated by it. He was such an old, old chap, Saint Andrew, and so untidy, with straggling hair, a long unkempt beard and a robe that looked as if it could do with a good scrub. From the ground at his feet nettles sprouted – perhaps they were meant to be thistles – and a lumpy blue-black rain cloud compressed his silvery halo. His eyes were the sharpest part of the portrait. Red and piercing they glared straight at Kirsty so that she could not shake the feeling that it was Saint Andrew who was judging them and not Mrs Agnes Frew.

If she had not been so exhausted Kirsty might have given Craig a sign that this place made her uncomfortable and that she would prefer to find another less genteel lodging for their first night together. She kept still, though, because she was afraid that Craig would take her at her word and continue his search for a boarding-house all night long. Hour upon hour they had tramped Glasgow's streets, moving away from the proximity of the glass-roofed cathedral of St Enoch's railway station, across Argyle Street and, left, along Bothwell Street and eventually into St Vincent Street.

Kirsty had only known where she was by observing the name-plates at corners for Craig did not see fit to inform her of their destination, if he had one. Kirsty had been dazed, not enthralled, by the size of the city. She had been deafened, choked and generally jostled and had had no opportunity to pause before the great gaslit stores, the 'Bonanza' sales, window displays of incredible richness and variety.

Every conceivable commodity was for sale in Glasgow, weird and wonderful objects as well as food and drink and clothing. Corsets, artificial limbs, anchors, metal chimney cowls were all shown off behind glass, like treasures in a museum. Meat by the ton and beer and spirits by the gallon, gaudy hoardings and posters for theatre shows, craft shops exhibiting violins and bath taps, cabinets and laces; Kirsty could not take in a tenth of it all as she dragged along by Craig's side on his tour of hotels and boarding-houses.

He would pause on the pavement outside an establishment, study its tariff board and dinner menu, complain about the price and lead Kirsty away before she had a chance to offer an opinion. She did not know what rate was expensive, what was cheap. It was not her money that would pay for their room and board. Craig had eyes only for notices that offered *Rooms*. But he rejected each and every one of the accommodations with a shake of the head, and went on, lugging the canvas grip and holding Kirsty by the arm. It grew dark. Dusk accumulated in the smoke, settled over the long streets and roadways. Pedestrian traffic on the pavements grew heavier. Gas-lamp lighters trooped about with long poles on their shoulders and brought a golden glow to the closes and the lanes. On Craig went, dourly, until St Vincent Street had been left behind and they were tramping along Dumbarton Road.

At length Kirsty put her foot down. She stopped dead in her tracks, like Nero.

"Craig Nicholson, I'm starved," she said.

"Oh! Aye, I'm hungry myself."

"Can we not find somethin' to eat in this town?"

He frowned. Realising that Craig would be quite incapable of making up his mind which tea-room, restaurant or pie-shop should have their custom she grabbed him by the arm and whisked him into the first place that advertised *Sit Down Suppers* and from whose doorway wafted a delicious effluvium of pan fat.

It was hardly the Grand Hotel. Four or five wooden tables and a dozen wooden chairs, no customers; the man in a dirty apron who emerged from behind a curtain in the rear of the shop did not exactly brim with welcomes. He told them what there was to eat in a dialect so coarse that it was all Craig and Kirsty could do to make sense of it.

The choice of fare was strictly limited but Kirsty was so hungry that a dish of fried haddock, boiled potatoes and white beans seemed like a royal feast, a cup of black-brewed tea like finest champagne. She concentrated on appeasing her appetite while Craig ate with an air of distraction and gazed out of the window over the wooden half-partition.

"What are you lookin' for, Craig?"

"I think we've come west."

"West?"

"Do you not remember Mr Douglas?"

"Who's he?"

"Did you not go to Sunday School at Bankhead kirk?"

"You know I didn't. I wasn't allowed."

"Aye, that's right. Well, Mr Douglas was my Sunday School teacher. He told us all about Glasgow. He used to come up here for prayer meetin's an' Bible study. He said the nicest part o' the city was the west end. Told us about this place he stayed in."

"How long ago was this, Craig?"

"Nine years, ten maybe."

"Perhaps it's changed since then."

"Nah. It would be the place for us, if I could find it."

"What was the name o' the street, where Mr Douglas stayed?"

"Nineteen was the number. Funny me rememberin' that."

"An' the name o' the street?" Kirsty prompted.

"Walbrook Street. Aye, that's it."

"But where *is* Walbrook Street?"

"Somewhere near here," Craig said. "I think."

It did not occur to Kirsty any more than it did to Craig that they might dare to become passengers upon a municipal horse-tram or even to hire a cab to drive them to the destination that had become so obsessively fixed in Craig's mind.

Kirsty said, "Look, you'd better ask somebody. It's gettin' late. We might be miles from Walbrook Street."

"Good idea, Kirsty," Craig said. "But who can I ask?"

"Ask the man when he comes for the money."

In spite of his apparent truculence the man from behind the curtain turned out to be amiable and helpful. He led Craig out on to the pavement and, observed by half a dozen small boys who seemed to find the scene entertaining, pointed out directions with a great many zig and zags and rolling motions of his fat hands.

Craig thanked the man profusely and, taking Kirsty's arm once more, hurried her along the road in a more cheerful mood.

"It's not far, Walbrook Street," he told her.

Dumbarton Road was broad and bustling but navigation seemed to come naturally to Craig and he turned confidently from the main thoroughfare into a maze of short, tenemented side streets. Finally he rounded a corner marked by a small clean-cut church, into a row of trim terraced houses set behind patches of what had once been grass. There was only one 'side' to the street. Even Craig paused at the sight of the spectacular skyline that towered over the green privet hedges. Cranes and masts and ships' rigging and the blank gables of sheds and warehouses were cut from the odd beige glow that never seemed to leave the Glasgow sky.

"Is this Walbrook Street?" said Kirsty.

"Aye. I never thought I'd be here."

"Like Mr Douglas?" said Kirsty.

"Well, hardly," said Craig. "I mean, we're not goin' to a prayer-meetin', are we?"

Number 19 was only fifty yards along the street from the kirk corner. It had a plain black door and a transom of dove-grey glass and a low step of some marble-like material. It struck Kirsty as queer that such a fine row of houses would be sited in the shadow of quays and dockland cranes.

There was a bell-pull with a wrought-iron handle, above it a painted board of no great size: *Accommodation for Gentlemen – No Mercantiles – No Commercials*.

Craig hesitated. He stepped on to the step with Kirsty clinging to his arm, rang the bell and waited, stiff and tense and silent, trying to appear as un-mercantile and un-commercial as possible.

The outline of the woman was abruptly there in the open doorway, as if she had been seated behind it like a porter.

"Aye?" she said.

"A – accommodations?" Craig stammered.

"I am vacant, as it happens. How long are you?"

"What?"

"Staying?"

"Oh," said Craig. "Three nights, at least."

"Step inside, if you please."

The place had the same sort of smell as Baird Home dormitories. For that reason it seemed unfriendly to Kirsty as she followed Craig over the threshold into the hallway.

Old Saint Andrew was quick to draw her eye. For the rest there was a huge lump of oak furniture, a sideboard perhaps, two plants with longboat leaves, and just the peep of a gas jet under a glass funnel to give light to the ground floor.

"I am Mrs Agnes Frew. Names?"

"Mr Craig Nicholson an' – an' Miss Barnes."

"Not related?"

"No, we – we're here to get married."

"Are you, indeed? Not in my house."

"No, I – I – we – Two rooms," said Craig.

"Have you a recommendation?"

"What?"

"I prefer references," said Agnes Frew.

"Mr – Mr James Douglas," Craig stammered.

"Mr Douglas?"

"From Bankhead, in Carrick. He told me—"

"Oh, that Mr Douglas."

Mrs Frew smiled. Kirsty assumed it was a smile. The woman was small and prim and seemed coated with a fine white powder about the face, head and shoulders. Her hair was gathered into tight, girlish buns worn like ear-muffs, hair that was neither quite white nor quite blonde. Her complexion too was bloodlessly pale. The only hint of colour was about her eyes which, as they were not back-lit like those of the patron saint, were pink and dull. It was impossible to guess at Mrs Frew's age for she had the immutable and unchanging quality of wax statuary.

"Mr Douglas," said Craig, "told me to come here."

"Presbyterian?"

"Aye," said Craig.

"Regular?"

"What?"

"On the Sabbath?"

"Never miss a Sunday at Bankhead kirk." Craig answered with such sincerity that Kirsty was almost tempted to believe him.

She was unprepared for the woman's question to her.

"Pure?" Mrs Frew enquired.

"I – I don't understand what you mean," said Kirsty.

"Before marriage?"

Craig cleared his throat. Kirsty wondered if he would take umbrage at the personal nature of the question and would defend her against its unpleasant implications.

She was a good Christian girl, even if circumstances had prevented her attending the kirk very often. She bristled with resentment. Craig said nothing, however, merely gave her a nudge with his elbow to indicate that the question would have to be answered.

"Aye, Mrs Frew," Kirsty heard herself say.

"Mr Douglas," said Craig, "would not have sent us here otherwise."

Mrs Frew gave another smile, as crimped and enigmatic as the first. "Mr Douglas knows how I am on purity. Blessed are the pure in heart, the Good Book says."

Craig said, "For they shall see God – if I'm not mistaken."

Mrs Frew was delighted. "You are not mistaken, Mr Nicholson. And the meek shall inherit the earth, will they not?"

"They will, they will, ma'am," Craig unctuously agreed.

46

"That's the way of it," said Mrs Frew. "Now, it's one shilling and sixpence for each room, each night, which includes clean sheets and a breakfast. Half past seven o'clock in the dining-room: I would prefer it if you paid me in advance, since Mr Douglas hasn't been here for a while."

They still had not strayed one foot from the vault-like hallway and no evidence of other guests had been seen or heard.

Stepping closer to the tiny gas jet, Mrs Frew held out her hand, not graspingly but close to her bosom, white against the ribbed black bombazine blouse.

Craig had already separated a single five-pound note from the sheaf in his trouser pocket and he tugged it out now and laid it solemnly across the landlady's palm.

She looked down at it, smiling. "Three nights?"

"At least," said Craig.

"All paid in advance?"

"Aye, we'll collect the change before we leave."

"A sound arrangement," said Mrs Frew.

Any hopes that Craig might have nurtured of creeping into his beloved's bed were dashed by the disposition of the rooms as well as that of the landlady. Kirsty was led upstairs while Craig, to his consternation, was left to cool his heels in the hall. His room, it seemed, was situated in the basement while Kirsty, like an angel, was to take her repose much higher up.

Mrs Frew said, "I see you've no luggage."

Kirsty had already learned the value of a fib. "My basket's bein' sent on."

"Came away in a hurry, did you?"

"A bit," said Kirsty. "Craig – Mr Nicholson – he has to see about a job tomorrow. I came along with him to buy my trousseau."

Mrs Frew might have continued her line of enquiry if Kirsty had not paused on the half-landing to admire the picture.

Saint Andrew had indeed been rendered in stained glass, coloured lumps of the stuff fastened by lead beading into a wooden frame fixed to two long wooden feet. The stand was set upright before a second small gas jet which flared quietly and unflickeringly behind it.

Noticing Kirsty's interest Mrs Frew paused on the steep dark stair above her.

"Is it not beautiful?"

"Aye, it certainly is," said Kirsty.

"My husband made it. Specially for me," said Mrs Frew. "Before he died, of course."

Below in the hallway Craig smothered laughter under a sudden bout of coughing while Kirsty, lips compressed, followed the woman upward into a region as dark as sin.

It was, as it happened, a pleasant if musty room. There was a narrow wooden bed with a headboard of polished mahogany and a spread of imitation silk. As soon as she had lighted the oil-lamp – no gas this high in the house – Mrs Frew removed the bedspread, folded it expertly and slid it into a large brown paper envelope which she popped into the bottom drawer of a tallboy. On top of the tallboy, Kirsty noticed, was a mirror, no fly-blown shard but a big clean square on a stand that could be tilted. She had seen drawings of such things in journals and had always longed to have one of her own. The wash-stand had a top of white marble upon which stood a jug of clean water and a basin. There was even a flowered dish to hold a piece of dry soap and a rail upon which were draped two towels. Tucked discreetly beneath the wash-stand was a chamber-pot in a pattern that matched the soap dish.

Kirsty sighed. It was, without doubt, the most elegant room she had ever been in, more austere, perhaps, than the parlour at Bankhead with its stuffed furniture and shelves of bric-à-brac, but more stylish too, in Kirsty's opinion. Her weariness sloughed off at the sight of the bed, its pillow in a slip of cream lace. Though there was no fire lighted in the miniature grate the lamp itself spread a warm glow and softened the angles of the ceiling which jutted in all sorts of directions and of the heavy brocade curtains which hung on brass rods across the window bay.

"View of the river," Mrs Frew said.

Kirsty gave the landlady a genuine smile.

This was not how she had imagined her first night in Glasgow, not by a long chalk. Oddly, she was relieved that she would not have to spend it in bed with Craig. She was happy to be alone, to savour the luxury of Mrs Agnes Frew's establishment without having to contend with other novelties, with Craig.

The woman, who had been observing her closely, said, "You're just a country lass, are you not?"

"Aye, ma'am. I am."

"What is he to you?"

"He'll be my husband, as soon as we can be married."

Mrs Frew breathed gently, hardly even a sigh.

"You look too young for that sort of thing," she said.

"I'm eighteen, Mrs Frew."

"I did not marry until late in life. It took my Andrew five years to persuade me." She breathed out again. "I must say that in retrospect there are times when I think I should have done it sooner."

Kirsty did not know what to make of the woman. She was disconcerted by the fleeting revelation of lost happiness.

She said, "Has he been gone long; Mr Frew, I mean?"

"These fifteen years."

"I'm sorry to hear it."

"Oh, no need to sympathise. I've no regrets. I have my comforts, and the Lord sustains me."

"Aye," said Kirsty, without cynicism, "I imagine the Lord is a great comforter."

"Do you say your prayers?"

"Sometimes; not as often as I should."

"Do you attend religious worship?"

"When I can."

"You'll know, then?"

"Know what, Mrs Frew?"

"Perils and pitfalls," said the woman. "Pitfalls and perils. Traps for the unwary. Watch him." She turned down the quilted cover and gave it a neat dextrous flick that exposed a perfect triangle of cream linen sheet. "There can be a terrible strong corruption in young men."

In the lamplight the woman's eyes had become even pinker but her paleness had been lessened by the glow of the wick-flame.

Before Kirsty could find words to defend Craig, Mrs Frew said, "Breakfast. Half past seven. Prompt and punctual."

"Yes, Mrs Frew."

The woman withdrew to the corner by the door. She left the lamp, would risk finding her way down three flights of steep steps without a light to guide her.

Kirsty gave the landlady a cheerful goodnight. She was relieved, though, when Mrs Frew went out and closed the door behind her and she was free at last to let her excitement have its head.

She was drawn to the window as if by a magnet. She parted the curtains and stepped into an alcove that was almost as large as the bothy at Hawkhead.

From this vantage point the city seemed less diffuse and somehow much grander. Her room was tucked under the eaves. Wisps of grass and weed had found root in the gutter, hung down like hair over the glass and fluttered in the breeze off the river.

Beyond the privet hedge Kirsty saw a park of some sort, very flat and precisely bordered. There was a pavilion with a Chinese tower into which was set a huge round clock. She could make out the face perfectly and read the time; twenty minutes to ten o'clock.

If she had been at home in Hawkhead she would have been in bed by now, lonely as well as alone. Here in Glasgow she did not feel that sort of loneliness. Suddenly her heart was beating hard in her chest. She spread her fingers over her breast. She had never been so happy. In Carrick she had been nothing but the girl from the Baird Home, Clegg's lass. Here in Glasgow she could become what she wished, a new person, wife to Mr Craig Nicholson.

The whoop of a steam whistle disturbed her thoughts.

Into sight came an engine spouting sparks. It passed along the plain between park and quays and drew behind it, clinking and chuckling, a caravan of coal wagons which rolled on monotonously until Kirsty grew bored with waiting for it to end.

Below on the pavement a middle-aged man and woman walked a pet dog, a terrier, strolled arm-in-arm along Walbrook Street. Perhaps Craig and she would walk like that, taking a breath of air before bed. Four dark-skinned men, heads wrapped in white scarves, scurried past the house, muttering to themselves. A two-wheeled cab, drawn by a lean, high-stepping horse, whisked under the lamp-standard and Kirsty glimpsed a taffeta skirt and a pair of jet black boots on the board.

It was all too much for her. She stepped back into the clean, well-furnished room. She could not believe that it was her room, at least for a time, that she might sleep in the bed, wash in the basin, sit before the mirror. The pleasure of it had to be expressed somehow.

She pirouetted, arms above her head, her patched old skirt swirling, her auburn hair shaking loose a little from its braids.

Glasgow, she felt, was a warm and welcoming place where a young wife might settle and be happy.

Tomorrow, she would learn the truth.

TWO

The Narrow Place

Kirsty had no idea where they were going when they left Number 19 or what particular plans Craig had made for the day.

She had slept well, undisturbed by the strange noises that floated over the shunting-yards and the dockside. She had not wakened until seven o'clock, a half-hour after her usual time of rising. On the ground floor the dining-room contained eight chairs, a sideboard and a long dark-oak table. There appeared to be no other guests in residence but the breakfast, served by a girl of about Kirsty's age, was substantial. Mrs Frew, who made only one appearance 'upstairs', was not quite so wispy and pink as she had seemed by gaslight. Politely she enquired if they had slept well, was gratified to hear that they had, asked what they would care for for breakfast and whether they would 'care to partake of an evening meal'. There was no development of that confidential rapport which had shown itself for a second or two in the bedroom and Kirsty was puzzled by the woman.

Craig, however, was much less sensitive to the subtleties of Mrs Frew's character and, as soon as they had turned from the path and had taken a few steps along Walbrook Street, he said, "Old bitch. We'll have to get out of there quick as we can."

"She seems quite nice to me," said Kirsty.

"*Nice!* Not her. I know her sort. Nobody else there, did you notice? Not bloody surprised. Like a damned mausoleum, yon place."

"Craig, where are we going?"

"To look for things."

"What things?"

"Well, since you told her you had a 'basket' on the way, we'll have to buy you clothes, won't we?" Craig said. "You can't go on wearin' what you stand in."

Kirsty was confused. The prospect of having money to purchase clothing was enormously pleasing but there was a disgruntled and grudging mood on Craig this morning that she believed might stem from regret at yesterday's impetuous gesture, at quitting Dalnavert's secure existence just for her sake. She said nothing. They reached the corner by the church and, walking quickly, rounded out of Walbrook Street into the busy thoroughfare of Dumbarton Road.

Craig said, "I'll need to look for a job of some sort."

She was sensible enough to realise that she must let Craig make the running. He looked untidy, for some reason, and fatigued, as if he had not slept well. The grousing, grumbling note remained in his voice.

"We need a place to ourselves," he said. "Anywhere that's private."

Kirsty said, "Should we not stay where we are at least for a day or two?"

Craig squinted at her. "I thought we were supposed to be gettin' married? It's not my idea o' marriage for you to be in the attic an' me in the bloody cellar."

"We'll look for some place, Craig. It's a good idea."

Her response seemed to placate him and, for the first time that morning, though it was broad daylight and the pavement was populated with women, children and elderly men, Craig took her arm in his, drew her against him and kissed her on the mouth.

Kirsty put her modesty aside, let her lips linger.

"I can't wait," Craig said. "Last night was a torment."

Kirsty said, "What can we afford, Craig?"

"Somethin' decent," Craig said. "Some sort o' place where we can be man an' wife."

It was, so she told herself later, all Craig's fault. If Craig had not encouraged her to ignore the cut-price stalls and bargain-basements that abounded on the nether edge of Anderston and Argyle Street and accompany him instead to the block-long fashion house of Allardyce and Prosser where, on annual pilgrimages, his mother bought all her clothes, then the spending spree might never have begun.

Armed with a paper street map that he purchased along with a newspaper and a packet of cigarettes, Craig confidently led his lady-love to Charing Cross and into Sauchiehall Street, a distance of some two miles from Agnes Frew's boarding-house. Here, on the sharp corner of Spring Street, eight great pavement-level plate-glass windows displayed modes, mantles and millinery.

Wise in the ways of retailing, Messrs Allardyce and Prosser did not clutter their spacious floors with household goods and domestic commodities to distract and depress their customers with reminders of life's harsh realities. Within the precincts of the fashion house reality was full-length mirrors and racks of gowns. Between the broad glass-topped counter slender plaster models were decked in handmade laces and Swiss embroidery, in frilly little capes of *peau de soie* and coats of chiffon *glacé*, tea-jackets and Empire gowns, delaine blouses, slips and stoles and nainsook camisoles. Lighting was discreet and indirect, 'trying-on' rooms plush and private. The assistants, all female, had been selected for their looks and trained to flatter, cajole and serve as conspirators in acts of outrageous extravagance.

Stunned by the window displays, Kirsty could hardly believe her ears when Craig instructed her to walk inside and buy whatever she fancied, plus a hand-sized luggage basket to give truth to her lie to Mrs Frew. Shopping for anything except 'buttons and pins' was a heady new experience for Kirsty. She had never had a penny to call her own, had never enjoyed the exhilaration of shopping for its own sake, an exercise that she was soon to learn lay on a higher plane than mere acquisition. Even so, at that stage it was still Kirsty's intention to restrict herself to buying stockings, summer-weight drawers, two vests, a night-gown and, perhaps, a one-and-ninepenny skirt to replace the rags she had travelled in. Craig was airily insistent; buy something nice and suitable for city wear. She was no farmyard skivvy now, was she? Soon, indeed, she would be marrying a city gent, though how that transformation would be accomplished was a question that remained unanswered.

Naturally Craig would not be caught dead inside such a repository of feminine culture. He hung about on the pavement, his back to the windows, paced up and down, smoked three of his five cigarettes, watched a gang of labourers tear up cobbles and a tar-boiler pour out pitch, eyed the pert and pretty misses from the professional offices and ogled the elegant ladies as they climbed in and out of cabs and carriages and showed their ankles, all very aware of themselves. He had told Kirsty to take her time, to set the goods she wanted to one side, come out, tell him how much she had spent and he would give her the money. He still had a market mentality. He did not trust swanky city shopkeepers any more than he trusted Irish horse-traders. He expected Kirsty to be absent for about ten minutes or a quarter of an hour; Craig had never been in a clothing store with his mother and had no notion of the sort of haze that can descend on a girl under such circumstances. Kirsty was gone for well over an hour. She emerged – at last – glowing.

Craig said, "About bloody time."

She looked jubilant, radiant.

"How much?" he enquired, realising that no matter what sum she had spent it would be cruel to go back on his word. "What's the bad news?"

"It's – it's seven pounds an' eight shillin's."

"*What!*"

"But Craig, you told me—"

"Aye, aye."

Stoically he dug into his trouser pocket and took out one of the fivers and three single pound notes. Glancing furtively this way and that, as if he expected to be picked up for soliciting a lady's favours on a public thoroughfare, he slipped the money into her hand. Kirsty kissed him on the cheek and, laughing, whirled and shot like an arrow back through the shop's swing-door.

"Seven bloody guineas!" Craig murmured under his breath, "Dear God!" and lighted another cigarette even though his throat, unused to such indulgence, was sore and constricted.

The essential folly was a powder-blue costume with a shaped bolero jacket and a mermaid skirt. It was totally impractical, hardly the sort of rig she could wear to scrub steps or polish brasses. But she could not resist the appeal of the garment or the patter of the smart Glaswegian counter-hands, who *oohed* and *aahed* and assured her, when she tried the costume on for size, that she would knock all the lads for six in that one. Kirsty convinced herself that Craig would adore it as much as she did, would be proud to be seen with her in the powder-blue.

After spending three pounds and fourteen shillings on the original items, spending more seemed as easy as sweeping a floor. She flitted from department to department with an almost proprietorial air and purchased a pair of quite sensible shoes, a useful long coat of showerproof cloth, similar to Mrs Nicholson's, and a plain – well, plainish – hat. Finally she bought a dress-hamper in buff wicker, had the assistants accumulate her purchases at the counter in the gown department and total up the cost.

It did not strike Kirsty that she had acted irresponsibly or that Craig, in not clipping her spendthrift wings, was being irresponsible too. In due course she emerged from the door of the fashion house accoutred in all her finery, lugging the basket and an extra brown-paper parcel. She had a suspicion that it hadn't been quite 'proper' to put on the new clothes there in the shop and carry her old ones away but she no longer cared. She cared even less for customs and good manners when she saw the effect that the outfit had on Craig. She slipped her arm through his and made him turn around. His mouth opened, and his eyes were round as saucers.

"My God, Kirsty! What've you done to yourself?"

"Do you not like it?"

"Aye," he said, inspecting her. "Aye, you're a corker, a real corker."

"It cost an awful lot o' money, Craig."

"It was worth it," he said.

"What do we do now, Craig?"

He shrugged. He had formulated no plan for the rest of the day, had only a vague notion that he must soon look for work.

Kirsty said, "Then can we get somethin' to eat, dear? Shoppin' fair makes you hungry."

"No sooner said than done," Craig told her, and led her off along Spring Street in search of a tea-room.

In the end the day perished. Not to be outdone, after a 'luncheon' fit for a king in Miss Godfrey's Restaurant, Craig had decided that he too must have a rig suitable for a Glasgow man and had paraded Kirsty about, toting the wicker basket and the parcel, while he inspected gentlemen's fashions in shop windows within a square-mile radius of Charing Cross. Finally he bought a new cotton shirt, a necktie, a pair of brown shoes, a striped blazer and cream-toned flannel trousers. He put each item on as he purchased it, folding his own garments into a new canvas carrier, then the couple gravitated back towards Walbrook Street, drifting along dusty pavements amid the bustle of the town to which they did not yet, somehow, belong.

With legs aching and back twingeing, Kirsty hobbled on in the unfamiliar constricting skirt. The pavements of the streets became hard and less yielding as the day went on and even Craig, for all his fitness and stamina, was ground down, as much, he claimed, by the racket as by the walking. They found a place to sit at last, not a park but a patch of sour grass against a high dirty brick wall, a bench of wood and iron that seemed so old that it might have been a fossil.

They were no more than a half-mile from Walbrook Street, Craig said, and Kirsty, with inexplicable relief, recognised the skyline. Goods stations and mineral depots crammed the area, a delta of iron rails thunderous with tank engines and shunters and those interminable caravans of trucks and coal wagons. Beyond lay the sheds and moorings of the Queen's Dock. The sun had gone in and a grey wind swirled about the back street chasing paper scraps and cindery dust and carrying the raw sounds of foundry hammers and timber saws to them. But to sit, even there, was a relief. Craig slumped elbows on knees, lit his last cigarette and inexpertly blew little puffs of smoke at the ground.

Kirsty kneaded her calves with her hands, trying to unknot the muscles. Her new shoe, on her right foot, slipped off and hung suspended from her toe. She looked at it disconsolately, saw that the leather was already scuffed about the toe and that the heel had a scar on it. Away to the left an empty tram rolled along the street, the horses lathered and exhausted, heading for the terminus and their stables.

"What time does she put out the supper?" Craig asked.

"Half past six."

"It must be near that now."

"Only ten past five," said Kirsty.

"How do you know?"

"I saw a clock."

Craig blew more balls of tobacco smoke.

The new boater was tilted back, exposing dark hair curled over his brow. He did not look like a gentleman. In the ill-fitting, carrot-striped blazer he seemed like a boy dressed up.

"We'll go back there," Craig said "For tonight."

"I thought we were going to stay there until you found—"

"Not now," he said.

Kirsty noticed that he did not attempt to meet her eye. She was not tempted to touch him either and leaned into the arm of the bench which, she noticed with indifference, was pocked with rust and had already deposited a dusty smear upon the material of her bolero.

Craig shivered. He watched the wind swirl trash up the lane and lag it against the barred gate of a coal yard. Perhaps, Kirsty thought, he was remembering the field at Dalnavert; he would have put in a long, useful day on it and now, with the sun lowering westward, he would be preparing to head for the farm, for a hot supper and a warm fire and crack with his sister and brother. Hawkhead, Bankhead, the rolling hills of Carrick seemed so far, far, far away. She too felt pangs of homesickness, though, God knows, she had never been happy there. But at least it had been her place and she had known what was expected of her and what pattern each day would bring.

She reached out and put an arm about Craig. Startled out of his reverie, he glanced at her and then caught her head and brought it to him, her lips to his mouth, their hats tilting awkwardly. He kissed and cuddled her, rubbed his chest against her breasts but it was done without real desire and the moment of forced passion ended with a sudden deafening shriek as, somewhere behind the brickwork, a steam klaxon sounded.

Craig leapt as if it had been a police whistle and Kirsty flinched too.

Seconds later, from a gateway hidden some hundred yards down the lane, a crowd of women and girls emerged, twenty or more, shawled and aproned, all in a hurry to quit the work place. They swamped the lane, four, five, seven abreast, some with arms linked, some walking with elbows clenched to their chests, indrawn, scowling.

Craig and Kirsty gaped.

The girls were followed by men, young and old, and a handful of boys no older than Gordon. They sped past energetically. The men were dusted with a strange white coating which, in the March breeze, whirled from them like ectoplasm as if their spirits were being released as well as their bodies.

There was a threatening sense of purpose in the workers as they crammed the lane, heading fast away from the factory, but some, the younger girls and men, had time enough to notice the odd-looking couple on the bench, to laugh, wink and point them out. Chirping noises were addressed in their direction, catcalls, cutting sarcasm: "Hey, Jenny, see the gingerbread man. Aye, him in the strippit coat there. Thinks its the Groveries, so he does, him an' his wee budgerigar. *Cheep, cheep, cheep.*"

Craig shot to his feet, bristling at the insults; then sat down again.

Taking a clay pipe from his mouth, spitting, a man shouted, "Lost yer yacht, sonnie, eh?"

This comment was taken up, swelled into a snatch of song: "*Sailin', sailin', over the boundin' main.*"

Nobody stopped for conversation, polite or otherwise, and Craig and Kirsty were obliged to remain where they were, rigid with embarrassment like a couple clamped into village stocks. In three or four minutes the bulk of the crowd had departed.

"What – what do they do?" Kirsty whispered.

"Search me," Craig answered.

Still Craig and Kirsty did not move to escape. They stared down the lane, craned forward, watching as an old man with a club-foot came limping out of the gate. Hands in pockets, pipe in mouth, he clumped towards them, paying them no attention at all.

"Sir?" Craig got to his feet, took off the daft boater and left it on the bench. "Sir, what do they make in there?"

The eyes were not inquisitive, the expression was neither friendly nor hostile.

"Pots," he answered tersely.

"Pots?"

"Crocks, pots, china-like."

He glanced at Kirsty. There might have been a softening of the bunches of tight muscle under his powdered moustache; Kirsty could not be sure.

"Sir, would there be work goin' there?" Craig called out.

"Aye, for skilled hands." The old man with the club-foot went on at his clumping pace. "No' for a bloody farm labourer – or his pretty lassie."

Taken aback, Craig sat down again.

"How did he know? How the hell did he know?" Craig asked, bemused.

"Your voice, perhaps," said Kirsty.

"He knew I was a bloody hick, just by lookin' at me."

"Craig, it was only a guess."

Craig got to his feet again.

Men in bowler hats were coming out of the gate now, a handful of them and one or two neatly dressed chaps upon clean, green-painted bicycles, trousers shaped to their calves by wire clips.

"No work for a farm labourer, eh?" Craig muttered and, snatching up the wicker dressing-case, left Kirsty to collect their parcels and follow him back to Walbrook Street and the shelter of Number 19.

It appeared that the Reverend Vass was a frequent guest at Mrs Frew's establishment. He was treated more like a first-born son than a man of the cloth and was attended throughout the meal not by Cissie, the maid, but by Mrs Frew in person.

If Kirsty and Craig were somewhat in awe of the religious gentleman from Edinburgh the same could not be said for the fourth dinner guest, Hugh Affleck, Mrs Frew's brother. He was a tall, red-cheeked man of about fifty, clean-shaven and dry, with merriment, as well as a trace of slyness, in his bright blue eyes.

Kirsty was fascinated by the ebb and flow of conversation between the gentlemen but, at first, took no part in it. By certain remarks made by Mr Affleck she gathered that Mr Vass was a scholar and orator who had travelled from Edinburgh to address the Society of Biblical Research in one of the University buildings that very evening.

"Will old Stewart be there?" Mr Affleck asked the minister.

"Professor Stewart will be in the chair."

"Oh, so there's to be a debate afterwards, is there?"

"The meeting is not open to the public," said Mr Vass quickly, evidently to forestall any mischief that Mr Affleck may have had in mind.

"I see," said Hugh Affleck. "It'll not be much of a debate in that case since all of you there will be of one mind."

To Craig Mrs Frew said, "Did you enjoy that, young man?"

"Aye, I did."

"Custard?" said Mrs Frew.

"Aye," said Craig. "I like custard, thanks."

Kirsty watched the ladle dip into the glass bowl. She wondered how such a thickness had been achieved. She could never get custard to stand like that and even Mr Clegg, no epicure, had complained that it was more like lentil soup than a decent pudding. But out it came, standing firm on the ladle, and held shape when it was put into the plate, like a mountain floating in a lake of apple juice.

"Here," said Mrs Frew, dumping a pudding-plate before her brother. "See if that'll shut you up."

"Full cream, I see," said Hugh Affleck. "My, my! You should be honoured, Mr Vass. Only very special guests get the full-cream treatment."

The Reverend Vass did not deign to acknowledge the remark and made no comment concerning the richness of the pudding which he put away with great efficiency in two or three mouthfuls. Like Hugh Affleck, Kirsty allowed the custard to melt in her mouth, savouring its blend of sweetness and sharpness. Glancing at her, Hugh Affleck held her gaze and winked.

"Positively sinful, ain't it?" he murmured.

Kirsty chuckled and nodded while Mr Vass and Mrs Frew regarded her with a hint of condescension.

Without preliminary Hugh Affleck said, "Now, it's a pity you hadn't been orating on the benefits of Christian marriage, Mr Vass. You could have taken an eager pair for your audience, unless I'm much mistaken."

Craig flushed, pretended that he had not heard. Kirsty, however, was flattered to learn that she had acquired a 'bridal look'. The new powder-blue costume had obviously given Mr Affleck his clue.

"I'm not married yet, Mr Affleck," she said.

"'Deed you're not," Hugh Affleck said. "My sister does not take 'doubles'. She's no more keen on havin' married couples under her roof than she is on Lascars or travellin' salesmen."

"Hughie," Mrs Frew warned, "I'll not stand for that talk."

"What talk? By God, Nessie, there are times when you carry decorum too far. I mean, we're all married here, or have been. I didn't notice that you barred the door against randy old Andy when he was alive and kicking."

For a moment Kirsty thought that Mrs Frew was about to pitch the custard-dish at her outspoken brother's head.

Mr Vass prudently intervened. "May I have a drop of tea, Mrs Frew, if you will be so kind? I see that the enemy has caught up with me and I must leave very soon for the university."

"I'll have a word with you later, Hughie," Mrs Frew said, and went out of the dining-room to obey the minister's request.

Mr Vass turned in his chair and peeped out of the window. "It remains dry, if blustery. I shall walk to the edifice on the hill, I believe."

"You'll be late returning, I expect."

"Your sister has kindly agreed to leave the door unbolted and to put the key on a string behind the letter-box."

"Aye, that should do it," said Hugh Affleck, "so long as you're sober."

The tea-pot was a huge knobbly affair of silver, and Cissie trotted out all the paraphernalia of jugs and bowls and tongs. Mr Vass attended with alacrity, downed a swift cup and, dabbing his lips with his napkin, made his excuses and left.

Good manners might dictate that Craig and she quit the dining-room too now, but Kirsty lingered, not knowing where they would go or how they would while away the evening.

It was far too early to retire to their – separate – rooms and she did not feel like strolling Glasgow's hard pavements for another couple of hours. It did not occur to her that the city had theatres and musical concerts, lectures and peepshows that Craig and she might attend at the cost of a shilling or two. She sipped her tea, brooding a little.

Mr Hugh Affleck, however, did not seem to be in a hurry to be off. From his vest pocket he took a silver case, clicked it open and offered it to Craig. Sanctioned by a nod from Kirsty, Craig helped himself to a cigarette, a strange oval-shaped one, and accepted a light from the match that Mr Affleck held up. Next, Mr Affleck stole from the table, stooped by a sideboard, opened a door and came back to his chair carrying a bottle of Teacher's Old Highland whisky and two glasses.

"You'll have a taste, Mr Nicholson?"

Craig hesitated. "Aye, why not? To be sociable."

"Just a wee drop, Craig," Kirsty said.

"Not used to it?" said Hugh Affleck, as he dispensed the whisky into the glasses. "Aye, it took me many a year, and much secret practice, to acquire a head for the stuff. Still, it sits down quiet and obedient after a buster. I'll say that for Nessie, she can cook a man a dinner fit for a king." He lifted the glass. "I'll drink a health to the pair of you, then."

"Many thanks." Craig lipped the amber liquid in his glass cautiously. He had downed pints of beer in the pub at Dunnet often enough but he had a fear of spirits and the hold they could put on a man, a lesson learned from his father's example. "The truth is, Mr Affleck, I'm more concerned wi' findin' work than findin' a minister to marry us – at least for a week or two."

"So you're prospecting for employment, are you?" said Hugh Affleck. "Tell me, what possessed you to come to the city without a job to fall into?"

"My father felt it was time I struck out on my own," Craig answered. "The farm where I was brought up would not support two families."

Kirsty was surprised at Craig's glibness.

Hugh Affleck puffed on his cigarette. "You've no craft, no trade?"

"None, outside farm labour."

"There's plenty of stock in Glasgow, you know. More mutton, beef and pork in this fair city than you'll find grazing in all of Ayrshire. Pigs from Ireland, sheep from Australia, cattle from the Argentine."

"I'm not sure I want—"

"Slaughterhouses at Hill Street, Scott Street and over at Victoria Street too," Hugh Affleck went on. "There's a Dead-Meat market in Moore Street. Home-fed and foreign carcasses galore. In addition there's the cattle mart itself. Thousands of hoofs and horns sold every month. And that makes no mention of the Plantation quay or Shieldhall where imported animals are unloaded into lairages."

Craig sipped his whisky thoughtfully. The air over the table was thick with tobacco smoke and sharp with the smell of the whisky. It seemed to Kirsty that Craig had already acquired a degree of urbanity that would cause him to resist work in musty straw and cow-splatter.

"Since you seem well acquainted wi' the employment situation, Mr Affleck, perhaps you can tell me how well these sort o' jobs pay."

"Ah, there's the rub, son," Hugh Affleck replied. "They pay only what they are worth, which isn't much. There are more country lads in Glasgow than there are jobs for them. Supply outstrips demand; therefore, low wages."

"I'm after somethin' better," said Craig.

Mr Affleck said, "What are your priorities?"

"A job, a place to stay, marriage," said Craig.

"It might not be so easy."

"Och, I'll take practically anythin' to get started."

Mr Affleck nodded. "Provided it's not on the docks or in the mart?"

"I've had enough of cattle."

Mr Affleck finished his whisky, poured himself another and, without offering a second dram to Craig, put the bottle away in the cupboard.

Standing by the sideboard, he said, "I'd better go through and placate my sister. Perhaps we'll meet again. I'm here for supper, sometimes, on Thursdays."

"We'll be gone," said Craig, "before next week."

"If you can find a place."

"Don't tell me there are no rooms to rent in Glasgow?"

"Precious few," said Mr Affleck.

"In that case why isn't this house full?"

"Because my sister has no need of the income and does not put herself out to attract residents," said Hugh Affleck. "I'd say that you pair were fortunate to be taken in. Our Nessie's very fussy."

Craig dabbed the coal of his cigarette into a porcelain ashtray.

"Anyway," said Hugh Affleck, "I wish you both well. Who knows, perhaps we'll bump into each other, since Glasgow's such a narrow place."

"A small world?" said Kirsty.

"Oh, very," Hugh Affleck said, and went out into the hallway and left the young couple alone.

There was a smell of spring threaded in the smoke reek and the dull metallic odour of the river. It seemed to exude from the hedges, plane trees and worn rugs of grass that lay before the houses. Arm in arm, like the couple she had seen from her window,

Craig and Kirsty strolled the length of Walbrook Street and back again. There was a light in the pavilion and, by peering through a gap in the hedge, Kirsty could see a handful of men within the building, gathered at a table; a committee in session.

Tonight, even with Craig's arm in hers, she felt unsettled, the mood caught from Craig. He was quiet, almost sullen, and would not be drawn into a discussion of his prospects.

"Perhaps Mr Affleck's right," Kirsty said, "about taking what you can find to get started."

"I've seen cattle slaughtered," Craig said. "I want none o' that trade."

"The docks then?"

"I want somethin' better – for both of us."

"How long will it take to find a job?"

"There's enough in the kitty, still," he said.

They walked on, in silence. The rattle of traffic came from Dumbarton Road, behind a rampart of tenements, but Craig seemed almost afraid of the thoroughfare, of its attractions.

Kirsty said, "At least we're comfortable where we are."

Craig said, "I don't like it."

"I thought the supper was—"

"It costs too much," Craig said. "Two rooms like that."

"Mr Affleck seemed to think—"

"Him!" said Craig with derision. "To hear him talk you'd think I was nothin', that that sister of his was doin' us a big favour by takin' us in. God, it would cost us thirty-five bob a week to stay there."

"Aye, it's a lot."

"Two rooms," Craig said.

"We – we spent too much, Craig. I shouldn't have bought—"

"You deserve fine clothes. I don't grudge it."

"I know, but—"

"What time is it?" he interrupted.

"About half past eight."

"I'm tired. We'll go back now."

They walked back to the boarding-house, passing the lighted windows of the terrace residences, seeing the lamps glowing warm behind the curtains, observing the quiet comings and goings of the folk who lived there, hearing, outside one house, a singsong to the strains of a piano and a violin. He did not kiss her at the door but found the key on its string by fumbling through the letter-box, fished it out, opened the door, pushed in.

The gloomy hall seemed friendlier now, almost familiar,

though she had been there only one night. Kirsty thought of her room and the privacy and pleasure of it. She would be sorry to leave Walbrook Street, even though she realised that Craig was right; it was too expensive and could not be permanent, was not the place for them. He gave her a peck upon the cheek and watched her from the hallway as she ascended the staircase past the gaslit stained-glass screen. Just as she reached the bend in the stairs, where it grew dark, a door opened to the left of the hall and she heard Mrs Frew enquire who it was there, heard Craig's voice; the low sullen mutter of conversation. No doubt he would be reassuring Mrs Frew that he was not about to sneak upstairs, to make her his wife before marriage. Kirsty sighed. She had hardly thought of that subject all day long. She listened while the voices went on and on, paused for a minute, and then continued. She could not imagine what Craig would have to say to the woman, what he might want from her.

In due course she heard doors close, heard the stairs to the basement creak, and it was quiet within the house again. She went on up to her bedroom and took off the powder-blue costume, hung it on a hanger and brushed the skirt carefully. Already there was mud around the hem. She took a duster to her shoes, put them under the bed, seated herself upon the edge of the bed, hands in her lap. The freight-yards did not seem so noisy tonight. Perhaps she was growing used to the din of trains, the rumbling of wagons. She did not feel sleepy, though her legs and back still ached from the long day upon Glasgow pavements. She glanced from time to time at the costume on its hanger, at her reflection in the mirror, felt empty, almost bored. Mr Affleck had called Glasgow 'a narrow place'; perhaps he was right.

It was around ten when she heard the street-door open. She had been at the window only minutes before, staring out at the docks and the sky and had seen no pedestrians in the street. Perhaps it was Mr Vass returning from his lecture at the University, though he had claimed that he would be late and she did not think that ten o'clock was 'late' for a city person. She parted the curtains and stepped into the alcove once more.

The wind had dropped, cloud had lifted, the sky had its own shine to it, deeper than the reflections of the city's lights. And there was Craig, boater upon his head, striped blazer buttoned, walking rapidly along the pavement away from Number 19. Kirsty felt suddenly cold. She clasped her arms about her body, shivering. Craig knew nobody in Glasgow. She imagined that he was seeking company, hurrying to a public house or, worse, to find a girl, a woman, one of the kind she had heard about so often, one of the kind that her mother had been.

Frantically she knelt by the window and fumbled with the brass handles. The window seemed to weigh a hundredweight and rose reluctantly as she thrust against it. Craig was almost out of sight before she managed to open the window and push her head and shoulders through the space and, craning out, looked towards the church corner.

Hands in pockets, hurrying, Craig crossed Walbrook Street at the corner. He did not, as Kirsty expected him to do, turn into Dumbarton Road. He headed for what seemed to be a blank brick wall and, as Kirsty watched, bewildered, stopped on the pavement before it. It was only then that she noticed the pillar-box. Craig took a letter from his pocket and put it carefully into the box, turned and came diagonally back across Walbrook Street, heading for the boarding-house.

Immediately Kirsty withdrew. She closed the window. She knelt in the alcove, forehead pressed against the cold glass until she heard the street-door open and close.

Craig must have borrowed paper, envelope and ink from Mrs Frew, had even purchased a stamp from her, perhaps. He had written a letter in the privacy of his room and had slipped out to put it in the mail. Kirsty knew at once that the letter would not be addressed to Craig's father but to his mother. In it, perhaps, he begged for understanding and forgiveness, inviting Madge Nicholson to come hotfoot from Carrick to drag him home again.

For hours Kirsty lay awake, fretting, fearful that Madge Nicholson would divulge her whereabouts to Mr Clegg and that he would come for her or, more probably, would report her to the authorities. It had been too good to last, her escape with Craig, like a dream come true. She should have known better than expect it to last.

When, over breakfast, Craig told her his plan she was too relieved, and too confused, to put up an argument, and meekly let him take her into town to be fitted for a wedding band.

The ring, Craig said, would make all the difference. It would make it very much easier to obtain a room to rent if they presented themselves as man and wife. Nobody would ask impertinent questions, would doubt that they were legally married. Look, Craig said, how it cost them twice as much money at Mrs Frew's. If, he said, they had had a wedding ring Mrs Frew would not have asked if they were man and wife but would have thought they were on their honeymoon, or something, and they might have saved the best part of four shillings. God knows, he said, they would soon whack through the rest of the stake unless they behaved sensibly; that meant saving every penny from now on, and that meant finding a place of their own at a reasonable sort of rent. The wedding-ring would be an investment, part of the saving. Nobody would ever guess that they weren't married since no landlord would ask to see the marriage certificate. Wasn't it just common sense, Craig said, to put the cart before the horse for a while so, once they were settled and had saved a bob or two, they might have a stylish wedding, all legal and proper, and a proper honeymoon too?

He made no mention of the letter. Kirsty did not have the temerity to ask him about it. She was too taken aback, too confused by his long harangue, hunched over the breakfast cups, to put up arguments against his plan. She wanted to be his wife and if it was not possible to be so under law then she must accept the next best thing. Craig was right. Who would know the difference?

The ring was bought from a small shop in Argyle Street. The jeweller was all attention, even although the plain golden band was not by any means expensive and the bridegroom indicated that he wanted one off the shelf, one that fitted, and that it would not be necessary to leave it to have it engraved.

"An' when's the happy day, sir?"

"Next Wednesday," Craig said.

"Ah, wedding bells, wedding bells. Be a big event, will it?"

"Big enough," said Craig.

"All the relatives?"

"Put it in a box, please," Craig said.

"Of course, sir, of course."

The jeweller, a man in middle life, small and pale and shabby, took Kirsty's hand and held it while he eased the gold band from her finger.

Craig paid in cash, of course, and Kirsty turned away as he laid two pound-notes upon the worn wooden counter. The jeweller snapped the ring into a tiny box upholstered in purple velvet.

"Do this way, sir?"

"Aye, that'll be fine."

Craig put the box into his pocket, collected nine shillings in change and they were out in the dusty street again and heading rapidly away from the shop.

Kirsty had not imagined that her 'wedding day' would be at all like this. She had not dwelt on the meaning of it, only on its trappings, of being, for one day, a special and distinctive person, loved and admired by all. But there was no romance in Craig Nicholson. He was too gauche to guess at Kirsty's needs. He did not suggest a wedding feast in a smart restaurant, did not even lead her to some shady and secluded spot in one of the parks, to make a ceremony of it. He stopped her by a shop-front under the spidery bridge that spanned Argyle Street and carried trains into Caledonian Central.

The moment, however perfunctory, would remain vivid in all its details until Kirsty's dying day. Pigeons swooped and crooned among the girders overhead. Horse-drawn trams clashed past on their lines and carters' voices echoed raucously, accompanied by the grumble of the big, iron-rimmed wheels on the cobbles. All about them were the real folk of Glasgow, not the west-enders, all moving, moving like a sluggish tide along the pavements of Argyle Street in the gusty March morning.

A contretemps with beer barrels and two burly draymen had drawn a crowd. Kirsty could see a policeman's hat among it and, yards along the road, cowered down by the stinking wet wall of a fishmonger's shop, a raddled female clad in a cape of cracked brown tarpaulin, barefoot and filthy, sucked on a bottle. The thunder of a train overhead bore down oppressively and droplets of brown water flicked across her cheek.

"Take it," Craig shouted. "Here, take the damned thing."

He gripped her wrist and turned it, turned her hand palm uppermost and put the little box upon it.

"Put it on, Kirsty," he cried.

The yell of steam from high above was heathen and barbaric and the hiss of brakes jolting the carriages to a halt at the platform within the station echoed in her head. She squeezed her eyes shut, trying not to cry, holding the little box of purple velvet in her fist.

"Put it on," he shouted, "then we can start."

Jostled by a gang of four men in aprons and flat hats who marched line abreast along the pavement, Kirsty stepped back and away from Craig, separated from him.

She found a refuge of sorts by a broken pipe which splashed into a drain in a niche between a flesher's and a grain-store. She opened the miniature box with her thumbnail and picked out the hammered gold ring. She glanced up at Craig on the pavement's edge, separated from him by the strutting apprentices. Across the street she saw a dray-horse making water, a young girl in a bulging shawl, an infant knotted against her breast, and the vagrant by the fishmonger's step suck from her bottle once more.

Kirsty shoved the ring on to her third finger. She held up her hand, fingers spread, to show Craig that she had done what he expected of her.

"There," she mouthed.

Craig nodded, elbowed his way to her.

"It looks fine," he shouted.

"Aye, it does."

Taking her firmly by the arm he pulled her after him. The little velvet box dropped from her grasp and was lost, whisked and kicked into the gutter by passing feet. Kirsty checked, dismayed, then yielded. Empty, the box meant nothing. The ring itself was tight and snug against her knuckle.

They struggled out of knots of pedestrians and paused at the corner.

Kirsty hoisted herself on tiptoe and shouted into Craig's ear, "Are we married now?"

"Near enough, Mrs Nicholson," he said, gave her a kiss upon the brow, and groping for her hand, led her on into Union Street without further ceremony or delay.

Eighteen carats of hammered gold conferred no immediate blessing on Craig and Kirsty Nicholson.

Housing was at a premium in Glasgow. The city was grossly overpopulated and various schemes by the city fathers, the City Improvement Trust for instance, to stimulate the private market had foundered on high interest rates and a chronic shortage of social conscience. Programmes of municipal improvement had swept away many of the stinking vennels and closes, slums that had grown cheek by jowl with the elegant eighteenth-century façades, but nothing worthwhile had replaced them. Piecemeal conversion of middle-class mansions and the flinging up of the odd tenement had done little to provide dwellings for working-class families. 'Model' lodging-houses, of municipal design, furnished shelter for more folk than ever found a home in council tenements. This urban phenomenon, as is the way, tickled the private sector, much to the detriment of the artisans who packed every neuk and cranny and had these 'made-down' houses bursting at the seams.

Houses of less capacity than two thousand cubic feet were officially inspected and registered and a metal ticket was fixed to the lintel stipulating the number of occupants permitted by law.

But such a law had no meaning for immigrants and wanderers and the homeless citizens of the Empire's second city. None of this history of municipal mismanagement mattered to Craig and Kirsty. All that concerned them was finding a place of their own, a room to rent at a price they could afford.

Local shops plastered their windows with advertisements for accommodations, wanted and on offer. It did not take Craig and Kirsty very long, however, to realise that the wording of the advertisements were masterpieces of literary sytle, of hyperbole and euphemism. *Comfortable Bed for Single Gent on Night Work* meant a doss in a corner of a kitchen shared with other shift workers. *Sleeping Quarters for Respectable Family*: six by eight feet in somebody's single-end, with hammocks on a pulley and children under five tucked up in baskets by the stove.

All that Friday Kirsty followed Craig on another of his interminable and indecisive treks about the west side of Glasgow. What Craig sought, of course, was the equivalent of a farm labourer's cottage within the confines of the city; a mirage. By late afternoon, bone-weary and dazed by the realities of the housing situation, he was desperate to find any sort of room at all. He would have had them in a box-bed in the lobby of a house in Cawdor Street even if Kirsty had not at last drawn the line.

She was aware that Craig wanted her in bed with him. But she was also aware that, in spite of their extravagances, they were not yet strapped for cash and could afford to spend another night or two in Mrs Frew's boarding-house.

"I'm not goin' in there, Craig," Kirsty snapped.

"It's just for a week or two. It's only three bob a week."

"It smells."

"When did you become so bloody fussy?"

"About ten minutes ago," Kirsty retorted. "I'm not sharin' with those folk."

"They're all right."

"Are they?"

"I suppose you'd rather be back in Walbrook Street?" Craig said.

"Aye, I would. Far rather."

"Sleepin' alone?"

"Not there, Craig. Not in any o' the places we've seen."

"It's not my bloody fault we can't find a room for rent."

"It's not mine either," Kirsty said. "I've done what you asked. I'm wearing a weddin' ring, Craig Nicholson, but I'll not spend my – my weddin' night stuck in a cupboard with ten strangers listenin' to our every move."

"Damn it, Kirsty, we could be weeks in Frew's."

"So we could."

"Money's—"

"I know how much is left," Kirsty told him.

They were standing on a lofty and exposed corner of a hillside street that looked down upon the docks. She had at last seen the Clyde in all its glory but she was too fatigued and far too angry to pay it much heed.

The properties here were old and crumbling and had the rat-infested, soil-streaked atmosphere of a slum. The March wind moaned in the closes and battered the broken fence of a Monumental Stonemason's yard and carried not only din but grit and grime from the yards on the riverside. It was only a quarter of a mile or so from Walbrook Street but it seemed to Kirsty like a nether world, not one raised up. She clung tenaciously to the solemn comforts of the boarding-house and resisted Craig's impatience and impracticality.

The prices they had been asked to pay for dosses, for bunks in communal rooms, for beds shared with strangers had appalled him too. Mrs Agnes Frew's charges had come to seem much more reasonable during the course of that day.

Craig leaned against the tenement wall. The stench of burnt cabbage, oozing from one of the windows, enveloped him. Against the sky, dwarfed by it, eight or ten children played in the gutter. Ragged and shrill, legs bowed, heads over-large, they had no individual identity and seemed, Kirsty thought, like mere daubs on that canvas sky. She had a horror of settling for a bed in a corner in a tenement here, a fear that Craig would take day labour, that she would give birth to children who would become like the little creatures on the horizon, stunted and ugly through no fault of their own. Even at their worst the communities of Dalnavert, Bankhead and Dunnet had offered nothing as bad as this.

She said, "No, Craig."

"Christ! For a stray from the Baird Home you're bloody fussy."

"Maybe that's why."

"What?"

"If I'd been more fussy, Craig, I might not have chosen you."

He had put a cigarette into his mouth and had a matchbox in his hand. Her statement, however, gave him halt. He paused, the cigarette dangling from his lip, his eyes round.

"Not have *chosen* me?" he said.

"You heard me."

She defied him. Already the city of Glasgow had woven into her some of its fibre. She would hear talk, later, of how the men and women of that place were losers in the world, pacified by poverty, content in their misery. She had no sense of it all in those early days and would not admit even a drop of such fatalism into her thinking. She was no servant now. She was a wife, albeit nominally, and she had a ring on her finger to prove it. She put her hands on her hips and cocked her chin.

"How much is left?" she demanded. "Exactly."

Craig did not have to fumble notes and coins from his pockets, did not have to take a tally.

"Eight pounds, eightpence," he told her.

"Three weeks," she said.

"Eh?"

"You know damned well what I mean," Kirsty told him.

Her strength astonished him. He had not expected it, had not recognised that quality in her before now.

Craig scratched his head, looked at her and then, embarrassed, gave a half-laugh. "We could find another place like Frew's, if that would suit you. Let on we're man an' wife.'

"Have you nothin' on your mind but bed?" Kirsty snapped. "You're frightened o' your marriage duties, is that it?"

"I'm frightened o' startin' on the wrong foot," Kirsty said. "Listen to me, Craig Nicholson; what sense is there in takin' a bed in that filthy place when we don't know how much we can afford?"

"Eight pounds'll not last for ever."

"I'm well aware of that. But suppose you find a job somewhere, a job that pays well."

"Fat chance."

"See," Kirsty shouted. "See, you've started makin' excuses."

"Go on."

"There's work to be found. There must be. Good, honest work that offers a decent wage. I'll bet there's work for a strong girl too."

"You?"

"Aye, what's wrong with that?"

"Some rich man's servant, I suppose."

"Let's stay where we are. At least we get properly fed."

"For how long?"

"Until we find out how much we'll have comin' in."

She softened. She stepped to him. He was shaking his head, the unlighted cigarette wagging in his mouth. She put her hands on his shoulders, almost as if she intended to shake sense into his silly head. She did not know why it should be but she felt stronger than she had ever felt in her life before. Her awe of Craig had diminished now that she had learned more about him.

Craig had been protected against harsh reality. He had been coddled, spoiled, was comfortable only when doing what he was told. She realised now that he would never have run off with her if his father had not coaxed him to do it. Kirsty wondered if the wedding ring gave her a strange new kind of power over him, like a fairy tale gone wrong, or if Craig was right in his assessment and she feared the hour when he would take her and possess her as a husband does a wife.

Her emotions might be cloudy but her manner was positive.

"Don't you see?" she said.

"I suppose so."

"It would be so much better to begin with a room of our own."

"Of course it bloody would. I'm not denyin' it."

"But not in a dismal place like this, Craig."

"Beggars can't be choosers."

"We're not beggars, Craig. You've bought me a ring, told me I'm your wife, so I want some of the things a wife has a right to expect from her man; a house, for a start."

"Aye, that's all very fine an' dandy but—"

"In the meantime," said Kirsty, "we'll go back to Mrs Frew's."

Suddenly Craig capitulated. He let Kirsty take his arm.

She said, "Tomorrow we'll start again."

"Start what?" Craig said.

"Looking for work in earnest," said Kirsty.

THREE

A Boy and Girl Romance

Craig was dead set against seeking employment in a cattle mart or on the docks. He had no aversion to working with horses, though, and embarked optimistically on a tour of carriers' offices in search of a post.

It did not take him long to discover that the four large firms who handled road haulage for the railway companies had no interest in a green hand without a 'Society' ticket and that even smaller establishments were only on the look-out for lorrymen who could freight fragile and dangerous cargoes and navigate the crowded city streets without falling foul of the strict police regulations. Undaunted, Craig lowered his sights. In local yards wages were meagre and hours longer but the turnover in hands was greater and a Society ticket not always an advantage. He learned that Sunday morning was the time of the week when bosses were sure to be on the premises. On Sunday morning carters were expected to clean the stables, tend their horses and repair damage to conveyances; and, of course, collect their wages. But Sunday brought Craig no job either and he came back to the boarding-house that evening in a disconsolate mood.

No less than three ministers shared the dining-room table with Craig and Kirsty. They were not particularly friendly and paid no heed to the young couple, exchanged tedious kirk gossip over the plates and teacups. Kirsty had knotted her wedding ring to a leather bootlace and wore it, hidden, about her neck. Craig approved of the secrecy. He was less concerned now about finding a house than he was about finding a job. But it was Thursday before he tramped out as far as Greenfield, a nondescript little burgh that nestled between Partick and Whiteinch. Here, in Kingdom Road, he discovered the premises of Maitland Moss, general haulers and deliverymen, and, nothing loath, wandered in through the open gates.

The yard was stuck like a half-closed drawer in a tallboy of red tenements. It was flanked by the Kingdom burn which oozed out of a conduit for a lungful of air before vanishing into a big iron pipe for a final crawl to the river. The ammoniac reek of stables was very strong but Craig, a farm lad, did not find it off-putting. He stepped quickly over broken cobbles on to hard-packed cinders. To his left was a wooden shed, raised up on posts and reached by rickety stairs. None of the tenements' windows looked down into the yard, only cliff-sized gables that reared to the chimney-pots high overhead.

"What the hell're you doin', pokin' about here?" roared a deep, rasping voice.

Craig started guiltily.

"I'm lookin' for Maitland Moss."

"For what reason?"

The man was concealed in the shadowed mouth of a stable stall and did not show himself.

Craig swallowed. "I'm after work."

"What's your name?"

"Nicholson."

"Age?"

"Twenty."

"Where are you from?"

"A farm, near Dalnavert."

"Where's that?"

"In the Carrick, near Girvan."

"What's brought you to Glasgow?"

"I told you, I'm after work."

It struck him as strange that the shouted conversation attracted no attention, that the yard, apart from the man with the gruff voice, was deserted.

"What d'you know about horses?"

"I can plough," Craig answered.

"I'm no' needin' a bloody ploughboy."

"Look, I can tend horses an' I've driven carts, long an' short, for years. Is there work here for me or is there not?"

"Keep your hair on, sonny."

When the man emerged from the shadows he was grinning. He was the swaggering sort, muscular, with a powerful bull-neck showing in the collar of his open-throated shirt. Moleskin breeks clung to bulging thighs and a broad leather belt with a brass buckle was slung low about his waist. He wore no scarf or muffler but had on his head an old round-crown tweed hat that perched on a tangle of bushy brown hair.

"Are you Mr Maitland?"

"Not me."

"Mr Moss, then?"

"Same bloke; Maitland Moss."

"When can I see him?" said Craig.

"Never," said the man, still grinning. "He never dirties his shoes comin' down here. Why should he? He's got me t' run the show for him."

"Are you the – the boss?"

"Danny Malone. Hirin' and firin' is my business."

"Well, will ye hire me, Mr Malone?"

"Pay's rotten an' the hours are weary."

"I'm used to that on the farm."

"You've a decent pair o' shoulders on you, an' a snappy sort o' lip which will stand ye in good stead when you're arguin' wi' a copper at a junction. Ever been in trouble wi' the law?"

Craig frowned at the question.

He shook his head. "Nah, never."

"Ye won't like what I'll do to you if you're lyin'."

"I'm tellin' the truth, I swear."

"All right, then, I'll take ye on a week's trial; how's that?"

Craig's throat was tight with excitement but he was not without guile. "Is that week's trial with or without pay?"

"If I tell you it's without pay what'll ye do?"

"Walk," said Craig.

"Walk where?"

"Home."

"Where's home?"

"Lodgin's in Walbrook Street."

"Walbrook Street; very posh for a farmer's laddie. Are ye married?"

Craig did not hesitate. "Aye."

Malone grinned again and stuck his thumbs in the sagging belt.

"Married to some juicy wee country lass, I'll wager," he said.

"Do I get the job or not?" said Craig.

"One week's trial, with pay by the day. The rate per rake's damned low, I warn you. Mr Moss likes his profit."

"What is the rate?"

"On average you'll take home about sixteen bob."

"I thought the minimum rate was—"

"Minimum rates are for Society members – an' that ain't you, sonny," Malone told him. "Anyhow, this is no Society yard. We want none of that sort here. Come on now, are ye in or out?"

"In," said Craig. "Do I have to sign a paper?"

"Christ, no!" said Malone.

"When do I start?"

"Tomorrow morn. Five o'clock."

"I'll be here," Craig promised.

Malone did not offer his hand to seal the contract.

"Have you bairns?" he asked.

"Nah."

"Tryin' hard, though, I'll wager."

"What's that got to do wi' you?"

"How do you feel about puttin' in a spot o' night work?"

"If it pays extra, I'm more than willin'."

Malone placed a beefy hand on his shoulder.

"Are ye no' scared some dirty dog'll sneak into your bed when you're gone?" Malone suggested.

"Let him try," Craig said, with more belligerence than he felt. "I'll kill any bastard that tries it on wi' my wife."

Malone laughed. "That's what I like to hear; a man that can look after his own."

Still laughing he gave Craig a dunt with his elbow to direct him out into Kingdom Road, no longer a footloose stranger but a man on the verge of employment.

From Gallowgate to Saracen Cross, from Hogganfield to the Whifflet you were never more than a short step from the door of a place that sold strong drink, from premises where a man might slake his thirst and find relief from the grinding monotony of toil in manly company. Tucked away between the vaults and inns and public houses, however, so obvious as to be invisible, were other oases of comfort and consolation for the citizens of the west. Never a voice was raised to protest the extent of the vice that they fostered and no church took militant stand against them. No society was ever formed to fight a demon that rotted teeth, pitted the gut, puffed up the pancreas, shrivelled the liver and gradually depleted the body of strength by cheating it of true nourishment. Temperance was never preached to those poor wights who fell victim to sweet tooth, who each day craved a taste of sugary confection and who, if they did not get it, grizzled and girned for want of the treat. Fortunes were made from the national addiction. Vast commercial empires were founded and sustained on satisfying the demand for all things sweet, and great wedding cakes of profit were erected on columns of pure cane sugar.

While the average wife was a dab hand at scones, baps or pancakes she somehow baulked at baking cakes, felt perhaps that she could not compete with the products of commercial bakeries, examples of whose art appeared by the hundred score on stencilled boards every morning, oozing treacle and fruit syrup, glistening with icing and sugar crystals. What ordinary mother could duplicate such magic, could reproduce the mouth-watering artefacts that tempted you just with the sight of them lined up on a tray in Dougie's Dairy or Mr Kydd's wee corner shop? Few women were bold enough to try. For that reason rogues like the Oswald brothers flourished and girls like Kirsty Nicholson were employed in long bleak sheds to turn out cakes in volume like so many artillery shells.

The Oswalds had several retail outlets of their own where each of their nineteen varieties of cake was displayed in the window on a separate little silver tray against a bank of more ordinary teabreads and soft pastries. In fact, Kirsty had been on the point of going into the shop to part with a penny for a delicious-looking chocolate cup when the notice had caught her attention. Hands, it stated, were wanted in the Oswald Brothers' Vancouver Street Cakery; no experience necessary. As work of any kind was at a premium Kirsty was surprised to find no queue of eager lassies clamouring for jobs when she presented herself at the 'Cakery' the following morning.

She knocked on a big painted door round the back of the building and was greeted by a narrow-shouldered baker in a filthy canvas apron who shouted at her and rudely directed her to the front gate. From there she found her way into the sheds where girls were 'assembling' cakes on long trestle tables and sorting them on the boards to fill the day's printed orders. Kirsty had put on plain clothes, not her powder-blue, and was glad that she had been sensible, for any hint of 'posh' would have lost her the job before she had even started.

It was not, of course, either of the Oswald Brothers who 'interviewed' her for the vacant position but a heavy-set and menacingly swarthy woman named Dykes. Mrs Dykes was in charge of all female staff, responsible for keeping the girls hard at it from the start of the shift at a quarter past five in the morning until last orders had gone out and the 'rooms', as the sheds were called, had been swept and sprinkled.

Mrs Dykes asked Kirsty several desultory questions about her age, marital status, place of residence and proneness to infectious diseases. Kirsty answered truthfully, except that she replied to the question regarding her status only by holding up her left hand and showing Mrs Dykes the ring which she had taken from its thong and slipped on to her finger after she had left Walbrook Street that morning.

It was apparent that Kirsty's answers were of no real importance, that she might have given her address as the Govanhill lazaret for all the difference it would have made. She was fit enough to stand for seven hours at a stretch and that was all that mattered to Mrs Dykes and the brothers Oswald.

The catch was the wage; a miserly six shillings for a six-day 'half shift'. Kirsty was not so green as to suppose that a shilling-a-day rate was not usurious, an exploitation of the female labour market's need for part-time employment. She accepted, nonetheless, and listened while Mrs Dykes reeled off company rules and regulations.

She would be docked threepence for lateness.

She would be docked two days' wages for every one day that she failed to report for work without prior notice.

She would not, of course, be paid for a day or any part of a day in which she had to leave the sheds for any reason and for any purpose other than to answer a call of nature.

She was not allowed to take her apron or mob-cap home.

She was – glory be – permitted to buy misshapen cakes at half-price and a bag of a dozen bread rolls at a one-penny discount.

To all of this Kirsty agreed, nodding.

Vancouver Street was a long walk from the boarding-house but Kirsty had received so little recompense for her labour at Hawkhead that she felt flattered to be offered money at all. Six shillings was not so bad. Indeed, when Craig found regular work they would be able to afford to rent a nice room and she would be free to devote every afternoon to shopping and housework.

"Are ye takin' it, hen?"

"Yes, please," said Kirsty, an answer which, by its eagerness, drew a funny look from Mrs Dykes.

"Report for 'trainin'' at five tomorrow."

"Friday?" said Kirsty.

"Somethin' wrong wi' Friday?"

"No, oh no. Friday's fine."

She thanked Mrs Dykes again and went to the door without really studying the girls at the tables or noticing the rusty girders or sweating plaster or the edging of grime to the floor. She had a job, would earn a wage, and that was all that mattered to her there and then. Elated, she set off with the vague notion that she might find Craig in the street and tell him at once of her good fortune.

During the week's stay at Walbrook Street Kirsty had acquired an awareness, rather than knowledge, of the geography of the territories that snuggled along the Clyde, the wards and parish boundaries marked by steeples, towers, green parks, that flanked the length of Dumbarton Road. Greenfield was new to her, however, for she had not been this far west before.

For Partick folk burgh status lent pride and collective identity but Greenfield was too small and insignificant to be separated from its lively neighbour. It did not even have a proper view of the Clyde, for warehouses blocked out the wharves and an embankment of the Lanarkshire and Dunbartonshire railway line bottomed the little burgh like a rampart. Beyond the railway lay Hedderwick's repair and fitting yard where, on a few narrow acres, shallow-draught vessels were keeled and equipped. A new block of flats, in beautiful red sandstone, peering disdainfully down on the junction of Kingdom Road and Canada Road, might have suggested to a casual stranger that this was a high-class area but a few steps into the hinterland and the smoke-blackened, weather-worn façades of old whitestone tenements would rapidly dispel the notion that the burgh was in any way 'posh'.

Kirsty walked down Kingdom Road's chasm of tenements and hunchbacked cobbles, turned into Banff Street and, skirting the tenements' dingy backcourts, popped out into the bottom end of Canada Road where it sloped toward a tunnel in the railway embankment. Curiosity led her through the dripping stone arch into St John Street, a long cobbled street which fronted the wharves and shipyards.

Through the open gate she glimpsed the interior of Hedderwick's yard, the river regulated by a series of locks, and a long 'thing' on a slipway that looked for all the world like the rotted carcass of a cow over which men scrambled as if to strip the last of its flesh from its bones. Two gatemen in tall hats glared at Kirsty and quickly closed the big gate as if they feared that she might learn secrets that it was not given to a mere woman to know.

Precious little to see along St John Street; Kirsty returned through the tunnel to Canada Road.

Quarter of a mile or so from the base of the street a little crowd had gathered outside one of the tenements. The bustle and hubbub seemed threatening and Kirsty's initial impulse was to slip down one of the lanes and avoid the commotion. But she strolled on, intrigued by the reason for the gathering, saw children and a handcart piled high with furniture and bundles of old clothes, and wondered what tinkers could be doing so far into the city. They were not tinkers at all but tenants caught in the humiliating ritual of an eviction.

At first Kirsty could not make out what was going on for the language was so guttural and alien that she could hardly understand a word of it. A constable, tall and distinctive in his uniform, presided over the proceedings and seemed calm and passive in the midst of the rabble. It took Kirsty several minutes to sort out the cast of the drama; the landlord, his agent, a municipal officer, members of the family, and three, possibly four, male lodgers who had also lost their billets.

More bundles were slung on to the handcart and two small children were hoisted on board and a runny-nosed toddler of indeterminate sex was lifted up and perched, howling, on the very top of the pyramid. Women leaned from tenement windows and gathered in closes and bawled and catcalled as if the performance was taking place on the stage of the *Empire* and not on a public thoroughfare. The landlord and his agent appeared no more respectable than their tenants and, far from being bullying, seemed to be very upset by the whole squalid affair.

"Ah'm sorry, Mrs Skinner, but ye canny say ye wisnae warned," said one of the men in a whining tone, while his agent, also small and seedy and drooping, patted his shoulder and muttered words of sympathy as if injury was being done to the landlord and not his tenants.

"See you, McCoig, you's needin' hung," cried a crow-voiced wife from one of the windows. "Ye're a greedy bastard, puttin' the law on them, an' her wi' an ailin' hubby tae."

"Hangin's too bloody good for him."

"Aye, so it is but."

McCoig, the landlord, denied the accusations.

"It wisnae me, I tell ye," he bleated. "God, but she was well warned. How could she no' pay the three quarters owin'? I mean, God, she's got four lodgers in there tae."

But the crowd was not to be appeased.

"*Who was it notified the Sanny man, eh, McCoig?*"

The 'Sanny man', municipal officer in charge of Health and Sanitation, entered the fray.

"It was, I assure you, a random inspection," he cried.

"*McCoig brung ye in. Deny it if ye can.*"

"Never you mind, Dougie. Never you heed them," the agent, a brother perhaps, muttered soothingly. "Right's on our side."

"RIGHT? WHAT BLOODY RIGHT?"

"I never reported nobody." Douglas McCoig appealed to the

officer, who, in black suit and bowler hat, exuded an air of superior wisdom. "Tell them it wisnae me, Mr Manfred."

"BLOODY MIDAS, SO YE ARE."

Mr Manfred had no more respect for landlords than he had for the tenants who packed their miserable apartments far in excess of the numbers laid down by burgh law.

Mr Manfred snapped, "Think yoursel' lucky you weren't fined, Mr McCoig. You knew fine what was goin' on. Thirteen folk in a wee single-end, for God's sake!"

"I never counted them."

"It was your responsibility, Mr McCoig," said Mr Manfred, then, waving an arm imperiously, shouted, "Now, you lot, stop shilly-shallyin'. I haven't got all day to waste."

A young man in shirt sleeves, cheeks aflame, flung himself out of the crowd and might have assaulted the Sanny man if the police constable had not rolled from the wall with the swiftness of a leopard leaping from a rock. He caught and restrained the young avenger and growled, "Enough out o' you, lad, unless you're anxious for a spell on bread an' water."

Persuaded not to press his grievances with his fists the young lodger, released, took shelter behind Mrs Skinner who had by now wrapped her broad-hipped body in a voluminous tartan shawl and had picked up an infant and a toddler to complete the image of martyred and unrepentant motherhood.

She was in her thirties but looked older. Sallow, haggard, with ash-grey circles around each eye, she displayed no lack of energy and in a high yapping voice snapped out orders that every member of the Skinner clan jumped to obey. "Bring him down then. Go on, Jimmy, fetch him down. Gi'e him a hand, Bert. I'm no' leavin' this spot till I see him right." She hoisted a child into the crook of each elbow and shrugged the shawl expertly around them to cover their skinny bare legs.

"POOR THINGS. LOOK'T THEM. ARE YE NO' BLACK ASHAMED, McCOIG?"

Douglas McCoig did indeed appear to be ashamed. He hung his head and could not bear to look as the procession emerged noisily from the close. Mr Manfred was not so squeamish. Hands on hips, coat-tails thrust back, he watched every move with a tiny hard-edged smirk.

Kirsty inched closer. Nobody paid her the slightest attention for every eye was fastened upon the close mouth and a hush, broken only by the wailing of the toddler atop the handcart, fell over the multitude.

Seated stiffly on a ladderback chair, Mr Skinner was carried from his ancestral home. He had a shawl about his shoulders and wore no overcoat or jacket. His collarless shirt was open to show a shrunken chest and the emotional palpitations of his Adam's apple. He was not ashamed of his tears. He did not hide his face in his hands, kept his fists closed tight on the chair knobs as he was rocked out of darkness into daylight. He wore no shoes or boots and his trousers had ridden up to his shins to expose pale, hairy legs. In his lap was a chamber-pot and a cut-glass vase.

The young lodger, Jimmy, was weeping too, and the other attendants looked grim and funereal as they put the chair down on the pavement directly in front of the Sanny man.

Mr Manfred did not flinch. He was not afraid to confront a victim of officialdom face to face.

"Got the key then, Mr Skinner?" he demanded.

It was too much, too cold, for the neighbours. Shouting broke out anew and fists were raised. One wife lost balance, shrieked, and was only just saved from tumbling over her window-sill and beaning some poor soul on the pavement below. Even Kirsty, a stranger, felt a lump in her throat when Mr Manfred stuck out a lilywhite hand and once more demanded the key.

Slowly, hesitantly, Mr Skinner dipped a hand into the chamber-pot and brought out a long iron key. He placed it across the officer's palm with all the dignity of a general surrendering a battalion's colours.

Mr Manfred heaved a sigh. "Right, on your way. You have my letters to the supervisor so you'll not be turned away."

"The Model!" wheezed Mr Skinner. "Who would have thought it'd ever come t' this that a Skinner would be sent tae the workhouse."

Mr Manfred leaned forward. "I thought you'd be used to it by now, Skinner. Anyway, it's a model lodgin' not the workhouse."

Mr Skinner stiffened, straightened, sniffed and said grandly, "Minnie, take our poor homeless weans awa'."

Hands gripped the shafts of the cart. The child on top, shocked into silence, grabbed desperately at the bundles as the pyramid of belongings listed to starboard. Lodgers levelled the cart and flexed their muscles. Mrs Skinner's brood gathered, big-eyed, about her skirts. Mrs Skinner glared venomously at Douglas McCoig and spat on the pavement at his feet. "Hell mend ye, McCoig. May ye be damned for this day's work."

McCoig winced, hung his head and did not look up until the woman led her children off, followed by the laden cart and finally by Mr Skinner raised up in his chair on willing shoulders. With a nod of satisfaction Mr Manfred gave the key to the agent who pocketed it promptly and discreetly.

The police constable had strolled away in the wake of the procession but whether it was to attend their welfare or just to see them safely off his beat Kirsty could not be sure. She had been distracted from watching the family's departure, her attention caught by the key. A key meant a lock; a lock meant a door; and a door meant an apartment. It dawned on her at that moment that there was a vacant room in this tenement in the Greenfield and that the owner of the property and his letting-agent were standing not ten yards away. Stayed by a certain guilt, she did not immediately obey her inclination to rush forward and accost the landlord on the spot.

The crowd dispersed. Windows slammed shut. The men loitered by the close to watch the Skinners recede. The children clung to Mammy's hands or to her skirts, dragging and trailing and girning, and the cart swayed and lumbered ponderously with the little toddlers still hanging grimly to the bundles. But the ladderback chair and its occupant had vanished. It was not until Kirsty stepped back that she saw what had become of them. The chair was propped against a wall, vase and chamber-pot beneath it, and above them was the gilded sign of the Vancouver Vaults, Canada Road's most salubrious public house. Bearers and borne had apparently been unable to resist a last refreshment there and the police constable had apparently felt duty-bound to accompany them to see that they came to no harm.

Kirsty gave a little gasp, laughter and relief. Her guilt evaporated instantly. She dashed into the close of Number 11, where the McCoigs had gone, and followed their voices upstairs to the top landing.

Mr Colin McCoig, cousin not brother, was on the point of inserting the long key into the lock while Douglas watched him gloomily.

Panting, Kirsty said, "Sir, can I have a word wi' you?"

The men looked round and Mr Douglas said, "Aye, lass, what is it ye want?"

"Is it for rent, this house?"

The cousins exchanged a glance and Mr Colin raised an eyebrow before he answered, "As a matter o' fact, it is. But it'll not be vacant for long, dear, not in this neck o' the woods."

"What size is it?" said Kirsty.

"It's a single-end," said Mr Colin.

"What's that?"

"God, are you from China?"

"A single-end's a kitchen wi' a bed recess," Mr Douglas explained.

"Were *all* those folk livin' in one room?"

"That," said Mr Douglas, "is what all yon stramash was about. The Burgh Council won't allow it. Three adults an' three children under twelve is their maximum."

"Did you not know?" said Kirsty, ingenuously.

Again the cousins exchanged a glance and Mr Colin cleared his throat. "Obviously the room'll need a bloomin' good scrub but, otherwise, it's in perfect order. How many of a family have ye got, dear?"

"Me an' my husband, that's all."

"Aw, you're newly-weds."

"Aye."

"Both workin'?"

"Yes." Kirsty had learned the value of a little white lie in the right place at the right time. "Yes, he's a carter. I'm employed at the bakery."

"Which bakery?"

"Oswalds'."

"That'll no' pay much."

"My husband earns a good wage. He works hard."

"No doubt, no doubt he does," said Mr Douglas McCoig, as his cousin pulled him to one side and whispered in his ear.

Mr Colin said at length, "The rent's four shillin's per week."

Kirsty said, "Can I look at the place?"

"Not at this very minute," said Mr Colin. "We have to check in case it needs repairs, see."

"Is it furnished?"

"It has all the furnishin' that newly-weds need," said Mr Colin. "Come on now, dear, make up your mind. I can get a shillin' a night for the place if I farm it."

Kirsty hesitated; the rent did not seem unreasonable when she weighed it against her takings from Oswalds. The fact that Craig did not yet have work did not unduly bother her and she gave no thought at all to the long-term commitment.

Firmly she said, "I'll take it."

"One month's rent's required in advance."

"Well, I haven't got it on me."

"When can you get it?"

"By tonight."

"Come tonight then at half past seven – with the cash."

Kirsty was suddenly desperate to obtain occupancy of the single-end, gulled into imagining that it would be impossible to do better. She touched her wedding ring. It was on the tip of her tongue to offer it as a pledge of good faith that she and Craig would be there that evening with sixteen shillings in cash. But she could not bring herself to do it. She looked at Mr Douglas who seemed still to have a drop of charity in him.

"Promise me you'll keep it for us."

"We'll keep it lass," the landlord answered. "Until eight o'clock."

"We'll be here," said Kirsty.

She dropped a curtsy to the men, turned and skipped away down the stairs, her heart singing.

She had a job. She had a house. She had a husband. The dark and dragging threat of Hawkhead snapped like a worn thread and fell from her, leaving her light-hearted and light-headed.

Behind her, echoing down the stairwell, came Mr Douglas's shout: "No dogs, no cats, no parakeets, remember."

And Mr Colin's parting shot: "An' bring the bloomin' readies."

Kirsty did not hear them.

She was already out in Canada Road and running like the wind to find Craig and tell him her wonderful news.

It was almost midnight. For Craig and Kirsty the day had been filled with uncomfortable novelties. Saturday would bring them no rest and no respite and on Sunday they would have to tackle the kitchen in earnest to put it into habitable state.

"Kirsty," Craig said. "Is that not enough?"

Pale with exhaustion, he leaned dejectedly against the jawbox, the small stone sink under the window, a claw-hammer in his hand. Since he had returned from the yard at nine o'clock he had been trying to clear the bed recess into which the Skinners had fixed three tiers of bunks. Back at Dalnavert he had always enjoyed working with his hands but there had been space on and about the farm; here there was none and the physical limitations seemed to accentuate the frustrations that had been building in him almost since the hour he had left home. It was all very well for Kirsty. She had been used to squalor. He had been brought up decently and to his way of thinking this place, even if it was 'their own', was no better than a slum. He blamed Kirsty for it and cursed his own weakness for not holding out for something better. What had his dad's hard-earned money bought – a black iron range, a gas jet in a frayed mantle, a cold-water sink, a table, three chairs and a fragment of worn carpet. Kirsty seemed confident that she could create a comfortable home out of it, especially since they both had jobs, but he did not trust her word, was not convinced by her enthusiasm.

It had all been so different from what he had imagined it would be and he could not cope with the swings in his moods, the strain of responsibility and uncertainty. When he had packed the bags and left Walbrook Street, for instance, he should have felt glad to be shot of the stuffy boarding house but, in fact, he had gone with a little pang of regret and had been quite touched, though he had not shown it, when old Frew had given them a gift of bed linen and a pair of good wool blankets. He wanted things to be printed down in black and white, to know what was good and what was bad, as he had done at home in Carrick, but everything contrived against such simplicity and he felt as if he had moved not just from the country to the city but from one dimension into another. He *had* to cope, *had* to shape up to it, to fulfil his vague, rash promises and become not only a man but a provider, to keep his end of the bargain in the hope that Kirsty would keep hers.

His first day on the job had been harrowing and his agitation came out of fatigue. At Dalnavert he would have come home to a hot meal and a warm fire and a chair in which to rest his bones. He had trudged home from the yard with a similar expectation only to find chaos. Supper was a hasty affair, a meat pie and mushy peas, for Kirsty had work for him to do. She had been busy all afternoon, had purchased pots and pans and crockery from the Partick Bazaar, had found a coalman to lug two bags of best domestic upstairs and fill the bunker in the tiny hall, had made a determined start on cleaning. The kitchen was pungent with the smell of carbolic and lukewarm suds. The fire smoked. The frayed gas mantle stank like a singed hoof.

"What was the job like?" Kirsty had asked.

"All right."

"Where did you go?"

"No place very special."

"What did you deliver?"

"Nails. In kegs."

"What else?"

"Just nails. All day."

"What sort of horse was it?"

"Just a horse, a dray."

"Did you have the reins?"

"Nah, I'm only a porter."

"What's the driver like?"

"All right."

"Is he young?"

"Nah."

Sensing his reluctance to talk, Kirsty had asked no more questions. He was glad of it. He did not want to seem weak by complaining about the hardship of the carter's lot and was not sure that she would understand why he hated it so much, with the din of traffic in his ears and the monotony of loading and unloading the tubby kegs, his driver, Bob McAndrew, treating his discomfort as if it were a great joke.

He had made an effort, though, to be civilised.

"How about Oswalds'? What was it like?" he had asked.

"Fine," Kirsty had said.

He had nodded and turned his attention to the problems of the bed recess and the dismantling of all that clumsy woodwork with nothing but the hammer that Kirsty had bought for him out of the kindness of her heart. He could not understand why she was so cheerful. With her auburn hair tucked under a mob-cap and her sleeves rolled up, she fairly fizzed with energy. No doubt she was anticipating a night of love, locked in his arms. The truth was that the events of the day had drained him of all desire and he contemplated Kirsty almost objectively. It was for this girl, to possess this girl, that he had quit Dalnavert, surrendered the security of his family and given up the only sort of life he had ever known.

Fleetingly he yearned for the company of his brother and sister, for his mother's sharp discipline, forgot the rebellion that had been simmering in him for months before Kirsty had appeared out of the darkness and the strange adventure had begun. He felt as if his father had cast him out, not given him his freedom, and he resented it. Much of his vague, youthful, moody resentment of being made to face the reality of responsibility settled, inevitably, upon Kirsty, who, on her knees on the bare floorboards, plied the scrubbing-brush with a vigour that mocked his fatigue. Hands all rough and red, face flushed, hair straggling, she paddled in greasy suds. He did not want her to do it, to have to do it. He wanted her to be sweet and soft and yielding, as fragrant and unblemished as a girl in an advertisement for Starlight soap. He blamed himself for not making it so and was angered at his impotence in protecting her from the coarse and common realities that sullied everything.

Dolefully, guiltily, he contemplated her round bottom, swelling hips and the shape of her breasts heavy under her blouse. There was no drop of passion in him. He did not see that he could avoid disappointing her again and wondered if he would ever be able to fulfil himself in her eyes, make of her the wife he wanted her to be. If he had been less raw, less gauche, he might have thrust the hurt and anger to one side, might have recognised that tenderness needed no dressings or ceremonies, might have touched her, lifted her up and taken her in his arms and told her that everything would be all right, have shown her that there was love entangled in his pride. But he had seen none of it, had no models, and in his confusion snapped at her, "Kirsty's for God's sake, can it not wait till tomorrow?"

She glanced over her shoulder, gave him an uncertain smile. "I'll not be long, dear."

Oh, God, she assumed he was eager to get her into bed.

"Come on, mop up that mess," he told her.

"I'll just be—"

"*Now, Kirsty*," he snapped.

She got to her feet, plopped brush into pail, carried the pail to the sink and emptied it, lifted the new, tousled mop and whisked it over the wet boards.

Craig leaned on the wall by the bed recess, watching her blearily.

She wrung out the mop under the cold-water tap, rinsed the pail and turned it up to dry.

"Soon be finished, Craig," she told him cheerfully.

This was his wedding night, his honeymoon. He sighed, took his grip from under the bed and went out into the hallway. He changed from his work clothes into a clean shirt and, standing there, stared down at his body. He placed a hand tentatively on his parts and experienced no response at all. He tiptoed out of the house and scurried down to the water closet on the half-landing, praying that he would not meet any of the neighbours. When he got back, tense and shivering, to the kitchen he found that Kirsty had managed to make up the bed. There was no mattress yet but she had tucked a blanket over the hard boards and folded the new linen sheets, fashioned a pillow out of one of Mrs Frew's wool blankets.

Craig stared in horror and gave a little inaudible groan when Kirsty discreetly lowered the flame of the gas to relieve the kitchen of its starkness and bring in at least a touch of romantic mystery.

Did she not realise how tired he was, that he would have to be up again in about four hours and would be jolting on the board of a horse-cart in five, heaving bloody nail-kegs about? He ached with weariness and craved only sleep. Never before had he appreciated such trivial luxuries as a pillow, a mattress and a bed that he could call his own.

"Pop in, dear," said Kirsty.

"What – what about you?"

"I'll be with you in a minute, Craig."

Cautiously Craig fitted himself into the makeshift bed. He sighed, rested his neck on the flat pillow, slid out his legs, turned on his hip, tucked up his knees, stared at the scarred and yellowing paper on the back wall.

He closed his eyes. He took a deep breath, tainted with smoke and carbolic soap. He sighed again and with an effort of will, forced himself to fall asleep.

Kirsty was neither surprised nor disappointed to discover that Craig had fallen asleep. She had expected as much. She had not even taken her brand-new nightgown from its tissue wrapping and wore only her usual clean, patched shift. She gave her hair attention with the brush and then went softly to the side of the bed and knelt by him. He was curled up against the back wall, snoring fiercely. She had never seen him so tired and dejected and felt guilty about it, believing that she had somehow disappointed him.

She got up, stretched and glanced about the kitchen.

All her chores had been done. The fire was banked, kettle put on the hob; the tea-caddy, porridge pot and salt shaker were placed where she could find them in the drowsy bumbling half-light of the morning hour. She had even remembered to put the butter dish and milk jug in the cold stone sink. She would be first up, of course, at four o'clock.

She picked up the nickel-plated Peep-o-Day American alarm clock that Craig had bought as an essential item and set it as he had instructed her to do, listening to the tiny fairy-like *ting* of the bell cup and the whirr of its interior mechanism. She put the alarm on a chair and the chair close to the bed recess. All she could see of Craig was a lock of dark hair above the cowl of the blanket and one bare foot at the other end of the bed. She slipped carefully in beside him.

She wriggled into position, adjusted her bottom, made herself as small and unobtrusive as possible. She longed to be able to put her arms about him, hug him to her, but did not dare in case he wakened and supposed that she was putting him under an obligation.

Tomorrow would be better for him; she would make sure that it was better.

She slid an arm along his flank and was soothed by the passive touching. She snuggled closer to her man who did not stir, not even when she kissed him lightly on the earlobe and sleepily whispered her goodnights.

Kirsty arrived at Oswalds' in the calm primrose dawn of a fine April morning. Mrs Dykes was waiting to give her a change of occupation. Saturday was a busy day in the Cakery. Rich, poor and in-between families were all given to perking up their tea-tables with cakes and fancy confections and orders would be thick on the spikes. Kirsty had quickly mastered the routine tasks of the packing-room, guided by Letty, a skinny tubercular girl of about her own age, and Mrs McNeil, a square-faced, square-bodied woman of forty or so who, now that she had borne a family, had returned to work to help make ends meet.

Letty was chatty but Kirsty could not understand half of what she said for the girl had a real Glasgow accent and gave no quarter in her prattle. The work on the boards was simple but fraught with pitfalls for a novice who had not yet learned the names for all the cakes and who could not always decipher the scribbles on the order slips.

"Letty, what does that say?"

"Dozen coconut buns, dozen snowballs, two dozen fairy cakes, three dozen almond slices," Letty would interpret in her incredible accent, adding, "A wee board'll dae ye."

Kirsty would find a small board, would move along the flour-dusted iron racks that backed the packing-tables and pluck out the appropriate number of cakes and place them on the board in neat rows. She would then lick the original order slip, slap it to the side of the board and carry the board to the 'vanman's table' where it would be picked up by a delivery boy or one of Oswalds' carriers.

Kirsty had assumed that her tasks would remain the same from day to day, varied only by sessions of cake-making when seasonal demand was high. She was surprised when, on that first Saturday, Mrs Dykes led her away from the tables only moments after she arrived.

"Can you count?" said Mrs Dykes.

"Aye, well enough."

"What's four times four?"

"Sixteen."

"Go into the store. Tommy'll tell you what to do."

The flour store lay between the sheds and the bakehouse and Mrs Dykes' son, Tommy, was waiting for Kirsty there.

On seeing her, Tommy grinned, showing large white teeth and pink gums. He was probably about her own age, Kirsty judged, but his gawky arrogance made him seem like a child pretending to be an adult. From the first she could not take him seriously. He wore a flannel vest and a brown apron. His arms were thin and hairless and his ears stuck out like the handles of a chamber-pot.

He said, "So you're the new one, eh?"

"Aye."

"You've to do what I tell ye."

"What's that?"

"Measurin' the mixes. It's no' every lassie gets to do it but my mam has you marked as a smart one, so just you listen to me." From behind his back Tommy Dykes produced a metal scoop attached to a short wooden handle. "See this? This is a two-pounder."

He handed her the utensil, stepped to the side and slapped a hand on the lid of a wooden bin, chest-high and some six feet in breadth. A dozen such bins lined the storeroom. Two wooden tables occupied the centre of the room.

"See this?" Tommy said. "Cornflour."

The bins were coated in the ubiquitous grey dust that seemed to infiltrate every corner in Oswalds' Cakery.

Kirsty nodded; she had already noticed the printed sign above the bin which identified its contents. Tommy put a hand on her waist and steered her to the left.

"See this? Oat-flour."

He gave her a squeeze and guided her on.

"See this——"

"Rice flour," said Kirsty.

"How'd you know that?"

"I can read, Mr Dykes," Kirsty told him, nodding at the sign.

Tommy grunted and led her to the tables.

Upon them were a series of large metal bowls of different sizes.

Tommy said, "I heard a rumour that ye were bonnie. I'm the man for freckles."

"I'm married, Mr Dykes."

"Call me Tommy, eh!"

"Show me what I've to do."

"Ever seen how a doughnut gets made?" Tommy asked her.

"I can't say I have."

"Like this." Tommy made a gesture with fingers and thumb. "I'll show ye later, if ye like."

"I don't think I do like, Mr Dykes."

Tommy shrugged off the rebuff. "Suit yourself."

"I'm here to work, Mr Dykes," Kirsty reminded him.

"Aye, right," he said. "See this? These are mixin' bowls. You take flour out o' the bins an' put it into the bowls. Simple, eh!"

"In what proportions?"

Tommy did not understand.

Kirsty said, "The measure, the recipe?"

"Oh, aye." Tommy dipped a hand into one of the bowls and brought out a slip of paper identical to the order slips used next door. The pencilled message upon it was, however, more legible. "Four rice. Two oatmeal."

"Is that all?"

"It'll just be a wee batch or a special order," said Tommy. "The bakers'll add in the sugar an' stuff. You only get t' do the basic. Another thing; don't forget to remove the recipe from the bowl before ye put the flours in. The bakers get fair wild if bits o' burnt paper spoil the risin'."

"Where do I put the bowls when they're filled?"

"On the table; just leave them on the table," said Tommy. "Don't take them into the bakehouse whatever you do."

"Why not?"

"Women aren't allowed in the bakehouse."

Kirsty did not question that answer. The bakehouse would be man's domain where masters of the trade held sway.

"Will I be doin' this job every day from now on?" said Kirsty.

"Naw, just till Lizzie Weekes gets back."

Kirsty put her hand into the big smooth bowl and fished out the recipe; six rice, ten corn. It could not be easier.

"You can leave me to it, Mr Dykes."

"I'm here t' see you do it properly."

"Oh!" said Kirsty.

She did not trust Tommy Dykes one bit and kept a wary eye on the young man as she lifted up the metal bowl and made to carry it to the flour bin.

Tommy exploded. "*What the bloody hell do ye think you're doin'?*"

Startled, Kirsty almost dropped the bowl. "What's wrong?"

"Don't *lift* the bowl. You never *lift* the bowl, y' stupid cow. Take the flour from the bin to the bowl. *Never* the bowl to the flour."

"But why?"

A Boy and Girl Romance

"That's the way it's done. The *right* way. If I see you liftin' a bowl again I'll belt your bloody lug."

"That you'll not do, Mr Dykes. Lay a hand on me an' you'll regret it."

"I'm in charge o' all the girls here. They do what I say."

Kirsty was not intimidated by his bluster.

She said, "How old *are* you, Mr Dykes?"

Tommy blustered even more.

"Don't be so bloody impudent," he told her. "Get on wi' your work, chop-chop."

Kirsty tucked the recipe, folded once, into the breast pocket of her apron, took the two-pound scoop to the flour bin, opened the lid and peered inside.

The rice-flour was like fine snow. It had a pleasing sensual texture but an unappetising colour. She held up the lid with her elbow, awkwardly dipped the scoop into the flour. Carefully she extricated the levelled scoop from the bin, let down the lid and returned, without spilling a drop, to the table and carefully padded the quantity of flour into the bowl.

Tommy watched her, arms folded, a scowl on his face.

She returned to the bin and repeated the procedure.

She felt cut off in the flour store. She could hear the clang and clatter of oven doors and male voices from the bakehouse and the prattle of the girls in the sheds, even the whistling of vanmen from the lane. But she could see nobody at all, and could not be seen.

Tommy said, "That's two."

Kirsty said, "I know it's two, Mr Dykes. I *can* count."

"Freckles," Tommy said. "I like freckles."

Forth and back between the tables and the bins Kirsty went, while Tommy lolled and scowled and grinned and passed remarks that bordered on or infringed the limits of decency. Kirsty had little choice but to put up with it. She would have preferred, of course, to be standing next to Letty and Mrs McNeil, for this work was no less monotonous than filling trays and she did not have Tommy to contend with next door.

Tommy Dykes' knowingness was a mask for uncertainty. He was, Kirsty estimated, not much above sixteen and had no status at all in the bakehouse. The point was proved when a figure appeared in the archway between store and bakehouse, a small, flour-speckled, sepulchral man with a booming bass voice. "TOMMY FOR CHRIST'S SAKE, GET THAT STUFF IN HERE."

By now Kirsty had filled recipes for fourteen of the mixing bowls and had only four left to complete.

At the man's command Tommy grabbed the nearest bowl and ran with it into the bakehouse. Kirsty went on with her job, listening intently for the howl of protest that would tell her that Tommy was not so smart as he thought himself to be.

"*Idle bugger. Get your bloody mind aff the dames, Tommy, or I'll belt the hide aff your back wi' my strap, so I will.*"

Kirsty could not restrain herself. She gave a little smothered chuckle of satisfaction not untinged with malice.

Tommy ran back into the store, shouting, "See you, ye cow, did I no' tell ye to put the—"

Ready for him, Kirsty shouted back. "No, you did not."

"I did, I told you—"

"You've been hangin' over my back all mornin'," Kirsty cried, "so how did you not notice I was doin' it wrong?"

Hands on hips, the baker watched the argument from the archway. Kirsty could not tell whether he was amused by or angry at her tirade against Tommy Dykes.

"It's all bloody wasted. God, it's all ruined. You never marked the bowls wi' the recipes," Tommy wailed. "How are we supposed to know what's what?"

"Oh, is that what's botherin' you, Mr Dykes?"

"Botherin' me? Botherin' me?"

"Take it easy, Mr Dykes."

Kirsty fished the neatly folded recipes from her pocket. She had kept them in strict sequence and had no doubt at all about the accuracy of the procedure as she walked briskly down one side of the tables and planted a paper slip in the hillock of flour in each of the bowls. She walked up the other side of the tables and finished the planting with one slip left.

"The one you took away, Mr Dykes," she said, holding the slip up before him.

He swiped the paper from her grasp, opened it and stared at it.

The baker called out, "Fetch them in here then, Tommy. At the bloody double."

"I think your ears are blushin', Mr Dykes."

Grabbing the bowl Tommy ran off into the bakehouse without another word.

Kirsty completed her work with the scoop and filled the last of the bowls after which she was dismissed to the room again to finish her shift at the tables. Her fingers were soon sticky with icing and she settled to the task, glad to be in the company of other girls and women.

Letty leaned towards her. "Did Tommy try for a wee feel then?"

"Aye, but I managed to put his gas in a peep," Kirsty answered.

Letty sniggered. "He's a daft big bugger, so he is."

For several minutes, while Mrs Dykes prowled close, they worked in silence, laying out snowballs, rock cakes, ginger diamonds, chocolate cups and clusters; then Kirsty leaned towards Letty and asked, "By the way, what happened to Lizzie Weekes?"

Letty stiffened slightly and exchanged a glance with Mrs McNeil, but neither deigned to answer and left Kirsty, unfairly, to find out about Lizzie for herself.

As he hurried to the stables on Sunday morning Craig was in a black mood. He was aggrieved at being called out to do menial work in the stables and irked at the realisation that he had blown money that would have been better saved. He detested the straw boater now, the striped jacket, regarded the wedding ring too as a wasteful expense; nobody cared a hoot whether Kirsty and he were married or whether they were not.

To his surprise, however, the morning's labour cheered him up no end. The yard was abustle with carters, vanmen, boys and horsemen. There was a camaraderie here that he had not expected to discover and, since Mr Malone did not employ Society or Association members, everybody pitched in equally. Malone was the boss, though, of that there was no doubt. His word was accepted as law. He allocated the Sunday jobs just as he did the weekly rakes and had in his gift, as it were, the plum piece of Sunday work, a trip on the manure cart to Beattock's farm near Canniesburn where there were pretty daughters and servant lassies and the 'dung crew' were treated to dinner at the farm and might stay as long as they liked, enjoying the country air, provided they fed and watered the dray-horse on their return to the yard and did not disturb old Willy Ronald, the resident horseman, who bedded very early.

Most important of all Mr Daniel Malone wore about his shoulder a big fat kidskin satchel out of which, about noon, he would take the weekly paybook and the money due to each man and check the total and shell out the chink.

For most of the morning Malone occupied a stool in a corner of the yard close to a well-fired brazier. He would sup strong tea from a can and smoke fragrant and expensive Havana

Delmonicos and summon his special chums to him now and again for a joke and crack and, for most of the time, seemed affable and amiable. But Craig had one glimpse of the sort of man that Mr Malone could be if he was crossed, and the scene was the only cloud over the pleasure of the shift and left a wariness in Craig that Mr Malone's overtures never quite managed to erase.

After grooming, the horses were run round the yard for Malone's personal inspection. Old Willy stood by him to offer his expert advice and between them they were quick to spot an injury or an ailment which had not been reported. One carter, a youngish man, had, it seemed, failed to bring to Willy's notice a puffy swelling on the hock of a dray that he had been driving for most of the week. Willy's sharp eyes detected it before the horse had taken hardly a step on to the cinders. He tapped Mr Malone's shoulder and Mr Malone flicked away the butt of his cigar, put down his tea-can and got to his feet.

Harry Shaw, the carter in question, knew what to expect. He tried to retreat. But Malone, too swift for him, shot out a big fist, caught him by the collar and sank a punch into his belly with such functional force that Harry had all the breath knocked from him and could only gurgle and gasp and slump on to his knees on the cinders.

Some carters looked away, others watched furtively. A few went on working as if nothing remarkable had happened.

Malone put a vice-like hand on Harry's shoulders.

"Harry, you should have told me about it."

"I – I – forgot, Mr Malone."

"Forgot be buggered. You took a stick to the animal."

"Naw, I swear, naw."

"Don't bloody lie to me, sonny."

"It kicked itsel', Mr Malone."

Malone entangled his fingers in Harry's hair and jerked him back so that he could look down into his face. "It's a capped hock, Harry. When did it happen?"

"Last – last night, Mr Malone."

"Did y' not ask Willy to treat it?"

"I – I forgot."

"You seem to have a right bad memory these days, Harry. Where were you yesterday? Bath Street, was it?"

"Aye," Harry confessed. "Aye, on the long hill."

"You took a stick to it?"

"Aye. But he's no' lame. It's only swole."

Malone released his grip on the scarlet-faced young carter. Near to tears, Harry scrambled to his feet.

Willy had already led the limping animal quietly away.

In the stable doorway Craig leaned on his shovel, hardly daring to breathe lest some undetected 'crime' on his part was brought to light during this period of inquisition.

"Ten shillin's, Harry; that's the price of forgettin'," said Malone.

"But, Mr Malone, I've got weans to feed—"

"Christ, sonny, will you argue wi' me?"

"Naw, naw, but—"

"You'll be docked ten shillin's. Think yoursel' lucky to still have work. Now get out o' my sight."

Harry Shaw crept off into the shelter of a stable where old Willy had already begun to prepare the horse for surgery, a minor but dangerous operation done with a heated needle. If Willy was careful and skilful, which he always was, then the beast would be fit to pull a light cart again by the week's end.

Malone seated himself on the stool once more, grinning. He dug a fresh Delmonico from a leather case kept in his inner pocket. He struck a match and rolled the cigar end in it, lighting the tobacco evenly while he squinted this way and that through the smoke. Craig did not quite have the wit to turn away before Mr Malone's gaze alighted on him.

"You, Nicholson, the farmer's boy, come over here."

Craig put down the shovel and nervously went over to the brazier.

Malone smiled. "Do you know what yon idiot did wrong?"

"Aye, he took a stick to the beast's hocks."

"Rapped the poor creature to make it step the pavement, I expect," said Malone. "You'd never do somethin' that daft, would you?"

"Not me, Mr Malone."

"Farm lads would know better."

"Most o' them would, aye."

"I hate to see an animal maltreated. It's the horses earn the fees here, no' the bloody men." He shook his head. "Still, I was young mysel' once an' I know how hard it can be to make the day's rakes in time. Some days the horse seems against you, as well as tram-drivers an' gate-keepers an' terminus men. But that's all part o' the carter's trade, sonny, an' such trials have to be endured."

"Aye, Mr Malone."

"You'll get some pay today, wi' the others."

"Will I? I thought—"

"Ach, I'm told by Bob McAndrew that you're a willin' lad, so I'll pay you for the two days at full rate. How's that?"

"That's grand," said Craig.

"Aye, in this yard we look after our own, Craig, as you'll find out."

"Thanks, Mr Malone."

"Buy the wife new knickers."

Craig nodded and, dismissed, returned to mucking out with renewed vigour. He would receive only four or five shillings, of course, but he was gratified to be at last on the earning chain. Whistling, he put his wariness of Daniel Malone to the back of his mind and told himself that there were worse places to be on a fine Sunday morning than the stables in Kingdom Road.

Kirsty had not been idle. Brasso, blacklead, sugar soap and Cardinal polish were the tools of her trade and by the time that Craig returned from the stables she had the kitchen shining like a new pin. Dinner was a hot beef stew, a queen's pudding to follow. Craig shifted the lot, including seconds, and told her that it was the best tuck-in he'd had since he'd left Dalnavert.

All morning the spring sunshine had tempted Kirsty, made her eager to be out of the stuffy kitchen and in the open air. Benevolently Craig agreed that a long walk would do them both good. He put on his flannels and jacket while Kirsty, in the hall, changed into her powder-blue costume, and young and jaunty, they sallied forth together arm in arm.

Even among Greenfield's legions of the godless the Calvinist tradition lingered on. There was a degree of respect for the Lord's Day, a leaning towards good togs and sobriety. Wives who normally hung their bosoms over kitchen windows would on Sunday sit behind net curtains, aspidistras and canary cages to watch the world go by unseen. Children who would shriek and thunder through closes and across backcourts six days in the week would, on peril of a warmed lug from Mammy, mooch quietly about the street and contain their energies as best they could. Bairns were not so much brought as sent to Jesus. Brushed and scrubbed and stiff in best pinnies and flannel breeks, collection pennies clutched tightly in their fists, they would toddle in sedate little gangs to the Band of Hope mission house or to one of the neighbourhood's Sunday Schools or, smart as paint in Boys' Brigade uniforms or Guildry caps, would march off to an afternoon church parade. The din of industry and the raucous sounds of the street traffic would be mellowed and the air itself seemed cleaner on a Sunday. As Kirsty and Craig came on to Dumbarton Road the marching-song of a boys' brass band floated from the distance, cornets, horns and euphoniums fading and fluctuating until only the thump-thump of the big bass drum could be heard, steady as a pulse, from Partickhill.

Craig did not make for the West End park or Botanical Gardens. He turned west along Dumbarton Road, and Kirsty, who was just glad to be out and about, hugged his arm and matched her step to his as they headed along the thoroughfare into unexplored territory.

New tenements fronted shipyards and foundries, and on the right side of the road were neat new terraces with little oblong gardens to separate them from the pavement. Greenfield and Whiteinch soon fell away 'behind and the road broadened and green fields and blue hills could be glimpsed behind the buildings. Capaldi's ice-cream barrow occupied a strategic corner near the Evangelist Hall, a wooden building plastered with 'holy' notices like a bargain store, jumping with the enthusiasm of the Saved. From a swarthy man with huge moustachios Craig purchased two ice-cream cones. Kirsty had never tasted ice-cream before. She adored the cold, smooth, sticky-sweet taste and texture of it. She licked delicately while Craig munched on his as if it were a carrot. They turned casually into a side street that narrowed to a lane that in turn reached down to the riverside behind the stand of brand-new tenements.

The river appeared to have been cut out of the buildings and pasted unevenly against pasture. A herd of Ayrshires grazed in hazy sunlight and Kirsty, seeing them, experienced a sudden little flit of longing for Carrick's rolling dales and friendly, empty hills.

"Craig, where are we?" she asked.

"God knows!" Craig said. "I thought we'd take a look at the river."

Tall black-iron railings marked off a platform of sand and gravel that jutted from the line of the bank. One long green-painted bench, surrounded by litter, occupied the space, but Craig did not sit down. He made at once for the railings and gripped them like a prisoner. Cautiously, Kirsty followed. The water of the Clyde gurgled thickly below her toes. She stared at it, fascinated. She felt as if she were on a ship that might at any moment detach itself from the shore and carry her off. She pushed the last of the cone into her mouth and, like Craig, closed her fists about the railing. She had never seen such an assured piece of water, though it was rough and ugly and mud-coloured and its banks were shored with greasy stonework from which protruded pipes and conduits that oozed ribbons of livid effluent like banners draped across an arm. All along the curve of the wall were cranes and gantries and the ribs of ships under construction, and the hulls of ships ready to be launched. Downriver, modest in the haze, she glimpsed the little towns and villages that clung to the Clyde and sucked on its industries. She stared and stared into the muscular brown water that flexed and stretched and coiled below her and could almost feel herself drowning in it.

She started slightly when Craig looped an arm about her waist and pressed his body against her bottom.

She turned her head. He kissed her ear, her cheek, her lips.

Tenement windows glittered in the afternoon light. She felt as if a hundred pairs of eyes were watching her, as if all the wives that dwelled in the courts that overlooked the Clyde had stepped quick to their kitchen windows to grin and wink down at her and shake their heads ruefully at the memory of some moment of wooing that stung their memories still.

Flushed, Kirsty did not resist. She let Craig squeeze her against the railing, poised above the water; kiss her; kiss her; press his hips against her belly.

"Come on, Kirsty. Let's go home."

"But—"

"Please, Kirsty."

She yielded without reluctance. She had slept against him and not felt this strange and unfamiliar response in her nerves. She had dreamed about him without being thus aroused. But she was ashamed of it happening in broad daylight, in public, and was glad to pull away from the river and into the lane, Craig's hand locked about her waist.

They returned to the main road and caught the first horse-tram that rumbled along, not even waiting for it to halt. They seated themselves inside, knee to knee. Craig held her hand and everybody, even little girls with plaited hair and buttoned capes, seemed to know what was going on, and Kirsty did not know which way to look and how to stop a blush colouring her cheeks.

The ride cost a halfpenny each. It seemed interminable.

They got off at last at the head of Kingdom Road and ran down it and turned into Canada Road, hand in hand, out of step now and breathless. They reached the close of Number 11 and clattered upstairs. Craig could hardly find the lock with the key but fitted it at last and pushed the door open with his knee at last and pushed Kirsty inside. He closed the door behind him with his heel. He pushed her against the bunker, hands upon her breasts. He thrust against her. She could feel his hardness. His passion was not practised, not skilled. When he put his hand down to her thighs he searched her face in perplexity as if he expected her to castigate him and throw him off.

Laughter echoed from the stairwell outside. Children stampeded past the door, giggling. Mr Mills, the landing neighbour, shouted at them and reminded them that it was Sunday.

Kirsty disentangled herself from Craig's arms.

"Wait," she whispered.

"I can't wait."

"Just for a minute, till I close the curtains."

"Do you – do you want to do it too?"

"Yes."

She slipped from him into the kitchen.

The fire seeped grey smoke that hazed the kitchen. The sun, having soared over the wall of tenements, tinted the air a smoky gold. Even when Kirsty tugged down the paper blind and closed the curtain there was still a glow of light in the room. The voices of children could still be heard and the thump-thump of the marching band in the far distance, blowing itself back to supper. Nervous, breathless, Kirsty removed the powder-blue costume. She draped it on a chair. She slipped out of her blouse and shift and stepped out of her drawers. She was naked now in the haze. She hesitated, not knowing what Craig would expect from her or how he would come to her. She wondered if she should put on the nice new nightgown, fresh-smelling from its scented tissues.

Craig knocked uncertainly on the kitchen door.

"Kirsty, I'm – I'm ready."

She scrambled into bed, slid beneath the sheets and clasped the blanket to her chin. It was all happening so suddenly, so urgently. She was moist, though, and her breasts tingled. She realised that she was still wearing her stockings. Hastily she skinned them off and kicked them to the bottom of the bed.

Craig opened the door.

"Are you ready, Kirsty?" he hissed.

"Yes."

He was still dressed. He had removed only his jacket, not his shirt or trousers. She had been curious to see him. She clutched the blanket to her throat as he advanced to the side of the bed.

Stooping he brushed her hair with his fingertips and kissed her.

"Are you sure you're ready?"

"Yes," she said, "yes."

He showed a concern that Kirsty found both irritating and touching. She had been prepared for masculine roughness, for pain and perhaps humiliation but Craig did not seem to know where to begin. Kirsty drew down the blanket, let him see her breasts. He kissed her again, put a hand to her breast. Would he be put off by her freckles? Would she be big enough to please him? She did not know what would happen next. He edged into bed, still dressed, incredibly modest for a man.

Kirsty wriggled closer to the wall but Craig made a tent of sheet and blankets and fumbled off his shirt and trousers, pushed them to the floor. Cramped in the hole-in-the-wall he touched her accidentally. She flinched at his hardness.

"Sorry, sorry," he apologised, embarrassed by his awkwardness.

He eased himself down beside her, his face by hers on the pillow. She saw that he was unsure and would have taken the lead in love-making if only she had known how. She raised herself. She kissed him. The touch of his secret flesh had rendered her clumsy. She was afraid to cuddle him or rub against him in case he became too roused. She felt his fingers insinuate between her knees. She resisted out of instinct, then yielded, opened her thighs to his explorations. She winced when he found the opening. She held her breath. She tilted her hips, receiving not rejecting him.

"Is this – this the way?" he asked.

"Yes. It's all right, darling. Yes."

There was pain, a swift stinging pain. She gasped, gasped again as she felt warmth there and a sudden horror that her body had gone out of rhythm. She caught herself. She knew what it was. She opened her eyes and looked down at the line of her body, glimpsed Craig's muscular stomach and dark tangle of hair as he lowered himself into her. She bit her lip, gasping once more.

Beads of perspiration dappled Craig's brow. His arms about her shoulders were slippery. He felt huge within her but not sore. She was no longer afraid, not now that it had begun. His hands stroked her back, cupped her buttocks. She was out of step with him, all at sixes and sevens. Suddenly she wanted it to be over, over and out of the way so that she might hold him quietly in her arms. He slapped down against her. She felt a strange exciting tug deep in her stomach. She heard herself groan, heard Craig panting as he beat faster and faster and faster and faster, chest slapping against her breasts. It was as if she had become someone or something else. She hated his frantic detachment even while caught in sharp expanding sensations. She pinned her arms about his waist to hold him to her. She felt him jerk and jerk and gasped when he gasped. Then he slumped, arms on each side of her head, face buried in her hair.

"God, oh God!" he groaned.

Kirsty lay motionless, waiting.

He pushed himself up, looked at her, smiled, kissed her brow.

"All right?" he asked.

"Yes," she said. "But be careful."

"What?"

"How you – how you come out."

"Oh, aye."

He checked, withdrew slowly until he was clear of her and then he gave a laugh, rolled to one side and folded his arms above his head. His hair was plastered to his forehead in scalloped curls. His eyes were lazy-lidded. He grinned, proud of himself, smug and satisfied. He did not seem to need her now or share her desire for closeness.

"Well," he said, at length, "how does it feel to be Mrs Nicholson?"

"It feels fine," Kirsty said, and, a moment later, clambered from the bed to make them both a cup of tea.

Oswalds' Special Easter Cakes were nothing more than two crown-sized pieces of biscuit gummed together with a dab of fruit puree, given a lick of sugar-and-water with a small shellac brush and stuck with a 'flower' of dyed icing. To add distinction, and justify the extra halfpence on the price, the cakes were arranged by the dozen in tiny baskets of thin wicker which looked enticing in the windows of local grocery stores and confectioners' stalls.

If the weather had held fine Kirsty might have enjoyed making and packing the 'seasonal fare' but the warm sunshine of the weekend had given way to a snarling north-easter that drove rain across the Greenfield and made spring seem very remote indeed. She had been sent back to the packing-tables out of the flour store, though the mysterious Lizzie Weekes had not yet returned. Kirsty did not know who was doing the measuring. Letty, when asked, shrugged indifferently as if to say that she did not care so long as it wasn't her.

The week progressed in monotony and discomfort. The stone floors of the rooms were swept by icy draughts that chilled the feet and legs and made the back ache. Mrs McNeil was much affected and had to scurry away to the closets in the yard every quarter of an hour or so, much to the amusement of the younger girls who whistled and cheered the poor woman's every trip out of doors. Kirsty plied her bristle brush, charged with sugar-water, and patted floral shapes on to hard biscuit until her whole body felt sticky and the cloying taste of icing made her gag. Sunday seemed like a dream now. Rain lashed the shed roof, wind moaned in its girders and the cake racks never seemed to empty. Even Letty had little to say for herself and the hours of each shift dragged by leadenly.

At home things were not much better. Now that he had 'found the way', as he put it, Craig could not get enough of her. He fondled, handled and examined her as if she were a pet and not his wife and, though she did not deny him, Kirsty resented it a little, particularly as he remained modest and would not let her see him or touch him, not even in the full heat of love-making. On Thursday morning she awakened to discover that her bleeding had started eight days before it was due. Embarrassed, she got up, dressed and made breakfast. Craig seemed oblivious to her condition. She did not enlighten him. She fed him and saw him off to Maitland Moss with hardly a word. She felt thick and sluggish and had to exert will-power to don her coat and scarf and leave the warm kitchen for a walk through rain-splashed streets to the Cakery.

Mrs Dykes was waiting to direct her to the flour store again for, with the weekend coming, there was pressure on the bakers to increase supplies and 'her Tommy' could not do it all by himself. That much was true. The unsavoury Tommy did not have a spare moment to practise seduction. Harassed, he rapped out an order for fifteen bowls at four scoops of rice-flour to each bowl and left Kirsty to it while he loped away into the bakehouse.

Wool-headed and awkward, Kirsty lifted the lid of the bin – it seemed to weigh a ton today – and peered down at the flour banked against the bin's back wall, all tamped and clotted and damp. She was obliged to balance on her stomach to reach down to it. She had the obsessive fear that Tommy Dykes might steal up behind her and put his hand where it should not be. Today of all days she would die of humiliation if he did. But she filled seven bowls before Tommy showed himself, running, to whisk the bowls away and yell at her to get a bloody move on, Mrs High-and-Mighty, if you don't mind. She yelled after him, "This bin's near empty," but Tommy had gone and, victim of some crisis that had beset the masters, did not immediately return.

Kirsty pushed up the lid, leaned over, stretched down and poked the scoop into the flour in the corner.

At first she thought it was an imperfection in the flour itself, a stain – until the stain moved. It gave a puckering to the bulky stuff and a queer little surge. Frowning, Kirsty touched it with the tip of the spoon. She released a miniature landslide from the wall into the corner, a thick, dense, furtive covering which, after a second, also moved. She made a quick stiff stab with the tip of the scoop and lifted it up.

The grey mouse clung to the scoop by tiny grey forepaws.

Dusted with flour, wriggling and frantic, it swung in the air, chittering in anger or alarm, then it fell with a soft plop into the flour below.

Instantly a dozen mice were visible. Burrowing and wallowing into the broken nest in the bin's corner, into gaps in the boards of the floor, they submerged and surfaced hideously.

Kirsty screamed. She flung away the scoop, kicked to fling herself clear of the bin. The lid slapped down, pinning her. She screamed. She heaved upward and projected herself backwards with such terrified force that she tripped and fell to the floor.

With the image of that writhing mass of flour-soaked vermin printed in her mind she felt her gorge rise. She imagined the mice swelling like yeast, swarming over the rim of the bin, over her legs and thighs. She clapped her hands to her mouth to check her retching and stumbled to her knees.

Tommy came running from the bakehouse, Mrs Dykes from the rooms. Neither had need to ask Kirsty to explain her outburst. Lizzie Weekes, and umpteen other girls, had taken sick because of it, because of the mice. With an arm about Kirsty's waist the woman helped her through the store and out by a side door into the back yard, held her while she choked and was finally sick. With an iron fist Mrs Dykes kept Kirsty's head extended over a puddle of brown rainwater.

"That's right, that's it," she crooned. "Good, good."

A heavy, snatching cramp began in Kirsty's stomach. Icy cold sweat started on her brow. She pushed the woman from her and stiffly straightened herself. She wiped her face with her hand, shaking.

"There's a cold tap by a trough round the back there," said Mrs Dykes. "Wash yourself off, girl. I'll wait for you."

Kirsty, trembling, did as bidden. She found the old iron trough and ran clean water from a brass tap on a spout and wiped away the traces of sickness as best she could. She washed her face and rinsed her mouth. She could not stop shivering, though, and the cramp had not decreased. She returned to the yard by the side door.

"Better, hen?" Mrs Dykes asked.

"Aye, a bit."

"I thought, since you were a farm lass, you'd be used to such things."

"I – I didn't expect—"

"Ach, ye canny keep the damned creatures out."

"In – in the bins?"

"Only at the bottom," said Mrs Dykes. "What's wrong wi' you? Are you still feelin' sick?"

"Aye."

"I suppose you'll want to go home?"

"Aye."

"Go, then."

Kirsty put a hand to her brow and clenched her knees together to force herself to stand up straight. "Am – am I bein' sacked?"

"Don't be daft," said Mrs Dykes. "Come back tomorrow."

"Not – not for the flour—"

"The packing-room," said Mrs Dykes. "You're no' fit for the flour store after all."

"What about today? Do I get paid for it?"

"Naw, hen, you sacrifice the shift."

"But I've worked for five—"

"It's the rules."

"In that case," said Kirsty, "I'll stay."

The woman uttered a *huh*, squinted at Kirsty, then gestured towards the door with her thumb.

"Suit yourself," she said. "But if you're sick in there—"

"I won't be," said Kirsty.

"Find a clean apron, then."

Kirsty nodded, made her way back into the room where, pale and shaken and sore, she took her place between Letty and Mrs McNeil and worked out the shift's end assembling Easter cakes.

Craig came home late. Playfully he tossed his cap into the kitchen before him. Kirsty was at the sink, stirring cold water into the potatoes to stop them from burning in the pot. She flinched when the cap came skittering across the floor.

"How's my wee honeysuckle tonight then?" Craig asked jovially.

Kirsty did not answer. He came up behind her, put a hand about her and cupped her breast.

She drew away from him angrily.

"What's wrong wi' you?"

"It's the wrong time, Craig."

"It's only five past eight, for God's sake. I had one pint o' beer, that's all."

She could smell beer on him, cloudy and sour. She pulled away further, to the oven in the range.

She had to tell him what was wrong but she did not know how to do it, what words to use. She felt tearful, in need of affection. But she would not throw herself into his arms. She went on preparing and serving dinner. Craig would not understand why the discovery of mice in a flour bin had made her sick. She really could not talk of it, try to make him see the difference between vermin in a bakery and vermin in a barn. She felt separated from him because she could not let him make love to her.

After dinner she went out into the closet on the stairs, seated herself in the darkness and had a good cry. When she returned to the kitchen she found Craig engaged in writing a letter.

"Is that to your mother?"

"To Dad."

"He never replied to the others."

"He's no' much of a letter-writer."

"Are you tellin' him you've found work?"

"I am."

"Are you givin' him our address?"

"Why should I not?" said Craig. "Don't look so bloody po-faced, Kirsty, old man Clegg'll not make trouble for you now. It's too late."

She hadn't been thinking of Clegg or the Baird Home officers. She collected dishes from the table and put them into the new enamel basin by the sink.

"Craig, would you not like to go back to Dalnavert?"

Craig glanced round at her. "Would you?"

"No."

He gave a shrug. "Neither would I."

"Do you like it here, with me?"

Craig said, "Mr Malone tells me I'll have a cart o' my own soon. That'll mean more money. Come the winter I could be drawin' as much as twenty-three or -fourshillin's every week."

She poured water, lukewarm, from the kettle into the basin, washed the dinner dishes and put them away. She set out the things for breakfast, clinking them down inches from Craig's letter pad. She felt all up and down with him, angry and hurt, as if he were to blame for what had happened at Oswalds'.

Pencil, new and sharp, poised over paper. He had written only a few lines in spite of the time he had been at it.

How long could she live without Craig, without the money he brought in? Not long, not in a house of her own. She could see his reflection in the long glass of the window as he sat back, head tilted, staring up for inspiration at the strings of damp washing that dangled from the pulley overhead.

"Craig, I'm goin' to bed."

She wanted the day to be over, to end.

"Best place for you, in this mood," Craig muttered.

He had divined the reason for her shyness without having to be told.

She went into the hallway and undressed. She put on a pair of old drawers under her nightgown and came back into the kitchen to find that he had completed the letter, had addressed the envelope and was in process of licking the stamp.

She touched him, kissed the side of his neck. "I'm – I'm sorry."

"Not your fault," he said, "I suppose."

It was an hour later before he came to bed. Kirsty was still awake, not even drowsy, too tense and overwrought to find sleep easily.

Craig climbed over her to the inside place by the wall, settled, his back to her. Kirsty studied the kitchen. He had neglected to smoor the fire in the grate, to turn down the gas, to draw the curtain over the window.

She should get up and do these things but she feared that Craig would resent it, would take it as criticism. She closed her eyes. She wanted to hug him, hold him, share an intimacy that had no sexual end. But he inched away as if he sensed what was on her mind. She shrank down into her burrow in the mattress, tears in her eyes.

Outside, rain pattered upon the window pane, a broken gutter splashed water into the backcourt and, much closer, the tap drip, drip, dripped, not maddeningly but with a steady soothing regularity as if the appointments of the house had more sympathy for Kirsty than had her man and, in substitute, sang her their own soft lullaby.

Bob McAndrew was old enough to have been Craig's father. He was thick about the midriff, had a full walrus moustache and smoked a dainty clay pipe that was all bowl and no stem. The pipe hung upside down and dropped occasional gouts of ash into his lap, an occurrence that did not seem to bother Bob at all, though he would usually remove it dedicatedly from his mouth at that point and spit to one side, to the peril of any poor pedestrians who happened to be near the cart.

"Ever been across the river?" Bob asked, after they had been on the road for ten minutes or so.

"Where do you mean?" said Craig.

"Renfrew?"

"Nah," said Craig. "Is that where we're goin'?"

"It is, it is."

"Is that not a bloody long way to carry a load o' light wood?"

The cart had been loaded when Craig had arrived at the yard, a stack of planed timber loosely stacked and roped, so light in fact that it could be drawn by a filly that was usually reserved for the 'Valuable Goods' van.

Bob said, "The contractor got it cheap, so it's worth the carriage fee, see?"

Craig, in his innocence, thought no more about it for a while but hung on to the rail by the front of the board while the filly clopped round the corner and into New Clyde Street.

The wind was still stiff but rain had gone out of it and it was a fresh invigorating morning that made Craig feel sappy and full of beans; a nice morning to be clipping along on a deep-sided two-wheeler behind a sprightly chestnut filly heading for the ferry.

"What are we to carry báck, Bob?" Craig asked.

Bob McAndrew extracted the pipe, spat.

"I dinna ken," he said.

Bob did not know what the return cargo would be; unusual for a carrier to be so vague about loads and schedules. Craig, with just the faintest prickle of suspicion in him, did not press the point, put no more questions to his mentor and looked about him at the passing scene in silence.

Moist and brilliant with early sunshine the skyline was dominated by the Plantation's heavy cranes and steam-powered coal hoists. In the streets that radiated from the quays there were milk floats and cleansing carts and the rainbow jets of 'hosers' flushing away cattle muck. The cobbles ran red and brown and the smell brought Craig a sudden unexpected memory of mornings at Bankhead. Nostalgia faded swiftly enough, however, when the cart ground down the stone ramp below the mouth of the

Kelvin and straight on to the larger of the steam ferries that plied the Clyde.

Bob and he were early enough not to have to queue for passage on the deck, for the vessel could carry but eight horses and carts at a time. The Clyde was running high and strong and, while Bob attended to the filly, Craig leaned on the taffrail and watched the iron-girdered craft slip out into the current and slide away from the familiar shore, drift and twist and nuzzle in again, under the towering walls of a rigging-shed, to bump its bumpers against the Govan wharf.

Bob took the reins and let Craig lead the filly up the ramp from the ferry wharf but when the young man went forward towards the road Bob called to him, "No' that way," and summoned him back on to the board.

"There's a better way, Craig. The old towpath. It's o'er narrow for a big cart but it'll accommodate this wee thing fine."

"Is it quicker?"

"Aye, out o' the traffic. Clear o' the polis."

Craig thought nothing of the remark for carriers and coppers were natural enemies. One officious constable could cost a carter a fine or late-fee or even his job if the firm was strict and the delay long. Bob guided the filly about the gable of an old lime-washed building on to an unpaved ride.

Craig settled again, enjoying the sun on his back and the unhurried, countrified pace. Bob told him that the towpath weaved a right-of-way from the Highland Lane to Renfrew and that forty or fifty years ago it had been a busy thoroughfare when the Silk Mill and the Plantation House were operating, before railways stole the business and shipbuilding yards spread out along the shore. The path nipped away from the river wall whenever there was a yard, ran adjacent to long lines of tall wooden buildings and under the jibs and rigs and ribs of ships on their berths, came back faithfully to the river whenever it could to give Craig a glimpse of the brown, broad water and the far distant hills.

Once he roused himself, sat up and pointed.

"Hoy, Bob! Yonder's the Greenfield."

Smiling at the young man's pleasure in the prospect, Bob said, "So it is now, so it is. I wonder what it's doin' away over there, eh?"

From this perspective Greenfield parish appeared small and undistinguished. Even so, Craig eagerly picked out landmarks and pretended – and Bob did not have the heart to correct him – that he could see Canada Road and the tenement in which he lived.

The cart rolled on for four or five miles. It was just after seven o'clock, still early, when it turned away from the towpath and nosed up a lane into a high street.

"Is this Renfrew?" Craig asked.

"It is."

The market town, a little port, was neat and quiet and sedate. Not exactly on the river, its commodious steamboat wharf was set apart from the burgh centre. The town hall was imposing and the parish church had a fine slender spire and the whole place seemed genteel and well-heeled, though it was no longer as prosperous as it had once been, Bob said, and had only been saved from ruin by the broadening of the Clyde basin and the arrival of steam engineering.

Bob turned out of the high street and headed west through a scattering of new villas on to a flat back country road guarded by trees.

"Where's the yard, Bob?"

"It's no' far, no' far at all."

The inn was half hidden by the tree line, a small, squat building in a disreputable state of repair.

There was a coachyard to the rear with a high plastered wall about it. The inn itself sported no hanging sign but a weathered board on the wall spelled out, in blistered blue letters, a story of better days: *The Belltree Inn – Refreshments for Travellers – Carriers – Horses – Livery & Beds*.

There were no hints of any of these advertised services. Hens clucked about the doorstep and a barefoot laddie led a couple of cows along the road towards a pasture gate. Beech trees and elms gave the yard shelter from the wind and from prying eyes. Bob pulled the cart into the yard and reined it to a halt. He looked round cautiously at rusty churns, a midden, a broken barrow, kegs and crates, barred back windows and a closed door. There was something odd about this run, Craig realised. He kept his mouth shut and asked no questions. For two or three minutes there was no sound save that of the wind stirring budding leaves, the lowing of cattle from an unseen field and the arrogant crowing of a cockerel. Bob smoked a fresh fill of tobacco, spat frequently, did not dismount from the board; then he stiffened slightly and cocked his head.

Craig had heard it too, the chuckle of wheels and the *clop* of hoofs; a gig or trap. It did not enter the inn yard but stopped out of sight at the front of the building. A minute or so later the back door of the inn opened and a man stuck his head out. He was tall, not young, had a thick square beard and wore a chequered vest under a Norfolk jacket. A pearl-grey bowler was set at a jaunty angle on his head. The sporting gent made a discreet signal to Bob who handed the reins to Craig and climbed down to the ground.

"Do just as I tell you, son, an' keep mum," Bob said.

"All right," said Craig.

"Tie up the filly an' off-load the planks. Pile them up neat against the wall there."

"Right."

"Give her a rub an' a drink. You'll find a pump an' bucket round the side there."

"Is that all?" said Craig.

"I'll attend to the rest o' it."

Craig did as he was told to do. The filly was obedient and he had her tied, dried and fed very quickly.

He took off his jacket, for the sun was spring warm. From the corner of his eye he had seen the toff and Bob shake hands before they had gone into the inn. There was not hide nor hair of the publican or any other residents. He unloaded the long, light, pine boards and stacked them against the wall of the yard, watched by a pair of magpies and three or four white doves that had fluttered, crooning, on to the inn roof.

Beneath the pine boards Craig discovered two square wooden crates and a padlocked box, laid on a rug of thick buckram. The crates were roped tight.

Bob had not mentioned a secret cargo and Craig did not know if he was expected to unload it too. He was apprehensive, uncomfortable and, turning, found that the toff was watching him from the back door, a glass in his hand and a cigar in his mouth.

The toff called out, "Leave the boxes, boy. Just water the filly like a good chap."

Craig headed at once for the alley between the inn gable and a wall. Here, as Bob had said, was a rusty iron pump and a bucket, and stables; stables that were so neglected they were beginning to decay. Craig cranked the pump, filled the bucket with brownish water and then, after glancing this way and that, stole to the front of the building and peeped out into the road.

It wasn't a gig but a large, shiny dog-cart with a sleek Shetland pony in the shafts. Craig paused long enough to admire the rig then came back into the alley, lifted the bucket and returned to the back yard.

It did not surprise him to discover that the wooden crates and padlocked box were gone.

He watered the filly, put on his jacket and seated himself on the cart's tailgate to wait for Bob.

Ten minutes later a young girl came from the inn with a tray in her hands. Bob had sent him out some breakfast; a glass of ale, three slices of beef and brown bread and butter. The girl was young and would have been pretty if she had not had a cast in her right eye. Her blouse was unbuttoned at the throat and her breasts were plump.

"What's your name?" Craig asked her.

"Marie."

He studied her, saw her differently now that he had become a husband, a man. He fancied that he knew all her secrets. He told her to hold the tray while he lifted the glass and drank the ale. He wiped his lips with his wrist.

"Marie; that's a nice name," he said, and winked at her.

Perhaps she knew what was in the crates and the locked box and the name of the toff and what the toff and Bob were doing inside the inn; he was tempted to question her. But the turned eye was disconcerting, the fold between her young breasts even more so.

He stared at her; and she let him.

Heat and heaviness between his legs; he would not be able to exploit that energy, not now and not tonight.

He snatched the tray from her hands and slid it on to the bed of the cart, snapped at her, "What the hell are ye lookin' at?"

She stuck out her tongue at him, thin, pink and moist, swung on her heel and left him.

Craig watched the lithe hips under the skirt, the shape of her buttocks and, with a degree of annoyance, thought of Kirsty, who had somehow cheated him. Just thinking of Kirsty at all made the heaviness increase. He pushed himself from the tailgate with a little silent snarl and, standing, ate the breakfast that had been sent out to him while Bob was inside doing business with the toff.

Kirsty put on her apron and pulled the cotton cap over her hair, took her place at the table beside Letty and Mrs McNeil. They were still on Easter cakes, the racks thick with biscuits, the boxes crammed with flowers of dyed sugar. She tried not to look towards the archway, towards the flour store in case the sight of it made her squeamish. She ran out two lines of biscuits, pulled her brush from the water jar and reached towards the puree dish.

Letty caught her wrist and told her in a whisper, "Lizzie Weekes is dead."

113

"What?"

She had never clapped eyes on Lizzie Weekes. She had no idea whether the girl had been plain or pretty, young or old, dark or fair, yet she had shared with that girl the experience of the flour bin and had somehow ascribed to Lizzie a nature so sensitive that she had been ruined by the store's contaminating secrets.

"When?"

"Last night," said Letty.

At the other tables the girls were picking over the same piece of news like crows at a meaty bone, giggling, some of them, as if it were scandal and not tragedy.

"She must've been very sick after all," said Kirsty.

"Sick, nothin'," said Letty. "She done herself in."

"May God forgive her all her sins," added Mrs McNeil.

"Killed herself?" Kirsty exclaimed. "But how did she—"

"Drank a bottle o' caustic."

Letty's fingers flew over the cardboard biscuits, dabbing puree here and there. The process of manufacturing Easter cakes went on while she imparted, out of the side of her mouth, the sordid details of Lizzie Weekes' death.

"She was in the family way," said Letty.

"Four months gone," put in Mrs McNeil.

"It was startin' to show," said Letty. "I heard it was a marrit man done it to her. But he wouldn't dream o' leavin' his dear wife. I heard he was a toff from a big house in Dowanhill."

"How did she meet him?" said Kirsty.

"Got picked up by him in the Groveries last summer."

"Well," said Mrs McNeil, "Lizzie told me she was sure he was mad in love wi' her."

"Cabbage!" said Letty derisively.

"Aye, she'll burn in the eternal fires o' Hell for her love, I'm thinkin'," said Mrs McNeil with a nod.

"That sort o' mortal sin's only for you Catholics," said Letty. "Lizzie was no bloody Pape."

"Catholic or no'," said Mrs McNeil, "she placed her soul in jeopardy an' must pay the price."

Kirsty slapped two biscuits together, dabbed them with the heel of her hand and, changing the brushes, pumped the bristles into the bowl of sugar and water. Gossip and argument had dulled the first edge of shock and sorrow. She had a wedding ring on her finger and a good man at home. She felt righteous and protected. She had avoided the trap of illicit love and felt entitled to listen to stories about the silly girl, as if suicide were no more than mischief.

Kirsty said, "I thought it might've been Tommy."

"Tommy! Tommy Dykes!" Letty shrieked. "God, there's a chuckle for ye. Tommy hasn't got the spunk for makin' babies."

"How d'you know?" said Mrs McNeil.

"Take my word for it; I know."

"Have you been out wi' Tommy Dykes?" said Kirsty, and grief drifted obliquely from her mind to be replaced by something alive and intriguing.

"Aye, I have – kind of," Letty confessed. "I met him one night at the *Temple*."

"Is that a church?"

"Naw, naw, naw," said Letty. "*The Temple o' Fame*."

"A hall of Varieties," Mrs McNeil explained. "It's down in Black Street near the Cross."

"Anyway, I was down there wi' my cousin Jeannie. They were doin' plays at the *Temple* that week; *Still Waters Run Deep* an' *The Hunchback*. I fair liked the hunchback. It was about this mannie who—"

"Get on wi' it, Letty," said Mrs McNeil.

"Anyway, we were in the top gallery – so was Tommy."

"The *Temple*'s no' a place where decent girls should go alone," said Mrs McNeil. "It's just beggin' for trouble."

"'Course it is," Letty admitted. "Why do ye think we go there? Anyway, there was Tommy. He'd had a drop too much an' he was beezin'. Our Jeannie had got hersel' a click; a brass-founder, no less, from Beardmore's. Very well-spoken."

"What about you and Tommy?" said Kirsty.

"He said he'd walk me home. No sooner are we out o' Black Street than he was haulin' me up a close."

"How could you?" said Mrs McNeil. "Anythin' might have happened."

"I told you, Tommy was beezin' wi' drink. I knew I was safe enough. Anyway, he tried t' get his hand – you know."

"I've heard enough o' this," said Mrs McNeil, but did not draw away from the conversation. "It's disgustin', that's what it is."

"Aye, disgustin's the word," said Letty, "since the daft beggar couldn't."

"Couldn't what?" said Kirsty.

"Couldn't – you know."

Kirsty laughed. She could imagine Tommy Dykes, red, gawky, fumbling, and how Letty would put him through the hoop for his failure to be a man. She laughed again. The girls at other tables all seemed to be laughing. Kirsty looked up, heard them, saw them, felt laughter choke in her throat.

How callous she had become, how coarse.

She felt her eyes grow misty with sentimental self-pity.

She wiped her nose with her wrist, stickily.

"What's wrong wi' you, for God's sake?" said Letty.

"Got a cold comin' on," said Kirsty.

"Then kindly keep it to yoursel'," said Mrs McNeil. "I can't afford t' be off sick."

"Who can?" said Letty and then, uninvited, rattled on with her tale of the seduction that never was.

Bob chose to return by a different route. He drove through the town and down to the riverside where the Renfrew ferry crossed to Yoker. While they waited for the boat to come over the far shore Bob fished in his pocket and brought out two half-crowns. Without show or formality he handed them to Craig.

"What's this?" Craig said.

"Gratuity."

"Is this the rake?"

"Naw, we chalk up the rake in the usual manner; that's a bonus."

It had been a very fishy deal and Craig was no longer in doubt that the boxes hidden under the timber contained stolen goods which had been sold off to the sporting gentleman. The fact that he had been a party to something illegal did not bother him much. Bob McAndrew would not be behind the deal; it would be Mr Malone, and Craig, though wary of the man, took a certain pride in the fact that he had been 'trusted', if that was the word, by the boss.

"Look," Bob said, "if anybody asks you where we were this mornin' just tell them we went to Bellshill."

"Where's that?"

"Lanarkshire."

Craig said, "Who's liable to ask me?"

"Och, you never know," said Bob. "Best no' to talk of it at all; not even t' your wife. You know how women chatter."

"Aye," said Craig.

Bob said, "Once we're over the river I'll let you drive, if you like."

"I'd like that fine."

He was given the reins as soon as the cart had cleared the ferry ramp on the Yoker side of the river. He had driven carts on Dalnavert and at Bankhead and knew what to do.

Day shift had begun in the yards and graving docks but the long stretch of the Dumbarton Road was for the most part bounded by fields and light on traffic. In less than an hour they were back in Greenfield.

Bob let him navigate into Kingdom Road and right into the gates of the yard so that Mr Malone, leaning on the rail at the top of the stairs to the office, could see how proficient he was. Though pleased with himself Craig did not put the morning's events out of mind and did not miss the enquiring glance that passed between wily old Bob McAndrew and Mr Daniel Malone or Bob's discreet signal that all had gone smoothly, exactly according to plan and that the Maitland Moss gang had found a new recruit.

Unlike many of her fellow citizens, Kirsty did not regard religion as a springboard for bigotry or as something which disbarred you from all pleasure and condemned you to glum sobriety. Going to church was an act of free will as far as Kirsty was concerned; she had never been allowed to leave Hawkhead on Sunday to make the long walk to Bankhead kirk and had thus been excluded from its socials, picnics and soirées, as well as its services. Now that she was her own woman she felt entitled to take three hours of a Sunday morning to herself and, while she'd never have squandered them by lying idly in bed, she felt justified in attending Christian worship while Craig was at work at the stables.

Kirsty had no firm opinion of the advantages of one denomination over another but had it in mind that it might be nice to bump into an acquaintance. Thus she headed for Walbrook Street and the sedate little church on its corner which seemed, from the outside, more hospitable than the smoke-stained kirks that were crammed into side-streets in Greenfield or the huge and daunting edifices that towered over sinners along Dumbarton Road. She liked the gentle name of the Walbrook Street church – St Anne's – and the feeling that the lead-paned windows gave her and the fact that the building was not composed of soaring verticals but of warm corners and gaslit vestibules, all tinted, of course, by memories of Number 19, where she had first tasted independence.

She had gone but half the distance to Walbrook Street when the first bells rang out. Soreheads found the bells infuriating as they turned over, groaning, in bed or hunched over a late breakfast. To Kirsty, though, they seemed cheerful and encouraging. Her blue mood lifted for the first time in days and she squared her shoulders and lifted her head as she walked along and thoughts of the flour store and poor Lizzie Weekes fell from her.

It was almost as if Mrs Frew had known that she was coming. As Kirsty approached Number 19, the door opened and the woman emerged, dressed all in black, save for a blood-red bow upon her hat. She fumbled with a purse, an umbrella and an enormous bible as she turned to lock the house door with her latchkey; Sunday, of course, was Cissie's day off.

Kirsty hesitated, embarrassed by her temerity. Perhaps Mrs Frew would have no time for her now that she was not a guest in the boarding-house. Perhaps Mrs Frew might not care to be seen in the company of a young woman who was not her social equal. However, she had come this far and must risk a snub.

"Mrs Frew, Mrs Frew."

The woman had just stepped on the pavement. She turned, without a smile.

"Oh, it's you, is it?"

"Aye, I was just passing, so I thought I'd—"

"Passing?"

"On my way to church," said Kirsty.

"Are there no churches in Greenfield?"

"Well, I've always liked the look o' St Anne's."

"One church is as good as another," said Mrs Frew. "Does the Lord not tell us that where one or two are gathered in His name there will He be?"

Nonetheless Mrs Frew did not object when Kirsty fell into step with her and together they made their way towards the corner.

"Why are you wearin' that?" said Mrs Frew.

The powder-blue costume was not the most suitable outfit for the Sabbath but it was the only decent, matching garment that she possessed.

Kirsty said, "Is it too gaudy?"

"You're young enough to get away with it, I suppose," said Mrs Frew. "And you're married now, I see."

Kirsty had not had the ring off her finger since leaving Walbrook Street.

She nodded. "Yes. Yes, Craig an' I are married."

She held her breath, sure that she would be interrogated, found out in the lie and that her tenuous friendship with the widow would end before it had properly begun. But Agnes Frew was shrewd enough to hold her tongue; what she did not know would not harm her moral sensibilities. She put no questions about the ceremony and appeared to accept Kirsty's white lie at its face value.

"Are you settled in Greenfield, then?"

"Yes."

"Have you a house?"

"A single-end – until we can afford better."

"Does he have work?"

"We both work. I do a half-shift at Oswalds' Cakery an' Craig's with a firm of carriers."

Mrs Frew did not seem to be listening. She held her head high, nose pointed at the church.

Suddenly she said, "Take my arm."

"Pardon?"

"Take my arm, Kirsty. It'll not look so bad if you're with me."

Obediently Kirsty slipped her arm through Mrs Frew's and so arrived at the door of St Anne's where the ushers, Mr Brown and Mr McKay, stood rubbing their hands, smiling, bowing, nodding to all the gentlemen and ladies who climbed the four steps to the stone archway.

From within came the soft persuasive sound of an organ and the old dry fragrance of teak and cedar, leather and plush velvet. Involuntarily Kirsty hugged Mrs Frew's arm as they climbed the steps.

Mr Brown, or was it Mr McKay, beamed at her ruddily and said, "I see you've found a helper, Mrs Frew. Aye, there are times when I feel I could be doin' wi' a hand up these steps myself."

"I am not infirm, Mr Brown," said Mrs Frew.

"'Course not," said Mr Brown, who knew the widow's foibles only too well. "Welcome to St Anne's, lass. Hymnary?"

"Thank you," said Kirsty and self-consciously followed the widow through the inner door.

It was not in the least like Bankhead kirk, not narrow and austere.

Mrs Frew took seats in a middle row left of the aisle and Kirsty seated herself on the padded leather bench which, though firm, was more communal than Bankhead's upright pews. She looked about her at carved and graceful pillars and woodwork and stained-glass windows which depicted Jesus the Good Shepherd and Jesus the Fisher of Men and, as the organ played, she felt calm and serene.

It would have been lovely if she could have been married here, coming down the aisle on Mr Sanderson's arm in a dress of ivory white while Craig and his brother Gordon, in black frock coats, waited by the steps. But she could not marry in St Anne's, or anywhere, for, in the eyes of the world, she was already a wife.

Mr Graham entered, his black robes floating behind him. He was followed by a small, barrel-shaped man in a tight three-piece suit of absolute black, the senior elder and clerk. Mr Graham was contrastingly tall and lean, with a hawk nose and two sprigs of hair on his cheeks. He wasted no time and, after a murmured prayer, announced the first hymn.

Kirsty rose with the rest of the congregation and gave a tiny start of surprise when the first massive chords rolled from the organ which had previously been so quiet and was now rousing. She filled her lungs with the sound of it and, glancing down at the words in her hymnary, sang with the rest: *Hosanna, loud hosanna.* She had a strong clear voice and could hold the tune without effort and, uninhibited, felt herself buoyed up by the chorus, loosed, for a time, from concern about Craig and Oswalds', racks of Easter cakes and poor Lizzie Weekes. She was glad, very glad, that she had come to St Anne's and hoped that nothing would prevent her from coming again.

Kirsty was home long before Craig who did not arrive until after two o'clock. She had, however, taken pains to prepare a cold roast beef dinner for him and had bought a jar of the big brown pickled onions that he loved. He came cheerfully into the kitchen and gave her a peck on the cheek by way of greeting. Today he smelled of horses as well as beer.

"You're all dolled up," he said.

Hopeful that he might take her out to the park, Kirsty had not changed out of her Sunday best.

"I went to church," she told him.

"Church? Why?"

"I felt like it."

He seated himself at the table and reached for the pickle jar.

"Craig, wash your hands please."

Without argument he got up and went to the sink. "Is that what goin' to church does for you?"

"Pardon?"

"Is cleanliness no' next to godliness?"

"Your mother wouldn't let you sit at her table after you'd been muckin' out stables, would she?"

"What the hell's she got to do wi' anythin'?"

"I didn't mean to bite your head off," Kirsty apologised.

She filled the brown earthenware teapot from the kettle, fitted on its knitted cosy and put it on the cork mat on the table. Sleeves rolled over his forearms Craig returned to the table and picked up his fork.

"Are you mad because I've been drinkin'?" he asked.

"It's up to you what you do."

"Christ, I only had one or two jars in the yard."

"So that's what goes on on Sunday mornings."

"Mr Malone offered them. I couldn't refuse."

"How hard did you try?"

"Mr Malone seems to like me."

"That's good."

"He's offered me extra work."

"Paid work?" said Kirsty.

"Aye."

Kirsty put the plate of beef and cold potato in front of Craig, and a dish of tomatoes. The tomatoes had cost her a fortune for they were imports from the south, but the dinner-table would look bare without them.

Craig reached out and took one, cut it dextrously into quarters and began to eat.

"Night work," said Craig, his mouth full.

"When?"

"Tonight."

"Sunday?"

"Aye, I'll be goin' out about ten."

"For how long?"

"Dunno. As long as it takes."

"What sort of stuff do you carry at midnight on Sunday?"

Craig folded a slice of bread and pushed it into his mouth. The beef, potato and tomato had all vanished, though she had not been niggardly in her serving.

"I think," Craig said, "it might be a moonlight flit."

"It's not against the law?"

Craig grinned. "Not if ye don't get caught."

He got up from the table, seated himself in a chair by the fire, lit a cigarette and picked up last night's *Evening Citizen*. When Kirsty brought him a cup of tea he accepted it without a word.

"The weather's quite nice," she said. "Are we goin' out for a walk?"

"Nah, I'd better catch forty winks."

She hid her disappointment.

It was the only time that she felt close to Craig, that she belonged to him; not in bed, not seated on his knee while he fondled her but 'promenading' on Dumbarton Road or in the park. If he had to go out late tonight, however, he would be in need of rest.

With a sigh she said, "It's just as well. I've things to do about the house."

"Do them quietly, dear," Craig told her.

Tomorrow afternoon, after her stint at the Cakery, she would have her time in the wash-house in the backcourt, use of the big tub and boiling water and a share of the drying-lines that latticed the 'green'. She had already accumulated a pile of sheets and towels that had to be done. 'Arrangements' regarding use of the wash-house and a stair-cleaning rota were made by Mrs Bennie, empress of the close community and a woman even more formidable than Mrs Dykes.

Kirsty had asked, innocently, if she might do her 'turn' at cleaning the stairs and scrubbing out the lavatory on a Sunday. Mrs Bennie had been outraged by the very suggestion. Nobody, she declared, nobody, not even that slut McAlister – who had a family of eleven – would dream of sweeping stairs on a Sunday. It had to be, had always been, Tuesday for the occupant of the top floor right; and that was that. Life in Number 11 Canada Road was a far cry from Kirsty's dream of a cottage with a rose trellis and a vegetable garden, and 'marriage' to Craig was not all kisses and cuddles. It would never be like that, she realised, though the girlish dreams persisted from time to time. Canada Road was certainly better than Hawkhead, however; better than slaving for Clegg or living in a room in Dalnavert and squabbling with Craig's mother day in and day out.

Craig heaved himself out of the chair, took off his boots and rolled on to the bed. He lay on his back, hands above his head and stared at the pock-marked plaster florets high above his face.

Making as little noise as possible, Kirsty washed dishes and set the table for tea.

When that was done she took off her apron and went over to the bed. Craig's eyes were closed. On impulse she leaned over and kissed him on the brow. His eyes flew open, startled. His hands flew to her shoulders not to pull her down but to push her away, as if he was afraid of affection.

"When'll you be – fit again?" he asked.

"Fit?"

"You know what I mean."

"Oh," Kirsty said. "In two or three days."

His voice was husky with vexation.

She wanted so badly to please him and knew that it pleased him to make love to her. The truth of it was that she wanted him now more than she had ever done before but she would have to learn to put up with this trick of nature as part and parcel of being a wife. It seemed, though, so wanton and unfair. It was easier for Craig. All he wanted was money, and to make love to her. She envied him his easy desires. She did not really know what she wanted. She had grown out of girlhood all too soon and into complicated womanhood without, it seemed, acquiring volition of her own.

She drew back from him, from the bed.

She seated herself and lifted her mending-basket. She did not feel at all inclined to spend the afternoon with her new darning-egg and slippery needles, repairing Craig's stockings and cardigan.

She wished that she had accepted Mrs Frew's kind invitation to return to Walbrook Street at half past four o'clock and take tea there, after Mrs Frew had given lunch to her reverend guests. But Kirsty had reluctantly turned down the invitation out of a sense of wifely duty, out of loyalty to Craig and in the hope that he would want to spend the afternoon with her. She could hardly appear at the boarding-house now, out of the blue.

She sighed, unspooled a length of coarse brown wool from the ball and threaded a wetted end through a darning-needle.

In the recess Craig snored rhythmically.

He wakened at six. He ate supper. At nine he left again for the Kingdom Road and his share of the night work that Daniel Malone doled out to trusted accomplices and young lads too green to know exactly what was going on and what treasures they carried through Greenfield's dark streets in the back of the covered van.

Around ten, tired, dispirited, and with the bloom long gone off the day, Kirsty went to bed alone.

FOUR

Night Work

Summer was marred by persistent rain and blustery winds. Steamer cruises on the Clyde, trips to the seaside, band concerts, minstrel shows, Masonic picnics, twilight dances in the parks and most annual Gala days fell victim to unseasonable weather. Even folk like Craig and Kirsty who had not yet discovered the pleasures of the summer city felt cheated by wet grey skies and, before August was out, Kirsty found herself looking forward to winter's crisp cold days, dry frosty evenings and nights spent before a cosy fire.

The span of time between April and autumn, measured out in occupational and domestic routines, seemed long and monotonous. On the last Friday in every month Mr McCoig would call for the rent. Every Wednesday evening Jack Dunn would clump up the stairs with two bags of best coal and hold out his grimy black hand for payment. Every Tuesday night Kirsty would sweep out the stairs and close from top to bottom and scrub out the lavatory on the half-landing. It did not seem so terribly different from the routine of farming, except that it was more diverse, and that it was shared; and in the sharing of it Kirsty learned that there were worse things to be than a Baird Home orphan or a farm servant, that there were levels of despair and poverty below any that she had imagined.

Mr Kydd of the corner shop allowed tick but only to the tune of three shillings and would grant no extension to that limit no matter how a woman begged. Charlie Phillips, whose cart carried milk in the mornings and fish in the evenings, gave no tick at all, not even on Thursdays, not even to Mrs McAlister who had eleven mouths to feed off one wage and would have taken a dish of fish-heads if she could have had them on credit, who would even have gone round the backcourt with Charlie if he had fancied her which, of course, he did not since she was as skinny and pop-eyed as a filleted cod.

"That woman," Mrs Bennie would snarl, "is dirt. Give her the loan o' nothin', Mrs Nicholson, or you'll have her scratchin' an' clawin' at your door mornin', noon an' night."

But Mrs McAlister never 'scrounged' from Kirsty or from anyone in the close and Kirsty's sympathy was kept to herself, separated by the height of the building, though she observed with shame the hungry state of the children that crouched about the door of her ground-floor neighbour, heard them wail and whine like little banshees when Mammy was 'busy' with the marble-white infant that had been born in March; wept tears for her lack of charity when, late one Friday night in July, the marble-white infant died in its sleep and was taken away in a box by Doctor Godwin. Mrs Bennie claimed that it was to make sure by examination that murder had not been done but Kirsty felt that Doctor Godwin had removed the tiny corpse only to ensure it had a decent burial at no cost to the McAlisters.

The landing on the top floor of Number 11 was shared with Mr and Mrs Mills, models of rectitude, whose children had long ago gone off to seek fame and fortune elsewhere. The wife was snow-haired, plump, deaf as a post. The husband was fat, bandy-legged and smug as an owl. They existed on a wise little fund that Mr Mills had accumulated through the Northern Life Insurance Company during his forty-six years as a janitor in their offices in Gordon Street. In Mr Mills' book any person who had not possessed his degree of perspicacity, who had not used his youth and prime to make ready for old age, was a fool and a wastrel. Mr Mills' reaction to news of the death of the McAlister babe was to declare that if the child had been insured at birth then its passing would not have been in vain.

Alone in the kitchen Kirsty would listen to the noises of the tenement, an orchestra of small strident sounds, and wonder just how soon she would be absorbed into it, no longer protected by her youth and her daily job at Oswalds'. She was not chained by children to the house in the tenement now, but soon, in all likelihood, she would be. The prospect frightened her.

She confided her fears to Mrs Frew one dreary afternoon in August when she had gone to take tea with the widow in Walbrook Street.

"It's the way of the world, my dear," said Mrs Frew. "It's a woman's lot to suffer."

"Have you—?"

"No, I could not carry a child," said Mrs Frew. "It was Andrew's dearest wish, of course, that our union might be blessed. But the Lord did not see fit so to do. Andrew had five by his first wife before she fell into her final, fatal illness and, after many years of pain – borne with fortitude, I might add – was called to her rest."

"What happened to the children?"

"Andrew saw the boys to school, found husbands for the girls as soon as they were of an age."

"Where are they now?"

"I hear nothing from them."

"That seems a bit cruel, Mrs Frew."

"It was not my doing. They were too well cared for. Spoiled, if you ask me. I was not 'accepted', you see."

"Did they resent you?"

"They resented the fact that I was their father's only source of comfort and consolation during those years of trial."

Kirsty cleared her throat. "You – knew him before—"

"I was a friend, a church friend, that's all," put in Mrs Frew quickly. "We shared mutual interests. There was nothing indecorous done between us, I assure you. We waited three years after Evelyn's death before we took the plunge into marriage."

"I thought Mr Affleck said—"

"Hughie's a born liar; the bane of my life since the day he was born." Mrs Frew switched from wistfulness to sharpness in an instant. "We come from good stock, you know, though you'd never guess it to hear our Hughie talk."

"What does Mr Affleck do?"

"He's educated, I'll say that for him. He was always more learned than he looks. He could have gone far as a scholar, but he had no taste for the sedentary life."

"What job did he find?"

"He works in the City, for the City."

Kirsty waited for embellishment but Agnes Frew said no more on that score, reached instead for the big silver teapot and returned to talking of her husband and the position she had once held in society.

By the second week in September Kirsty was convinced that she was pregnant. She said nothing to Craig but 'stole', if that was the word, ten shillings and sixpence from the purse that Craig kept hidden under a board under the bed and, on a Monday afternoon, as soon as she was released from Oswalds', walked to Dumbarton Road and climbed the steep hill to the handsome sandstone mansions of Dowanhill Gardens.

She had decided weeks ago that if her suspicions were correct she would not put herself into the hands of the district's midwife, Mrs Curran, though the woman had a good reputation and had been trained in her profession, nor would she creep into the tiny damp waiting-room in Banff Street where Doctor Godwin, the same practitioner who had attended the infant McAlister, took his 'down town' surgery three nights in the week.

Kirsty had learned from Mrs McNeil that Doctor Godwin's main practice was conducted from his house in Dowanhill Gardens, had learned too, from listening to all sorts of gossip, that anyone who valued their privacy did not entrust themselves to the Banff Street place with its thin walls and ill-fitting inner door but struggled to scrape up the half-guinea fee that Doctor Godwin charged those who made the climb uphill in search of a consultation.

She was admitted by Doctor Godwin's wife, a woman of severe aspect but with a kindly voice, and taken directly through an echoing hallway to a room at the rear of the house.

Doctor Godwin was disconcertingly youthful, very clean and very slender, smooth-shaven and might, if he had had any hair at all upon his head, have been judged handsome.

"And you are?" he asked, from behind his polished desk.

"Kirsty Nicholson."

He wrote the name down upon a pad of paper with a fat pen, looked up, smiled reassuringly.

"Address?"

Kirsty told him.

He said, "That's just round the corner from my room in Banff Street."

Kirsty said, "Yes, Doctor. I know that."

He nodded, made no mention of the half-guinea fee. "What's wrong with you?"

She said, "I think I'm expectin' a baby."

He lifted the pen again and, without awaiting her answer, made an amendment to the note upon the paper pad, saying, "Ah, so it's *Mrs* Kirsty Nicholson, is it?"

"Yes."

"First pregnancy?"

"Yes."

"How long have you been married, Mrs Nicholson?"

"Five months, an' a half."

Smiling, he opened a drawer and took out a rubber-limbed instrument. "Well, let's see what's what, shall we?"

His examination was thorough, his questions frank.

Kirsty responded with equal candour, tried not to blush or hesitate but was too embarrassed to feel much pleasure when, at length, the doctor confirmed that she had conceived and was indeed some nine weeks into a normal pregnancy.

While Kirsty dressed, Doctor Godwin returned to his desk, made more notes and then, with pen still poised, told her what to expect by way of 'changes' in her bodily functions and in physical discomfort. Rising, he went to a deep cupboard at the back of the room and, still talking, busied himself within it. He enquired about her husband, the nature of his occupation, talked about the 'responsibilities' a mother-to-be had to an unborn child, warned her against lifting heavy weights, against 'straining' and, still out of sight, against allowing her husband to be too 'strenuous' after the lights were out. He came out of the cupboard with a brown bottle in his hand, gave it to her, took her half-guinea, told her that the peppermint mixture would relieve any inclination to sickness, told her to call upon him again if she should feel it necessary, here or in Banff Street as she preferred, and assured her that, if she wished it, he would attend her personally during the final weeks of her confinement and deliver the baby at home.

"Is there somebody who can look after you for a day or two?" Doctor Godwin asked as he ushered her towards the door.

"My – my husband."

"I meant a woman; your mother, say."

"No."

"Nobody?"

She thought fleetingly of Mrs Frew but discarded that notion immediately.

"Nobody," Kirsty said, "except my husband."

"I'll have a word with him," Doctor Godwin promised.

"When?"

"In due course," the doctor said and, reaching past her, opened the door and turned her over to his wife who saw her politely out into the Gardens once more.

Puzzled by her lack of any very definite emotion, Kirsty walked carefully down the long hill into Partick.

She thought, strangely, of her own mother, her real mother, wondered if she too had experienced this odd sort of nothingness when she had first discovered that a baby was on the way; if she had been filled with joy or with rage. By the time she reached Canada Road, however, her emotional vacuum had begun to fill with trickles of doubt and apprehension. She seemed to see the

streets clearly for the first time, the squalor that lurked behind
dowdy curtains and unwashed windows, to scent the stink of
poverty from the closes. She hated the thought that her baby
would be born to this inheritance, into such a world. Why such
snobbish nonsense should impress itself on a brat from the Baird
Home who had known nothing but slavery to a farmer in the wilds
of the Carrick hills was a puzzle in itself. She fretted over that
question too as she entered the close of Number 11 and climbed,
puffing a little, upstairs.

The moment she got indoors she brewed a pot of tea, buttered a
slice of bread and, still wearing her coat and hat, seated herself at
the table.

She examined her feelings cautiously; not tearful, not sorry for
herself, she felt, if anything, annoyed that everything would be
changed by the baby's coming, turned again on its head. She felt
secretive too, not ashamed but possessive; yet through her
grievance came little twinges of fear, like the pains in a tooth
touched by cold air.

The job at Oswalds' would be sacrificed. She certainly did not
regret that, but with it would go the six shillings that helped lift
them above the line of most of their neighbours. There would
be an extra mouth to feed and, even with occasional 'night
work' from Danny Malone, Craig brought home no more than
twenty-two shillings a week. She should have been happy this
day of all days but all she could think about was money or the
lack of it, and how, after the baby arrived, they would be pushed
to make ends meet, would become like everybody else in the
Greenfield.

She drank a second cup of tea, ate a second slice of bread and
butter then got up and fished the doctor's brown bottle from her
shopping basket and hid it behind the pipes in the box below the
sink. She did not want Craig to find it, to ask questions before she
was ready to give answers. No doubt she would have to tell him
the glad tidings soon but she would choose the time with care,
catch him in just the right mood.

She did not imagine that Craig would desert her even though
she was protected by nothing more legally binding than a
wedding ring. No, she was afraid for Craig, of how he would stand
up to the burden of responsibility, to fatherhood; afraid too that he
would write to Dalnavert and that Madge Nicholson would come
hot-foot to Glasgow to snatch away her grandchild.

Suddenly impatient with her own silly imaginings Kirsty
buttoned her coat again, found her purse and shopping basket

and, with a deep settling sigh, went out to walk down to Mr Kydd's to buy something nice for tea.

August was a quiet month in Mrs Agnes Frew's boarding-house. The academic year had not yet begun and a majority of parish ministers had gone off on 'exchanges', seeking a breath of country air or a sea breeze to blow away the cobwebs. Nessie Frew would not, of course, entertain her brother's suggestion that she open her doors to city visitors or holiday-makers pausing in Glasgow before heading out to the coast.

There was no meat upon the table that night but the dish of macaroni-and-cheese was tasty enough and the fig pudding to follow was positively delicious. Sister and brother ate at a dropleaf table in the kitchen, for Cissie, who had never shaken off her winter's bronchitis, had been shipped to an uncle's farm on Islay in the hope that two weeks of fresh milk, sea air and rest would quell the wheeze once and for all and restore her to full health.

Sister and brother ate and talked and, in due course and roundabout fashion, Mrs Frew informed Hughie of her young friend's altered state.

Hugh Affleck did not so much as raise an eyebrow.

He said, "I think you've developed a soft spot for that girl, Nessie."

"She's decent, well-spoken, and a Christian."

"Can the same be said for the husband?"

"I've heard nothin' to the contrary. He seems to treat her well enough."

Hugh Affleck applied a dollop of Worcester sauce to a second helping of macaroni and spread it carefully with the blade of his knife.

"Is it Canada Road they live in?" he asked.

"Yes, in a single-end," said Mrs Frew, wrinkling her nose.

"Bottom side?"

"Number eleven, I believe."

Hugh Affleck made mental note of the address.

He had met the Nicholsons only once, in April. He had not clapped eyes on either the girl or boy since. Nonetheless he had been kept abreast of their progress by his sister to whom other folks' affairs were a substitute for a lack of activity in her own. He regretted that Nessie and his wife, Beatrice, did not rub along and that he could not persuade his daughters, Gladys and Patricia, to visit their forlorn old aunt. The girls bitterly resented her 'preachiness', referred to her, cynically but not without wit, as

'Auntie Modern'. Nessie, in turn, regarded her nieces as frivolous and flighty and, though she did not say it in so many words, as downright sinful in their lack of Christian fibre.

Hugh Affleck said, "How long until her baby arrives?"

Why he should feel that the girl's pregnancy made any difference to his plans for the Nicholsons Hugh Affleck could not be sure. But it did. He recalled the girl vividly; freckled, cheerful, pretty, candid but not silly. Though the boy had not seemed to him to be the stuff from which criminals are made, Hugh was wary of snap judgements; in his time he had bumped into many charming characters who hid murderous natures behind their smiles.

Nessie Frew answered, "March, I believe."

"Is she also employed?"

"I told you, Hughie – in Oswalds' cake place."

"Rather her than me," said Hugh Affleck. "I wonder what miserly pittance they pay her there."

"I have not had the temerity to enquire, Hughie."

"Have a guess."

"Ten or twelve shillings a week, I suppose."

"Less."

"Less?"

"Oswalds' is another of those damned—"

"*Hughie!*"

"Well, it is; a slave market, a sweat-shop."

"It suits Kirsty. She is not required to work all day for her wages, she can attend to her housekeeping in the afternoons."

Hugh Affleck did not argue the point. He finished off his macaroni, watched his sister slip on a pair of cotton gloves and, stooping, bring the fig pudding all brown and steaming from the oven. Discreetly he took a little notebook and the stump of a pencil from his pocket and, while Nessie was busy with serving, jotted down the Nicholsons' address.

Sergeant Hector Drummond knew better than to do his drinking in public houses within a five-mile radius of Ottawa Street police station. He had been a bachelor in Barracks far too long to be blind to the disasters that overtook coppers who could not wean themselves from the whisky bottle. Besides, the mere whiff of a constable in a Greenfield drinking-parlour was enough to send half the customers scuttling for the exit and push the other half into pugnacity, for the police were unloved and unappreciated by all and sundry. The rank and file of the Greenfield force nipped up to a cosy public house in Glasgow for company and a quiet pint, in mufti, of course. But he preferred to spice his drink with a breath of fresh air and popped down on the train to *The Railway Arms* at West Kilpatrick, a rural hamlet fifteen miles down the Clyde shore. It was here too that Superintendent Affleck might be found when he was in the mood for a dram and an evening of shop talk with his old companion from the Burgh.

If the weather had been kinder that late August evening the pub would have been packed but with dusk coming early on melancholy grey rain there was only a handful of agriculturals at the bar. They paid not the slightest attention to the sergeant who, though he sported not one item of uniform, still managed to look, somehow, like a policeman. His taste in plain clothes had been shaped by a thousand hours in heavy serge and he did not feel comfortable in anything less sober and confining. He wore a high-collar, off-the-peg suit from the Greenfield Co-operative Society's warehouse and boots with soles like boiler-plates and a cap as flat as a cowpat that sat, without tweak or rake, dead level on his cropped grey head. He had been in the pub for half an hour, nursing a pint of draught bitter and a dram of Old Highland, before Hugh Affleck arrived.

Hugh Affleck took off his coat and hat, hung them where he could keep an eye on them, and carried his drink from the bar to the little table by the window.

"So it's yourself, Hughie, is it now?"

"It is indeed, Hector."

Drummond and Affleck had been young beat-constables together back in the dim and distant, though even then it had been obvious that Hughie, with his 'background' and education, would rise to better things. Off duty, however, rank was set aside and the men met on equal terms, friendly and easy.

Hugh Affleck wasted no time on casual chat but got down at once to business; and the business on hand concerned those notoriously ugly villains William Skirving and Daniel Malone.

It was common knowledge to detectives in the City of Glasgow as well as Greenfield Burgh that Malone and Skirving were 'the brains' behind a whole parcel of robberies, housebreakings and assaults, but it had so far proved impossible to lay them by the heels and muster sufficient evidence to bring a case to court. They were not much smarter and no less vicious than the brutes who nobbled tallymen in dark closes or bashed in the heads of bookies' runners but they had, somehow, bought the loyalty of their accomplices and had even spread corruption into the ranks of the police. Behind Skirving and Malone were clever and unscrupulous gentlemen who provided a ready-made market for gold, silver and works of art, stolen treasures beyond the scope of the average burglar and one which made Skirving and Malone's criminal endeavours highly lucrative. One of those gentlemen, Hugh Affleck believed, was none other than Maitland Moss.

Because Danny and Billy did not now prey on 'average' citizens but concentrated on the mansions of the well-to-do, all sorts of idiotic tales were put about concerning their derring-do and they were regarded with awe and admiration; a nonsense, of course, for Malone and Skirving were and always would be nothing but violent, ruthless men who would cut anybody's throat for ten bob.

Hugh Affleck hated them, coldly and professionally. It galled him that he had not been able to lay a glove on either of the villains in spite of several years of effort and endeavour. He was sure that the carriers' quarters in the Kingdom Road was the capital of Malone's shadowy empire and on two occasions had placed plain-clothes detectives in work there. Though they had been groomed for the job and were experienced in such operations, Danny had sniffed them out almost at once and had given them marching orders without apology or explanation. It was murmured that somehow or other Danny had known what was going on and had been on the look-out for 'narks'; and that meant that a copper in Glasgow or the Greenfield had been paid for the information, and relations between the officers of Greenfield Burgh and the City of Glasgow had become somewhat strained because of it.

At last, though, fate seemed to have dealt Hugh Affleck a high card and he had brought the sergeant here tonight to advise him on how he might best play the hand.

"Is it sure you are, Hughie, that the youngster is deeply enough involved in Malone's dirty work to be of use to you?" said Sergeant Drummond.

"I'm not that sure of anything, Hector, but he's got eyes and ears and he might be persuaded to use them on our behalf."

"How might that be done?"

Hugh Affleck shrugged. "In my opinion the young man is fundamentally honest. He's a country lad, not long in Glasgow and I've the feeling that he knows right from wrong."

"Will you threaten him, is that it?"

Again the detective shrugged. "I might do a bit of that, yes, but I think I can persuade him where his duty lies."

"If it's done badly," said the sergeant, "the youngster will simply tell Malone and we'll have stepped back instead of forward."

"I'm well aware of that, Hector," said the detective. "But I have to take the chance."

"What can the lad tell you?"

"How Malone transports stolen goods about the streets, for one thing."

"Which policemen are being paid to turn a blind eye?"

"Improbable that the lad will be privy to that sort of information," said Hugh Affleck. "What he might be able to do for us is put the finger on Malone, tell us in advance when a job is to be done."

"If you could catch either one of them red-handed," said the sergeant, "they might blow the gaff on all the rest."

"It's possible," Hugh Affleck said, "but I doubt it. Danny and Billy have both served time—"

"No," the sergeant corrected. "Malone has never been in prison. He has been up on three charges, when he was younger, but nothing has ever stuck."

"Yes, of course. I always tend to think of them as a pair."

"They are separate individuals," said Sergeant Drummond. "I feel that loyalty might evaporate if only they could be caught with blood on their hands. Billy and Danny might not be daunted by a stretch behind bars but the thought of the rope might loosen their tongues."

"Murder?" said Hugh Affleck. "Oh, they're capable of it. In fact, I'm damned sure that Billy has killed more than one man in his day but I wouldn't want to set a trap that put any life at risk."

"Och, no," said the sergeant.

"And I would much prefer to have them arrested within the jurisdiction of the City of Glasgow."

"It would be a High Court trial in any case."

"Probably," said Hugh Affleck. "But I'd like to make sure."

"What do you expect from this youngster, from Nicholson?"

"I'll have to talk to him."

"Would you use him as a witness?" said the sergeant, frowning.

"Only if I could be certain that he would be safe."

"If I were a youngster I'd be too scared of retribution to put my nose in a witness box, even if Danny and Billy were locked up tightly."

"Nicholson may not know that he'll be in danger."

"Will you not tell him?"

For a moment Superintendent Affleck did not answer, seemed to ponder his reply.

The sergeant said, "Look what happened to your last informer."

"I've no wish to discuss that matter."

"You never even told me his name."

"I told nobody his name," said Hugh Affleck.

"Where is he now?"

"Vanished."

"Vanished into the Clyde in a weighted barrel?"

"Perhaps. I don't know about Malone," said Hugh Affleck, "but Billy Skirving would certainly knife a nark as quick as winkie."

"So it's dangerous."

"I don't deny it." Hugh Affleck sipped his whisky and stared bleakly out across the river, shrouded in rain and almost dark. "What sticks in my gullet, Hector, is that Skirving and Malone are so damned cocky. They strut about as if they were above the law, as if they owned the Greenfield. By God, but they must have made a packet of money from sale of the stuff they've stolen."

"Aye, the Ming stem cup – what was it valued at?"

"Four hundred pounds."

"And yon Dragon vases?"

"Five," said Hugh Affleck. "The solid silver wine-cooler from Lord Cunningham's house; God, you could hardly lift it with a crane. I mean, it's not all being melted down. It's being sold intact to foreign collectors, I'm sure."

"By Maitland Moss?"

"Oh, probably," said Hugh Affleck. "And I find that very ugly, very ugly indeed; the idea of a couple of brutes like Skirving and Malone thieving precious articles on the instructions of a so-called gentleman, and none of them caring a jot whose head gets smashed in the process."

"In my personal opinion," said Sergeant Drummond, "I think you will be very fortunate to bring Mr Maitland Moss to trial at all."

"I know it, Hector. I'll settle for putting Skirving and Malone behind bars for a long, long time."

"Catch them in the act?"

"Exactly."

"Use the youngster – Nicholson – to help you set them up?"

"It's the first real bit of luck we've had."

"Aye, but will this young man agree to help us?"

"I won't know until I've talked with him."

"When will that be, Hughie?"

"Soon," Hugh Affleck answered. "Very, very soon."

It came as a great shock to Kirsty to find Mr Affleck on the doorstep. There was no twinkle in his eye, no teasing in his manner. He seemed taller too, and younger. When he informed her that he had come on business and not as a friendly visitor, Kirsty's apprehension increased.

"What sort of business?"

"I'm a policeman, Mrs Nicholson."

He held out a black book the size and shape of a postcard; his name was prominently printed upon a certificate of identity attached to the book's forepage.

"I have credentials," he said, "as you can see."

"Mrs Frew didn't tell me what you did," said Kirsty.

"Nessie's somewhat ashamed of my profession."

"What do you want, Mr Affleck?"

"To talk to your husband."

"You'd – you'd better come in."

She led him into the kitchen. She noticed how he glanced about the room, casually but with intent, as if he were looking for something.

"My husband – Craig's not home yet."

"How long will he be?"

"I'm expectin' him soon."

"May I wait?"

Kirsty could contain herself no longer. "What's Craig done, Mr Affleck? Tell me, please."

"He's fallen in with bad company."

"It's that man, that Malone, isn't it?"

"Why do you say that?" Mr Affleck said.

"He gives Craig money, extra money. Money for night work."

"Night work?"

"Moonlight flittin's, shiftin' furniture for folk who don't pay their rent. Is that a crime?"

"A misdemeanour," said Mr Affleck. "Nothing serious."

"Are you an inspector, Mr Affleck?"

"Superintendent."

"Is that not a high position?"

"Fairly."

"Then you're not here because of moonlight flittin's?" said

Kirsty. "What are they movin' in the night-time? Is it stolen goods?"

"Possibly."

"Oh, God!"

He patted her arm consolingly and put other questions to her. Kirsty answered him as best she could. She tried to hide the fear that she was being disloyal to Craig. If she was calm and truthful she might somehow save Craig from punishment, from prison. The quarter of an hour before Craig arrived was like a bad dream. Rain pattered on the window, the clock ticked, pots bubbled on the range just as they had done before Mr Affleck had knocked upon the door, but everything had changed; her existence was suddenly threatened. She was not sure how much uncertainty she could stand.

It had been bad enough screwing up her courage to tell Craig about the baby. He had not reacted with delight, had backed away, had eaten his supper with hardly a word. When they had gone to bed she had wanted him to make love to her but he had backed away, sat up, arms folded, and had talked in a stern voice about money. He had barely mentioned the baby. Kirsty had cried, in spite of her resolve not to, and Craig had got up and made her tea and brought it to her and had sat by the side of the bed and held the cup for her and murmured to her to turn off the waterworks, that he didn't really mind about the baby, after all. Eventually he had climbed back into bed and had put his arms about her and held her, awkwardly, and, at that moment, Kirsty did not know whether he loved her at all or, what was worse, whether she loved him.

"Is that your husband now?" said Mr Affleck.

She heard the clump of boots on the stairhead, got up quickly and ran to the door to open it before Craig could use his key, to give him warning.

"What's up wi' you?" Craig said "You're white as a bloody sheet."

"There's a man here to see you."

"A man? What man?"

"Mr Affleck."

"Mister who?"

"From the boarding-house."

"Oh, aye. What does he want?"

"Craig, he's a policeman."

In that split second Kirsty had seen guilt in Craig's eyes, a flash of panic, and realised that he had not told her the truth about what went on at the carriers' yard or what things he was required to do for Daniel Malone. She clutched at his arm as if to prevent him from bolting out of the house.

"What have you told him, Kirsty?" Craig hissed.

"I didn't tell him a thing."

"Jesus Christ!" Craig said, under his breath.

He squared his shoulders and went into the kitchen where Hugh Affleck waited, seated on a kitchen chair with his back to the bubbling pots in which the dinner was wasting. To Kirsty's surprise Mr Affleck rose and offered his hand and Craig, nonplussed by the gesture of friendship, shook it.

"Sorry to call on you at this late hour," said Mr Affleck, "but I'm making enquiries into a certain matter that I think you might be able to help with."

"What certain matter?"

Kirsty removed the pots from the range and took an ashet pie from the oven and set the dish on the side of the hob to keep warm. Behind her she heard the man and her husband speak, haltingly but without heat.

"Concerning what goes into and out of Maitland Moss's yard."

"All sorts o' things come an' go," said Craig.

"Late at night, Craig."

"I don't know nothin' about that."

"Come on, Craig, let's not waste time beating about the bush," said Mr Affleck. "You do some of these night runs."

"Did *she* tell you that?" Craig turned angrily to Kirsty. "Did *you* tell him that?"

"Your wife didn't have to tell me," said Mr Affleck. "Good God, son, I'm a policeman. I know a lot about a lot of things."

"Why are ye askin' me then?"

"Just how well do you know Danny Malone?"

"He's the boss o' the yard where I work."

"Does he ride with you?"

"Nah."

"Who is your regular driver, Craig?"

Craig hesitated. "Mostly it's Bob McAndrew."

"Does McAndrew take the reins on late-night jobs too?"

"Sometimes. Sometimes I do the drivin'."

"Who else?"

"I don't know, do I?" said Craig.

"Peter Gilfillan?"

"Nah."

"Jock Middleton?"

"Nah."

"Have you ever met a man – not a carter – named Skirving?"

"I have not."

"All right, Craig, now tell me what you carry on these night jobs."

Craig drew in a deep breath. "I don't know."

"Craig – " said Kirsty.

He rounded on her furiously. "It's the bloody truth; I *don't* know. All I do is collect the cart or the van at the gate o' the yard an' drive it to – well, to some place."

"What sort of 'some place'?" said Mr Affleck.

"A corner, or outside a shop."

"What happens then?" said Mr Affleck quietly.

"Somebody comes out an' loads it."

"'Somebody'?"

"Mr Malone; or Bob."

"Bob McAndrew?"

"Aye."

"And then?" said Mr Affleck.

"I drive the cart to where I'm told."

"Who rides with you?"

"Sometimes it's Bob. Sometimes it's Mr Malone."

Mr Affleck paused before he put the question. "Where do you go with the cart?"

"Different places."

"*Different* places; not to the carriers' yard?"

Craig said, "Sometimes we stop outside a close an' the stuff is off-loaded."

"Do you help with the loading?"

"No."

"Never?"

"Never. I'm no' allowed."

"All right; where are these places?"

"All over."

"In Hillhead, say, or Partick, or—"

"In the Greenfield," Craig answered.

"Could you tell me where they are?"

"Streets. I don't know rightly."

"All right. Now what's carried?" said Mr Affleck. "You must have had a glimpse of cargo at some point."

Craig shook his head emphatically. He had not removed his duffel and sweat beaded his brow and upper lip. He was, however

139

talking more freely now, as if he could not check the need to unburden himself.

"I haven't," Craig said. "Look, it's always in boxes or wrapped in tarpaulin."

"How much of it?"

"Usually no' much at all."

"How large?"

"All shapes an' sizes," Craig said.

"Are you never stopped by the police?"

"Aye, quite often."

"Really!" said Mr Affleck. "In the Greenfield?"

"On the Dumbarton Road, in Partick."

"And what happens?"

"The copper looks in the back o' the van, shines his lamp an' that's it. He signals us on. Bob an' me."

"He signals you on. Lets you leave?"

"Aye."

"Where is Danny Malone?"

"He goes away, walks away. He hardly ever rides on the cart or the van."

"Craig, why do the police constables let you go?"

Craig said, "Because there's nothin' to see in the bed o' the van."

"I don't follow you," said Mr Affleck.

"When you lift the back canvas, the van's empty."

Hugh Affleck opened his mouth and raised his eyebrows and, slumping back in the wooden chair, slapped his fist down lightly on the table. "Good God, of course! It's got a false bottom."

"I think so," Craig confirmed. "On the small van an' on the deep cart. Neither vehicle's used durin' the day."

"Good God!" said Mr Affleck again. "I wonder who dreamed up that ruse?"

"Mr Malone, I expect," said Craig.

"What payment do you get for night work?"

"Five bob, usually."

"Didn't it strike you as strange that Malone pays that much for – what – three hours' work?"

"I never thought about it."

The quiet manner was gone immediately. The transformation startled Kirsty. Mr Affleck's hand shot out and gripped Craig's wrist and he was drawn forward, unresistingly, until his elbows were braced on the table and Mr Affleck's face was only inches from his own.

"You *did* think about it, Craig. You thought about it all the time. What you did *not* do was face up to the fact that you were abetting criminals. Am I not right?"

Craig swallowed, his Adam's apple bobbing. He did not try to free himself from the superintendent's grasp.

"Five bob's a lot o' money," he said.

Mr Affleck said, "Five bob could land you ten years in jail."

"All I did was drive a van."

"All you did was pretend to be ignorant."

"I'm not bloody ignorant."

"You're doing a fair imitation of it, I can tell you," said Mr Affleck. "Now this is your lucky day, Craig. This is your one and only chance to extricate yourself from what might well turn out to be a right old mess."

"What d'you mean?"

"I want your co-operation."

"Co-operation?"

"You know damned fine what I mean," said Mr Affleck.

"You want me to nark."

"More than that."

"More?"

"I want you to help us catch your pal Malone."

"Catch him yourself," Craig said, defiantly but without conviction.

"Oh, don't think I can't," said Superintendent Affleck. "Don't think for one minute that because your pal Malone has evaded the law until now he'll evade it much longer. Next time one of the Moss vans gets stopped it'll not be some daft copper. Oh, no, no! It'll be a very smart inspector and a couple of detectives that'll be there. Believe me, they won't be fooled by false bottoms. They'll have that cart stripped and in pieces – and then where'll you be?"

"What," said Craig, "if I tell Mr Malone?"

"God, you're more ignorant than I took you for," said Mr Affleck. "I come here to give you a chance to save your neck and all you do is side with this brutal villain. Do you know *anything* about Danny Malone?"

"Not much," Craig admitted. "The men like him, though."

"Don't be such a damned fool, Craig. The men are *afraid* of him. And they have cause, believe me."

"It's your lot, the polis, that folk are scared of."

"No, no," said Hugh Affleck. "The police may not be popular but it's not fear that makes it so."

"What is it then?" said Craig.

Hugh Affleck considered his reply. "A kind of power, I suppose. It's the strength of the society that we impose, the discipline that people don't even know they need."

Craig gave no sign that the man's words had impressed him or even that he had grasped their significance. "Listen, you're not goin' to tell Malone we've talked like this, are you?"

"Do you see; you *are* frightened of Malone. Why don't you rid yourself of that fear?"

"Christ, are you jokin'?" said Craig ruefully.

"You can help. Help me, the police force, and yourself into the bargain."

"I can't see how it would help me one wee bit."

"As it is you're one step from becoming a real criminal."

"Get away wi' you," said Craig. "I'm not fallin' for that one."

"Would you not rather be on the right side of the law?"

In spite of himself Craig was impressed by Hugh Affleck's manner even if the logic of his plea cut little ice. There appeared to be something vital at the core of the man's argument, an authority that reminded Craig, just a little, of Mr Sanderson. He experienced a sudden tilt of attitude, a grudging respect.

Hugh Affleck was quick to spot the change. "Come on, Craig. Be sensible."

Kirsty moved towards Craig and put her hand on his shoulder. He twisted round and glanced at her enquiringly but he did not draw away. Indeed he leaned into her a little and covered her hand with his to hold her there, close by him.

He cleared his throat. "What do you want me to do?"

"Help us catch Malone."

"How?" Craig said.

The scratch and flare of a match wakened Kirsty at once. She rolled over. Craig was crouched in a corner of the bed recess, blanket up to his chin, a tobacco-tin lid on his knees. He puffed on a cigarette, hiding the glow in his cupped hand.

"What's wrong, dear? Can't you sleep?"

"Nope," he told her.

"What time is it?"

"'Bout three, I think."

"Will I get up an' make tea?"

"Just go back to sleep, will you?"

She struggled into a sitting position, too sleepy yet to judge his exact mood.

"Are you worried?" she said.

"I'm worried in case Malone realises I'm lyin' to him."

"If he does," said Kirsty, "we'll just have to move."

"Aye," Craig snorted, "wi' me in a coffin."

"Is Malone as bad as Mr Affleck says he is?"

"Worse."

"If you want to," Kirsty said, "you can hand in your notice; or not show up at the yard again."

"If it wasn't for the baby, I would," Craig said.

"The baby's not due for months," Kirsty said.

"How can you know what Malone's like?" said Craig. "Christ, the very way he eyes you up."

"You're frightened, aren't you?"

"Don't you bloody start."

"Why did you ever get mixed up with him in the first place?"

"For the bloody money, o' course."

It always came down to money in Craig's book. Even so, she felt closer to him than she had done for months. He seemed to have no basis for pride, and no pride in anything worthwhile and in consequence needed her more.

Craig said, "I wish she'd write to me."

Kirsty was taken aback. He was thinking of home, of his mother. She should not grudge him that, perhaps, under the circumstances.

She said, "I'm afraid she hasn't forgiven you, Craig."

"Knowin' her, she never will," Craig said. "I wish Dad would write, though, or Gordon."

"They know we're all right."

"Aye, but we're *not* all right, are we?"

Kirsty drew up her knees. Her breasts were less tender this past week. She could feel the gradual quickening of the child inside her, though. She had no words to tell Craig what it felt like, what it meant to her, how the texture of her feelings was changing with its growth.

"Are you sorry you came away wi' me?" Kirsty said.

"I'm sorry we ever went to that damned boardin'-house," Craig retorted. "Sorry we ever clapped eyes on bloody Affleck."

"It's not his fault."

"It's not my bloody fault either."

"Craig, is it the baby? Do you not want the baby?"

"Aye, of course I do."

She slipped an arm about his waist. He did not draw away as she had expected him to do. He was shuddering, though it was not cold in the kitchen. She laid her cheek against his shoulder.

He said, "Are you cryin' again?"

"No."

"You are," he said. "You're cryin' again. Why the hell're you always cryin' these days?"

"I canna help it."

"It's me should be doin' the cryin'," Craig said.

"I'm frightened too," said Kirsty.

"You don't have to do it, what Affleck asks."

"We could – could run away."

"No."

"Craig—"

"*No.*"

"I wouldn't mind if we—"

"I made a mistake, all right. But I'll live wi' it. Even if it means losin' the job. Even if it means gettin' my neck broke."

"Craig—"

He disentangled his arm and stabbed out the cigarette into the tobacco tin, grinding at it until not a grain of the coal remained alight. He slumped back, head thudding against the corner wall.

"God, but I'm tired," he said. "So damned tired of it all."

"It'll be over soon," Kirsty whispered.

"One way or the other," said Craig.

It was that time of a Saturday evening when at the end of a hard week's work Glaswegians were at play. The streets were loud with the last of the shoppers and the first of the boozers, and factory girls and the office girls dolled up in warpaint were on the loose in search of sweethearts, and young men, by no means unaware of their value, were downing a few sweet pints before sauntering forth to the *Temple* or the *Tivoli* or up town for a taste of blood-and-thunder at the *Grand* or the *Hippodrome*; or, for those who hadn't two bawbees to rub together, a ramble for free to the fish-fry at Anderston Cross where lots of liberated lassies congregated in the hope of swapping kisses for a poke of lukewarm haddock or a bag of peas and vinegar.

Even in Walbrook Street there was a certain Saturday clatter with cabs and carriages clopping off to concerts or supper parties or carpet dances or to 'grand stag banquets' at the *Bodega* or the *Silver Grill*.

Mrs Frew, all alone in her back parlour, was only dimly conscious of the hum of traffic from the streets outside, and of her loneliness. For a year or two after Andrew's death Saturday had been a difficult and tearful day of the week until she had hit upon the idea – Hughie's suggestion, in fact – of taking in guests, a favoured few with impeccable credentials, and had thus found purpose and a not-too-demanding routine. But that particular Saturday night her guest had eschewed the taking of dinner at her table in favour of a chop-house snack.

She had sent Cissie home. Later she would poach herself an egg, would go early to bed with a glass of sherry, perhaps, to help her sleep. Meanwhile she sat at ease by the fire, an old Kashmiri shawl draped across her thin shoulders, and immersed herself in the latest 'Ouida' to come her way, a two-shilling edition of *Puck*. Mrs Frew was as addicted to reading as was her brother but unlike Hughie, who displayed his library proudly on shelves all over the house, she kept her collection hidden in the left-hand side of her wardrobe. She was embarrassed by the fact that she enjoyed sensational, sentimental novels, and authors like Wilkie Collins, Justin McCarthy, Sarah Tyler and Walter Besant.

She had just reached a chapter entitled 'His First Betrayal' when the jangle of the doorbell made her start. Shedding her shawl, she hid it under the chair, went along the gloomy corridor and into the hall.

She called out, "Who is it?"

The answer came, "It's me, Nessie. It's Hughie."

She opened the door and admitted him.

"What is it? What's wrong? Is it one of the girls?"

"No, no, Nessie. Nothing like that."

"What is it, then? What are you doing here?"

"I was just passing. Thought I'd drop in."

He closed the door carefully and followed her down the hall and into the parlour.

"Have you had dinner?"

"I'm expected at home for dinner, Nessie."

"Oh!"

"Sorry, old girl. I'd stay if I could."

She turned, hands folded at the level of her waist and gave him the steady penetrating stare that all Afflecks had inherited from their formidable dam. "Not even takin' off your coat, I suppose?"

"You're right, Nessie. It isn't a casual visit."

"What is it, then? Come along, out with it."

"Now I don't want you to worry—"

"Worry? About what?"

"About what I'm going to ask you to do—"

"Ask me to do?"

145

" – because it's only a precaution and there's no need to get yourself all upset about—"

"All upset?"

"Will you listen to me, Nessie, please?"

She pursed her lips. "I'm listening."

"In my professional capacity—"

"Huh!"

"Nessie! In my professional capacity it has come to my ears that a gang of villains has sussed out—"

"In English, please, Hughie."

"A gang of villains has it in mind to rob this house."

"*What!*"

"Be calm, be calm, Nessie, please."

"There's nothin' of value here."

"Oh, but there is, Nessie. It's the silver they're after, I think."

"Papa's silver; I didn't think it was particularly valuable."

"Take my word on it, Nessie, please."

"Am I to be murdered in my bed for Papa's old soup tureen?"

"That's why I'm here, Nessie."

"How did you come by this information, Hughie?"

"Via an informant."

Mrs Frew understood perfectly well. From Wilkie Collins and other writers she had acquired a sizeable vocabulary of underworld terms and a knowledge of criminal methods that would have surprised her brother. The matter was clearly serious. She nodded curtly.

"I can't, of course, tell you my informant's name. That isn't on. But I can tell you that I have found this chap to be very reliable with his information in the past."

Nessie Frew said, "The panels."

Hughie frowned. "Eh?"

"Not the silver, Hughie. It's Andrew's stained glass they'll be after."

"Of course," Hughie said, smacking a fist into his palm. "That's it. You've struck it. It isn't the silver at all – though they'll take that too if they do gain entry – it's the stained glass they're after."

"Worth a great deal more than silver."

"Yes, oh yes," Hughie agreed. "I should have thought of it. However, the important thing is that we have a very fair and accurate idea of their intentions. We know when they will make their strike, and how."

"*Modus operandi.*"

"Exactly," said Hughie."

"What do you require me to do?"

Nessie Frew had no great opinion of her brother's character and had nurtured a grievance against him since he had dropped out of Edinburgh University and had chosen to be a policeman rather than a minister of the Gospel, but she was not altogether daft. Hughie had not risen to his present august rank without brains and the ability to apply them. She trusted him implicitly.

Hughie said, "I want you to go away for a night or two."

"Leave the house unguarded?"

"Of course not; I'll be here."

"Alone or with colleagues?"

"With colleagues."

"To catch the crooks red-handed?"

"That's it, Nessie."

"Where shall I go?"

"Beatrice will—"

"I could go to Greenock and call upon Edith."

"I thought you didn't rub along with Edith either."

"She is our sister, and she is old. Yes, I'll go and visit Edith."

"I'm sure she'll be pleased," said Hughie.

"I'll write to her tonight. When do you expect this – this thing to happen?"

"On Friday."

"Will there be shooting?"

"Good God, Nessie, no."

"Won't they come armed?"

"Not with pistols," said Hughie.

"Shall I move the stained glass?"

"I doubt if it's necessary," Hughie said. "They'll be grabbed and nabbed before they can do any damage, I promise."

Mrs Frew sniffed. "I've heard your promises before."

"Look, we've been after this gang for months. Now we have a chance to catch them and put them behind bars. You would be doing a great service not only to the Glasgow Police but to the public at large."

"Friday? Next Friday?"

"Yes."

"I'll go to Greenock on a morning train and stay over with Edith."

"Guests?"

"Only one."

"Will you find him alternative accommodation?"

"You may leave that to me, Hughie."

"Don't tell him – whoever he is – the truth; I mean, make an excuse, Nessie. I want no hint of this to leak out, not to anyone."

"What about Cissie?"

"Tell her only that you're going away for a couple of days. Send her home."

"Yes, that's best."

"Not a word, now, not to a living soul."

"I'll move St Andrew, I think," said Mrs Frew.

"Good idea," said Hughie. "Put him in the attic for a while."

"Will you help me?"

"Of course."

She managed, one way and another, to keep Hughie with her until after eight o'clock. He was patient and obedient and, if she had pressed him, might even have risked the wrath of his wife, Beatrice, and taken off his coat and sat down and had supper with her. But she did not ask it of him. St Andrew was safe away in an upper room and the tall panel that dominated the drawing-room, which depicted in wonderful detail Jesus walking on the water of the Sea of Galilee, had been manhandled upstairs too.

Eventually Hughie had taken his leave, reassured that she would do all he asked.

She poured herself a little thimble of brandy as soon as her brother had gone. She was pleased with herself, pleased that she had given him no sign of the dreadful excitement that was in her at the thought that she would participate in bringing a 'gang' to justice, that her quiet sanctuary would become a battlefield in the war between good and evil.

Excitement fizzed and bubbled inside her and she did not return to 'Ouida' but sat, nursing a second thimble of brandy, and gazed into the parlour fire. She was flattered that Hugh had confided in her. She would not, of course, breathe a word about it to Cissie, to anyone; except perhaps to Kirsty who was her friend and could be trusted. She might just mention it in passing to Kirsty on the way home from church tomorrow.

But next morning Kirsty Nicholson did not turn up at St Anne's though Mrs Frew waited by the steps until the last possible moment and, disappointed, had to keep the intriguing secret to herself.

Raw and rattled, Craig climbed the steps to the 'office' above the yard like a man going to the gallows. He was not in the least flattered that he had been chosen by Hughie Affleck to play a leading role in the capture of Danny Malone. His feelings towards Malone had been ambivalent all along and he still had respect for the man's daring defiance of the law. As it was he had been forced into an alliance with the law. At least Affleck's plot would keep him out of jail, though he could not imagine that Danny Malone would fall for it or be caught by plodding blue boys from the burgh.

If it hadn't been for Kirsty he would not have shown his face near Maitland Moss, might have scurried back home to his mammy and told nobody his reason for returning to the life of the farm. But he could not take Kirsty back to Dalnavert, not in her condition, and he could not bring himself to abandon her.

Taking a deep breath Craig rapped on the weathered door.

Mr Malone was alone inside the office. Craig had watched and waited all morning for the boss to go up the steps and unlock the door. Now that he stood on the rickety wooden landing, though, he felt as if every eye in the yard was upon him and that *Treachery* was printed on his back in letters of fire.

"Come in."

It was a shabby tumbledown sort of room with a desk, a table, a high cabinet of open pigeon-holes, a wooden armchair and a kitchen chair. The fire, unlighted, was packed with cold ashes and the place stank of gas and horses. Danny Malone, puffing on a Delmonico, was seated in the wooden armchair behind the desk, feet upon the window ledge.

"Can I talk to you, Mr Malone?" Craig said, gruffly.

"I'm all ears," Malone said. "Take a pew."

Craig licked his dry lips. He had rehearsed what he was going to say but the words stuck in his throat now like dry oats.

"What're you so bloody scared about?" Danny Malone swung his feet from the window ledge, the swivel chair shrieking, and planted them on the desk. "I'm not goin' to eat you, lad. Out wi' it."

"Remember," Craig began, "remember how I stayed in a lodgin' in Walbrook Street, before – before I moved to the Greenfield?"

"Aye, a posh place."

"I've been thinkin'," Craig went on.

"About what?"

"Silver."

"You mean money?"

"I mean silver plates."

"In this house in Walbrook Street?"

"Aye."

"What reason have ye got for tellin' me this?"

"I'm – I'm green, Mr Malone, but I'm no cabbage. I've an idea what goes into the vans I drive on those night jobs."

Malone seemed neither surprised nor dismayed by Craig's acumen. He puffed on the cigar, blew a wave of thick blue smoke over his nether lip. He squinted at Craig quizzically through the haze.

"Has Bob been talkin' out o' turn?"

"Nah," said Craig. "Bob never had to say anythin'."

"Have you seen the silver plate?"

"Where?"

"In this house in Walbrook Street?"

"Aye. I never thought much about it at the time. But – " Craig hesitated.

"But what?"

"I – I thought you might be interested."

"How can you be certain it's genuine sterling silver?"

"It has marks on it; the stamp."

"Who owns the house?" said Malone.

"Her name's Frew. She lives there alone, except for a servant," said Craig. "What's more, she'll be out all night on Friday. The place'll be empty."

"How do ye know that?"

"My – my wife, she goes to the same kirk as the Frew woman."

"An' the Frew woman told your wife the house would be empty?"

"Nah," said Craig, "but she told her she was goin' to visit her sister in Greenock an' wouldn't be at the prayer meetin' on Friday, this Friday."

"So your wifie goes t' prayer meetin's, eh?"

"Aye, sometimes."

Craig squirmed a little on the hard wooden chair. He hated it when Danny Malone mentioned Kirsty, even casually, for Malone pronounced the word 'wife' in a dragging, leering tone. Craig had heard stories, some envious, about Malone and his women, how he bedded a young thing in a house in Regina Street while keeping a wife and weans tucked away downriver in the village of Cardross. Craig did not find such behaviour admirable or manly and he did not envy Malone his women; one wife was more than he could handle.

"Does it on her knees, eh?" said Malone.

Craig said, "It's an empty house wi' a load o' silver plate in it.

Number nineteen, Walbrook Street, opposite the bowling-green."

"You said there was a servant."

"She goes home every night."

"What for are ye tellin' me all this, Craig?" said Danny Malone, still squinting through cigar smoke.

"Because it's there for the takin'," said Craig.

"Take it then."

Craig forced a grin, got up. "That's fine, Mr Malone. I was hopin' you'd say that. See, I didn't want you to think I was queerin' your pitch or anythin'."

"You'll get nabbed, sonny."

"I'll chance it."

Malone swung his feet to the floor and leaned forward. He rested his elbows on the desk and even put down the cigar, balancing it carefully in an empty tobacco tin.

"How will you move it?" he said.

"I'll only take what I can carry," said Craig.

"Aye, an' maybe leave the best o' it behind."

Craig shrugged. "It'll be enough for me, whatever I get."

"How will ye get in?"

"Through the back kitchen window."

"Barred, I'll wager."

"Not barred," said Craig.

"How—"

"I looked, didn't I?"

"You've a right insolent mouth on you, Nicholson."

"Look, Mr Malone, why do you think I left Carrick?"

Puzzled, Malone frowned.

"Because I had to," Craig said. He shrugged again. "It was gettin' just a bit too hot down there, if ye know what I mean."

"You mean—"

Craig said, "Let me just say, Mr Malone, that I know a bit more about night work than I learned drivin' a cart for you."

"Your wife, your 'prayer meetin'' wife, I'll bet she doesn't know what a bad lad you are?"

"Think I'm daft enough to tell her?" said Craig.

It hung, at that point, in the balance. Craig knew that he had been inspired in his performance, was pleased with his invention about his reason for fleeing from Carrick and he had sense enough not to embellish it. He tried to appear close and tough, to encourage Malone's doubts about him.

Malone plucked up the Delmonico between finger and thumb and took a long pull at it, sucking smoke into his lungs.

"If you had it done proper you could clear the whole house," said Malone at length. "You could have a cartful. Aye, an' a sure market for the silver, if it's any good at all."

"Is that a proposal, Mr Malone?"

"Aye."

"That's what I came for," said Craig.

"I could see that the job's done properly."

"Right you are."

"I could see that it's done wi'out you bein' put at risk."

Craig grunted, said, "An' have you tell me later there was nothin' in the bloody house worth sellin'? Nah, nah, Mr Malone. I'll be there to earn my share."

Malone laughed loudly.

It was done, accomplished; the bait had been swallowed.

Malone got up suddenly, came around the desk and draped his arm over Craig's shoulder, hugged him, laughed again.

"I got caught like that once," Malone said. "God an' Jesus! It was a lesson well learned, though, I'll tell ye. I was only about your age too when I was taken for green."

"I'll bet you weren't taken twice, though, Mr Malone."

Malone's laughter was dense and unaffected. It would probably be heard in the yard, in the stables; Craig wondered what the men would think of it and if they would respect him for becoming so 'pally' with the boss.

"I've never been taken since," Malone said. "An', by God, I'll never be taken again."

Craig said, "What about this job on Friday night?"

"Easy-peasy," Malone said.

"Is it on, then?"

"It's on," said Danny Malone.

Although the baby was not due for months, Kirsty imagined that she could feel it stirring in her womb and, in the course of that weekend, developed a fear that was almost a phobia that she might somehow be hurt and that the health of her child would be affected. She became tense and jumpy. At Oswalds' she shouted at Letty for tugging her playfully by the arm. In the street she was tense and alert, afraid of barking dogs, neighing horses and rough-and-tumble urchins. She was also suddenly and acutely aware of all the poor, daft, big-headed bairns that trailed about, noses running, on their mothers' hands and, in the night, suffered restless dreams about them.

In the end, on Monday, she went to the consulting-room in

Banff Street and tearfully blurted out her fears to Doctor Godwin who patted her arm, gave her a tiny bottle of brown syrup – four drops in water daily – and assured her that she was strong and healthy and that her baby would be equally sound in wind, limb and mental faculty.

The impending 'plot' weighed heavily upon Kirsty. She was short with Craig and hated herself for not offering him sympathy for the dangerous ordeal that lay at the week's end. Most of all, oddly, she experienced a tremendous weight of guilt at having missed Sabbath worship at St Anne's. She felt that God would strike a black mark on her attendance record and hold it against her, punish her for her omission.

Pagan superstitions, old wives' tales, rose and mingled with her other oppressive worries. She did not know who to blame for any of it – and so blamed Providence, promised in her prayers to be honest and kind and loving if only nothing bad happened to her husband and her baby.

She wanted no part in the deception that would lead the man, Malone, to prison; but she could not stand back from it now.

Mr Affleck was waiting inside Mr Kydd's corner shop on Tuesday afternoon. How long he had been there or whether he had followed her, unseen, from Oswalds' gate Kirsty could not be sure. He loitered by shelves of tinned biscuits and gave no sign that he recognised her when she stepped over the threshold from the street.

Two old women, strangers, were gossiping with Mr Kydd, a slim effeminate man with thin sandy hair and gold-rimmed glasses. Kirsty sidled past them, past the counter's tray of brass weights, past the scales on which the potatoes were weighed, past thick soft sacks of oats and brose meal and dark sea-green racks of kail and cabbages; stood staring at tins of tea and bottles of coffee essence.

Mr Affleck's voice, a murmur in her ear: "Has your husband heard anything definite?"

Without turning, Kirsty answered, "It's to be Friday."

"What time?"

"He didn't say."

"Malone didn't say?"

"Craig didn't tell me. He'll not know."

"All right, lass. Listen; tell your husband to remain outside with the van if he possibly can. When he hears the first blast of a police whistle he's to drive off as fast as he dare, commensurate with safety, of course. Got that?"

"Yes."

"If, by any chance, he's forced to enter the house, tell him to make sure he remains on the ground floor, near the door. As soon as my men appear he's to run out into the street. If he's stopped by one of my men tell him to put up no resistance. I'll see to it that he's released. Got that?"

"Yes."

"We'll be stationed in number nineteen by dusk, so he need have no fear if Malone elects to come early."

"What," said Kirsty, "what if somethin' goes wrong, if the plans are changed?"

"In that event go to Ottawa Street police station and give a message to Sergeant Drummond. Only to Sergeant Drummond, not to anybody else, in uniform or out of it. Got it?"

"Will the sergeant—"

"Yes, he'll get in touch with me immediately."

"Is there anythin' else?"

"That's it," said Mr Affleck.

He stepped away and selected a long tin of Bath Olivers from a shelf. As he squeezed past her on his way to the counter, however, he gave her elbow a squeeze and murmured, "Thank you, lass."

Kirsty bought a quarter pound of loose tea, two wan-looking kippers from the enamel tray by the ham-slicer, four eggs and a pat of fresh butter. As she paid for her purchases and Mr Kydd wrapped them she heard one of the women behind her say, "Know who that was?"

"Who?"

"Him that just went out."

"Naw, I never saw him right."

"He used t'be in the polis, in Ottawa Street. I heard he was up in Glasgow now."

"In the polis?"

"Aye."

"Get awa! Wonder what he wants in here."

Without glancing up, Mr Kydd said, "Bath Olivers," and leaning over the counter carefully slipped the provisions into Kirsty's shopping bag and, as he withdrew again, gave her a little knowing wink.

By Thursday evening Craig's nervousness had reached such a pitch that Kirsty relented, put aside her own dread and found herself cosseting him as if he were an invalid. She bought a piece of frying-steak for his supper, carried a jug of beer from the Windsor

Road off-licence, paid for with money that she had been saving to buy baby clothes.

Craig came home early. He was not his usual boisterous self but, cowed and furtive, slipped into the house and seated himself at the table in silence.

He asked Kirsty if she had been in touch with Affleck that day. Kirsty shook her head. Craig gave a little growl and put his hand over his eyes. "I don't know how I got into this."

"You took money, Craig."

"Who in their right mind would turn down money?"

"It'll soon be over, dearest," Kirsty said.

He looked so youthful, dark hair tousled, eyes dark and perplexed, his skin with a sallow tan. She put her arms about his neck and hugged him.

"Where's my supper?" he said.

She had fried potatoes to go with the steak and broke an egg on top of the meat. She served the plateful up to him, poured him a glass of beer from the jug. He did not seem to notice that she had taken trouble to please him. He ate in dour silence.

"I'll get no wages this week," he said, at length.

Kirsty said, "Why won't you?"

"Malone'll be in the bloody clink, won't he?"

"I hope he will," said Kirsty.

"An' Maitland Moss isn't goin' to pay me for puttin' him there."

Craig mopped his plate with a piece of bread, lifted the beer glass and carried it to the chair by the grate. He lit a Gold Flake and seating himself stared, scowling, into the fire.

"We couldn't have gone on," he said. "Affleck's right; sooner or later I'd have been nailed along wi' Malone. It wouldn't have been right, not wi' a baby comin'."

She had saved a piece of steak for herself and ate now, standing, forking the pieces into her mouth without appetite. She could not be sure if Craig was apologising for his foolishness or if, somehow, he was accusing her of collusion in his misfortune. His tension was palpable. She hoped that he would not crack, would not blurt out the truth to Bob McAndrew or Daniel Malone and spoil Mr Affleck's well-wrought plan.

She put the plate on the table, wiped her lips on her handkerchief and hugged him once more. Craig sighed and patted her hand; and, at that moment, a fist thudded loudly on the outside door.

Kirsty started away and Craig stiffened.

"Who can that be?" Kirsty said.

"Maybe it's Affleck to tell us it's all off."

"I'll go an' see."

Kirsty opened the door with trepidation and confronted the man on the landing with a welling of pure fear.

"So you're the wee country wife, eh?" said Danny Malone.

"Who – who—"

"Is he in, sweetheart?"

"It's only – only Thursday."

"Aye, I know what day it is," said Danny Malone. "Is he out?"

"No, but—"

"Here, I'll see for myself."

Malone brushed past her and went into the kitchen.

Shocked, Kirsty hesitated. She looked out of the door, saw nobody on the landing, on the stairs. She hurried back into the kitchen, leaving both doors ajar.

She had missed the first exchange but was not long in the dark about Malone's purpose and intention.

Craig was on his feet, protesting. "But it's only bloody Thursday, Mr Malone. You said—"

"I know what I said, sonny, but I've changed my mind. Get your clobber on. We're goin' now, right now."

"I bloody told you it had to be Friday."

"I know what you bloody told me," said Malone, "an' that's why we're pullin' the job tonight."

Craig did not move.

Kirsty said, "Craig, what – what is it?"

Malone said, "Did you no' tell her?"

Craig said, "Nah."

Malone chuckled. "Well, sweetheart, it's a spot o' night work, that's all. Nothin' for you to wet your drawers about."

Malone perched himself on the table and, uninvited, poured himself a glass of beer from the jug. He wore a pullover of dark brown wool, a quilted vest buttoned tightly over it. He was not as Kirsty had pictured him, was smoother, less physically coarse. She began to understand why Craig had fallen under Malone's spell.

"Come on, sonny. Clobber up. The van's waitin'."

Kirsty took a deep breath. "Hurry up, Craig. Mustn't keep Mr Malone waitin'."

Malone turned his head and studied her, a grin kinking the corner of his lips. "No prayer meetin' tonight?"

"What?" said Kirsty.

"Naw, it's Friday for prayers, right?" Malone said, still grinning. "If you lived in my house, sweetheart, I'd make sure your prayers were answered. Be more than the Holy Ghost would come upon you, eh?"

"I don't know what you mean, Mr Malone."

"Aye, sure you do."

She saw him clearly, revealed by sexual assertiveness. He did not doubt that he could, if he wished, have her. Malone was a bully in a society that had grown accustomed to being bullied, that associated aggression with power and power with masculinity. The very size of his fist, as he clasped the beer glass, seemed larger than life now. He had no fear that she would tell anyone in authority that he had called here; Malone assumed that Craig was man enough to keep his wife under control.

Craig, seated, was lacing his boots.

"Come on, sonny, shake it a bit. We haven't got all bloody night," Malone said, kicking the spar of Craig's chair.

Craig said, "She'll be at home tonight, ye know, the widow woman."

"Ach, it'll no' matter."

"There might be guests an' all."

"Guests?"

"Men stayin' there," Craig answered.

"What," Kirsty forced herself to say, "are you talkin' about?"

"Nothin', sweetheart," Malone told her. "Nothin' to bother your head wi'."

One minute later, without farewell, they were gone.

Kirsty had no opportunity to tell Craig of her intention. Malone had skilfully kept them from being alone together even for a moment. Malone had strong suspicions that Craig was in cahoots with the police but not strong enough, apparently, to cause him to turn his back on the robbery.

Kirsty pulled on her shawl and shoes and hurried out of the kitchen on to the landing. She leaned over the banister and listened, heard no sound at all from below. She locked the house door and ran downstairs, paused at the close mouth, hugging the wall. She could not be sure that Danny Malone or one of his henchmen was not positioned outside ready to pounce on her the moment she left the close.

She slipped back from the close mouth, down four shallow steps into the backcourt. Light fell from the tenement windows but wash-houses and middens were pits of pitch-black shadow. She made her way between them, found a gap in the railings that divided one court from another, squeezed through it, darted across the Windsor Road backs, out into the road itself, turned right and headed, running, for Ottawa Street.

The police station was a handsome sandstone structure that should have soared up like a church or department store but seemed to have been chopped off by a roof of black slate and an apologetic little coping. Its windows showed the shadows of interior bars and the glass was etched to obscure the cells within. The steps that led up to the door were bathed in stark white light from an arc over the transom. For all her panic and urgency Kirsty drew up before the forbidding doorway and hesitated before pushing through it.

Directly to her left was a half-open door; Kirsty had an impression of a packed room beyond it, men's voices and a haze of blue tobacco smoke. On a long bench in the main chamber two big constables flanked a tiny waif of a man who, far from being intimidated, twittered curses with the desperate anger of a habitual offender who feels he deserves special treatment.

"Put a sock in it, Jimmie. Ladies present," said one of the constables. "What are you after, miss?"

"Sergeant Drummond?"

"That's him."

"Aye, that's bloody him, hen," the waif shouted and might have added more by way of character reference if one of the flanking constables had not extended a large arm across his gullet.

Kirsty made her way across the empty floor to the desk.

The man there wore no hat and his grey cropped head made him seem less daunting. His cheeks were smooth and ruddy, as if he had shaved recently. An open ledger and a stand of inkwells were on the desk before him.

"Sergeant Drummond?"

"Aye, miss, and what can I be doing for you?"

"I'm – I'm Kirsty Nicholson."

One eyebrow cocked. The sergeant flicked his gaze from her anxious face to the constables on the bench.

Kirsty whispered, "Mr Affleck said I was to talk to—"

"Wheesh, lass," the sergeant murmured. "Step this way, if you please."

He opened a gate in the counter-top and admitted Kirsty to the inner sanctum, ushered her before him into an office furnished with a small table and two wooden chairs. He did not close the door but stood by it, from which position, Kirsty fancied, he could spy on the constables on the bench and also keep watch on the desk.

"You may talk now," Sergeant Drummond said.

"You know about Mr Affleck an' Danny Malone?"

"I do, I do."

"Malone came tonight—"

"*Tonight?*"

"Yes," said Kirsty. "He came unexpectedly about a quarter of an hour ago an' took Craig – took my husband – away with him."

"To do the job?"

"Yes."

"I see," said Sergeant Drummond quietly. "Very well, Mrs Nicholson, if you will be good enough to wait here I will place a telephone call to the City of Glasgow headquarters in the hope that Superintendent Affleck is still upon the premises."

"What if he's not?" said Kirsty.

"One bridge at a time," said Sergeant Drummond, and went out again.

Kirsty stepped to the half-open door. She could see the constables across the counter-top. One had muffled the prisoner completely by cupping a fist over his mouth while the other, the elder, had gotten to his feet in something bordering alarm. They were hissing at each other angrily, but she could not hear what they were saying. Distantly she heard a bell ring. She assumed that it was something to do with a telephone, though she had never used such an instrument. After a minute or so the elder constable whirled and headed for the station door, passed out of her sight. A minute after that Sergeant Drummond, apparently unruffled, reappeared.

"Fortunately," he told her, "I was able to make contact with Superintendent Affleck. He will attend to the matter personally. I take it, Mrs Nicholson, that it was to Mrs Frew's house in Walbrook Street that Malone was headed?"

"It couldn't be anywhere else, could it?" said Kirsty.

"Did Malone say it, in so many words?"

"Yes," Kirsty answered. "Yes, he did."

The sergeant nodded. "Go on home then, Mrs Nicholson."

"But – but what can I do?"

"You can do nothing, lass," the sergeant said. "The rest of it is up to us."

The van was a trim affair only six feet in length and forty inches wide at floor level. The brass lamps that were mounted on each side of the half-cab were unlighted and the whole rig, including the canopy, was painted black and jade, the horse dun-coloured. In the shadows the van was almost invisible.

To Craig's relief Bob McAndrew was not on the board. He had heard of Billy Skirving, though, and gathered that this was the man. He wore dark brown moleskins, a duffel jacket and stocking cap and carried an Indian exercise club. He had a thin, pinched, vicious face and eyes as hard as iron rivets. Lingering respect for Malone melted when Craig looked into Skirving's eyes, and he knew that all the fine tall tales he had heard about Billy Skirving and Danny were lies. He wished that Mr Affleck had warned him about Billy too for he sensed that here was a man without pity or any drop of compassion.

"You," Skirving told him, "drive."

Craig climbed nervously on to the board and took up the reins. Skirving was by his side and Malone was in the rear of the van, crouched, his face only inches from Craig's ear. Malone told him in a hoarse whisper to keep the pace easy until they got into New Clyde Street and then to let it out. Neither of the men spoke again as Craig steered a course out of Greenfield and on towards Walbrook Street.

He was more frightened than he had ever been in his life. He had separated himself from them by agreeing to help Mr Affleck. He did not regret it for he saw now that Hugh Affleck had been right, that he would have slipped down inch by inch into an association with men of this calibre until he either became like them or was broken by his own weakness. He did not want to be exposed as a coward. On the other hand he was cut off from both sides. He was being used by Affleck just as he was being used by Malone, and nobody cared a damn about him or what might happen to him.

The resentment gave Craig a peculiar kind of strength and he tried, vainly, to formulate a plan that might prevent them reaching Mrs Frew's house. He did not even know where the police stations were or how to summon aid. He had been drawn into this mess out of ignorance and he vowed, as he tugged and flicked the reins, that he would not be so stupid again, never again. All he had wanted was a better life for himself and for Kirsty but he realised now that he had been deluded; there was no easy route to fortune. He wished to God he had been more patient and wiser in the ways of the world. But it was too late now. He was stuck with Skirving and Malone, embroiled at last in a situation that demanded courage and control, even if it was a deception, a treachery.

It was only about half past nine. Glasgow's citizens were still out and about, shops and pubs full lit, the streets, even back streets, were busy. They seemed to reach Walbrook Street suddenly. Suddenly the van was running along it towards Number 19.

Malone said, "Keep drivin'. Don't stop."

Craig did as instructed without protest. He drove on past the sober façade of Mrs Frew's boarding-house; a dim light in the dining-room, all other windows dark; no sign of Superintendent Affleck or his constables, of course, and not a person within a hundred yards of the step.

"Turn in here," Malone told him.

"Turn where?"

"Into the lane," Skirving snarled, "by the bloody kirk."

Craig braked carefully, reined, positioned the van and ran it into the narrow gap between the wall of St Anne's and the terrace gable. It was a place of smells and darkness which the horse liked no more than Craig did. The beast whinnied and would have shied if he had not predicted the movement and forestalled it with the rein.

"There's somebody here," Craig said huskily.

"Sure, there'd better be," said Danny Malone.

From the shadows a voice hissed, "Is that yoursel', Danny?"

"Who in hell's name would it be?" Malone clambered from the back of the van. "How long have you been here, Tom?"

"Like you told me, Danny, since half past six."

Craig recognised the watcher; Tom McVoy, a carter from the yard, one of Malone's pals. He too was dressed in a seaman's jacket and stocking cap.

Malone said, "Did you see anybody go in or out?"

"Not a bloody soul."

"Back and front?"

"Keppit an eye on both, Danny," McVoy answered, then said, "Is that young Nicholson up there?"

"Aye, it's me," Craig heard himself say. .

"Are ye holdin' your water, son?"

"Aye, Mr McVoy."

Malone said, "You get off now, sonny."

"Am I not drivin' the van tonight?" said Craig.

"I thought it was your tickle?" said Malone.

"Aye, you're going t' be in there," said Skirving and prodded Craig in the ribs with the handle of the Indian club.

"Tom?"

"Aye, Danny?"

"Take the reins."

Reluctantly Craig climbed to the ground and handed charge of the vehicle to Tom McVoy.

He hesitated, thought of making a break for it then and there, glanced down the lane to the open street. Malone's fist closed on his arm and drew him roughly aside as McVoy skilfully turned the horse in the corner of lane and church wall, nosed it back towards the street and drew to a halt once more.

"Right," said Malone. "No sense in dawdlin'. You'll take the back, Billy. The window'll yield, won't it?"

"Aye," Skirving said. "I scouted it last night."

"Nicholson an' me, we'll take the front."

Craig said, "The front door! But she'll recognise—"

"Wrap this round your chops, sonny." A woollen scarf was thrust at him. "Anyway, she'll have precious little chance t' see your face."

"What d'you mean?" said Craig, but received no answer.

Skirving was by his side, breathing into his face. He smelled of onions. "Look, you, just do what Mr Malone tells ye. I'm beginnin' t' think you've a reason for no' wantin' in on this tickle at all."

"I've never done robbery before."

"High time ye learned then," Skirving told him.

"Come on, come on." Malone caught Craig by the arm, dragged him past van and horse and out into Walbrook Street.

To Craig the street seemed to teem with people; a couple strolling with a dog on a leash, three gangling boys kicking a cloth ball against the bowling-green fence, a hansom clipping towards the city with the driver, high and alert, staring down at him.

"Walk casual," Malone told him.

In the uncurtained window of a terraced house Craig saw a pair of young girls in pretty floral frocks standing before a music stand and singing their hearts out. By the mail-box, where he had posted his first letter home, a fat girl in a servant's cape loitered flirtatiously in the company of a kilted soldier. Exposed and ashamed and scared, Craig kept step with Daniel Malone as they walked along Walbrook Street and mounted the steps to the door of Number 19.

It was Thursday; Craig clung to the fond hope that Hugh Affleck might be dining with his sister; then he remembered that Tom McVoy had been on scout since dusk, had seen nobody leave or enter the boarding-house.

"What the hell's wrong wi you?" Malone hissed. "Pull up the muffler I gave you an' chap on the door."

Fumbling, Craig took the scarf and wrapped it about the lower part of his face.

"The bell; ring the bloody bell," Malone snapped.

Malone too had wrapped a scarf about his nose and mouth and, with cap pulled down, was effectively masked; only his eyes showed, fierce and red in the catch of light from the gas-lamp.

Craig rang the bell.

The couple with the dog had gone. The servant and the soldier had vanished too. The gangling boys had drifted away from the fence and were punting the ball along the gutter, heading for Partick.

The wool, wetted with warm breath, clung to his lips.

"Again," said Malone impatiently.

Craig closed his fist on the wrought-iron handle of the bell-pull and gave it another strenuous tug. He stared at the plain black door and then lifted his eyes to the dove-grey transom in which a light showed.

Malone's fist pinched his arm above the elbow, holding him rigid and motionless directly in front of the door.

It opened.

Mrs Frew confronted him.

She blinked.

Malone pushed Craig past the woman and, in almost the same motion, struck her, cuffed her economically with a short sweep of his right forearm. He stepped after her as she staggered against the interior wall, and kicked the outside door shut with his heel.

"Bolt it," Malone shouted.

Mrs Frew was gagging, contorted features turned in Craig's direction, eyes wide. It was light in the hall; she had brought a lamp with her and had left it on the stand by the umbrella rack.

"Don't," said Craig in a soft pleading whisper as Malone, with the same economy of effort, struck the old woman again.

She slumped on to the iron rack and pitched headlong to the floor, the rack crashing with her. She rolled over, flopped on to her back, twitched and was still. She did not look like Mrs Frew any more.

"She never recognised you, sonny," Malone said. "I told you you'd nothin' to worry about."

"Is she dead?"

"Snoozin'," said Malone. "Now will you bolt that bloody door."

Craig fumbled with the long bolt, would have left it loose if Malone had not been watching. He shot it into the lock. He was trapped in the house with the thieves, had become an accomplice to violence.

"Right, where's this bloody silver?" said Malone in a normal, natural voice, not a whisper.

Craig did not answer. He was fascinated by the sight of the old woman on the floor. She had no shred of dignity in that position. Her false teeth jutted out hideously and her skirts were thrown up to expose wrinkled stockings and skinny bare thighs.

Malone grabbed him, shook him. "The silver stuff, where is it?"

From the rear of the house came the muffled sound of breaking glass – Skirving. Why, Craig wondered, had it been necessary to smash into the kitchen? Why had Malone not simply strolled through the hall and unlatched the kitchen door?

At that moment Cissie, shrieking, shot from the shadows at the top of the basement steps. It had not occurred to Craig that the servant girl would still be in the house at this hour of the night for she was usually dismissed about eight. Pursued by Billy Skirving, Cissie darted towards the main staircase. She made but three steps before Skirving caught her round the waist and threw her down. He pinned her, his knee in the small of her back, and closed a hand over her mouth. Craig could still hear her muffled screams.

"Stick the bitch a good 'un Billy, an' shut her up," said Malone.

"Leave her alone," Craig said.

"Never mind about her, you, where's the damned silver?"

"She's only a servant," Craig said.

"I'll have your friggin' guts, sonny if you—"

"*I said not to hurt her,*" Craig shouted. "*Leave her alone.*"

Skirving had taken the Indian club from the breast of his jacket and held it poised. Knee still embedded in Cissie's spine, he looked down and grinned. "Fancy her, son? Alive an' kickin'?"

Tearing himself free of Malone's grasp Craig stepped nimbly across the hall and caught the upraised club. He seemed to do it in spite of himself; once he had broken the inertia, however, had acted of his own free will, deception was over.

Malone, of course, understood.

"*You bastard!*" he snarled.

Craig held tightly to the Indian club. He had no notion of where his strength came from; a second ago he had been weak and limp. But that feeling was gone. Flushed by outrage, his body felt hot and powerful. He dropped to one knee and snapped Skirving's arm across it. He heard Skirving cry out. Cissie, released, screamed piercingly and scrabbled up the staircase. Craig thrust his hand into Skirving's face and pushed the man's head back, forcing him down with one hand, then rolled to one side and got to his feet. He saw Skirving's hand on the stair, like something severed. He stamped on it with all his force; and Cissie, still shrieking, scrambled on to the first landing out of his sight.

"Christ!" Malone said, "I should've known you were one of them."

If he could get past Malone he might make it to the door. Once he was in the street he could surely raise the alarm. Cissie was out of reach of the robbers now. Squirming on the landing stairs Billy Skirving was too occupied with pain to pose a threat.

Malone lashed out at him. Craig stepped back.

Everything seemed lucid in the light of the lamp on the hallstand, pristine in its clarity. Even so he did not see the short iron bar in Danny Malone's hand until it struck him on the crown of the shoulder. Numbing fire spread down his arm. He heard himself utter a throaty grunt of astonishment. He shrank from the weapon that was poised to smash in his skull.

Numbness seemed to spread into his brain, a cloudy sensation, red and sick. He ducked. The iron bar struck hunched muscles on his upper back. He charged into Malone, hands outstretched. He found Malone's face, the scarf, dug his fingers into it and squeezed, squeezed as he might squeeze the heart of a great soft cabbage. The iron bar flailed against his back and buttocks without leverage or force. He rammed Malone into the wall. A strange plaintive yammering came from Malone's lips but Craig did not let go. He bunched his fists until his wrists ached and his arms trembled.

"Open up, open up."

The voice was deep.

The long bolt on the door rattled furiously in its socket.

"I am an officer of the City of Glasgow Police."

Pounding fists sounded on the door. Involuntarily Craig slackened his hold on Malone who, with a sudden surge, threw off the young man and ran for the kitchen.

Craig reached the door, found the bolt and shot it open. Hugh Affleck charged past him, yelling, "Where is he? Where is the bastard?"

"There," Craig pointed. "Both of them. That way."

Hugh Affleck charged on into the kitchen. Three burly uniformed officers followed him and, ignored, Craig slid out of the house. Shoulder, arm and neck were knitted with pain but he no longer felt cloudy and sick. He stood on the top step, looked right then left along Walbrook Street.

Directly opposite Number 19 a hansom cab was drawn up, its door flung wide on its little hinges. Close behind it was a high-sided two-horse black van with the City of Glasgow arms painted upon the side, and a policeman seated on the lofty board. The black horses were lathered and panting. Both cab and police van were pointed towards Partick, away from St Anne's corner.

Craig wiped his mouth with his knuckles. He had lost his scarf in the scuffle, but did not care who saw or recognised him now. He was still sizzling with the thrill of the fight. Heart hammering, he watched the corner by the church, saw the horse emerge from the lane with a feeling, almost, of relief.

Discreetly the van turned into Walbrook Street and headed towards the maze of lanes and streets that led to Dumbarton Road. Craig watched with amazement; the rig moved so slowly and sedately that it hardly seemed to be there at all. If it had come plunging out of the lane it would have attracted immediate attention and pursuit by the constables. As it was, in three or four minutes it would be out of sight and once more Danny Malone would have escaped the law. Craig had no doubt at all that Danny Malone was crouched down under the canvas canopy.

The arrival at speed of a hansom cab and a police van had brought the good folk of Walbrook Street hurrying to windows and doors. On one step the pretty singing girls clung to the arm of a bearded man in a silk smoking-jacket. Servants peeped up through the railings of half-basements while an elderly gent in tasselled nightcap craned from a bedroom window and demanded an explanation of the racket that had wakened him from slumber. Craig was oblivious to all of them. His gaze was fastened on the distant rig. Once into Harbour Road or Portside Street, Malone would slip from it and be lost and McVoy would swing the van on to Dumbarton Road all innocently, for he carried nothing to tie him to the scene of the crime.

Craig vaulted the iron railing and was running before his feet touched the pavement. He uttered no sound and gave no signal to the police to follow him.

Onlookers gasped, shouted, "See, there's one. There he goes," but no one attempted to stop him.

Bristling with energy, Craig ran as he had never run before. McVoy did not seem to notice him or hear the hue-and-cry. The little van appeared through white patches of gaslight, vivid for a moment then shadowy again. It picked up speed. Craig cut sharply left at St Anne's corner, pushed through a cluster of boozers at the door of a pub, pushed through a knot of Freemasons who had stepped out of their lodge, and cut sharply right down a narrow lane that brought him out at the very end of Walbrook Street just as the van came clopping round the curve that would carry it out of sight of witnesses.

Craig ran straight at the horse's head.

The animal shied and reared in the shafts. Craig ducked under the flying hoofs. The whip cracked about his ears. He side-stepped and came in again, too quickly for McVoy to react. Confused, the horse reared and pranced, shook the fly-weight van from one wheel to the other. Craig caught the horse's cheekstrap and, throwing all his weight into it, dragged its head down. The van tilted dangerously.

Standing up on the board McVoy yelled at and struggled to control the animal.

Craig tightened his grip on the strap and, by sheer brute strength, dragged the horse about. The van's wheels screeched on the cobbles. Suddenly he let go of the strap, drove his boot into the horse's belly, tripped and fell back. The van lurched and swayed violently and the horse bucked and plunged madly in the shafts, then, with eyeballs rolling white and its mane flying, went off at a gallop across the pavement corner and back into Walbrook Street. McVoy lost all control. Malone had had no opportunity to throw himself clear, of that Craig was sure. On his feet again, he limped after the runaway, saw the black police van thundering down Walbrook Street, two coppers clinging to its footboard, saw too that Superintendent Affleck had come out of Number 19 and was sprinting towards him.

The horse charged between the wall of a cottage and an old iron horsepost upon which the van sheared a wheel. It slumped on to the stump of axle, dragged to a partial halt, and slewed round. McVoy was thrown, not cleanly, the leathers twisted round his wrists. He was plucked from the board, dragged against the cruppers and shafts and, screaming, was jerked down on to the cobbles and dragged, dragged along the street until at last something gave way and his body was left still and elongated in the gutter.

Craig ran past Tom McVoy. He still expected Malone to jump for it and wanted to be ready for him. But Danny Malone had had no opportunity to gather himself and leap out of the careering vehicle. Finally the vehicle heeled over on to its side, the unfortunate horse pitched to its knees, and the van broke apart.

Superintendent Affleck reached the wreckage at exactly the same moment as Craig Nicholson, though neither acknowledged the other. Both were intent on the canvas flap, on the hand and arm that groped from the torn tarpaulin.

Dazed and bloody-faced, Danny Malone crawled out on to the cobbles.

Hugh Affleck gave a queer little laugh, breathless and panting. He dropped a knee upon Malone's spine, caught his ears in his fists and banged the man's brow down upon the stones, just once.

"Got you, you bastard," he said.

Sergeant Drummond sent a constable to fetch her from the house. The constable was a young man with a strange accent. He was truculent and unfriendly and gave Kirsty no word of comfort and only a minimum of information and stubbornly refused to answer any of her questions as they tramped back to Ottawa Street police office.

Craig was seated on a stool in a narrow half-tiled room in the station's basement. He was naked to the waist. An elderly man with a face like a fox-terrier was attending to his injuries. The man scowled when Kirsty was shown into the room and waved a warning hand to prevent her throwing herself on the patient in a fit of sentiment. Wincing, Craig glanced over his shoulder. He had a Gold Flake stuck in his mouth, was chalk pale, his eyes huge. She felt such a wave of pity for him that she longed to wrap her arms about him but waited obediently by the door until the surgeon had finished strapping Craig's shoulder with heavy cotton bandages.

At length the surgeon said, "He's got a cracked rib but no important bones are broken. He'll heal in no time."

"It's damned sore," Craig said.

"Bound to be sore," said the surgeon. "It'll be worse tomorrow, I promise you. Best stay in bed if you can."

The surgeon dropped scissors and a roll of wadding into a black leather bag, picked up the bag and locked it and then, without another word, went out, leaving Craig and Kirsty alone.

Awkwardly Craig took the cigarette from his lips. He coughed, winced, gave a groan. Kirsty cautiously approached him.

"It's all right," Craig told her. "They got Malone. Skirving too. Affleck took them away in the black van to the cells in Glasgow. It was best that I was brought here, apparently, since Affleck didn't want me near the prisoners."

"But what happened?"

Craig shuddered, winced once more. "She, your pal, she got a knock on the head."

"Mrs Frew? Is she all right?"

"Aye, she's no' dead or anythin'. Affleck took her to the hospital for attention. It was Malone hit her. Hit her twice."

"Could you not stop him?" said Kirsty.

"Huh!" Craig exclaimed, almost under his breath, and shook his head.

Kirsty had not touched him yet. Her initial impulse to comfort him had diminished into a strange kind of reticence. His nakedness and the neat cream-coloured bandage alienated her. Craig put the Gold Flake carefully back into his mouth and, at that moment, the door swung open and Sergeant Drummond came into the room.

"How are you feeling now, Nicholson?" the sergeant enquired.

"All right," Craig said. "Can I go?"

"Shortly," said the sergeant. "Finish your gasper first."

"What's the idea?" Craig twisted on the stool to face both Kirsty and the sergeant. "Am I goin' to be charged?"

"Och, no. No, no, nothing at all like that."

"Will I have to go into the court, be a witness against him?"

"I doubt it," said Sergeant Drummond. "But I cannot give you my guarantee at this stage, you understand. It will be depending on what the charges are and what the lawyers say."

"They didn't get away wi' anythin'," said Craig. "I mean, they didn't steal any silver."

"Did they not?" Sergeant Drummond raised an eyebrow. "I think you must have missed it in the confusion. You see, silver plate *was* found in the van, and a gold chain on the person of Billy Skirving."

"It must have been taken when I was lookin' the other way," said Craig, understanding the method at once. "What about McVoy?"

"Injured but not fatally."

"That's somethin', I suppose," said Craig.

"You will be pleased to learn that I am not required to take a statement from you at this time," said Sergeant Drummond.

"Is that another of Mr Affleck's clever tricks?"

"The Superintendent does not wish you to be seen to be involved."

"Bit bloody late, isn't it?" said Craig.

"He also suggests that you don't go back to work at Maitland Moss."

"What the hell am I supposed to do then? Starve?"

"Perhaps you could go home for a wee while."

"I live in Canada Road," said Craig.

"Back to your family, to the farm?"

"I'm not a charity case," said Craig. "I can't sponge off them. Anyway, I like it in Glasgow. I want to settle here."

"A holiday?" said Drummond, mildly.

"No holiday," said Craig, also without heat.

His anger seemed to have waned into a kind of stubborn resentment but Kirsty could not decipher his present mood at all. She did not know whether his pain was mostly physical or whether some great wound to his pride had been opened by the events of the evening. She had no true understanding of masculine pride, of its shapes and changes and its subtle manifestations, but she was learning almost day by day not to ignore its effect upon Craig's character and behaviour.

She caught him now, unaware of her scrutiny, as he studied the police sergeant with a sort of calculation, though what thoughts were clicking in her husband's mind she could not begin to deduce. He pushed himself to his feet, shook off an offer of assistance and struggled into his shirt. He left it unbuttoned, draped and loose over his left arm, and shrugged on his jacket, stuck his cap on his head.

"We can look after ourselves, thanks," Craig said, then, "Come on, Kirsty, it's time we were off home."

"Are you sure you can manage?" Kirsty said.

"I can manage," Craig answered.

He went before her to the door but the sergeant did not immediately stand aside.

"Will you not be changing your mind?" Sergeant Drummond said.

"About what?"

"Go home for a week or two; home to your farm, I mean."

"Stuff it," Craig said. "I'd be a laughin' stock. An' nobody's goin' to laugh at me any more; nobody."

The sergeant pursed his lips and gave a little sour nod before he stepped to one side and ushered Craig and Kirsty on to the stairs.

There were no prisoners in the office, no constables. But two sergeants, both bearded, both cold-eyed, stood behind the long desk. They watched in icy silence as Craig and Kirsty left the station and stepped down into Ottawa Street.

It was cold now, the sky clear, stars showing.

Craig shivered, wriggled deeper into his jacket.

"I'm starved," he said. "Bloody starved."

"There's ham," said Kirsty.

"Eggs too?"

"Aye."

"That'll do."

He began to walk, stiff and upright. Kirsty fell into step beside him.

"Craig—"

"What?"

"It'll be all right."

"By Christ it will," Craig said. "I'll make sure o' that."

He reached out suddenly, caught her wrist and brought her closer to him and, hand in hand, Craig and Kirsty Nicholson walked home through the cold night streets, back to their single-end in Canada Road.

FIVE

The Good Provider

Most of all it was their ferocity that surprised her. There were two of them, sisters, one not much above twelve and the other no older than fifteen. Their attack was sudden, an ambush near the gate of Oswalds' in the early morning hour. It was a dry dawn and the oblong puddles in the gutters had at last drained away, which was just as well for the girls' rush bowled Kirsty over and she sat down hard upon the pavement, arms wrapped instinctively across her belly.

The younger of the little harridans swiped a kick at her.

"Bitch, so ye are. Bitch, bitch."

Kirsty struggled to rise but the elder had danced around behind her, grabbed her by the hair and pulled her back. If she had not been so afraid of straining herself Kirsty would have fought back but her pregnancy made her vulnerable and the spitting fury of the girls had about it a tone of moral outrage.

"Because o' you, my daddy's deein'."

Understanding flared like a gas jet; they were the daughters of one of the villains, Skirving or McVoy.

Kirsty reached out and caught the younger girl a stinging slap upon the cheek. The child's rage turned at once into self-pity. She burst into tears. Wailing like a she-cat she stepped back from the affray while her big sister renewed her efforts to drag Kirsty on to the ground.

Letty came to the rescue. She had just turned into Vancouver Street – late too – when the commotion started. She came haring up the street, grabbed the assailant by the arm, yanked her away from Kirsty and, for good measure, administered a good round slap on the face that changed rage into hysterical tears.

The girls backed away.

Letty helped Kirsty to her feet. "Who the hell're they?"

"What do you want wi' me?" Kirsty shouted.

"Your man done it. He done for ma daddy."

"Their daddy? What're they bletherin' about, Kirsty?"

Kirsty did not answer Letty's question but shook her fist and advanced on the pair. Tears stained their faces and their noses ran. They looked pitifully dishevelled as they backed away from her, still mewing. When Tam Alexander, the Oswalds' gateman, came out of his shed into the street the girls turned tail and ran off around the corner and out of sight.

Solicitously Letty brushed Kirsty's skirt with the flat of her hand. "Are ye hurtit?"

"No, just winded."

Tam Alexander had come over too, not to enquire after Kirsty's welfare but to chase the young women into the sheds to their work.

"Who are they, Mr Alexander? Do y'know?"

"The McVoys," the gateman told her and, by his grim expression, indicated that he too knew of the night's arrests.

Kirsty limped into Oswalds', hanging on to Letty's arm.

Letty was all agog but Kirsty told her nothing.

At the tables, though, the girls swung round when she entered the room, glowered at her or shunned her with broad, obvious gestures. Kirsty could hardly believe that it was possible for news to travel so quickly, before shops were open, before men congregated at their lathes or benches or on the slipways of Hedderwick's yard. It was as if the tenements of Greenfield were connected by some sort of invisible wire along which news of Malone's arrest had throbbed, news too of Nicholson's treachery.

"Get on wi' your work," Mrs Dykes barked.

Tommy Dykes brought two bakers to the door of the flour store and pointed out Kirsty as if she were a specimen in a cage.

"Oh-oh!" said Letty. "You've been up t' somethin' naughty."

"Husband," said Mrs McNeil curtly. "Her husband's a nark."

"What?" said Letty, eyes like saucers. "A nark?"

"Sold Danny Malone an' Billy Skirvin' t' the coppers."

"Kirsty, is that true?" said Letty.

But Kirsty just shook her head and withdrew to the end of the packing-table. She was disgusted by the injustice of the situation and the community's reaction to it, a persecution, she reckoned, that would get worse before it would get better.

Broken glass was stashed in a tin bucket and Craig was perched on a chair by the window attempting to fit a piece of plyboard over the gaping hole. He had put the half brick, like a trophy, on the mantelshelf and had untied the surgeon's bandages to give himself more freedom of movement. He glanced round when Kirsty entered the kitchen.

"Happened about half an hour ago. Near took my bloody head off," he informed her.

"But why, why are they doin' this to us?"

"Because I got off," said Craig.

"Malone was a criminal. Surely everybody knows that."

Craig said, "Everybody hates the polis."

"Are you sure it's not a mistake?"

"Does it look like a mistake?" Craig nodded at the half brick. "We're on the bloody top floor, Kirsty. It took a man to throw that, not a mischievous wean. The bastards have it in for me."

"Me too," said Kirsty.

"What d'you mean?"

She told him about McVoy's daughters and their assault upon her person, about the silent treatment she had received from the girls in the Cakery. Craig climbed carefully from the chair and put his good arm about her to offer a modicum of comfort.

"Are you injured?"

"I'm hurt," said Kirsty, "but not injured. How long will they keep it up, Craig?"

"Christ knows!"

"I'm beginnin' to see why Sergeant Drummond urged us to get out o' the Greenfield."

"Bugger Drummond. Bugger them all," said Craig. "We're not leavin' here – an' that's flat."

Shortly after seven o'clock that same evening Colin McCoig turned up. He did not come alone. He was accompanied by a hulking brute of a man in a half-tile hat and Gladstone coat who, though not formally introduced to the tenants, was clearly another cousin of the landlord.

"What are you doin' here, Mr McCoig?" said Craig. "Our rent's no' due until next Friday. Have you made a mistake?"

"No mistake," said Colin McCoig. "Broken window."

"How did you know—"

"Damages must be made good or paid for."

"It'll be repaired," said Craig.

The sheer size of the man in the Gladstone overcoat frightened her and Kirsty retreated to the sink.

"Repaired by next Friday at the latest," said McCoig.

"Next Friday?" said Craig. "It'll be done tomorrow."

"Next Friday: I'm servin' notice," said McCoig.

"Notice?"

"To quit."

"What!" Craig shouted. "What reason have you got for tossin' us out? We've aye paid the rent on time."

"Landlord's privilege," said McCoig. "Read the lease agreement."

"Christ!" Craig shouted. "You're another one o' Malone's toadies."

"I don't know what you mean," said Colin McCoig stiffly.

Livid with rage, Craig stepped towards him.

The cousin shuffled quickly forward to interpose himself between landlord and tenant. Fists planted on hips he flipped back the folds of his overcoat. Stuck in his broad leather belt was an iron bar similar to the one that Danny Malone had wielded. Surreptitiously Kirsty put her fingers around the handle of the frying-pan. The cousin frightened her in a way she had never been frightened before.

Craig checked but did not back away. He folded his arms and squared up to the big man.

"I suppose you're another o' Malone's chinas too?"

"Danny's got your mark, sonny," said the cousin. "Danny knows it was you got him nicked."

"Danny got himself nicked."

"You're in thick wi' the blue boys."

"Beside the point," said Colin McCoig. "I need this room for — for other tenants. You've got seven days' grace, Nicholson. I'll be here to check the inventory next Friday."

"Stuff your bloody inventory," said Craig. "We're no' goin'."

"Aye, but you are, sonny," said the cousin. "By God, you are."

Craig took the tobacco tin from under the board under the bed and prised it open with a knife. He spilled coins on to the table, stirred them with his palm and immediately began to separate silver from copper.

Kirsty was seated at the table, hands tucked into her lap to hide her trembling.

"Well," she said, "at least we're not penniless."

"How long d'you think this lot'll last?"

"I've still got my pay from Oswalds'."

"Six bob a week'll no' even feed us, Kirsty, let alone put another roof over our heads," said Craig. "Besides, it wouldn't surprise me if Malone managed to put the arm on somebody at Oswalds' an' you wound up bein' sacked."

"How can Malone—"

"It's no' just Malone. He's got powerful friends."

"Craig, I'm—"

"Christ, woman, don't tell me again that you're sorry."

"I'm sorry."

"*Jesus!*"

"How much have we saved?" said Kirsty.

"Sixty-six shillin's."

Eight months ago such a sum would have seemed like a king's ransom. Living in Glasgow had taught her the value of money, however, and two months and a town rent would soon gobble up their savings.

"We could pawn things?" she said.

"What things?"

"The clock?"

"The clock would hardly raise the price of a pint," said Craig. "What I need is another job, one that pays better than cartin'. And I need it quick."

"Craig, are you certain that Maitland Moss will pay you off?"

He laughed. "Pay me off? God, I'll be lucky if he doesn't string me up."

"It's not right."

"It's the way the world wags, though," said Craig.

"Perhaps we should go home, back to Carrick."

She was testing him, the strength of his determination to stick it out, to stay with her here in the city. His hesitation suggested that he had not entirely put the idea from his mind. He frowned.

"Look, Kirsty, there's no sense in steppin' backward, is there?"

She shook her head.

He went on, "Or in lettin' ourselves be pushed. I'm man enough to resist that, at least. There are things I miss about Dalnavert, a lot o' things, but it's a dull life there wi' your feet in the mud an' little prospect of change."

"At Bankhead, though, you could—"

"I could be a head ploughman, aye, in ten years. Nah, nah."

She felt relieved, vastly so, though her anxiety about the future remained.

Craig said, "Here we are, Kirsty, an' for better or worse it's here we'll stay."

"But what'll we do for money?"

"Leave all that to me," said Craig.

It was no sort of day to fire the blood. Rain drizzled from gelatinous clouds and the city and its suburbs lay grey and still and sullen as Craig trudged up Kingdom Road towards the gates of Maitland Moss carriers' yard. He kept his hands out of his pockets and his chin up, though rain beaded his hair and formed a drip on his nose and he felt anything but aggressive and determined.

Nothing appeared to have changed in the yard. There was no visible activity and most of the carts had gone out. Indeed the only sound came from the forge where old Willy and a lad were repairing a set of springs. Craig marched boldly to the shed, marched boldly inside.

The reek of burnt hoofs and coke fumes caught at his throat. It was all he could do not to cough. He closed his throat on the choking sensation and waited, arms by his sides, until the lad spotted him and nudged old Willy.

Tongs in hand, bulky leather pad strapped to his forearm and a scarred apron covering his nether region, Willy turned.

"You, Nicholson!" he exclaimed. "By Jove, you've a brass neck showin' your face here."

"I've come for my wages."

"It's no' Sunday."

"I'm not waitin' for Sunday," said Craig. "Who's in charge now Malone's gone?"

"If you're caught here, son," said the horse-man, "they'll bloody flay you, so they will."

"Let them bloody try."

"Danny made money for half the men here," Willy reminded him.

"By theft, by robbery, by smashin' old widows in the mouth."

"He was pals wi' everyone, was Danny."

"How many o' Danny's pals did the coppers lift?" Craig asked.

"Och, the blue boys come wi' warrants all right, but they found not a blessed thing. Danny was too smart for them. Danny would never shop his pals."

"I want my wages," said Craig.

"Did the polis no' pay you, eh?"

"So you think I'm a nark, Willy; well, I'll tell you, I got nothin' from the coppers," Craig said. "Not a damned penny."

"You'll get nothin' from Maitland Moss either."

"Mr Moss?" said Craig. "Is he managin' the yard himself?"

Behind the horse-man, stuck in the jaws of the forge, a length of iron had turned from dull red to molten white. Craig stared at it, expecting it to melt completely and drip into the bed of hot coals even though the lad had ceased to pump the foot bellows and there was no draught to create heat.

"Mr Moss has t' do it until he can find somebody else," said Willy. "He'll never get nobody like Danny Malone, though."

"So Mr Moss had to get out o' his bed, did he?" said Craig. "Where is he, Willy?"

"Upstairs."

"Right," said Craig turning.

"Aye, you'd better get what you can an' clear out o' the Greenfield, son," said the old horse-man. "Word's out that Danny intends t' get you."

"How can he get me?" said Craig. "He'll be in the bloody clink for ten years at least."

"I wouldn't be so sure o' that," said Willy.

It was not Malone that worried Craig, but Malone's influence. The brick through the window, the attack on Kirsty, the landlord's cousin in the daft tile-hat; his betrayal had become public knowledge and it would serve no purpose at all to deny it.

Craig turned and, without another word to the horse-man, left the shed and crossed the yard to the stairs that led up to the rackety wooden office. He climbed them quickly, before his nerve could fail him, and knocked upon the door.

"What is it?" a voice called out.

"I've come for my wages."

"Who are you?"

"Craig Nicholson."

The door flew open.

Craig had half expected to be confronted by the sporting gent he had glimpsed at the *Belltree* that April morning in Renfrew but Maitland Moss, though out of the same drawer, had no whiskers, only a small bristling moustache. His jaw was blunt, his nose aquiline, his eyes as cold and grey as the Glasgow sky. He wore chequered tweeds of fine wool and finer cut and a high hard collar with a red silk cravat in the vee.

"Are *you* Nicholson?"

"I am, sir."

"What the devil do you want?"

"My wages, sir. Four days."

"By God, you've got gall!"

"My tally will be recorded in the day book, sir."

"I know where the tally will be," said Maitland Moss. "You'd best step inside."

He was younger than Craig had supposed him to be, not much over thirty. The office appeared unchanged, except that there was more paper scattered about and, in an ashtray on the desk, a slender cheroot smoked where once Danny Malone's fat Delmonico had rested. A gill bottle of Glen Grant whisky and a single glass were on the desk too. The fire and an oil-lamp were lighted. Maitland Moss did not invite Craig to sit down. He poured a dram into the little glass and drank it in a swallow. "Do you know what you've done, Nicholson?"

"I haven't done anythin', Mr Moss."

"How do you know my name?"

"Old Willy told me."

"Have you not seen me before?"

"No, sir, never."

Moss went on, "Not only did you cost me the services of a most excellent manager but you brought a gang of policemen to my house in dead of night and thoroughly frightened my wife and children."

"I did no such thing, Mr Moss."

"You were responsible for it."

"Am I not to get my wages?" said Craig.

"I've no stomach for your sort, Nicholson."

"My sort?"

"An ingrate. Mr Malone was generous enough to make you a place here and you reward him by telling some tall tale to the police."

"Tall tale! Malone was a thief."

"Yes, I thought you'd try to put the blame on Danny."

"He brought it on—"

Maitland Moss poured another dram and drank it too, taking it like a swift indrawn breath, hardly pausing in his harangue. "Look, Nicholson, I'm not interested in your sorry story. The truth is that you do not comprehend the delicate balance that exists between a man trying to earn an honest crust of bread and the tyrannical forces of a goverment that wishes all men to be made slaves to the state."

Craig shook his head in bewilderment. He had heard such stuff spouted around the yard but had not expected the master to uphold the same philosophy as his men.

Craig said, "What makes y' think I narked on Malone?"

"You were there on the night in question," said Maitland Moss, "yet you are not behind bars. Why would you be allowed to walk free unless you co-operated with the police?"

Craig said, "Have I been sacked, Mr Moss?"

"By God, Nicholson, you *are* a fool. Danny Malone liked you. He would have made a great deal of money for you if only you'd trusted him."

"Aye an' bashed old women on the head."

"You exaggerate."

At that moment Craig realised that he had no awe of Maitland Moss, only a certain cold contempt for the toff. He felt quite proud of himself and, with swelling confidence, heard himself say, "I'm here for my wages, sir, at Superintendent Affleck's suggestion."

Without even looking down, Maitland Moss yanked open a drawer in the desk, lifted out a cash-box and placed it before him. He flung open the lid.

"How much?"

"It should be about eleven shillin's, but the day book—"

Maitland Moss selected coins from the box and tossed them on to the desk where they rolled and flattened; four half-crowns and two sixpences. "Take your damned money and clear out."

Craig hesitated. He had been enjoying a feeling of equality with the toff, the novelty of being backed by a powerful authority. It was almost as if Mr Affleck and the Highland sergeant were in the room with him, standing silent but approving just behind his back. It was strange that he should think of them now without resentment or bitterness. This man, this rich man, was afraid of the police and, by inference, a little afraid of him too.

"Take it, damn you," Moss cried.

Craig smiled and slipped the coins from the desk and pocketed them. He had gained more than cash from this visit, though. Moss had yielded to him, had crumpled before his threat. It was beginning to seem that he was not so alone as he had thought himself to be.

Moss said, "Oh, yes, you think you've been smart, don't you? But you haven't heard the last of it. Danny won't forgive and Danny won't forget. Not all your pals on the police force will be able to protect you when Danny or Billy comes for you."

"More bricks through my kitchen window, eh?"

"That treatment will be very mild compared to what will happen when Danny and Billy are released."

"I'm told they'll be put away for years," Craig said.

"What did they promise you?" said Maitland Moss. "A wage, a house, a job? Was that the bargain? God, you're just the type; a sly young devil, wet behind the ears."

"I'm no copper," said Craig.

"Oh, don't lie. You didn't co-operate with Affleck for nothing. You're not that much of a fool."

"I just did what I thought was right," said Craig.

"God Almighty," Maitland Moss exploded. "Get out of my sight."

Craig was filled with a most peculiar sense of confidence, an arrogance that made him bold. He pointed his forefinger at Maitland Moss. "I think you'd best keep your nose clean, Mr Moss. It could be you that goes to clink next time."

"What the devil do you—"

Craig gave no answer, let the threat hang. He turned and left the office, went downstairs and crossed the empty yard. He hesitated at the gate, glanced back. He felt light-headed, almost faint with the thrill it had given him. He had got the better of a man like Maitland Moss, had made 'right' triumph. He needed no justification for his behaviour and had not had to prove that he was other than a daft country boy. Connection, however tenuous, with the forces of law and order had given him stature and strength. The more he thought of it, the better he liked it.

What had Moss said – *a wage, a house, a job?*

These were acceptable realities, things that he wanted and needed, things that would serve without question as motive and explanation for what he was about to do. The other aspects of it he did not dare dwell upon, though they, perhaps, were the factors that really steeled him to call his dues from Hugh Affleck, that gave form to his desire to 'get on', respectably, in life.

Strutting a little, Craig quit the carriers' yard and set out at once for Ottawa Street.

It had been one of those nights and, without doubt, it would be one of those days too. Hector Drummond had allocated himself extra shifts as Duty Sergeant for he could not afford to miss the visits of the big-wigs from the Burgh Watch Committee and high-rankers from Greenfield's Police Headquarters. The nabbing of Danny and Billy had set the cat among the pigeons with a vengeance and the sergeant was glad that they were being held in cells in Glasgow and not here, for he could not be quite sure that there would not be some sort of minor riot, a protest against 'police methods', though he doubted if it would come to that. In any case Skirving and Malone were housed in the big jail in the city and McVoy, under police guard in the Royal Infirmary, was in no fit state to make a dash for it.

Everybody was afraid that Danny and Billy would turn canary, would sing their black hearts out and bring scandal to the burgh and the force. Sergeant Drummond did not believe that corruption ran deep. Nonetheless two of his constables had failed to report for muster that morning and two more were acting very shifty. If they were wise they would resign rather than sweat out the weeks in the hope that Danny and Billy would not divulge their names as receivers of bribes. It was the bribery that had the place buzzing.

Lieutenant Strang, acting directly for Chief Constable Organ, had turned up late last night and asked a number of pointed questions. He had warned Sergeant Drummond and his cohort, Sergeant Stevens, that he would not be surprised if the individuals who comprised the Watch Committee decided to inspect the station in the next day or two and to keep all 'the lads' on their toes. Lieutenant Strang had not been wrong. Councillors had been in and out all morning, nosing and poking about, fishing for information on the arrests, even though Sergeant Drummond told them emphatically that the whole thing was being handled by the City of Glasgow and had nothing to do with Greenfield Burgh.

Though it had been almost thirty-six hours since young Nicholson had limped away, swathed in bandages, from Ottawa Street, in that time Sergeant Drummond had spared not a thought for the boy whose courage or duplicity – depending how you looked at it – had put the fat in the fire in the first place. He was surprised, and not a little dismayed, to glance up from work on the night-shift roster to find Nicholson standing before him, minus the bandage and with a simpering sort of grin on his face.

"Aye, young man, and what is it that we can be doing for you?"

"Tell me," Nicholson said, "am I to be charged with any crime?"

"I have heard nothing to that effect."

"Will I have to appear in the court?"

"Court?"

"To speak out against Malone?"

"I doubt if it will come to that," said Sergeant Drummond cautiously. "Superintendent Affleck would not be wishing it."

"So," said Nicholson, "there's nothin' against me."

"Pardon?"

"I want to join."

"Join?"

"I want to join an' be a policeman."

Sergeant Drummond drew back, as if the lad had threatened him with violence. "But – but—"

"You just said there was nothin' to hinder it."

"Why do you want to be a policeman?"

"Because it's secure."

"Secure?" Sergeant Drummond was aware that he was beginning to sound like a poll parrot. "I mean, what makes you imagine that it is secure?"

"I'm nobody's pal out there," said Nicholson. "Mr Affleck neglected to mention that fact when he conned me into shoppin' Danny Malone. Everybody seems to think I'm a bloody copper's nark – so I may as well be a real copper an' get paid for it."

"There is," said Sergeant Drummond, "a small matter of aptitude and basic educational requirements."

"I'm not scared o' hard work," said Craig Nicholson. "Anyway, I helped catch some criminals already, did I not?"

"Can you read?"

"Aye, of course."

"Write?"

"Aye."

"Add up sums?"

"Arithmetic; certainly," said Nicholson. "Even fractions."

"Are you sound in wind and limb?"

"Except for temporary cracked ribs, aye."

"No infectious diseases, lung trouble, bad feet, madness in the family?" said Sergeant Drummond hopefully.

"No, nothin' like that."

"Still, there are procedures."

Nicholson said, "How do I go about it?"

"You fill in a form, and send a letter."

"Have you got the form here?"

"Hold the cuddy a wee minute, son," said Sergeant Drummond. "First you must write to the Chief Constable and request an interview."

"I'll be doin' that," said Craig Nicholson. "Would it help me if I got a recommendation?"

"A reco—" Sergeant Drummond bit his lip.

"If Superintendent Affleck was to write a letter sayin' he thought I'd make a good copper?"

"Does Superintendent Affleck know you well enough?"

"He should," said young Nicholson.

"That nice young wife of yours," said Sergeant Drummond, "is this her idea?"

"Nah, it's my idea. I've tried it the other way an' it's not for me," young Nicholson said. "Now I feel I should try it your way."

"What are all these blethers?" the sergeant said, scratching his ear.

"It's honest employment, well enough paid, with prospects."

"That much, at least, is true."

Sergeant Drummond leaned his elbows on the counter and studied the young man thoughtfully. Perhaps it was not such a daft idea after all.

He sighed. "It is not an easy job, though."

"No job's easy," said young Nicholson.

"It has its own special difficulties."

"Such as?"

The sergeant sighed again. It was incumbent upon him to try to put the boy off, to tell him of the grinding monotony of the beat, of the routines of the station, spit and polish and self-discipline. Perhaps he should take him by the arm, lead him down to the holding-cells, show him old Tommy Watts who had not been sober in thirty years and who turned up regularly every Friday night to vomit all over the station floor, who would be charged at the Police Court come Monday, would vanish for thirty days, and would be back vomiting, cursing and pissing within twenty-four hours of release.

Perhaps he should put on his helmet and walk the boy along to the mortuary in Percy Street, show him the corpse that Constable McCrae had scraped off the railway line in the dismal light of dawn, a body without a head or feet, victim not of murder but of despair, just another suicide. Perhaps he should make young Nicholson camp on the bench for the rest of the day and observe the parade of grotesque and pitiful creatures that would shuffle through the station; men, women and children twisted by drink and violence, bigotry, poverty and neglect. But Sergeant Drummond knew that he was no good advertisement for any preaching that renounced the police force and, in lieu of sermons and lessons, he gave Craig Nicholson a copy of the application form and jotted down the address of Burgh Headquarters and the name of the lieutenant to whom he must write for interview.

"Now, it all depends whether there are vacancies," the sergeant warned, knowing perfectly well that recruits would be required within the week. "And it all depends on whether you are considered a good candidate. We only take the best in Greenfield, son."

"A letter from Mr Affleck, that would help, wouldn't it?"

"It would, it would – if he'll give it."

"I think he should," said young Nicholson.

"My, but you're bold, young man."

"I have to be bold," Nicholson said. "I've a wife at home, with a wean on the way. I've been sacked from my job and turned out o' my house, all because I assisted the polis."

"Because you got into bad company," said the sergeant.

"Maybe," Nicholson said. "If that's the case, I want into better company. What better company than the Burgh Police?"

At that moment, out of the corner of his eye, Sergeant Drummond caught sight of Mr Green, the Watch Committee's most vociferous critic, as he emerged from the corridor, beady and alert as always, saw too the braid of Lieutenant Strang behind him.

Sergeant Drummond straightened, said brusquely, "That'll be all, Mr Nicholson. We will be in touch in due course."

"Not too long, I hope," young Nicholson said.

"Not too long," the sergeant promised and directed him towards the exit door.

Craig lay on his back on top of the bed with a Gold Flake stuck in his mouth. Comfortably full of dinner, he had removed his boots and unbuttoned his trousers and he watched Kirsty lazily as she moved about the kitchen.

"They won't dare turn me down if I get a reference from a superintendent, from Affleck." he said. "If he snaps his fingers I could be in uniform an' drawin' a wage in a fortnight."

"I can't quite see you as a policeman," Kirsty said.

"Can you not? By God, I think I'm perfect material for a copper; tall, dark, fearless an' handsome – eh?"

"What does the job pay?"

"For the first month only fourteen bob a week but as soon as I'm out o' probation an' on to a beat then it earns twenty-three bob. Boot allowance on top, free uniform, a police house at a fiver a year rent."

Kirsty paused and glanced round. "Are you sure?"

"If you don't believe me, read the print on the back o' the application form."

"But the hours? The shifts are terrible, aren't they?"

"No worse than they are for a farm hand in the height o' the season." Craig propped himself up and grinned. "I'll be part of a fine body o' men, Kirsty. What's more I'll soon climb the ladder. You'll see, I'll soon get promotion."

"You talk as if it's all cut and dried."

"It is, near as damn it."

Kirsty experienced the lure of the job through him, could understand its attraction for her husband. But she was just glad that he had wrested, somehow, eleven shillings from Maitland Moss. Added to her wage from Oswalds' it gave them an extra seventeen shillings in the kitty, money that might come in useful in the weeks ahead, especially if Mr Affleck would not agree to propose Craig for the Burgh Force.

"Come over here." Craig held out one arm, beckoningly.

She crossed the kitchen to the bedside. The bruises where he had been struck by Danny Malone were dulled now but still extensive, spreading across his shoulder and upper chest, tan and purple. He did not seem to feel the pain, however.

It was three weeks since last they had made love. She did not know how to explain to him that her need for loving had waxed not waned with the changes in her body. Doctor Godwin had informed her that there was no danger to health in 'that sort of thing' until the fifth month. She looked down at Craig, at the bare flesh of his belly, at hard muscle and soft dark hair.

He slipped an arm about her waist, grinning.

"I want you to go an' see her," Craig said.

"What?"

"Your pal, Mrs Frew. Go an' call on her tomorrow."

"Is she not in hospital?"

"I expect she's out by now," Craig said. "Malone didn't hit her all that hard. Anyway, it's worth a try."

"She may not want to see either of us ever again, after what happened," said Kirsty.

"That's what I want you to find out," said Craig. "Butter her up a bit."

"But why?"

"So she'll persuade her bloody brother to write that letter."

"Why don't you just write to him at the Glasgow Police Office?"

"Nah, nah; a letter like that could easily get lost, if you see what I mean. I want to be sure I get that recommendation. God, our whole future hangs on it."

In his present cocksure mood there was no trace of apprehension, yet Kirsty sensed it at the back of his eagerness to be incorporated into the police force, to be protected by the rank and file of the law.

She said, "I'd intended to go to St Anne's tomorrow. I'll call in at Number 19 on my way home."

"Good," he said, nodding.

He eased himself down a little on the bed, resting the bruised arm and side. For a moment she thought that he was dropping off to sleep. She did not, however, seek to slip away, to return to her chores at the sink. To her surprise he placed his hand upon her stomach caressingly.

"I – I thought you didn't like that," she said.

"Slip your hand down an' you'll see whether I like it."

Kirsty hesitated then did as he requested. She touched the crisp black hair, the stem of his maleness which was both stiff and soft at one and the same time.

She said, "Do you want me to take my clothes off?"

"No."

"It's safe, Craig. The doctor told—"

"Just – just touch me."

Again she hesitated, but she could not refuse him, could not resist. She shut off her own need for tenderness and did all that he asked of her, wondering where he had learned these sexual tricks, until he quivered and gasped and expended himself.

"God!" he groaned. "You did that well, Kirsty. Must be in the blood."

A sudden sick feeling gripped her in the pit of the stomach. She stiffened, swung round, a moistened towel in her hands. "*What* did you say?"

"Nothin', dear. I enjoyed it, that's all."

"What did you *mean*?"

"Nothin', nothin'."

"You meant – you meant my *mother*."

"Nah, nah. I wasn't thinkin'."

"You *never* think," she shouted. "You just open your fat mouth an'—"

"God, what's wrong wi' you now?"

He turned on his side, drew the blanket modestly over his bare backside. Kirsty pitched the towel into the sink. The pot that had contained the dinner-time potatoes was there, half filled with cold water. Before she quite knew what she was doing she had hoisted it up by the handle, had taken four quick angry steps towards the bed and had hurled the contents over him in a great cold wave.

Craig yelled, shot to his knees as if he expected the pot to follow. He clutched the soaking blanket to his loins and shook water from his hair. "You bitch!"

"So you think my mother was a whore, do you?"

"She bloody was," Craig shouted. "It's the bloody truth."

The pot struck the wall above his head and thudded on to the bedding. Dragging the blanket with him Craig sought shelter in a corner of the recess, crouched, ready to leap away if she attacked him with another utensil.

What wounded Kirsty most of all was the fact that Craig did not realise how much he had hurt her. She did not know him at all; this was not the boy with whom she had left Carrick, with whom she had lain down in love on that sunny spring Sunday.

She stamped into the hallway, yanked open the cupboard.

Craig shouted, "What the hell is wrong wi' you, Kirsty Barnes?"

She stamped in from the hall again, buttoning a clean blouse over her breasts.

"*Nicholson*," she cried. "My name is *Nicholson*."

Relieved, Craig sank back against the wall. The lack of motive behind her attack had disturbed him. Now he thought that he understood.

"So that's what all the song an' dance is about," he said.

"What song an' dance?"

"You're mad because I haven't married you yet."

She stepped into the powder-blue skirt, hooked it up, thrust herself into the bolero jacket. She reached for the hat she had put upon the table, a frivolous item, relic of daft April days, days that had been put behind her and would never be redeemed.

"If that's all it is," said Craig, "I'll marry you next week."

"No, you will not," Kirsty said, flatly and without heat.

"Why not?"

"Because I don't want to marry you."

"But – but you're expectin'."

She flung open the kitchen door, almost striking him.

"You should have thought o' that before."

"I'm thinkin' of it now, damn it, Kirsty."

"Well, you're too damned late." She kicked her shoes out from under the table and hopped into them. "An' change that bed before I get back; it's soakin'."

"Where – where are you goin'?"

"Out," she said. "Out for a walk – by myself."

She went straight from Canada Road to the Kelvin Tea Room, invested a penny in the ladies' convenience there, seated herself on the pedestal and had a good cry in private; then she dried her tears, washed her face, tidied her hair, bought a cup of tea and a coffee bun, finished them and went out into bustling Dumbarton Road once more.

She knew where she was going, though it was not Craig's command that turned her towards Walbrook Street but bad conscience.

In response to Kirsty's tug upon the bell, the door was opened by a stranger, a woman of forty-two or -three, plump, with lustrous dark eyes and a small sensual mouth touched with a cherry rouge. She wore a tight-fitting Chesterfield coat that showed off her full figure and a stiff white shirt with a string bow tie in the collar. In one hand she carried a hat, a tiny 'French brimless'. It was apparent that she had either just arrived at Mrs Frew's house or was just about to take her leave.

"Yes?"

"I've called to enquire after Mrs Frew," said Kirsty.

"Oh, she's not so bad, not so bad."

The woman spoke with a trace of soft Irish.

"May I – may I see her?" said Kirsty.

"Are you Kirsty Nicholson, by any chance?"

"Yes, I am."

"Thought you might be," said the woman. "Do step into the hall. Nessie's havin' a lie down."

"Is she hurt badly?"

"Not so bad as all that," said the woman. "She's more shocked than injured, I'd say. She has a hard head, has Nessie. It runs in the family. I'm Beatrice Affleck, by the way. I believe you've encountered my husband."

"Superintendent Affleck?"

"The one and only."

"Oh, yes, I know him."

The woman smiled warmly. "Have you got a touch of conscience about all this?"

"Yes, I have," Kirsty admitted.

"It wasn't your fault. It was that daft husband of mine. He should never have got Nessie involved with criminals."

"Where's Cissie?"

"It was all too much for Cissie, poor soul. She handed in her notice without even collectin' her wages."

"Who's lookin' after Mrs Frew?"

"I am," Beatrice Affleck said. "Sort of."

"Does she not need constant nursin'?"

"She'll not have a stranger in the house. You know what she's like."

Encouraged by the woman's friendliness, Kirsty smiled. "Only too well."

"I suppose you do want to see her?"

"If it's convenient."

"Wait here. I'll 'announce' you."

Bea Affleck went into the ground-floor bedroom which lay to the right of the private parlour. Kirsty waited nervously in the hall. From within the room came the frail murmur of voice, a little cough, a little cry.

Mrs Affleck returned. "You're honoured. Follow me."

Agnes Frew was propped up in bed by a pile of lace-edged pillows. The room was as gloomy as the rest of the house. The monolithic window that overlooked the backcourt was partly curtained by a dark velvet drape and, through its folds, Kirsty glimpsed another glass-painting, not a saint but a sailing-boat. The bed was as narrow as a coffin. It floated on a sea of shadow, for the fire had only just been coaled and gas- and oil-lamps not yet lighted. The room was so funereal that it might have been the setting for a wake and not a convalescence.

"Go closer," whispered Mrs Affleck. "She won't bite."

The lace-trimmed bed-jacket and the lace cap that covered the widow's hair had the ivory hue of shroud linen. Her pinched features were bloodless, motionless hands were folded on the sheet that covered her bosom. Her eyes were closed.

"Mrs Frew," said Kirsty. "Mrs Frew, it's me."

There was no response, not a flutter of lids, not a purl of breath. She might have been dead.

"I'm real sorry to see you like this."

Under the bed-cap's lace edge a bandage was visible.

In a loud voice Beatrice Affleck said, "Nessie, say hello to your visitor."

On the bedside table were a fluted crystal wine glass, a silver pillbox, a jug of water, a Bible, spectacles, a bottle of yellow medicine and a sepia photograph in a scrolled silver frame; Mr Frew, big and solemn, posed against a Grecian urn in a jungle of potted plants.

"Come along, Nessie," said Mrs Affleck. "You're not deaf."

An eyelid flickered, opened; an eye surveyed the world.

Agnes Frew said, "Oh, so you came, did you?"

Beatrice Affleck sighed. "I'll make some tea, Nessie, shall I?" Without awaiting a reply she left the bedroom.

Kirsty stood her ground, though she was sufficiently intimidated to wish to follow Mrs Affleck out of the room too.

She cleared her throat. "Does it – does your head hurt?"

Mrs Frew managed to say, "One gets used to sufferin'."

Now that she had both eyes open, she seemed rather removed from ultimate martyrdom. "We are all born into the world to suffer an' I have had my fair share of it."

"Doesn't the medicine help the pain?"

"It cannot soothe the pain in my heart, the pain of bein' deceived by my own flesh and blood."

"It wasn't really Mr Affleck's fault," said Kirsty.

"Did *she* tell you to say that?"

"The man who hit you was a savage, Mrs Frew. He might have killed people if your brother hadn't caught him."

"He might have killed me."

"Craig – my husband – wouldn't have let him do that."

Mrs Frew struggled up on the pillows. "Tell me the truth, Kirsty; did Hughie deliberately send your husband in with the villains to protect me?"

Kirsty did not hesitate. "Aye, of course he did."

"That was brave."

"It was fortunate," said Kirsty.

"Did Hughie tell you to come here today?"

"I came of my own accord," said Kirsty, "because I was worried about you."

"Cissie's left me."

"So I heard."

"I don't want *her* lookin' after me." Mrs Frew jerked her head towards the door.

"Perhaps you could employ a nurse."

"You could come an' look after me."

"I have my work to go to, Mrs Frew."

"It's so difficult to find somebody you can trust."

"I'd like to, but—"

"For a week or two. With your husband. Free room and board."

For all that her job at Oswalds' contributed Kirsty knew that they would be better off here with a roof over their heads and a guarantee of two square meals a day. She saw at once that it would be a mutually beneficial arrangement and wondered if Hugh or Beatrice Affleck had put the idea into Mrs Frew's mind; wondered too what Craig would have to say about it.

Kirsty said, "My husband's hopin' to join the police."

"What?" said Mrs Frew. "Is this more of Hughie's nonsense?"

"No, but Craig would like Mr Affleck to sponsor him, give him a letter of recommendation."

"Kirsty, come and look after me."

"We'd need a place to store our possessions, such as they are."

"I thought you had a house?"

"We're bein' thrown out," said Kirsty. "The landlord was a pal of the man who biffed you."

Mrs Frew nodded as if the connections that bound them into their present situation had been destined from the beginning. "Every man's hand is raised against the righteous."

She raised herself upright in the bed and the lace cap slipped over her brow, giving her a tipsy appearance. She could not disguise her desire to have Kirsty come back to Walbrook Street.

Kirsty said, "If we do come, Mrs Frew, it would only be until you're better. If Craig is accepted as a constable we would hope to be allocated a police house in the not-too-distant future."

"*Did* our Hughie put you up to all this?"

"No, Mrs Frew, I swear he didn't."

"I don't blame your husband."

"Well, I'm glad of that."

Mrs Frew leaned forward, eagerly. "Did Craig punch that rascal on the snout?"

Kirsty, surprised, answered, "Aye, he did, as a matter of fact."

"David and Goliath; the Lord was on Craig's side."

"Perhaps He was at that;" said Kirsty.

"He'll make a good policeman, your husband."

"I hope Mr Affleck shares your opinion."

"When can you come, Kirsty?"

"Tonight, I suppose."

"Good. In that case, I'll make sure that Hughie calls tomorrow."

"Do you think you can persuade him to help us, Mrs Frew?"

The widow adjusted the lace cap and reclined upon the pillows, assuming once more a pose of pale martyrdom, spoiled by a wink.

"Just watch me, dear," she said.

She had not forgotten and would not forget his hurtful words but she knew that she could not enjoy, as rich women did, the luxury of sustaining anger. It, like so many things, had to be subsumed into the business of 'getting on with it', of settling and resettling, of finding shelter and food, earning a wage, taking another step on the road towards a better life. She entered the house fearful that Craig would have allowed his anger at her to smoke and smoulder but he, like her, had put their horrid quarrel behind him and did not refer to it at all. He had 'something to do', something to be at, and he seemed delighted at her proposal that, for a time, they move back into Walbrook Street. He was not contrite but appeared willing to sweep her along with him, to make enthusiastic bustle stand in lieu of apology.

"Will she chin her brother about writin' the letter?" Craig asked.

"She seems sure she'll manage to persuade him."

"Is it a condition? That we go to stay there for a while?"

"I think it is," said Kirsty.

"Right. It's fair enough."

By half past six o'clock Craig had them packed and ready to quit Canada Road. It was too whirlwind for Kirsty and she voiced her doubts and reservations. "But what about my job? What about Oswalds'?"

"Bugger that," said Craig. "We'll be fed and housed until such times as I'm signed on to the force. We don't need much money, at all, so the pittance you earned at the Cakery isn't going to matter."

"What about the McCoigs?"

"Told to get out, weren't we?"

"The inventory?" Kirsty protested. "The broken window?"

"McCoig won't be round until Friday. I'll have the window sorted by then. I'll be here when he comes."

"What if you don't get into the police?"

"Kirsty!" Craig exclaimed. "They wouldn't have the brass neck to refuse me."

Craig 'borrowed' a broken-wheeled barrow from a sweep's yard, carried their meagre possessions down to it and loaded them on board. With the homely items gone the single-end looked bare and dismal and Kirsty felt no tug of regret at leaving it.

Neighbours, of course, quickly became aware that something unusual was afoot and Daddy Mills was curious enough to pad out on to the landing.

"Are you doin' a flit?" the old man asked.

"Nah," Craig answered.

He locked the door, pocketed the key, lifted the canvas grip and tucked it under his uninjured arm.

"Looks to me like ye are," said Mr Mills.

"Holiday," said Craig.

"Does Mr McCoig know you're goin'?"

"None o' his business."

"But it is, it is."

From the turn on the stairs Kirsty watched. By comparison with the slow-witted, sententious old man Craig seemed as bright as quicksilver.

"Be back on Friday," Craig said.

"Where are ye goin'?"

"Never you mind."

"You *have* to tell me."

"Why?"

"In case – in case the place goes on fire."

Craig laughed. "On fire, for God's sake!"

"What'll we do if your house burns?"

"Blow on it," Craig said and, wasting no more time on old man Mills, hurried down the stairs and escorted Kirsty into the street.

Neighbours peered, scowling, from front windows and half-open doors as Craig dumped the grip on to the long barrow, shafted it on to its limping wheels and, with Kirsty at his side, fairly raced away from Number 11 Canada Road with its ghosts and dreams and stillborn memories; and its lingering threat of revenge.

Rather to Kirsty's surprise everything that Craig had planned came to pass, though not quite at the fast lick that her husband had predicted. Weeks accumulated into months. Autumn gave way to the fogs and bristling frosts of winter and the boarding-house in Walbrook Street came to seem less gloomy and oppressive and more cosy with each passing day.

Kirsty polished banisters and scrubbed steps, washed the glass-paintings with a chamois cloth, blackleaded the elegant fireplaces and kept the appointments of the dining-room agleam. She would not have minded living here for always, raising her children in the kitchen, being half-friend, half-servant to the lonely widow. Mrs Frew, however, had been true to her word. She had browbeaten her brother into writing a brilliant letter of recommendation to the Chief Constable of Greenfield Police. Mr Organ was nobody's fool. He knew fine well what rôle the lad had played in the capture of Skirving and Malone but he could not ignore a glowing testimonial from such a senior officer as Hughie Affleck and had no hesitation in interviewing Craig Nicholson and, finding him smart, in accepting him as a probationary constable.

Craig's progress into the Greenfield Police meant that their days in Walbrook Street would surely be numbered; burgh policemen were committed by regulations to reside within the parish to which they were appointed and to be part of the community they served. If Craig had been a bachelor he would have been obliged to stay in barracks with other recruits and

unmarried constables but, as a married man, he was permitted to
dwell with his wife until such time as the burgh found a house for
them. Craig did not talk much about his training. He was not lax,
however, was punctual on all parades and insistent that his
uniform, helmet and boots be kept in immaculate condition. He
even showed Kirsty how to iron the heavy knee-length shorts and
half-sleeved vest that he wore for gymnastic exercises and, in the
evening, no matter how tired he was, he would apply himself to
study the *Police Constable's Handbook* upon which he would be
tested and examined.

In due course, Craig Nicholson was inducted as a fully-fledged
constable, was marched around the parade-ground behind the
Percy Street drill-hall and had his hand shaken by the Chief
Constable, the Lieutenant and several councillors. The following
morning he made his first muster in Canada Road police station
and was shown, by no less a person than Sergeant Hector
Drummond, the extent of his beat and how to patrol it. Craig's
confidence was undiluted by modesty and doubt.

Kirsty could not deny that he looked every inch a policeman,
standing tall and dark and poised in uniform and helmet. She was
pleased enough to have him settled and to regard herself as a
policeman's wife.

If Craig and Kirsty had been forgiven by Nessie Frew for their
part in the robbery, Hugh Affleck had not. He no longer came for
supper on Thursday nights and turned up only once in that season
to reassure his sister that she would not be summoned to appear as
a witness in the Crown's case against Skirving, McVoy and
Malone. Written testimony would be enough, particularly as poor
Cissie had been put through the mill at Glasgow Headquarters
and had even been subjected to the hair-raising experience of
having to identify Skirving and Malone through a grid in the
cast-iron doors of the holding-cells.

Those members of the public, in and out of Greenfield, who
waited with bated breath for scandalous revelations of graft and
corruption were in the end doomed to disappointment. Danny
Malone and Billy Skirving, even the beleaguered McVoy, spiked
the authorities' guns by electing to keep their secrets to
themselves. They pleaded guilty to all charges and thus carried
the can for the toffs and sporting gents who had profited from their
labours over the years.

A day was fixed for the hearing before sheriff and jury but the
panel, all three, signed minutes and the Crown moved, therefore,
for immediate sentencing. No mitigations were offered, no

witnesses called. McVoy was given four years of penal correction. Skirving and Malone were sentenced each to twelve years' hard labour.

This sudden great weight of days was enough to cause even the indomitable Danny Malone to gasp and turn white as a sheet. He was taken down struggling, roaring, "Bastards, bastards. You'll never hold me," which gave press reporters one hard fact to salt their columns of priggish moralising.

Sergeant Drummond was the first person in Greenfield to receive the news from court. He did not wait for Constable Nicholson to tramp in from his relief point at the corner of Halifax Street and Wharf Road but put on his helmet and gloves and walked through the gathering dusk to meet the young man coming in.

"Twelve years, the pair of them," said Sergeant Drummond.

"How long did McVoy land?"

"Four."

"Did Malone say anythin', make any statements?"

"He said not a word, except to curse."

"Is Superintendent Affleck pleased with the result?"

"Pleased enough, no doubt," said the sergeant. "But I expect he would have liked more."

"To net Maitland Moss?"

"To see Danny hanged."

Constable Nicholson nodded.

"Next time," he said, without the trace of a smile, "next time, Sergeant, eh?"

For Kirsty the days rolled pleasantly by. Leaves drifted from the trees that flanked the bowling-green, the long window of the pavilion was shuttered against winter storms and the flagpole dismantled. Autumn harvests brought shop prices down. In spite of the wet summer greengrocers' tables spilled over with an abundance of fruit and vegetables. On Sundays Kirsty and Mrs Frew, now fully recovered from her ordeal, walked to St Anne's to sing praise to the Lord and receive spiritual balm from Mr Graham's sermons. Business at the boarding-house picked up. Every post brought letters from ministers and elders requesting rooms for such-and-such a night. Mrs Frew would record the names in her Guest Book and Kirsty would make sure that the rooms were spotless, the sheets fresh, that there was water in the jugs, oil in the lamps and kindling and coal in the scuttles.

To Kirsty, Craig also seemed contented with his lot, though he remained uncommunicative about his work. He said nothing at all about his first arrest, for instance, or his first appearance as a witness in police court.

It was Mrs Frew, a furtive reader of the *Partick Star*, who discovered Craig's secret. She let out a shriek that brought Kirsty running from the kitchen to the parlour where she found the widow on her feet and waving the newspaper above her head.

"Craig, it's our Craig. He's got his name in the paper."

"Where? Let me see."

"Did he not tell you?"

"No," said Kirsty, frowning.

She took the newspaper from the woman and read: *Greenfield Police Court: Assault: On Monday, before Bailie Wrayburn, James Reid was fined 30s, or 21 days, for assaulting Thomas Clark and a constable named Nicholson, on Saturday evening.*

"Was Craig not hurt?"

"He didn't appear to be," said Kirsty.

"He must have been in court."

"I don't know. He said nothin' to me about it."

"Still, it's very gratifyin' to see his name in the papers," said Mrs Frew. "Our Hughie's name was never out of the papers when he was on the beat in the Greenfield."

"Why didn't Craig tell me?"

"Too modest," said Mrs Frew.

Kirsty challenged him soon after he returned from work that evening. She showed him the item in the *Star* as he seated himself at the kitchen table in expectation of supper.

"Ach, that!" said Craig dismissively. "It wasn't important."

"Mrs Frew wants to know what happened."

"Old Reid was stottin' drunk," said Craig. "He's an old josser, about sixty, who got booted out o' the railway service for habitual drinkin'."

"Go on."

Craig sighed. "Am I not to get fed?"

"In a minute. Go on."

"I heard a commotion outside the *Vaults*. Tam Clark is Reid's boozin' chum but they'd had some sort o' argument an' Clark was on the ground, Reid kickin' him."

"What did you do?"

"Requested him to desist."

"Did he?"

"Nah," said Craig ruefully. "I had to stop him."

"It says you were assaulted."

"I wasn't sharp enough. The old bugger crowned me wi' a bottle."

"Craig, why didn't you tell me?"

"It was only a wee cut, treated at the station. It's healed now."

"An' the court?"

Craig shrugged. "Two minutes on Monday. Reid's son shelled out the thirty bob an' lugged the old josser away cursin' him' an' threatenin' to send him to the Inebriates' Reformatory if it happened again. It wasn't anythin' special, Kirsty."

Kirsty ladled soup from the big pot into a plate and put it before him. "What else has been happenin' that you haven't told me about?"

Craig blew gently over the surface of the broth and, lifting his spoon, shrugged again.

"Not a bloody thing," he said.

Chief Constable Organ was an innovative chap who had not only formed a Police Athletic Association but had even squeezed enough money from the Commissioners to build and equip a gymnasium in Cape Breton Road. He had also 'borrowed' Partick's new shift system which would shorten each man's duty to nine hours per day and allow more regular time off. Diehards were against the change but the Greenfield Commissioners had the proposal under review and were keen to move for its adoption in an attempt to reduce, if possible, the high incidence of drunkenness that the long shifts encouraged.

Craig heard talk about the station. He even discussed the proposal's merits with his fellow recruits in the locker room. He had not, however, been on the Force long enough to have strong feelings one way or the other. As a green hand – Constable Third Grade – he was not yet summoned on the beat during the hours of darkness, a nice refinement peculiar to Greenfield and one which recruits and raw young constables appreciated.

Filling off-duty hours, collected into a straight two and half days every seven, was a problem in itself. On a Saturday a man might take himself to the terraced steps of the football park to watch Greenfield Rovers play Linthouse or Morton or arch-rivals Partick Thistle; but an off-duty Saturday came around only one week in nine and, for the rest, there was such irregularity of hours that the majority of policemen found off-duty service even more tedious than pounding the beat and did what other loafers did, which was to hang about public houses and billiard halls in the dead of daylight hours, sleep their heads into engine oil or bicker incessantly with their wives.

Craig, however, had already seen evidence of the havoc that idleness could wreak to a copper's prospects. Being ambitious he was quick to seek other ways of occupying free time. He took advantage of a scheme that Mr Organ had set up for the improvement of the proficiency of his men, booked in as a beginner with a qualified instructor at Cranstonhill Baths and, shivering and unsure of himself, stepped reluctantly into the freezing pea-green water two or three times a week while boys half his age larked about with abandon and plunged in and out of the pond like porpoises.

Craig did not like it. He did not like being told what to do by the muscular man in the striped bathing-suit who seemed impervious to the cold and who would stand by him and cup his chin in a big unshivering hand and, holding him suspended, would shout, "Kick, kick, Constable Nicholson. You're not a wee puddock, man. Kick, kick, kick."

On his fourth morning on the beat Craig had been called to a ramp at the old ford at the bottom of Wharf Lane and had seen a corpse being dragged from the river. He had been obliged to stoop close, to grip the thing's swollen, suet-soft arm and help drag it up the steps, all dripping and sexless and unreal. So he kicked and kicked and spluttered out the water that got into his nose and promised himself that within a year he would earn three swimming certificates and would be ready to go for a life-saving medal, would be able to dive off the high dale that wee boys were forbidden to use, would not be afraid of plunging into the Clyde's coiling brown currents to save some poor soul from drowning.

Later, with skin wrinkled and eyes smarting, he would soak for ten minutes in a hot tub, knees to chin, and wish that he had already gone through it, had learned everything, knew all there was to know, was not young and uncertain any more, afraid of shouts in the street and dark closes and of what he might find, in the first foggy hour of his shift, lying dead and decaying in a midden or vennel or on the steep cinder slope of the railway embankment.

If only he had his own house, if only Kirsty had been as she was and not all fat and fussy with the baby in her, if he had his mam and his brother and sister close at hand, his dad to talk to, he might not feel as he did, might not prefer the cold pond or the gymnasium and the company of Archie Flynn, a big simple lad only six months down from the Isle of Harris who had joined the same week as Craig and who lived in the barracks in North Ottawa Street; he might not feel more kinship with Archie and with Peter Stewart, another shy Highlander new to the burgh, than he did with Kirsty, his woman, his wife.

Now that she had pulled the trick of womanhood and slipped from him into pregnancy Craig felt that he had nobody to look after him; he must learn to look after himself. Being a man, a policeman at that, he could not tell Kirsty of his fears, could not come close to her because of her swollen belly and swelling breasts, close enough to admit his weaknesses. At the end of the long shift he wanted to go home to his own fireside, to intimacy and fondness. But, though the grub was good, the bed clean, and they were saving money hand over fist, Walbrook Street offered none of these things. He experienced that vague sense of dispossession for which there is no name and for which, unreasonably, he blamed Kirsty.

With Archie or with Peter, in company with the lads at the station, he had no need of her. In the cold pond at Cranstonhill, in the gymnasium in Cape Breton Road, shivering or sweating it out, he could be free of the need of her, of the obligation to tell her where he went and what he did, and might blame his reticence, then and later, on the nature of the job.

What else has happened that you haven't told me about?

Not a bloody thing.

"Kick, kick," the instructor would shout. "Kick, Constable Nicholson," and Craig would thrash the freezing water and, within a month, had the hand away from his chin.

It seemed later than it was, for the boarding-house had no guests that night and Mrs Frew had retired to the back parlour, not in any mood of pique or unsociability but to apply herself to making up a list of friends to whom she must send a card at Christmas or New Year. It was, apparently, a procedure that required methodical concentration and the fortification of a large glass of port wine.

Craig had not arrived home and would, he had indicated, be later than his usual hour of nine, though for what particular reason Kirsty did not know; only the appearance of a wet bathing-costume wrapped in a sodden towel or of his gymnastic vest soaked with sweat would give her a clue.

The wave of energy that had buoyed her up over the past few weeks had ebbed since the weekend. She was concerned lest her tiredness presaged a fever or some dreadful turn in the course of her pregnancy that would impair the health of her child and, incidentally, ruin the little celebration that Mrs Frew had planned for Christmas in a fortnight's time. New Year would follow and she would be past the mark, into that spell which would end in birth and motherhood and another change in the tenor of her life. Somehow she fixed on New Year, on 1st January, 1897, as a magical date and convinced herself that nothing unpleasant would happen before that date.

If she had thought it through logically Kirsty would have realised that her fatigue stemmed from a long Saturday 'in town', an early tour of the departments in the Colosseum Warehouse whose advertisements in the *Star* had lured Mrs Frew and from whose laden counters she purchased the gifts required to appease the sensibilities of relatives she hadn't seen in years. Kirsty and Mrs Frew had wandered too into Johnston's Corner to admire the Dolls' Palace and keek at old Santa Claus as he dished out toys to good little girls and boys.

Mrs Frew had nudged Kirsty. "You'll be queueing up there with your wee ones before you know it, dear."

Kirsty had felt a strange warm glow at the prospect.

The day had been wonderfully rewarding but it had tired her physically and, with energy low, she had become depressed and imaginative.

Craig was out and Mrs Frew was seeking seclusion in the back parlour and, before she knew it, Kirsty had taken herself into the bathroom. She locked the door and brought out the framed mirror which Mrs Frew hid modestly in a cupboard and, with mirror propped on the bathrail, studied herself with furtive attention in search of a rash, a ruddiness or change in pallor that would confirm her belief that she was sickening for something horrible and would be lucky to survive the week.

She was swollen, fat as a piggie. Her eyes, she thought, seemed dull, her hair lacking in lustre. Even her freckles seemed to have expanded and become more prominent.

Kirsty swallowed and bent closer to her image in the glass.

"Oh, dear," she murmured. "What's wrong wi' me?"

She stuck out her tongue.

At that moment the doorbell rang and, thinking that it would be Craig and that he had forgotten his key, Kirsty hastily put the mirror back into the cupboard and, relieved to be thus diverted from contemplating her own demise, hurried out into the hall.

"I'll get it," Kirsty called, though Mrs Frew did not seem to have heard.

After nightfall fog had thickened rapidly in the valley of the Clyde. It had been lurking all afternoon, not the damp ectoplasmic mists that often filled the glens of the Carrick grazings in winter but a dour, ochre substance that was as dry and acrid as chimney smoke – which, Craig said, was what it really was. It was Kirsty's first sight of a Glasgow 'pea-souper'. It startled her. Street-lamps were obliterated, the bowling-green fence sunk, the railings, even the pavement, had all been absorbed. It lapped against the step and crept past Kirsty into the hallway in sinister swirls. She had an almost overwhelming impulse to slam the door to close it out, to close out the man who stood before her on the step.

He said, "You're not Cissie."

"No, I am not."

"Is my aunt not at home?"

"Your aunt?"

"Mrs Frew, I mean."

"Who are you?" Kirsty said.

"A lost soul," he answered.

He was not so tall as Craig, not quite so young. He wore a dark grey Cheviot overcoat and a long flowing scarf, a Greenlander travelling-cap tilted on his head, the cloth brim pearled with moisture. He was fair, with blue eyes, and when he smiled he showed even white teeth.

"I'm not really a lost soul," he said. "I'm David Lindsay Lockhart and I should have been happily rattling back to my digs in Edinburgh except that all the trains have been cancelled."

"You'd better come in."

He was not assertive, not thrusting, though she could tell by his voice and by the quality of his clothing that he was a high cut above her in standing and education. He took off the cap at once. His hair was smooth and dark blond, worn longer than was fashionable. He carried with him an old Bullion bag in scarred brown hide, held bag and cap in his hand while he waited, patient but amused, for Kirsty to do something.

She did not know why she felt so suddenly shy and awkward, tongue-tied and hesitant. From the moment that he had smiled she had sensed that there was no deception in him and that she need have no fear of him.

"Wait," she said, and carefully closed the front door, blotting out the swirling ochre fog.

Mr Lockhart seemed to be in no hurry to move out of the hallway, to find and greet his aunt. He swayed lightly on the balls of his feet and smiled again at Kirsty. It was the most candid and expressive smile that she had ever seen, a smile of sheer amiableness that reached into his eyes and made them twinkle.

Kirsty found her voice. "Is – is Mrs Frew really your aunt?"

"Actually she's a relative so distant that I do not know what to call her," David Lockhart answered. "My mother was her father's cousin; whatever that makes us. Aunt will have to do, don't you think?"

"I'll tell her you're here."

"Are there rooms?"

"Aye, lots of rooms."

"Good," said David Lockhart. "I've travelled from London today and I'm quite exhausted."

"Have you stayed here before?"

"Many times," said David. "What's your name?"

"Nicholson, sir."

"Sir? Oh, no, Mrs Nicholson, you mustn't call me that."

"How – how do you know I'm married?"

"Your wedding ring," he said. "In addition to which you are some six months gone with child, if I'm not mistaken; and my dear old terrible auntie wouldn't have you in her house if you didn't have a husband."

Kirsty wanted to laugh at his judgement of Mrs Frew but was at the same time embarrassed by his acknowledgement of her pregnancy.

David said, "Don't be put out, Mrs Nicholson. I'm a doctor, you see, and have delivered so many babies that I can spot an expectant lady at a thousand yards. What's your real name?"

"Real—"

"Christian?"

"Oh! It's Kirsty."

"I shall call you Kirsty, if you don't object."

"No, sir. No, Mr Lockhart."

"Now – where's Nessie?"

"In the parlour. I'll announce you, if you like."

"What a good idea."

Craig crouched over the fire and shivered. In cupped hands he held a mug of hot cocoa spiced with 'Bonnie Scotland', a cheap whisky that he had purchased, half-bottle size, from a late-night wine merchant's on his way home from the baths. He wore only lamb's-wool combinations. A blanket draped his shoulders and he looked chilled and miserable. Kirsty suspected that he was

nursing a virulent cold that had swept through the ranks in
Ottawa Street and had felled even the stalwart Sergeant Drummond. She had already filled a hot bottle and put it in the bed, had
offered him Jeffe Powder which he had gruffly refused. She dried
the supper dishes as quietly as possible, racked them and set out
the plates that would be needed to serve Mr Lockhart breakfast in
the dining-room.

Mrs Frew had welcomed the young man with open arms, had
taken him into the parlour and had told Kirsty to serve supper
there. She had had a sausage hot-pot on the go and had divided it
between Craig and Mr Lockhart, skimping on her own portion,
and a rich damson pie which she had coated with thick yellow
custard. Mr Lockhart had thanked her kindly for 'doing him the
honours' at such a late hour but Mrs Frew did not encourage
Kirsty to join the conversation. The old lady clearly wanted Mr
Lockhart all to herself; Kirsty could hardly blame her for that.

Out of the coat and scarf, relaxing by the parlour fire, Mr
Lockhart was a handsome man, easy and affable in his manner
and quick with his charming smile.

Craig said, "Who the hell is he?"

"I told you," Kirsty said. "He's a relative of Mrs Frew."

"Is he still in there wi' her?"

"I haven't heard him come out."

Craig said, "Aye, maybe he's her lover."

"Craig! For God's sake!"

"I've seen stranger things." Craig supped from the cocoa mug,
reached behind him, took the half-bottle of 'Bonnie Scotland'
from the table, poured liberally. "You've no idea what these old
birds get up to."

"You're talkin' daft," said Kirsty, offended. "Anyway, he's a
doctor."

Craig snorted. "So was Barret Deanes."

"Who?"

"The Partick Poisoner."

"How can you be so—I mean, you haven't even met Mr
Lockhart."

Craig did not answer. He drew his chair closer to the grate.

In silence Kirsty finished her chores. The clock on the shelf told
her that it was almost eleven. In seven hours she would have to be
up again. Craig, if he was well enough, would be off by a quarter
past seven.

Craig said, "What's the weather like now?"

Kirsty peered from the window. She could see only a grey

swirling substance that seemed to have replaced the darkness by something almost alive. She drew back.

"Well? Is it still foggy?" Craig snapped.

"I'll go to the door an' look," said Kirsty. "I want to lock up properly, anyway."

Craig nodded, got up, shivered, stretched and put down the empty mug. He lifted the whisky bottle. "I'd better hide this. I wouldn't want her drinkin' it."

Drawing the blanket about him he left the kitchen and padded wearily along the corridor to the servant's room where, in a big double bed manhandled down from the second floor, he and Kirsty slept.

"I hope you feel better tomorrow, dear," Kirsty said.

"I feel fine," said Craig.

She watched him go. She felt sorry for him, but also irritated. She picked up the iron poker, carefully stirred the coals in the grate, added a few lumps from the scuttle and a shovelful of dross, closed the iron doors and locked them in the hope that the fire would still be alight come morning.

For four or five minutes she pottered about the kitchen, making everything spick and span before she turned off the gaslight. In the half dark she could feel the fog envelop the building but it did not make her uncomfortable now. In fact all the worries that had beset her earlier in the evening seemed to have melted away; no accounting for her moods these days. She brushed her hands over her stomach to smooth her skirt, tidied her hair and went out into the corridor. St Andrew, back in place on the half-landing, glowered luminously down at her. She gave him a wink and paused near the parlour door, listening. Hearing no sound she went down the hallway to the main door, opened it and peered out into the fog.

It was thicker than ever, dense, mobile, all-enshrouding. The only hint of animate life came from deep within it, the muted lowing of a foghorn and, a moment later, the answering wail of a tugboat's hooter. She thought she heard a goods train tiptoeing over the rails behind the bowling-green but she could not be sure. Eyes smarting, she squinted into the grey-brown bank of fog in which nothing but the fog itself moved.

"Kirsty?"

Kirsty turned. Mr Lockhart – David – had slipped out of the parlour. He came towards her, smiling.

"Is it still bad out there?" he asked.

"Aye; worse, if anythin'."

"Is your husband safe home?"

"In his bed. He has a cold, I think."

"Does he walk to work?"

"Yes."

"That's just as well," said David. "I doubt if there will be much movement of traffic tomorrow morning."

"Are you hopin' to return to Edinburgh?"

"I must. I have a class at ten."

"A doctors' class?"

"No," David said. "Medicine's behind me, for the time being."

He leaned on the doorpost and looked at the invisible street then touched her gently on the shoulder. "Perhaps you should come inside, Mrs Nicholson. This stuff can be very sore on the lungs."

Kirsty stepped back. She did feel a little breathless, come to think of it.

"Let me do it," David said.

Kirsty watched him bolt the big main door and affix the safety-chain. He had fine hands, long-fingered and delicate.

"Do you require a lamp, Mr Lockhart?"

"To light me upstairs?"

"Aye."

"No, Kirsty. St Andrew will guide me."

"What time do you want your breakfast?"

"Early," David said.

"I'll serve at seven, will that do?"

He looked at her, one foot on the stair, one hand on the knob of the banister.

"Perfect," he said.

Craig felt as if he had swallowed a lighted blowtorch. The lining of his throat was raw and when he coughed, which he tried not to do, that rawness spread like fire down into his chest. He had no fever, fortunately, only an ache in the head and a general shiveriness that he tried to pretend was nothing more serious than a response to the weather, a dank grey-white day fog with spider-trails of frost in it. When he entered the muster room at Ottawa Street he was not surprised to find that two constables had not turned up and that another, Bill McFarlane, had staggered in from his beat in the wee small hours, very sick indeed.

It had been a quiet night at Greenfield, however. Villains were no fonder of being out in such foul weather than were ordinary God-fearing citizens. Whatever toll the fog would take in lives – and down-and-outs would die in droves before the blanket lifted – the discovery and carrying in of ragged corpses had not yet begun. Along the river reach few folk were to be seen. Hedderwick's stood silent long after the opening hour. On Ottawa Street and along Dumbarton Road the fog hung so thick and clinging that horse traffic moved about as silently as ticks in wool.

Sergeant Drummond did not report for duty. He sent a message with a lad to say that he hoped to return tomorrow morning, all being well. Sergeant Stevens, on extra duty, delegated Craig to relieve Constable Cropper at the junction of Kingdom Road and Grace Street. Here the Burgh Sanitation Department had dug a great gaping trench in the cobbles which would in due time contain a new main drain but which, with fog down, presented a serious hazard to life and limb. Tommy Cropper was damned glad to see his relief emerge from the fog. He gave Craig a nod and muttered a few words of instruction regarding the duty before, coughing too, he trudged off into the murk to sign himself off to breakfast and to bed.

Six iron cans marked the limits of the trench. Each had a duckbill snout and a trailing wick of teased cotton which burned with a great soft yellow flame. On the pavement close at hand was a tap-barrel from which the cans were refuelled with oil and a bucket which held several pine torches, cloth-headed and soaked in tar. The burned-out stobs of the flares that had seen Tommy Cropper through the long watches of the night had been stuck in the mound of clay that banked the trench. The stench of smoke wicks and tar, added to the reek of the fog, disorganised the senses thoroughly just as the whole routine of the burgh had been disorganised, with trams and cabs, carts and trains, mails and cattle and bakers' drays all lost and immobilised, and pedestrians stumbling about like shades in purgatory.

Craig hefted up a fresh flare, lit it from one of the cans and rolled the pole in his hands to make the tar burn evenly. Holding the flare away from him he patrolled the perimeter of the trench and called out, "Mind your step. Take care. Take care," until his throat ached.

He peered north up Kingdom Road towards Dumbarton Road, head cocked. He could see nothing, hear little. He did not even know if it was dawn yet and listened for the chime of the Burgh Hall clock.

Bong. Bong. Bong. Booonnng . . .

The notes wavered, distorted and were lost as a draught of air stirred the fog and made the flare hiss and sizzle. Craig swung round. A cart was crawling up Kingdom Road towards him. He raised the flare high and shouted, "*Go cautious, carter. Hole in the road. Hole in the road.*"

It was only when the horse coughed, a barking sound, that Craig realised that the cart was close to the pavement on the left of the road. He still could not see it. Behind him was the knee-high mound of clay and cobblestones that had been excavated; behind that was the trench, four or five feet deep.

The cart loomed suddenly out of the fog, cutting the corner.

"CAREFUL, MAN, FOR GOD'S SAKE," Craig roared.

He ducked to one side, staring up at the wheel, saw on the board old Bob McAndrew, pipe in mouth, a monk's hood of sackcloth draped over his shoulders.

"STOP," Craig shouted. "DAMN YOU, STOP."

His whistle was buttoned into his pocket, his baton in the holster at his side. He did not dare use the flare to protect himself in case he frightened the horse and made it flyte away; a runaway in the blind streets would be a dreadful danger to women and children. He swung the flare down like a flag of surrender and the cart jerked to a halt inches from him.

"Huh!" Bob McAndrew said. "So it's you, is it?"

The old man took the pipe from his mouth and spat a gobbet of saliva forcefully on to Craig's chest.

Rage surged up in Craig, a narrow burning hatred of the old fool. He would have flung the tar pole at him if he had not been in uniform, on duty. The discipline of the past weeks saved him. He stabbed the pole into the mound and swung round again, spittle like lace on his breast.

He said, "Do you want to spend the bloody day in a cell in Ottawa Street?"

"An' who'll take me there? You?"

"Fog or no fog," Craig said, "I'll take you there an' I'll see to it that you stay."

"On what bloody charge, son?"

"Malicious assault on the person of a constable," said Craig, making it up without hesitation. "Fifty shillings or twenty days."

He stepped on to the wheel and hauled himself up until he was close enough to Bob McAndrew to snatch away the reins. He could not believe that he had once ridden on that cart, had chatted to this old josser and thought him a friend.

"I heard you were on their side," Bob McAndrew said. "I heard how you'd joined the bloody polis."

"Drive slow, carter," said Craig. "An' if you ever as much as look at me again—"

"You'll what?"

"I'll have you."

Bob McAndrew shrugged. "Malone knows. He knows."

"Knows what?"

"That you're in the polis."

"I don't give a monkey's curse what Malone knows. He's servin' a stretch o' twelve."

"Maybe he is," said Bob McAndrew. "An' maybe he isn't."

Craig raised himself higher, thrust his chest out.

"Now, wipe it off," he said.

"What?"

"You heard me. Wipe it off."

"I'll be buggered if—"

"Nobody spits on my uniform."

"Wipe it off wi' what but?"

"Your hand."

The old man hesitated; his defiance crumbled. He put out a mittened hand and rubbed away the stain of spit.

He apologised. "I – I shouldn't have done it. You'll no' take me in, Craig, will ye?"

Craig looked down at his uniform and then sharply up at the old man. He felt cool and level and satisfied, more satisfied than he had ever been, even with Kirsty in the bed in Canada Road all those weeks ago.

Balanced on the wheel he craned forward until the brim of his helmet dunted Bob McAndrew's brow and he could smell the strong moist tobacco odour of the old man's breath, see the shrivelling in the old man's rheumy eyes.

"Tell them down at the yard, tell Moss too," said Craig, "that I'll have my eye on them. One wrong step an' I'll book them. Got it?"

"Aye, aye; right."

Craig leaned back. "Now get this rig on the proper side o' the highway an' drive with due caution."

"I will. I will."

"What are you carryin'?"

"Nails."

"Where's your porter?"

"Got none. We're short-handed."

Craig nodded, stepped to the ground. He put his fists on his hips. "Get on with you then, carter."

The old man flicked the reins and the horse plodded forward. Craig did not step back, did not yield an inch as the wheel rolled close to him and the cart crawled past.

"Remember what I told you," Craig shouted, and found that his throat did not ache any more.

He watched the cart vanish swiftly into the fog then turned, jerked the flare from the bank of clay, held it aloft and, strutting, resumed his morning watch.

When Kirsty brought the hot dish into the dining-room she found that David Lockhart had his head bowed in prayer. It seemed fitting, somehow, that he should give thanks to the Lord. He did not start up guiltily or curtail his devotions, was not in the least embarrassed by her intrusion. Kirsty waited by the door until he unclasped his hands and opened his eyes.

He looked up, winked, smiled. "And what have you brought me, Kirsty?"

"What you asked for – sausages."

"Pollock's finest, no doubt. Made by the mile; sold by the ton." Kirsty laughed. "You've been here before, I see."

"The finest sausages in the kingdom. Aunt Nessie cooked them with her own fair hand, I suppose."

"She insisted on it. I think she spoils you."

"She always has done; my brother and I."

"Oh, you've a brother." Kirsty put the plate before him. "Is he a doctor too?"

"Almost," said David. "He's a medical student here in Glasgow."

"What's his name?" said Kirsty. "If you don't mind me askin'."

"Jack; John Knox Lockhart to be exact. John Knox, can you imagine?"

Kirsty said, "Is he younger than you?"

"Absolutely; a mere boy, in fact," said David. "Tell me, has your husband gone?"

"Yes."

"Aunt Nessie tells me he's a policeman."

"Yes."

David reached for the cruet and ran a neat little pile of salt on to the side of his plate. Kirsty noted the sign of good manners; not like Craig who would sprinkle the seasoning all over his food.

David said, "I really would have preferred to breakfast in the kitchen."

"Aunt Ness—I mean, Mrs Frew would never hear of it."

"She used to let me, in the old days." David cut one of the four brown bangers into slices with his knife. "Of course, she didn't take in guests when Andrew was alive."

"What was he like?"

"Fun," said David. "And funny."

"Funny?"

"Very hearty. I liked him."

"Will you have tea or coffee?" said Kirsty.

"What's in the pot?"

"Tea."

"That'll do nicely, thank you," David said. "Are you leaving, Kirsty?"

"I – I'm not supposed to—"

"Oh, come on! I'm not a guest. I'm not stuffy old Vass."

"Do you know Mr Vass?"

"I've been lectured by that august gentleman several times."

"He's very clever, isn't he?"

"Very educated, certainly," said David, eating. "Does your husband like being a policeman?"

"He doesn't say much about it. It's a good secure sort of occupation, though."

"I've a great admiration for 'the polis'," said David.

"Why?"

"Nobody loves them but everybody depends on them."

"I don't understand," said Kirsty.

"They tell people what to do and stop people doing what they want to do."

"Criminals?"

"Society would soon go to pot if it wasn't for policemen."

"Are you, by any chance, a lawyer as well as a doctor?"

David laughed. He wiped his lips with the linen napkin. "I have a medical qualification. Now I'm studying Divinity at Edinburgh University."

"Divinity? To be a minister?"

"Of sorts."

"I expect that's why your aunt favours you so much."

With mannered efficiency he had put away the sausages and allowed Kirsty to pour him tea. He drank it, she noticed, without sugar or milk.

Rising, he turned to the window that overlooked Walbrook Street.

"I'm not going to make it, I fear," he said.

"Why don't you just stay?"

"Alas, I can't. I must make the effort. If it thins about lunchtime I'm sure the company will try to squeeze a train through." He turned. "Are you – will you be here for long, Kirsty?"

"Until we're allocated a police house."

"Perhaps I'll see you again."

"Yes," said Kirsty. "Perhaps."

"I wish—" he began, then gave a little shake of the head as if to censor any indiscretion that might have popped into his mind. "Jack and I are off to Inverness for Christmas but in the New Year I'm sure I'll be in Glasgow again."

She held the warm teapot in both hands. It had been a bitsy conversation but it had seemed, to Kirsty at least, to be charged with a rapport for which there was no sensible explanation. Clearly Mr Lockhart came from a stratum of society far above her own. There should have been no common ground between them, yet the old attitudes and responses did not seem to count – perhaps because David was a doctor and a minister in the bud. Kirsty tried to convince herself that it was only Christian charity that lay behind his interest in her. She fervently hoped that she would see him again, talk with him again before she became ensnared in motherhood and the setting up of a proper home in Greenfield.

"I must be on my way," David said. "I wish you well, Kirsty."

She stood like a daftie, teapot in her hands, tongue-tied as he hurried from the dining-room to kiss his aunt, put on his coat and hurry out into the grey, enfolding fog. It was strange, strange and troubling, this sudden new surge of feeling.

From the window she watched him hasten down the steps to the pavement. She wanted to call out to him, make some gesture, leave some mark or memory that he could carry away with him, but she felt coy and shy, and discovered, to her chagrin, that to this man as to no other she did not know how to say goodbye.

SIX

The Fostering Breast

Four days before Christmas Craig brought her the glad tidings.

"Guess what," he said, "we've been allocated a police house."

"Where?"

"Canada Road; the upper end," said Craig, grinning. "The building's only six years old."

"How big is the house?" said Kirsty.

"Kitchen an' *two* bedrooms, would ye believe."

"When do we take possession?"

"Well, it's supposed to be ours from the first o' the year but I've agreed to hold off entry until the end of January."

"Why?"

"Because o' the circumstances." Craig studied the buttons of his tunic and carefully began to unfasten them. "Because o' the family that's there at the moment."

"What family?"

Craig said, "Oh, some constable from Percy Street. I don't know him at all. Macgregor's his name."

"Dismissed?"

Craig shook his head. "Dyin'."

The kitchen was full of steam. She had put out washing on the lines in the backcourt that morning but there had been rain and she had brought it in again, draped it on the high pulley where, in the heat from the stove, it had given off a soft haze of steam for hours on end. If Craig had not been uncommonly prompt she would have had the place tidied and ventilated. As it was he had caught her unprepared. She felt a sudden wave of anxiety and seated herself at the table, her hands in her lap.

Craig said, "It's no' our fault. About Macgregor."

"No," Kirsty said.

Craig draped his tunic on a chair and seated himself too. He stooped to unlace his boots. They were caked with mud which, Kirsty had learned, indicated that he had made a patrol along the railway embankment late in the afternoon. She had an irrational fear that he would be mown down by a train, though Craig had

213

assured her there was not the slightest danger of that happening.

He looked up, squinting. "I thought you'd be pleased, Kirsty."

Kirsty said, "I am."

Craig said, "You won't even have to meet him, y'know."

"Who?"

"Macgregor."

"I – it's not that, dear."

"They're goin' home, back to Islay where they came from. Maybe he'll get better in the sea air." Craig paused. "If it's not that, what is it?"

"Everythin' seems to be happenin' at once."

"We'll have a couple of months to settle in the house before the baby arrives. I'll do all the heavy work, never fear."

"Aye," said Kirsty. "It'll be grand when we're in."

Craig removed his other boot, set the pair against the fender, not too near the fire. When the mud had dried he would take the boots out into the back yard and scrape off the caked dirt with an old penknife, bring them back for Kirsty to polish to a high black shine.

He did not draw his chair back to the table but remained by the grate, toasting his brow and his hands at the coals.

The stewpot bubbled.

"You don't want to go at all, do ye?" Craig said.

"Of course I do."

"You don't want to go with me."

"Craig—"

Three months ago she would have flung herself from the chair, would have wrapped her arms about his neck, would have fussed over him and given him reassurance. But tonight, now, she felt too selfish and too uncertain to play the comforter with conviction. Besides, Craig no longer seemed to need her.

Craig said, "You'd rather stay here, wouldn't you?"

"No. I'm your wife an'—"

"You're not my wife, Kirsty."

"I am," she said. "Everybody thinks I'm your wife."

"That doesn't make it a fact."

"Tell me about the house," said Kirsty. "Have you seen it yet?"

He turned his head and glowered at her. His dark eyes were sullen and secretive but there was no animosity in them. He seemed to see her now with disciplined control, that dispassion with which he observed the denizens of Greenfield's meanest streets and hovels, not with pity or disgust but with patient calculation.

"Aye," he answered. "Hector Drummond took me up there when the note came down from Headquarters that the house was for us."

"Tell me," said Kirsty, feigning enthusiasm.

"Top floor, of four. Eight families in the close. All burgh employees."

"Policemen?"

"Six lots of coppers at least."

"A – a community, then," Kirsty. "It'll be nice."

"It'll be safe," Craig said.

She did not ask him to explain, believing, wrongly, that she understood.

Later that night, after Craig had gone to bed, Kirsty took a late supper with Agnes Frew in the parlour.

"So you're leaving us, Kirsty," the old woman said. "I'll confess I'll be sore grieved to see you go."

"I'm not off to the moon," said Kirsty. "I'll still be at St Anne's every Sunday."

"After the baby comes that'll stop."

"Craig can look after baby for an hour or two."

"He'll be on duty."

"Not every Sunday," said Kirsty.

"This won't be your only child," Mrs Frew said. "You'll have more. Soon you'll be so tied to your family that you won't have time for the kirk, let alone me."

Though she suspected that the prediction might be true, Kirsty said, "Nonsense."

She had made a pot of tea and had buttered oatcakes. Seated on a spindle chair at the occasional table, she ate and drank with the delicacy of a lady born to the manor. The prospect of going back to Greenfield did not appeal to her. She no longer wanted a place of her own, to be alone with Craig night after night, listening to his silences.

"I know somebody who'll be sorry," said Agnes Frew.

"Hmmm?" Kirsty had been day-dreaming, teacup to her lips. "Who?"

"David Lockhart."

Kirsty was taken aback. "What's Mr Lockhart got to do wi' me?"

"I'd a letter from him this morning. He enquired after you specially; asks to be remembered to you."

"I hardly know the man."

"But you made an impression, Kirsty. He says he hopes to see you again next time he's in Glasgow."

Blushing, Kirsty asked, "How – how often is he in Glasgow?"

"From time to time."

"When he visits his brother, I expect."

"Oh, so he told you about Jack. You obviously got on well." Mrs Frew spoke with an archness that Kirsty did not like. "Jack's lodging's very small and he's prohibited from having overnight visitors. When David visits, the pair of them usually put up here."

"He – he seemed very pleasant," said Kirsty. "As a person I mean; a very pleasant person."

"Are you blushin'?"

"It's the heat in this room," said Kirsty quickly.

Mrs Frew tried not to smile. "That's what David said about you; the exact words – a very pleasant person."

"He's just being polite."

"He never said it about Cissie, and she was here for years."

"Mrs Frew, I'm—"

"Yes, yes," said Mrs Frew. "I know you're married. Even so, it's nice to be noticed by a gentleman, isn't it?"

"He could hardly fail to notice me, could he?" Kirsty glanced down at her stomach. "What does Mr Lockhart do?"

"After his ordination he'll return to China."

"China?"

"His parents are missionaries."

"China," said Kirsty. "When – when will he go?"

"In six or eight months, I suppose," said Mrs Frew.

"For – for how long?"

"For ever," Mrs Frew said.

"You mean he won't come back to Scotland?"

"His parents never did. Mission work is a calling, you see, a vocation. David and John were born to it."

"Born in China?"

"No. David was born in Inverness before his parents set off for Nanking. His mother was my friend as well as being a distant relative. She writes to me still from time to time. But somehow or other when furlough time comes around there are always reasons why they cannot leave."

"But David, his brother too—?"

"The boys could have been educated in China but Amelia and Richard elected to send them home," said Mrs Frew. "They were put into the care of Amelia's brother, George, and stayed with him in Invermoy while they attended Inverness Academy."

"Do all missionaries have to study medicine?"

"Of course not," said Mrs Frew. "Devotion to duty and strength in the Lord are all that's required, particularly for the China stations. David and Jack, however, are destined to take over the administration of the schools and hospitals that their parents founded, to run the North China Missionary Society in course of time."

Kirsty had no real notion where China was. She knew only that the people there were heathens, had slanted eyes and wore pigtails. She listened in fascinated interest as Agnes Frew talked of the vast and mysterious land across the seas; and suddenly Canada Road did not seem so far away after all. She wanted to ask the widow if she thought David would be happy in China but the question, she realised, had no validity. He had been born to it, his whole life shaped for service in a foreign land. She could not imagine the young man for whom she had cooked sausages on a foggy morning in Walbrook Street striding the hills of China, healing the sick and preaching the Gospel.

"*Chung-kuo*," Mrs Frew was saying. "The Middle Kingdom. That's what the Chinese call their homeland. The rest of us dwell in the Kingdom Outside. Isn't that ridiculous?"

Kirsty nodded, though she did not think it at all ridiculous.

Mrs Frew rose abruptly. She opened a little cupboard to the right of the fireplace, knelt and rummaged on the shelves for a moment. Idly Kirsty put the supper dishes on to the wooden tray.

Mrs Frew got up.

"See." She held out a book, a big soft quarto bound like a bible in black morocco. "It's all in here. All about China. David gave it to Andrew and me years and years ago, when he first stayed with us. Oh, he was hardly more than a child then. It was the first time he'd been away from his mother and father."

Kirsty took the book into her hands.

Mrs Frew had opened it at the flyleaf upon which was written in a large round script: *To Uncle Andrew and Auntie Nessie, With All My Love, From David. Christmas 1883.*

With sudden clarity Kirsty saw herself in the mid-winter of that year, when she was four years old, curled in the cot in the bleak and echoing dormitory of the Baird Home, crying into her pillow for the mammy she had never known, crying and trying to hide her tears.

"Take it," said Mrs Frew. "Take it and read it, dear. It's most informative."

"Thank you," said Kirsty.

She stared at the handwriting, the ink faded from black to sepia, the edges of the pages deckled yellow: *With All My Love, From David*.

She brushed her hand lightly over the paper as if to smooth it and, at that moment and for the first time, felt within her body a queer sharp little dig as if the new life inside her had served a reminder of its presence, had given her, in remonstrance, a sign.

Christmas celebrations began with a musical recital in St Anne's by the Greenfield Choral Association which performed a grand recitation of the sacred cantata *The Good Shepherd* and other gems from the seasonal repertoire.

Mrs Frew clucked approvingly over the choir's perfect balance and fine modulation of tone but Kirsty had no clue what lay behind her feelings of joy and exultation, why the music lifted her so and seemed to hold her suspended or why it made her raise her eyes to the vaulted roof and to the dim enigmatic shapes of painted glass in the depths of the nave, so quiet and tranquil and unmoved behind the heads of the choir.

When a quartet, composed of one lady and three gentlemen, sang *Love Divine, All Loves Excelling* Kirsty found tears trickling down her cheeks. She tried to hide them but Mrs Frew, dabbing her eyes with a handkerchief too, patted Kirsty's hand approvingly as if such a reaction was only to be expected.

The walked home, arm in arm, with Kirsty exclaiming, "Was that not wonderful?" and Mrs Frew saying, "It was, dear, it was," until they found Craig in the kitchen, trousers unbuttoned and boots off, slumped snoring in a chair before the fire with the remains of his supper still on the table waiting to be cleared away. Kirsty sighed, slipped off her coat and rolled up her sleeves while Mrs Frew, with a sniff, took herself into the parlour to sip a little glass of brandy before bed.

As Constable Third Grade, Craig drew Christmas Day duty. Dinner was postponed until late evening so that he might take his place at the head of the table.

With the goose cooking, pies and puddings all prepared and the dining-room table laid with silver and best linen, Kirsty put on her good new dress and took tea in the parlour with Mrs Frew. She drank two glasses of sherry while the tea was masking in the pot and was only saved from a giggling fit by the arrival of Hugh and Beatrice Affleck. They brought a gift for Nessie and a 'reminder' for Kirsty, an album of blank grey pages which, Hugh Affleck said, would soon contain photographic records of her babies and, in years not so far ahead of her, would give her something to look back upon.

For an hour they drank tea, ate sausage rolls and currant cake and laughed. Hugh Affleck was at his very best. He told hilarious tales against himself and against the dignity of the burgh police until the tears ran down Kirsty's cheeks. She was sorry when, at a quarter to six, the Afflecks explained to Nessie that they were dining with the Mackinnons at seven o'clock and had to pick up the girls at home first. Carrying their gifts, unopened, they took their leave.

"My nieces can't stand to visit me," said Agnes Frew when the house was quiet again, "not even at Christmas."

She looked so down in the mouth that Kirsty gave her a kiss and a hug and poured another glass of sherry to cheer her up.

Craig came home with cheeks flushed and a faint smell of whisky on his breath. He said that Hector Drummond had given them all a dram when they finished shift and had wished them a merry time but had warned them not to imbibe too heavily since they were all required on duty on Boxing Day when the wild boys of Greenfield, dogging work, were prone to brawl and booze and engage in acts of petty theft. Washed, Craig put on a tweed jacket and flannel trousers and knotted a ridiculous spotted cravat into the collar of his shirt. He looked, said Mrs Frew with uncommon candour, as if he had just moored his yacht at Plantation Quay.

Dinner was pleasant enough. Gifts were exchanged at the end of the meal. Craig had bought a pendant for Kirsty and a cameo brooch for Mrs Frew. He received from the widow a pair of smart black kidskin gloves which could be worn with his uniform in cold weather without offending regulations; from Kirsty a beautiful red rubber 'diving cap' and a pair of goggles to keep the water out of his eyes when he swam underwater. Kirsty's gift to Mrs Frew was a bottle of *Lily of the Valley* perfume. In turn she received a baby's shawl of Honiton lace so fine that it could be drawn smoothly through a silver napkin ring if not quite through Kirsty's wedding band. But after that the evening turned flat and listless, for they were all tired.

It was not much after eleven when, with the great mound of pots and plates all washed and put away, Mrs Frew retired and Craig and Kirsty were left alone in the kitchen.

On the shelf above the fire was propped a single card, a greeting from Mrs Frew to Kirsty and Craig.

Craig took it down and glanced at it. "Did the postman bring this?"

"No."

"What did the postman bring?"

"Some cards for Mrs Frew, that's all."

"Nothin' from Carrick?"

"No, Craig, nothin'."

He replaced Mrs Frew's card and lit a cigarette, holding the match cupped in his hand for a moment or two, watching the flame. He shook it out and flicked it into the hearth, inhaled, blew smoke through his nostrils.

Kirsty said, "Did you send them somethin', dearest?"

"Aye, somethin' for each o' them."

"Perhaps tomorrow—"

"I thought Dad might've written, since it's Christmas."

"Christmas doesn't mean much. He'll write at New Year, you'll see."

Craig shrugged, pretending that he did not care.

Kirsty put an arm about his waist and her head on his shoulder. Craig blew tobacco smoke over her head.

"She must've stopped him," Craig said. "Mother, I mean. She'll have put the kibosh on communication."

"When we're in our new house—"

"That's all I keep hearin'." Craig curled his lip sarcastically. "When we're in the new house. When the baby's born."

Kirsty disengaged herself. Though he had been cheerful all evening she sensed now that Christmas meant nothing to him, served only to rub the wounds of disappointment that he kept hidden from her.

"When we get married—" he murmured, and blew out a smoke ring. "When the bloody cows come home!"

"Craig," she said. "What's wrong wi you? Don't you like the job?"

"Aye, I like the job fine," he answered. "What I don't like is bein' away from it."

Kirsty gasped – "*Oh*" – and swung away from him. She found herself at the sink, a washing-cloth in her hand. She wiped the dry draining-board, wiped it again.

He came to her quickly, placed his hands on her shoulders and drew her round. Her belly protruded, keeping them apart. Craig held her at half arm's length. He leaned forward, kissed her.

"I didn't mean you, love," he said.

Kirsty blinked, striving to keep tears from trickling from her lids, praying that she would not weep.

Dispassionately Craig kissed her again, upon the tip of the nose.
Kirsty heard herself say, "I know you didn't."
Craig smiled, nodded. "All right then?"
"All right," said Kirsty.

They drank keg Export from the taps of the railway bar in the
North British station and warmed their fingers and toes at the
coals in the grate of the huge black iron fireplace that dominated
the refreshment room. Jack ordered a second half pint to wash
down the three smoked mackerel and the baked potato from
which he had made a second breakfast. He had every right to be
peckish; he had been up before six to struggle through from
Glasgow and had had only a heel of bread and a cup of coffee
extract in his lodgings with which to fortify himself for his journey
to the capital. There was snow in the clouds and a taste of winter
on the wind and the draughts that slithered through Princes
Street Gardens and down the steps from the Waverley Bridge
were snell enough to chill the blood of all but the most hardy
travellers who were on the road that Boxing Day.

The Lockhart brothers would have gone north before Christmas as was their habit – Jack had been free of Anatomy since
the 21st – but David had been invited to take part in a Christmas
Day service in St Giles. As the offer had come directly from his
Professor of Divinity, and the Reverend Matthew Walters was a
prime supporter of ecumenicalism and union in the Presbyterian
churches, it would have been churlish of David to refuse. Uncle
George would have missed their company at the festive board in
his house in Invermoy parish but he was a gregarious man with
many friends in the parish and no doubt he had found a hearth
upon which to plant his boots and a host with which to split a
bottle of good Madeira wine. He would have the boys for the New
Year, the best of Highland celebrations, but would have to
content himself with the knowledge that this would be the last
they would spend together; soon his nephews would be gone from
Scotland and he would not see either of them again unless he
packed his bag and shipped out for Shanghai.

Twenty-two months separated the Lockhart boys but they were
so alike in appearance they might have been taken for twins.
Jack was a little taller than his brother, a little leaner too. By
temperament he was less outgoing, perhaps because he lacked
David's ease of manner and had had to work harder at his studies,
at games, at making friends. There was no envy or animosity
between them, however. Jack accepted David's leadership while

David in turn had nothing but admiration for his brother's thoroughness and determination.

"Did the Lesson go well, then?" Jack asked.

"Seemed to," said David. "All I could see out there were grey stone piers and tattered flags."

"No congregation?"

"Pale faces floating in a fog of history."

"Oh, come now, David."

David grinned. "It's like preaching from a rock in the ocean, if you must know."

"Weren't you nervous?"

"Not particularly."

"I should have been."

"I was too cold to be nervous."

"Was old Matthew pleased, do you think?"

"He took me for supper afterwards with Guthrie and Pettigrew and old Neb."

"Neb? Really? Where did you eat?"

"At Guthrie's house."

"My, you are moving in exalted circles."

"Guthrie knew Father rather well in the old days. I think he was under the impression that I was a starving waif and that he was giving me a treat – like an orphans' tea-party," David said. "No, I mustn't be cynical."

"No," said Jack. "You mustn't."

"Still, it's odd how deferential these granite pillars of the kirk can be."

"What's your definition of 'deferential'?" Jack said.

"They seem to covet Father's life-style, his years in the field, acting for God. They regard mission work as *real* Christianity. They are under the impression that Mother and Father *suffer* all the time."

"Suffer? They love the work," Jack said.

"Of course they do," said David. "But the 'talkers' truly imagine that they sacrifice everything to minister to the heathen."

"Sacrifice a house in Marchmont Terrace, a generous stipend and the adoration of the old ladies of Edinburgh?" said Jack. "It sounds little enough to me – by way of sacrifice, I mean."

"Do you know what Neb told me – this, mark you, after a twenty-minute sermon on Disruption Calvinism – he clutched my wrist as if he were drowning in his own verbosity and quoted: *For every idle word that men shall speak, they shall give account*. And he keeked at me as if he expected me to absolve him from something

or other, as if the fact that I'd tramped the hills of China with Dad
had bestowed upon me some special grace."

"What nonsense," said Jack.

"Absolutely," said David; he paused. "Do you remember
much about China?"

"Of course; don't you?"

"This and that," said David. "When I think hard about it."

"Don't you think about it?"

"Not often."

"I do," said Jack.

"Are you dyin' to get back?"

Jack did not hesitate, did not ponder his reply. "Yes."

David said, "What do you remember?"

Jack laughed. "I remember the harmonium."

"The harmonium," said David. "Lord, yes, on the hill track
out of Honan. That must have been the very first time that Dad
took us both with him."

"When the donkey died."

"Yes."

"There we were with this gigantic great harmonium couped
over in the dust, Dad prancing round it, wringing his hands."

"He was very fond of that harmonium."

"Lord knows, it cost enough," said Jack.

"Yes," said David. "Do you remember how he had us all put
our shoulders to the wheel and heave it upright and then fitted us
into the shafts like coolies. He was not going to give in."

"What I remember," said Jack, "is how we had gone but a
quarter of a mile or so before we had a dozen willing helpers, not
even converts. They just seemed to appear, materialise, and
dragged the thing up the hill to Fanshi in no time at all."

"And Mr Wang, do you remember him?" said David.

"How could one forget him, with his bad temper—"

"And his opium kit."

"It always struck me as odd," said Jack, "that Dad would
entrust our language teaching to an opium-eater."

"Perhaps he didn't know," said David.

"Oh, he knew. Of course he knew. I think he had his eye
on a miraculous conversion. I wonder what happened to
Wang."

"He died," said David. "Mother wrote to us, don't you recall,
some six or seven years ago."

"The poppy finally killed him."

"Cholera, I believe "

"There wasn't much to kill; all skin and bone."

"Aye, but could he talk, could he tell tales!" said David.

The northerly wind surged across the platforms and rattled the doors of the refreshment room and the young men turned from the fire and glanced at them, almost as if they expected to see a Chinaman there, the spectre of Mr Wang summoned by the very mention of his name.

Two girls, escorted by their father, entered. They were young, pretty as painted china in loose sacque overcoats with facings of blue-black velvet and neat little boots with pointed patent-leather toes – twenty or thirty guineas each upon their backs – conscious of their breeding and their appealing style. Father was a musk-ox of a man, his belly filling his double-breasted overcoat, and the silk tile-hat set square on a bush of greying pomaded hair. He lumbered to a chair, seated himself upon it and raised one hand to summon service while his daughters settled themselves, giggling, and, within seconds, caught sight of the Lockhart boys and went into a dove-dance of flirtation.

"What do you think of them, David?" murmured Jack.

"I can't imagine them on skates, can you?"

Jack laughed. "Falling on their little bottoms – no, I can't."

"Are they still givin' us the eye?"

"In trumps," said Jack.

"I wonder why."

"Because we're handsome, well-set-up young fellows."

"What can come of it, though?"

"Nothing. It's amusement. Practice, I suppose. Come now, David, you haven't turned priggish on me, have you?"

"Certainly not," David said. "I just—"

"Papa is castin' a cold eye over us now."

"He can probably calculate our circumstances to the last farthing." David inched round in his chair and glanced casually at the family group. "By Gum, though, ain't he fierce!"

"Probably beats the servants."

"I wouldn't be surprised."

Jack put down his glass. "I do rather care for the little dark one, though."

"Can you see her in Fanshi in August?" said David. "Can you imagine her wielding a mopping-cloth in the baby-school?"

"No," said Jack reluctantly. "That I cannot do."

"They aren't for us, lad. Never will be, their sort."

"No harm in lookin', Davy."

"No harm at all," David conceded but turned again to face the fireplace and, with legs thrust out before him, settled his hands over his chest as if he intended to sleep.

"I'm glad I'm not Popish," said Jack. "Shouldn't at all like to be a priest."

"Celibacy may have its advantages," said David.

"I thought you liked Miss Dickie. Is that all off?"

"It was never on," said David. "Oh, Sarah's all right."

"I'll say," Jack put in. "More than all right."

"It's pointless, Jack. Pointless."

"Because we're going overseas so soon?"

David said, "I don't want to fall in love."

"I thought you liked being in love."

"I mean seriously."

"Dad loves Mother."

"I'm sure he does," said David.

"Made in Heaven, that one."

"Yes." David fished in his vest pocket and brought out a pocket-watch, clipped open the cover. "It's time to go."

"Must say I'll be glad to get home," said Jack.

David buttoned his overcoat and adjusted his scarf. "Do you mean to China, with Dad and Mother?"

"I meant Invermoy, actually," said Jack. "But yes, I admit that I will be glad to return to China, to be set on the right path at last."

"Can you remember what they look like?"

"Mother and Dad?"

"Yes. I can't, not clearly."

"I can; from the photograph."

"That's old. They'll have changed."

"We've changed, that's for sure," said Jack. "I doubt if they'll recognise you come August."

"If I go back," said David softly, "come August."

"*What* did you say?"

"I'm not sure I want to go back."

"I can't believe my ears."

"Oh, I expect I shall."

"It's not a matter of what you expect, David; it's what is expected of you."

"No call to get het up, Jack."

"After all the planning, the study, the money that Uncle George has laid out—"

"Come on, I think I hear our train."

"Bother the train!"

"You won't say that if we miss the connection at Perth."

"David, tell me that you didn't mean it, about not going back."

"I'll be in Nanking in August, never fear. Trained and ordained."

They moved across the refreshment room, David in the lead, his brown leather portmanteau clutched in his fist.

As they passed the girls, each sipping hot Russian tea from a glass, he stared at them deliberately and his sudden scowling attention made them flutter, flush and look away. He went on, Jack at his heels, out of the warmth and on to the cold reaches of the platform towards the great clouds of white vapour and roiling black smoke that hid the locomotive.

Jack caught him by the sleeve.

"David, the truth now."

"Jack, you idiot, I meant nothing by it."

"Word of honour?"

"Word of honour."

"Cross your heart."

Ruefully David studied his brother as steam hissed and billowed about them and then, with his index finger, he carefully traced the sign over his heart.

"Is that better?" David asked.

Jack nodded, grinned with relief, and let his brother steer him towards the waiting train.

Tickets for the Greenfield Burgh Police Annual New Year Concert were at a premium. Chief Constable Organ was a great one for fostering good relations with the public and the concert, under his patronage, had become quite an event in the burgh. On Thursday evening the Greenfield Hall would be packed, not only with officers, their friends and relatives but with a wheen of those ragtag citizens who spent most of the year cursing the police blue-blind but who, when it came to the bit, could not resist a cheap night's entertainment.

Craig had requested three tickets. He had received them at the muster that morning. It did not occur to him that he had never before taken Kirsty out for an evening that had to be paid for, and he was keen to surprise her, and old Frew, that night at supper. He had been careful to make discreet enquiries to ensure that the concert did not clash with some holy singsong at St Anne's.

On and off all morning Craig thought about it as he did his rounds of the streets. He took his dinner – paid for, of course – in the dingy back shop of Dinaro's Café which lay a few hundred yards off his patch. There he met up with Archie Flynn and Peter Stewart who were also taking their half-hour rest period.

Archie had 'found' a printed copy of the concert programme slapped to a wall near the *Baffin Bay* and had removed it before some urchin could deface it. The constables discussed the programme with enthusiasm, particularly the 'star' attractions: J. C. Wilson was a Negro who did 'eccentric dancing', whatever that meant; Mr Harry Lauder was a purveyor of humorous Scotch songs; and the beautiful Miss Phoebe Donaldson was a singer of legendary reputation who, only a couple of weeks ago, had reduced the stalwarts of the Partick Burgh Force to jelly with her rendering of *Tell Her I'll Love Her*.

"Not a dry eye in the house, so I heard," said Archie Flynn.

"Och, they would all have been at the whisky," said Peter Stewart. "It would be alcohol they would be sheddin'."

"I hear she's a real stunner," Archie said. "Fergusson's seen her in Glasgow. He tells me she's got the biggest pair o' globes he's ever clapped eyes on. When she hits her top notes, Fergusson says, she quivers."

"Quivers?" said Peter. "What quivers?"

"For God's sake, man!" said Craig. "What do you think quivers?"

"Not her bloody vocal chords," said Archie.

"You mean her—?" said Peter.

"Nearly pops out her dress," said Archie.

"My God!" said Peter, dusky-cheeked.

"All that an' music too for sixpence," said Craig. "Three cheers for Organ, eh?"

"Aye, if Phoebe does pop out o' her dress," said Archie, "they'll make him the bloody Provost on the spot."

They laughed uproariously and embellished on the theme of Miss Donaldson's lily-white bosom while they ate their fried-egg rolls and drank hot tea. But they also kept an eye on the clock in case Sergeant Drummond came to check on them.

Craig carried the laughter with him into the cold gusty streets. He did not feel cold, clad in lamb's-wool combinations and heavy serge uniform. He had stamina too now and did not tire in the course of the long shift.

One of Hedderwick's big wagons had broken an axle. The load had shifted and part of St John Street was closed. Craig jawed the workers and told them to get a move on, borrowed four bollards from the yard and set them up to signpost the diversion and kept himself warm and occupied for a full two hours steering cart traffic round into Banff Street until the repair was completed and the wagon hauled upright and driven off.

Night came swiftly, sullenly. Bruised winter gloaming showed up the prickling lights of the city. Spurts of fire from a foundry vent only made it more lonely. Craig stopped in a close that already had its gas-lamp lit, took out the three concert tickets and looked at them again. He thought of Phoebe Donaldson and wondered if her breasts were really bigger than Kirsty's and if they would feel as soft and heavy in a man's hands. Hastily he stuffed the tickets back into his pocket and plodded on to check on Joseph McGhee's pawnbroking shop and to inspect and sign the Pledge Book which was part of his daily duty. He found old Joe half asleep in his cane chair with the *Evening Citizen* on his knee and a little marmalade cat draped like a collar about his neck. He went on into Brunswick Lane to make sure that the apprentice at Hannah's Gas Appliances had fitted up the new set of shutters and padlocked them properly. There had been three break-ins at Hannah's in as many months, for copper tubing and lead sheets were like magnets to thieves. All was secure. The caretaker, Mr Pritchard, gave him a signal through the window of his cubby.

The embankment: trains rolled and chattered past one after another. It was not the time for suicides or accidents, not the quiet-line time when the glinting iron tracks brought out the daft and the despairing or children keen to risk their lives in dangerous play. Craig did not need a lamp tonight. He knew his way along the slope, could make himself stand without flinching only feet below the Dumbarton Express as it thundered past, the faces of passengers flickering in the windows like silhouettes in a kinegraphic machine. He came down into the street at the bridge, checked his watch and gravitated up towards the corner where Constable McNair would meet him and take over the watch.

He was twenty minutes early, did not want to loiter in case he was being observed by a sergeant or an inspector. He looked up to the corner and then went on up North Sydney Street, a nondescript three hundred yards which stole into Peter Stewart's beat at the corner where, beyond the long low sheds of a cotton-waste dealer's yard, stood a lone tenement, an old smoke-grimed stump inhabited, as far as Craig had heard, by peaceable tenants.

He was still some fifty yards from the building when he heard the scream. It was piercing and prolonged and sucked off into a gasping cry that made him think, just for an instant, that it came from the throat of a murder victim. Craig was already running.

Far off, not in North Sydney but up in the narrows of Friar Street, he saw a small crowd of men assembled outside the *Rembrandt*, a cosy little public house, saw them turn too. Sensing danger, he fumbled for his whistle. The hairs on the nape of his neck bristled when the scream broke out again, from above his head this time.

He stopped. He looked up. A white face, thin white arms jutted from a third-floor window. Craig asked no questions. He tugged his whistle from his pocket and his truncheon from its holster and went into the close and up the stairs three at a time. By the time he reached the second landing he could hear another sound, a man's voice, not deep and angry but shrill, pathetic. "*Oh, help, help, help me. Help me. Please, help me.*"

Craig recognised the voice; Peter Stewart's.

He paused before the half-open door, pushed it tentatively with his foot. "Peter," he called. "It's Craig. I'm comin' in."

He had no notion of what crime had been committed but the fact that Peter was in need of assistance tempered Craig's urgency with caution. He stepped carefully into the tiny hallway, glanced to his left. The girl was indistinct against billowing net curtains. She was no longer screaming, thank God. Her hands swung limply by her sides. Head cocked, she rocked back and forth on the balls of her feet crooning to herself in a sweet grieving whine that made the hair rise again on Craig's neck.

"*Craig. Here, Craig. Please, Craig.*"

The inner door was ajar. Craig tapped it with the truncheon and stepped into the kitchen.

There was never any question of criminal charges of negligence or neglect. The Cadells were honest, upright Christians. Father was a cobbler in a closet business on Dumbarton Road, as industrious and temperate as a man could be. He had gone that evening with his wife and five of his seven children to a prayer meeting at the Revivalist Mission in Scotstoun. They had left home only a quarter of an hour before the accident occurred. Irene Cadell was fifteen years old, a sensible girl. Eldest in the family, she was well used to caring for her brothers and sisters. No blame could be attached to Irene for what happened. No blame could be attached to anyone. A hundred thousand identical pots bubbled on fifty thousands hobs across the city. Innumerable children played on the floor below leaded ranges. Why little three-year-old Susan had reached up and pulled on the protruding handle of the pot would never be known. Perhaps she had stumbled.

Though Irene had been in the room with the child her back had been turned and the first thing she had heard was the clash of the big pot as it fell from the hob, her sister's shriek of agony as a quart of boiling water splashed over her head and shoulders.

Irene had run next door but had found the house empty. In panic she had flung open the bedroom window and screamed for help. By chance, sore chance, Constable Stewart had been approaching the tenement at that moment. He had sprinted upstairs and into the house to find wee Susan Cadell writhing upon the carpet, the pot upturned on the fender. She had been unable to utter a sound. She had swallowed a quantity of boiling water and that, coupled with severe shock, had rendered her mute. She was scarlet, blistering and blind. She plucked with her little fists at the collar of her dress while she rolled on her back on the sodden carpet.

When Peter had lifted her in his arms she had gone into a spasm, rigid and jerking, had stopped breathing. Peter later admitted that he had panicked. All that he had learned by rote in Sergeant Mannering's Ambulance and First Aid Class had vanished from his mind. Blood, wounds, he could have coped with – but not this drenched and choking child. Smothering her convulsions, he had called for help while the elder girl, her reason quite gone, had remained at the window, screaming.

"Put her down, damn it, Peter," Craig snapped. "Here, man, on the dry floor."

"Craig she's—"

"*Let her go, Peter.*"

"Take her. You take her. Please take her."

Kneeling, Peter Stewart thrust the child at Craig and Craig, stooped over, received the little body into his arms. She was still alive, still twitching. He had no clue as to whether she was choking from obstruction or from the scalding. First Aid: the child was not comatose but convulsive. He stretched her out upon the boards and opened her lips with his fingers, brought her tongue forward, a little soft moist thing against his forefinger, and she gave a snorting sigh and spluttered out some water.

"Peter, pull yoursel' together, for Christ's sake," Craig shouted. "Fetch me a cloth, a clean one."

Still on his knees Peter peered at Craig as if he did not understand the words. Craig turned, slapped him with loose knuckles across the cheek. "A cloth, a towel. An' a big blanket. Quick."

"Wha' – what?" Peter Stewart said.

The child was still twitching. Craig noted that a vast area of her head and upper body had been drenched. But water scalds, if he recalled rightly, did not penetrate down through the layers of skin; there might be hope for her yet if he could obtain immediate expert assistance. He left the child where she was, pushed Peter to one side, found the hole-in-the-wall bed. He ripped off a blanket and undersheet, spread them on the floor, picked up the child and placed her face down. He could not understand why she did not seem to react to pain, why she was so silent. He glanced towards the door. The elder girl was nowhere to be seen. Rapidly he wrapped sheet and blanket around the child. He left a flap of the top so that her face would not be covered. He lifted her as gently as possible in his arms, well supported. She was still twitching. Her head lolled against his forearm like that of a new-born baby.

He nudged Peter with his boot.

"Get up, man, for God's sake. I'm takin' her to the Western Infirmary."

Peter nodded, a glint of sense in his expression at long last. "Aye, that's—"

"You stay here with the other one. She's in a bad way too. Root out a neighbour. Find out where the family's gone. Might be the pub. Might be anywhere. Send somebody to find them and bring them back. Do you hear me, Peter?"

"Aye."

"On your feet then."

Peter scrambled up as Craig, the bundle in his arms, turned towards the kitchen door.

"Cr-Craig?"

"What?"

"D-don't t-tell anyone. Promise me you – you won't."

"Christ!" Craig said.

He ran out of the Cadells' house, downstairs into the street.

He was three hundred yards from Dumbarton Road. The Western Infirmary was the nearest hospital. He might, he supposed, have tried to find a doctor or have run the half-mile to Ottawa Street but he felt the child clinging to life through him, trustingly. He ran as fast as he could towards the thoroughfare.

Passers-by stepped hastily out of his path as if he were a ruffian; and Craig ran towards the lights of Dumbarton Road and, when he reached it, ran straight into the middle of the road through the growling traffic. He spotted a hack at the stance at the bottom of Peel Street. The cabbie spotted him at the same moment and reached for the brake and the whip to speed away from trouble.

Craig bawled, "YOU WAIT," charged across the road and, loosening one hand from the bundle, grabbed the horse by the snaffle.

"What the hell d'you think—" the cabbie began.

Very distinctly Craig said, "I am gettin' into your hack an' you are goin' to drive me to the Western Infirmary as fast as you bloody well can. Right?"

"Eh?"

"You heard."

"I never heard a word about who'll pay me."

"I'll pay you, you bastard. Now drive."

Craig hoisted himself into the back and sat back. He was winded, heart pounding. Sweat trickled down his spine. He did not dare look at the child. He convinced himself that he could still feel the pressure of her tiny fists as they clung trustingly to him. He snuggled her lightly against him and closed his eyes. He heard the crack of the whip, felt the surge of the hackney carriage as it started away from the kerb.

He kept his eyes closed.

He whispered, "There now, there now, my wee lamb. You'll soon be all right."

She died somewhere under Dumbarton Road's gas-lights, amid the bustle of the crowds.

Craig did not know that she was gone. He did not admit that he had lost her until he put her tenderly into the arms of a prim nurse in the great tiled hall of the Western Infirmary.

"What's this, Constable?"

"Scalding," Craig said. "She needs attention."

"She's dead."

"Don't bloody tell me that," Craig said.

The nurse held out the bundle, touched back the fold of cloth, and Craig saw that he had carried naught but a little corpse through the city streets, that he had been the trusting one.

"Now do you believe me, Constable?"

"I believe you," Craig said.

Kirsty said, "I hope your supper's not burned."

She took the plate of stew from the small oven and put it on the table while Craig took off his tunic and unlaced his boots.

"Have you been at the baths again?" she asked.

Craig shook his head.

"Then why are you so late?"

"I had – there was work to do."

"You're supposed to finish at eight."

"Things happen."

"What things?"

"I had a report to fill out."

"Oh! About what?"

"Nothin' much," he said. "Butter some bread, will you?"

She cut three slices from the morning's loaf and spread fresh butter upon them, put them neatly on a side-plate and laid it before him. He looked tired. There were ash-coloured bruises under his eyes and a furrow between his brows. He lifted his fork and stirred the stew and began to eat almost, Kirsty thought, mechanically.

"You'll want your tea now?" Kirsty said.

"Aye."

When she lifted the heavy kettle from the hob Craig twisted his head and stared at her, watched the stream of boiling water pour into the teapot, steam rising.

He turned once more to his supper, stiffly.

"Was it," said Kirsty, "a busy day?"

"Aye, it was," he said.

"I'll put a hot bottle in your bed."

"Aye, please."

She did not press. She realised that something had happened, something, perhaps, so unpleasant that he did not want to tell her of it. He was, she supposed, being protective since she was in a condition of expectant motherhood. She brushed his shoulder with her palm and he did not flinch away, did not stop eating, forking the food into his mouth and swallowing as if he did not like the taste.

"Is it all right?"

"It's fine."

She lifted his tunic from the chair-back, shook it out.

"Your jacket's wet," she said. "Is it rainin' outside?"

"It's dry," he said. "Cold but dry."

She waited. He did not tell her what had caused the dampness all down the breast of his coat or what it meant. She thought of the river, the ferry steps, the dark, mysterious quays, but the stain on his coat did not have the river's earthy, metallic smell; something else, something that made her nose wrinkle but which she could not identify.

"Craig—"

"Wait," he said. "I near forgot."

He unbuttoned the top pocket of his tunic, took out a brown

envelope and removed from it three tickets of yellow card. He held them out and Kirsty took them, read the print.

"A concert," she said. "Does this mean we're goin', Craig?"

"I thought you might enjoy it."

"I'm sure I will. The third ticket—"

"For old Frew, if she fancies it."

Smiling, Kirsty kissed his cheek.

"You're not a bad stick, Craig Nicholson," she said.

The Greenfield Burgh hall was a splendid monument to civic pride. In the fifteen years since it had been erected a good deal of money had been poured into expansion and decoration. The floor was of polished oak, the seats padded in leather. The gallery was a beautifully shaped horseshoe with mouldings in the Italian style. Glass-globed gas-lights added to the brilliance shed by six mammoth gasoliers that hung from the half-domed ceiling. The platform was framed by Corinthian columns, backed by row upon row of carved chairs which climbed to the impressive bronze pipes of the Thomas Mackarness Memorial Organ. An ingenious arrangement of red velvet curtains, painted flats, and potted plants from the Parks Department hothouses reduced the width and depth of the platform, however, made it a more intimate stage, complete with footlights, upon which performers, amateur and professional, would do their stuff.

The Chief Constable, in full evening dress, acted as Master of Ceremonies. Much as he liked the sound of his own rich tenor rolling round the hall he kept his remarks brief and the evening skipping along merrily.

J. C. Wilson was the first Negro that Kirsty had ever seen. She was taken not only with his coal-black cheerfulness but by the pace and agility of his 'eccentric' dance and the strange songs he sang while accompanying himself on an enormous banjo. Kirsty was not the only one to be impressed by J. C. Wilson. Mrs Frew was quite round-eyed and Craig's friend Archie Flynn got so carried away that he stuck his fingers in his mouth and whistled shrilly until Craig gave him a dirty look that made him stop at once.

In the foyer Kirsty had been introduced to Archie and to a young man named Peter Stewart. She had been surprised at how youthful they appeared, hardly more than children she thought, and was surprised to realise that they were no younger than Craig.

"An' this is Kirsty, my good lady wife."

"Pleasure to be meeting you, Mrs Nicholson."

"Aye, we've heard a lot about ye, Mrs Nicholson."

The young men's eyes were shy but appraising. She could tell that she impressed them and that Craig was proud of her, even in her present condition.

Sergeant Drummond made a point of asking after her health. He assured her that the 'new' house in Canada Road would be to her liking. He also addressed several words to Mrs Frew, bowing graciously and might, Kirsty thought, even have kissed her hand if her fingers hadn't been stuffed in a brown fur muff.

Kirsty was shown to other policemen too and, glancing surreptitiously round the rows before the gasoliers were dimmed, noted that she was as smart in appearance as any other woman in the group, except for the wives of the 'bigwigs' who occupied the front rows. She was flanked by Craig and Mrs Frew with Archie and Peter Stewart, both in uniform, left and right of her. She looked in vain for Hugh and Beatrice Affleck before the lights went down and the red velvet curtain, on a drooping wire, closed with a shiver and opened again.

She just had time to say to Mrs Frew, "Is your brother not here?"

"Somewhere," Mrs Frew whispered.

After the Negro dancer a section of the City of Glasgow Police Choir came on to a mixed reception of cheers and counter-cheers, to put it politely. But they delivered *The March of the Cameron Men* and *The Gathering* with such heartfelt and rousing sentiment that even those Glasgow keelies who thought that Prince Charles was the name of a racehorse cheered and clapped in patriotic fervour.

Abracadabra – an amateur magician from Maryhill Division – fared less well, poor bloke, for when he swept a pigeon from under his multi-coloured cloak it promptly flew up into the half-dome and, excited by all the attention, spotted several hats and hair-dos a hundred feet below its tail. It would not be cajoled down by Constable Abracadabra, though he tempted it with a broken biscuit and called out "Here, Sammy, come tae Daddy John then, there's a good boy," while suggestions from the body of the hall for disposal of the bird grew ever more ribald and inventive. Eventually Abracadabra left the stage in confusion and the pigeon, it was to be assumed, fell asleep. Apart from an occasional croon and the odd feather no more was heard or seen of it as the evening's entertainment progressed through bagpipers, fiddlers, comics, dancers and singers, and a faint restless murmur swelled among the males in the audience as Miss Phoebe Donaldson, second-top of the bill, prepared to reveal her talents to the

235

wondering gaze. To rapturous applause Chief Constable Organ made the introduction.

The red curtain closed, shivered, swished open to reveal two startled coppers caught in the act of shoving a grand piano out from the wings.

"By Jeeze, they're stealin' the furniture."

"Take that man's name, officer."

"Ye'd be better buyin' a bike, Davy."

Cheers, remarks and demands for an encore were stilled as a woman marched briskly into view. She was fifty if she was a day, gaunt and foxy and with a chest as flat as an ironing-board under a stiff-starched blouse.

"Is that *it*?" Archie cried. "Is *that* her?"

"That's the accompanist," Mrs Frew told him.

"Aw!" Archie nodded.

Silence; pin-drop silence.

Phoebe Donaldson came out like a flower of modesty, a woman of almost six feet in height, an Amazon in an evening gown of sky-blue silk, the bodice pouched, the collar low-cut with just a breath of chiffon on the décolletage. Pale-blue gloves covered her arms but her shoulders were bare and breathtakingly white and the shadow of the little 'salt-cellar' at the base of her throat ran directly into the deep soft shadow of her breasts.

"Dear God!" Archie moaned.

"A commanding presence, indeed," said Mrs Frew.

"Dear God!"

Miss Donaldson arranged herself in stage centre, hands folded below her bosom.

"Steady, lads," came Sergeant Drummond's muttered command and the men of Greenfield, all ranks, got a grip on their emotions.

A handful of notes flew from the fingers of the gaunt repetitrice. Miss Donaldson filled her lungs.

"Steady."

She sang.

In a rich vibrant contralto she sang *We'll Meet Beside The Dusky Glen* and *My Love She's But A Lassie Yet* and, as advertised, quivered deliciously when she lifted her chin to project the higher notes.

Applause was thunderous. They would not let her go even after *What Ails This Heart O' Mine*. It was, after all, her voice and not her figure that made Miss Donaldson special, a quality of pathos that plucked at one and all and made every eye grow misty

236

When she took her bow and left the stage the ovation was such that Mr Organ prevailed upon her to return, which she did with a pleasant smile. After a pause she struck into *The Vacant Chair* as softly as if she were confiding the pain of loss to each member of the audience individually.

It was in the middle of the third verse that Peter Stewart broke from his seat and, crushing past knees, bolted up the aisle towards the exit door. Craig went after him at once.

Nobody paid much attention for the air was moist in all parts of the hall and the rim of the balcony was marked by scuts of linen and lace, sniffings into handkerchiefs. For all that she too was affected something in the abrupt manner of Craig's departure drew Kirsty's attention from the figure on the stage. The instant that the last note floated from Miss Donaldson's lips she excused herself to Mrs Frew and, lost in the deafening ovation, squeezed out into the aisle and headed for the foyer.

Sergeant Drummond and Hugh Affleck had been quicker off the mark than Kirsty. She found the policemen gathered in a corner beyond the cloakroom door, Craig holding Peter Stewart in his arms, the young man sobbing as if his heart would break.

"Craig, what's wrong?" she said.

When he turned she saw on Craig's face an expression of such sorrow that, if he had been alone, she would have run to him and thrown her arms about him. But this mourning was a man's thing, secret and private. Sergeant Drummond gave her a warning scowl and Kirsty stopped in her tracks. Hugh Affleck had put an arm about Stewart's shoulders too and, as Kirsty watched, gently disengaged him from Craig and led him a few steps further into the corner of the corridor. Laughter from the hall, the music of a comical Scotch song; she guessed that Mr Harry Lauder, on stage now, would soon sweep away tears with broad, rough-hewn humour.

Craig glanced at her and looked down at his shoes, sheepish and guilty. He fumbled for and lit a cigarette and let Sergeant Drummond bring Kirsty an explanation.

"What's wrong?" said Kirsty. "Is he ill?"

"Och, no, nothing like that at all."

"Why is he so upset?"

"Did your husband not tell you of it, lass?"

"Tell me what?"

"Two days ago there was a girl who — well, she died, poor soul. Constable Stewart was present."

"And Craig?"

"Yes, he was also there."

"Why did he not tell me himself?"

"Some men——" said Hector Drummond; he paused. "I'm thinking that the best thing is for me to take them back to my lodgings for a wee drink. We had better not go to a place of public refreshment since we are in uniform. But my landlady will not object, I'm sure."

"Come to Walbrook Street, if you like."

"That," said the sergeant, "would not fill the bill."

Kirsty looked at her husband. "Craig?"

He gave no sign that he had heard her. He sucked in smoke and let it seep through his nostrils, hands in pockets. In the corner Hugh Affleck was talking quietly and intently to Peter Stewart who had stopped sobbing and was nodding his head.

She wanted Craig to tell her what had happened, to explain why he had kept it from her; yet she had a vague understanding of the system to which Craig now belonged and of his need to be among his own kind.

"I'll go home with Mrs Frew," said Kirsty.

"I'll see to it that he's not late," said the sergeant. "Leave it to us. There is nothing at all to worry about."

The pleasure of the evening had been dissipated. Kirsty turned on her heel, returned to the hall and, caring not for the *tuts* of annoyance, pushed past the knees and took her seat. She looked up at the little figure on the stage in his over-long kilt and enormous sporran; everything exaggerated. She tried to concentrate on the words, to pick up on the waves of laughter that swept the audience but it was too late. She was glad when the concert came to an end.

As the curtain fell, Mrs Frew turned to her.

"He was much affected," she said. "I suppose there was a death?"

In the seat by her side Archie Flynn shuffled restlessly. He might have slunk off without a word if Mrs Frew had not stayed him with a hand on his arm.

"Was there, Archibald?" she demanded.

"Er – aye."

"How bad was it?"

"They never told me much about it."

"Archie, what happened?"

"A wee lassie died; scalded wi' boilin' water."

"Was it murder?" said Mrs Frew.

"Naw, pure accident."

Mrs Frew sighed. "I suppose they'll be going for a drink somewhere."

Kirsty said, "Yes."

"Oh," said Archie. "Where?"

"Sergeant Drummond's house."

"Right," said Archie. "I know where that is," and, with a gruff goodnight, detached himself from the widow and hurried off into the crowd by the door.

She lay awake as long as she could, propped comfortably against the pillows and big bolster with a hot-water bottle against her feet. She sipped warm cocoa and, by the light of the oil-lamp, flipped over the pages of the book on China that Mrs Frew had loaned her. Anxiety, guilt and a faint irritating sense of having been shut out of Craig's life were soothed in the quiet bedroom with its solid mahogany furnishings.

She turned the pages, the quarto volume resting against her tummy, her knees raised. She looked at the funny Chinese names, the postcard-sized photographs and engraved plates that appeared on every page. There was a wall that stretched for a thousand miles; a wall that, in the photograph, looked unimpressively like the dyke that straggled over the Straitons from Hawkhead. She tried to imagine what the Great China Wall was really like, its size, its scale. But she could not make that leap. She was hampered by lack of experience. She turned to another page, saw the face of a Chinese pirate that reminded her so much of Mr Clegg that he might have been a long-lost brother.

Reaping the Rice Harvest: As soon as a boy grows old enough he learns to stand for long hours in the rice field, bent over to plant the seedlings in the ooze. Bare legs and a bowed back; only the broad straw hat added a touch of the exotic to the picture.

The Temple of Heaven, Peking. It was a bit like the bandstand in the Groveries, really. Feeling better, Kirsty snuggled down with a little grunt of amusement. The Temple of Heaven was nothing like the Kelvin bandstand. But she preferred to pretend that it was. She felt no desire at all, no itch in the legs, to travel, to see these strange and wonderful sights for herself. She had had all the novelty she could cope with, thank you, in this past year and in the year to come would have more of it, no doubt. For all that, it was nice to lie against the big wooden bedhead with the oil-lamp purring and the taste of sweet cocoa in her mouth and muse on the mystery of foreign lands. In her tummy her baby blew a little bubble that made her wince and change position.

The book fell shut.

She opened it again not at pictures or text – at the beginning, at the flyleaf, at the inscription.

She put her fingertips lightly against the paper and, closing her eyes, imagined that she could feel the writing against her skin, as a blind girl would. *With All My Love, From David.* She could not imagine him in overcoat and scarf in a flooded rice field or standing by the Temple of Heaven or walking along the Great Wall. She could only imagine him here and, with a little impatient *huh* at her silliness, closed the book again and put it firmly to one side.

She opened the door cautiously for Craig had made her aware that, even in broad daylight, you could not be too careful.

"Well," David said, "I see you're still here."

"For another fortnight," said Kirsty.

"And then you'll be off to a home of your own."

"Did Mrs Frew tell you all that?"

"She mentioned it in a letter, I believe."

"How long will you be stayin'?"

"Overnight."

"I'll make your room ready."

"Wait."

"What is it, Mr Lockhart?"

"Nothing," he said. "Where is Aunt Nessie?"

"Shoppin'."

"It's not inconvenient, is it, my dropping in without prior notice?"

"Oh, no. She'll be pleased to see you. It's been very quiet since the New Year."

"I – I didn't know that I would be in Glasgow, you see. It was rather an impulse, to call on my brother unexpectedly."

"John Knox?"

"The very same; you remembered."

"It's an uncommon name," said Kirsty. "Let me take your portmanteau up to your room."

"In your condition; certainly not."

"I'm not—"

"Take no chances, Mrs Nicholson, no chances at all."

"I keep forgettin' that you're a doctor."

"Well, after a fashion."

"You mean you're not—"

"Oh, yes, trained and qualified. I've done my stint of mending broken legs and curbing fevers but I don't really feel like a doctor."

"What should a doctor feel like?"

"Confident, in command of everything."

"And you aren't?"

"I've had no opportunity to cultivate that aspect of the healing art. Straight from the ward to the lecture room again. One minute, it seemed, I was lancing a carbuncle and the next I was debating Adoration, Confession and Supplication with a German-born professor with an accent like Scotch broth. Perhaps, Kirsty," he said, "you should close the outside door."

"What?"

"The door," said David.

"Aye," said Kirsty, and closed it.

"Do you know what I'd like, Kirsty?" David said.

"No, what?"

"A nice hot cup of coffee, if such a thing can be arranged."

"Will it do in the kitchen?"

"Perfectly."

"Come on then," said Kirsty.

David said, "You'll miss that young woman when she goes, Aunt."

"I admit it. I will," said Mrs Frew.

"You'll be on your own again."

"I've been on my own before."

"Why don't you employ some other girl, a resident?"

"It wouldn't be the same."

"No," David said. "I can understand that."

"David, why are you here?" said Nessie Frew.

"I came to see Jack."

"You didn't spend much time with him," said Nessie Frew, glancing pointedly at the clock on the mantelshelf above the parlour fire.

"We had supper together," David said. "But he's a wee bit under the weather since we came back from Inverness and I didn't want to keep him late."

"He's not ill, is he?"

"Heavens, no," said David. "The course of study has intensified, that's all. He's an obsessive worrier, our Jack. He believes that he might fail his examinations."

"Didn't you?"

"Oh, it crossed my mind," said David, "from time to time."

"You still haven't answered my question," said Nessie Frew.

"I thought I had."

"I may be old, David, but I'm not senile. What do you have to say to me?"

David hesitated. He sat back in the small overstuffed armchair, trying, it seemed, to find a comfortable position for his hips. He had a tumbler of whisky and soda-water in his hand for he had no stomach for sherry, and brandy, for some reason, made his lips swell.

"Out with it," said Mrs Frew.

"I'm – I'm considering – just considering, mind you – not going back to China," David said; he squinted at the woman anxiously. "I thought that I should – I mean, seek the benefit of your advice."

"What did your Uncle George say?"

"I haven't mentioned it to him yet."

"Jack?"

"Jack is, as you may imagine, aghast," David said. "He can't believe that the thought even crossed my mind. Everything is clear-cut for our Jack, always has been. The whole weary business of getting an education has only been a prelude to 'real life', to returning to China and taking up the work."

"Have you lost interest in the work, David?"

"It's not that. No, I haven't, of course not."

"Are you sure?"

"No, I'm not sure, not at all sure."

Neither approval nor censure showed in Aunt Nessie's expression. She seemed wary, as if he had put her on the spot, had forced upon her a responsibility which she could not shoulder lightly.

She rose, poured herself another inch of sherry from the decanter on the occasional table and returned to her seat. She put her knees together, her ankles together, straightened her spine and tucked in her chin.

"Have you lost your belief, David? Answer truthfully."

"It isn't a crisis of that kind, Aunt Nessie."

"Do you not have faith?"

"I ask myself – and this is the nub of it – 'How best can I serve?' "

"And what's your answer?"

"There are more sick bodies in Glasgow than in Fanshi."

"Sick souls too, David?"

"Yes, sick souls too."

"What's led you to this profound conclusion?"

242

"Observation."

"Is there a girl involved?"

He was taken aback. "No. No, I assure you—"

"What about Miss – what is her name?"

"Miss Dickie; Sarah Dickie."

"Won't she go with you to China, is that it?"

"No," said David vehemently. "That is *not* it. There was never anything serious – anything at all, in fact – between Sarah and me. My uncle and her father promoted a childhood friendship into something much more than it was. Sarah is infatuated with a farmer's son."

"And are you jealous?"

"She loves him," said David. "He's a pleasant chap with excellent prospects; a good God-fearing young man too. Perfect for Sarah Dickie. She could never be wife to a missionary, could never settle in China."

"You don't care for Miss Dickie, in other words."

"I don't – don't love her."

"No other?"

"No other." David shook his head. "It isn't that."

"David, what *do* you want; to doctor, to administer to the sick?"

"I truly do not know. It was a mistake, Aunt, I see that now. Being both doctor and minister – it's a different sort of thing."

"In a civilised country like our own, perhaps, but—"

"China is not uncivilised. Far from it. It's different, incomprehensibly different."

"Full of heathens parched for the living water of the Word. Jesus Christ cannot be hidden, David."

"Dozens of societies plough men and money into the work. The Baptists, the Friends, the Danes, the Americans. Heavens, Aunt Nessie, it's almost a hundred years since the LMS took a hold on mainland China."

"And still they are hungry for the blessing of His love," said Nessie Frew. "Your mother and father will be bitterly disappointed."

"It's their life, Aunt Nessie. Fanshi is their citadel, not mine."

"They gave up everything for God's work."

"Including their children."

"David, that's cruel."

"Uncle George, you too, Aunt – you mean more to me than Mother or Father. Jack and I have never been important to them."

"You are important to them. You'll inherit the Mission, the new hospital—"

"Make it bigger, make it better, make it more famous. Convert more benighted heathens than the Berlinners or the Evangelicals. Cure more cases of goitre and St Vitus' dance. Perform more surgical operations—"

"Please." She raised her left hand. "That's enough."

"I thought you might understand, might – might help me."

"Help you?" said Nessie Frew.

"Help me to find out what's really in my heart."

"Have you prayed, David?"

"Often, and devoutly."

"What did God say to you?"

David did not answer her.

She said, "Did you not listen to Him?"

David said, "They'll have Jack. He's twice the man I am, anyhow."

"They want both of you."

"I know."

"For God's work."

"For the glory of the Fanshi Mission, you mean."

"They must be told," said Mrs Frew.

"When I reach a final decision, one way or the other, I'll write to them," said David.

"I think you've already made up your mind."

"Aunt, if I stay, will you give me room here?"

"What?"

"If I decide to become a minister—"

"Not a doctor?"

" – and to apply for a parish—"

"Here, do you mean; in Glasgow?"

"There's nothing wrong with Glasgow," David said ingenuously.

"Well, certainly, yes, there must be plenty of work to do in this city, that's true." She drank her sherry in a single swallow, made a wry face. "Preaching. Serving the spiritual needs of the populace. But I thought that you—"

"I didn't say that I had lost faith, Aunt Nessie, only that I had lost my inclination to return to China."

"The ideal is—"

David said, "My one regret will be that I'll be letting Jack down."

"You won't try to change his mind for him, I trust."

244

"Absolutely not."

She turned the sherry glass in her fingers, looking at it and not at the young man.

David said, "Will you give me shelter, Aunt Nessie, for a while at least?"

"Yes, you *have* made up your mind," said Nessie Frew.

"Sort of, I suppose."

"Very well," she said. "I'll give you room here. When will you come, do you think?"

"In April," David said.

He had been up very early and, dressed in a soft tweed sports coat and flannel trousers, had seated himself at the kitchen table with Craig; Craig in dark serge uniform with buttons gleaming and the belt already clenched about his narrow waist.

Kirsty had seen them in apposition but not, as now, in contrast; it made her uncomfortable. She concentrated on cooking and serving breakfast and listened to their stilted conversation without comment. She sensed Craig's distrust of the 'toff'; he answered David's questions about the arduous nature of police work with a curtness that was almost impolite. He, Craig, finished his meal and hurried off, helmet in hand, with no more than a nod of farewell.

David said, "He doesn't like to talk about it, I see."

"Not to anyone, not even to me."

"I wonder why?"

"He doesn't want to worry me."

"Is it dangerous, do you think?"

Kirsty shrugged. "Things happen."

"Violent acts?"

"Yes."

Kirsty felt strangely reluctant to discuss details, those that she had gleaned, of Craig's occupation. David gave a little nod, as if he understood. A strand of fair hair stuck up untidily from his crown and Kirsty had to resist the temptation to smooth it down.

She removed the plates and ran them under the cold-water tap and put them in the basin in the sink. There was a wash to do and she studied the band of sky, tinged with daylight, that showed over the rooftops. In the window glass she could see David's reflection. Now that she was not looking at him he wore a serious expression, grave, not surly. When she turned around he started.

"I must be off too," he said.

"Did you see your brother?"

245

"Yes."

"Is he farin' well?"

"Well enough. He has to be examined at the end of this month and the prospect makes him nervous."

"Were you nervous when you were examined?"

"Of course," David said. He finished the tea in his cup and got to his feet. "Will my aunt be out of bed yet?"

"She should be," said Kirsty.

"I want to say goodbye."

"Will you be back soon?"

"No, not for – some time."

"I'll say goodbye too, then."

"The new house?"

"Aye, in a fortnight," said Kirsty. "When do you sail for China?"

"At the end of May – if I sail at all."

"I thought—"

"No, it isn't settled; not quite."

He offered his hand and she took it awkwardly. His skin was dry and warm and smooth, the grip strong. Questions clamoured in her mind but she bit her lip and held them back.

"Well," he said. "Goodbye again, Kirsty."

Sergeant Byrne had a brother who when he retired from the Force supplemented his meagre pension by doing removals. He stabled his cuddy and a four-wheeled cart in Whiteinch and pulled two or three hands from the street corner when he needed muscle to hump heavy furniture. He was a careful man, honest and dependable and Craig left the flitting to him.

Every inch of space in the four-wheeler was needed to take the Nicholsons from Walbrook Street back to Canada Road for Mrs Frew, in a fit of generosity, had scoured her attics and basement and had come up with an amazing number of items which, she declared, were superfluous to her needs and just cluttered up the place. Kirsty, she claimed, would be doing her a favour by taking them away. Tables, chairs, a double bed with mattress and a walnut headboard, brass oil-lamps, a brass coal scuttle, a brass log box, three Indian rugs with some wear in them still, a selection of vases in pretty glazes and a big box full of cutlery, Best Sheffield, and china. Kirsty protested, of course, but Mrs Frew was adamant and Craig hefted and hoisted the lots single-handed into the hallway from which, after he had gone off to do his duty, Sergeant Byrne's brother lifted them away into his cart.

It was an emotional farewell, as if she, Kirsty, were going to China and not just along to Greenfield.

Mrs Frew shed tears. Kirsty shed tears. They might have hugged each other half the morning if brother Byrne, with a delicate cough, hadn't indicated that he was ready to help Mrs Nicholson up on to the cart and wanted to be speedy in case the weather changed to rain.

Mrs Frew came out on to the step, discarding 'respectability' for once, and waved her lace handkerchief as the cart trundled off. Kirsty looked back over her shoulder and wept too as Walbrook Street slipped away from her and Mr Byrne and his three rough assistants exchanged glances but preserved a decent silence.

That night Craig came home from Ottawa Street to his own home at No. 154 Canada Road and found it, for the most part, all spick and span. He had already spent three evenings there doing a spot of painting and revarnishing, though the house had been left spotless by the departing tenant, had been inspected as a Police Dwelling by the appropriate committee man and signed off as sound and sanitary.

In view of Kirsty's condition, however, Mr Byrne and his boys had donated an hour of their time to putting up a bed in the front room, setting out rugs, tables and chairs just where Kirsty had wanted them and had even helped her unpack and stack away the stuff from the boxes. One of the lads slipped out and found a coalman who lugged three bags upstairs to the bunker in the hall. Though Mr Byrne had been paid in advance by Craig, Kirsty tipped him an extra two shillings, for so quick and thorough had they been that all was squared away by mid-afternoon and she even found time for a bite of dinner and a wee rest before she went out to shop.

It was strange to return to Canada Road, to look down its diminishing perspective and see, in the haze, the place where Craig and she had first lived as man and wife. She was apprehensive about meeting old neighbours but, that first afternoon, she did not. She came back with her shopping from Dumbarton Road and paused, looked up at the nice clean façade of the almost new tenement with its large windows and neat net curtains and roller blinds, with the sharp clean smell of lysol solution coming out of the close and the half-inch steps in front of each door on the stairs as white as snow. It was the same place, the same stretch of the Greenfield – and yet it was so very different.

She went on up, fumbled with the key and let herself into the apartment and stood for a moment, the basket and purse still in her hands, and looked into the rooms in the afternoon light and waited for the elation to catch her up, for the feeling of delight that she had anticipated in being a wife in her own home to rise within her. But, to her sorrow, it did not. She went into the kitchen and unpacked the basket and set about the business of preparing Craig's supper as if she had been here for months or years, as if the fine new house held no novelty at all. It would be different, she decided, when the baby came for it was a fine house in which to raise a family, spacious, clean and respectable, though it wasn't Walbrook Street and never would be, no matter how she worked to make it so.

Craig came home early. He was only five minutes' walk from the station now, and miles from Cranstonhill Baths. He found the fire blazing brightly and the table covered with glistening new oilcloth and the kitchen warm with the smell of supper. He gave Kirsty a big hug even before he removed his tunic and boots and he glanced at the list of eight things that she required him to do — repair the pulley rope, change the gas globe in the hall, and the like — and grinned and winked at her.

"Aye, Mrs Nicholson, I see you'll be keepin' me busy now we've a home of our own."

Kirsty, at the stove, managed a smile.

"Oh, I'll find plenty for you to do, Craig Nicholson, never fear," she said.

He wrapped his arms about her waist and laid his palms lightly on the apron that covered her stomach. He kissed her neck and watched over her shoulder as she ladled broth into a bowl.

"It'll be all right now," he told her. "You'll see."

"Aye," said Kirsty.

He gave her a gentle squeeze. "Don't you believe me?"

"Of course I do, daftie," said Kirsty, the ladle dripping in her hand.

She inclined her head and bussed him on the cheek and Craig, reassured, nodded and made his way to a chair at the table and waited to be served.

Seven families, in addition to the Nicholsons, occupied the close at No. 154 Canada Road. Mr McGonigle, tenant of the ground floor right, was a fireman at the Cyrus Street station. He had been a police constable until the Extension Act of 1891 at which time he had elected to transfer to the Fire Department to which he had been attached for six years. Mr Chapman, second floor right, was an inspector in the Office of Weights and Measures and had been employed in that capacity for twenty-three years. All the other breadwinners were coppers.

The Walkers, third floor left, had a sergeant for a daddy and an eldest son already in blue and four more pups all keen and eager to reach an age when they too might don uniforms and strut the streets of the Greenfield. Father's rank made the Walkers kings of the close and bestowed on Jess Walker all the airs and graces of a potentate's wife. Nobody seemed to like her much. Young Mrs McAlpine hated her and was quick to buttonhole Kirsty and try to enlist her as an ally in the sniping war. Kirsty was cautious. By discreet enquiries she learned that Joyce McAlpine's husband, Andy, was on 'his last warning for 'the drink' and would be summarily dismissed if caught boozing on duty again; learned too, from Mrs Swanston, the close gossip, that Andy McAlpine was prone to thumping his pretty little blonde wife but that he put on boxing-gloves before he did it since he did not want the neighbours to see bruises. The McAlpines had two small girl children and Joyce McAlpine confided in Kirsty, as if she was a bosom chum, that she would bear the bugger no more, would not let him near her when he was in an amorous mood, no matter what he did to persuade her.

Constable John Boyle and his wife Morven, leading lights in the Free Church, were humourless and unsociable. Upon their one child, Graham, they lavished the best education that money could buy. The boy marched off every morning in the distinctive uniform of a pupil of Kelvinside Academy and every morning endured the taunts of the hoi polloi with the stoicism of a martyred saint, his long foal-like face implacable, vengeance already simmering in his heart.

The Nicholsons shared the top landing with the Pipers.

"Pipers by name, pipers by nature," Constable Jock would cry cheerfully as he dashed downstairs of an evening in kilt and sporran, bagpipes swinging in a long black-painted wooden box; while Mrs Piper adopted as her war cry the odd phrase, "My, my, but it's a sair fecht for us weemen," and would greet all and sundry with that observation in lieu of more orthodox conversation.

Strange wails and strangled shrieks pierced the door of the Pipers' apartment at all hours of the day and night, for the Pipers were that worst of all creatures – Glasgow-born converts to the culture of the Gaels. While Daddy and the three boys wheezed into their chanters, Mammy and the three girls practised those weird, plaintive dirges known as 'mouth music' to the cognoscenti

Such musical enthusiasms might have been very commendable in a Highland glen where the nearest neighbour lived on the other side of a mountain but they played hell with peace and quiet in the confines of a close in the Canada Road.

Snapped out of a snooze in a chair by the fire Craig would start up and shout, "What's that, what's that?" and when Kirsty assured him that it was only the Pipers at it again he would growl and shake his fist at the wall and vow that some bloody night he would go in there and murder the whole damned lot of them; and then a snatch of song would rise sweet and lilting out of the bedlam and Craig would sigh and *tut* and, chastened, say, "Ah, well. Ah, well," and let the magic of the old art soothe the anger in his breast.

Public and private lives were so closely entwined in tenement society that Kirsty was not at all surprised that within a week or two of their arrival everybody in the close seemed to know all about them. It had not occurred to her that Craig had acquired a certain notoriety by the unusual manner of his entry to police ranks, that the capture of Skirving and Malone was an event not easily forgotten. To some Craig was a hero; to others a charlatan who had weaseled his way into the Constabulary by less than ethical means. For all that, Kirsty was accepted and made welcome. She found consolation in the company of women whose husbands' shifts were also essays in mystery and who were separated from the community at large by the very nature of their employment. On Sundays, rain or shine, Kirsty made a pilgrimage to Walbrook Street, drank tea with Mrs Frew before service and walked arm in arm to St Anne's with the widow. She could not, however, linger afterwards for she had a man to feed and a house to run and was slowed by the weight she bore before her as February progressed and the month of her delivery drew near.

It was on a dull and drizzling Tuesday about the middle of the month. Supper was over, dishes washed and dried, the kitchen all neat and cosy. Craig lay in his favourite chair, his stockinged feet on the end of the hob, a Gold Flake in his mouth and a novel, *Hunted Down*, open on his lap. Kirsty was sewing up frayed cuffs on one of Craig's shirts, squinting at the tiny needle and fine white thread in the gaslight when a knock sounded upon the door.

"Who can that be?" she asked, glancing up.

"Bert Swanson, maybe," Craig answered, stirring himself. "He said he might drop in to see if I wanted a few frames o' billiards down at the gymnasium. But I don't feel like it."

The Fostering Breast

Craig put down his book, yawned, stretched and went out into the hallway to open the door to the caller.

Kirsty returned to her stitching.

She heard voices, paused. She heard a peculiar sound, almost like a sob. She had just struggled to her feet, pushing herself from the chair, when the kitchen door swung open and Craig, a hand over his eyes and shoulders heaving, staggered into the room.

Hard on his heels came his brother Gordon.

"Craig?" said Kirsty. "What is it? What's wrong?"

It was Gordon who answered, for Craig waved her away and slumped at once at the table and hid his face between his arms.

Gordon said, "It's our dad. He's dead."

"Dead? But how – when—?"

"Last week, last Wednesday."

"Was he sick? An' why wasn't Craig told?"

Embarrassed, Gordon answered, "He – Dad just dropped. Nobody knew what caused it. He just dropped. He just dropped like a stone in the yard at the Mains. He just dropped down dead at the door o' the byre."

"Were you there with him, Gordon?"

"Aye, I was close enough t'see it happen. Straight down on to the cobbles on his face, he went. Split his brow wi' the fall. It was funny how he hardly bled at all."

"What was the cause?"

"Heart stopped."

Kirsty experienced a prickle of disappointment, not so much grief as selfishness. She had had a picture of Bob Nicholson with his grandchild on his knee, his small hard brown hands about the white shawl. She regretted that she had been cheated of the pleasure of that reunion, of repaying the man for his kindness to her, regretted too that her baby would never know its grandfather and that he was closed off for ever from them all and their future achievements.

"When will he be buried?"

"It – it was Saturday last," said Gordon.

Craig jerked up and whirled around, his expression fierce, eyes red and wet and glaring. "Christ, could some o' you no' have told me?"

"How could I tell you, Craig, when I never knew where you were?"

"I wrote—" Craig sniffed and wiped his nose on his wrist. "I wrote t' Da half a dozen times. Did he no' tell you?"

Gordon swallowed. "I – I don't think he got the letters."

Craig was on his feet. Gordon retreated half a step as if he feared that his brother was going to snag his head and knuckle him again as had happened from time to time when they were growing up.

"He must've got the letters," Craig said. "They were sent to him. All stamped. I mean – what about the gifts I sent at Christmas?"

Gordon shook his head.

Kirsty said, "If the letters didn't arrive, Gordon, how did you know where to find us?"

"She told me."

Gordon had changed. He was not as Kirsty remembered him. He had not grown taller but he had broadened out a little, had developed a crop of pimples about his mouth, had coarsened. He smacked no more of carefree ebullience but had the mark of the farmyards on him, long hours in cold byres. His nails were bitten down and rimmed with dirt; she wondered that Madge Nicholson had allowed him to slide into untidiness.

"Mam?" said Craig; changed question into exclamation. "Mam!"

Gordon said, "He often used t' say to me, when we were goin' to work, that he'd told you not to write. He said he knew you'd do the right thing by Kirsty an' would net a good job."

"He never even knew I was a policeman?"

"Nah."

"But the letters—" said Kirsty.

Craig dragged a chair to the table and pointed at it.

"Sit down, Gordon. She'll make ye some supper. Kirsty?"

Gordon glanced up, awaiting her invitation too.

Kirsty said, "Aye. You must be hungry."

"The letters," said Craig, "will be hid in one o' her drawers, slipped away under linen or blankets."

"Aye," said Gordon.

He wore his one and only jacket, apart from the suit he had preserved in the mothball-reeking wardrobe, flannel trousers, a scarf and a soft cap. He carried a little case, a thing of pasteboard and cord with a cheap tin lock, a lady's case, that he kept perched on his lap as if he were afraid that, even here in his brother's kitchen, some ruffian would sneak up and steal it from him. Kirsty felt a sudden terrific wave of pity for Gordon, saw that he was still shocked and suffering. She took the case from him and put it on the dresser, took off his cap and put it on top of the little case and then she put an arm about him.

Craig, fingers trembling, was in process of lighting a cigarette.

"Do you want one, Gordon?" Kirsty said.

"What?"

"A smoke."

"Gordon doesn't smoke," said Craig.

"Aye, but I do."

"Give him one, Craig."

She stood by Gordon's side while he extracted a Gold Flake from the paper packet that Craig held out to him, put the cigarette into his lips and craned forward to the match flame. Frowning, Craig scrutinised his brother as Gordon inhaled, as if he were watching a trick done by a trained collie.

"She'll not know you're on the gaspers?" he said.

"Nah." Gordon managed a grin, just. He looked up at Kirsty. "Thanks, Kirsty."

"How did you get here?"

"The train; then I walked."

Craig said, "She gave you the address, didn't she?"

"Aye," said Gordon. "She told me where the Greenfield was an' all. But she never told me it was so bloody far. God, man, I thought I was walkin' the length o' the Clyde." He glanced up at Kirsty once more, grinned. "It's some size o' place this."

"You get used to it, Gordon," said Kirsty.

Gordon said, "You're big."

"I'm due in five weeks."

"I never knew."

"Did *she* not tell you?" said Craig.

Gordon ran a hand over his hair, took the Gold Flake from his mouth and angled it between his fingers.

"Listen," he said. "She wants you back."

"Hah!"

"It's true, though. She sent me here t' tell you t' come back."

"If she got the letters, if she read them—"

"She did, Craig. By Christ, we both know that now."

"Well, if she did, then she knows I'm settled in work, wi' a house—"

Gordon interrupted. "She's taken on the farm."

"*What?*"

"Persuaded Mr Sanderson; told him you'd be comin' back."

"She can bloody well untell him, then."

"Right after the funeral, in the parlour on Saturday. She laid on a tea."

"Christ!"

"She had it all worked out, Craig."

"Did she no' cry?"

"Aye, at first. She cried louder, though, when she learned there was nothin' to come from the Burial Society."

"Twenty quid," said Craig, nodding. "He gave it t' us. He cashed it in."

Kirsty crossed to the stove and greased the small frying-pan with lard. "Who paid for the funeral, Gordon?"

"Mr Sanderson."

"God Almighty!" said Craig. "Did she ask him?"

"He's on the board o' the Burial Society. He knew the twenty quid was gone before Mam did. I think he was the one who told her the truth."

Kirsty said, "Will she have to pay it back?"

"Eventually," said Gordon. "As it is I'm to come off the day work."

"It's the bloody day work pays the bills," said Craig.

Gordon spread his hands, wafting smoke across the table. He appeared to be more comfortable now that he had shared the burden of responsibility with Craig and trusted his brother to extricate him, somehow, from the fate that Madge Nicholson had in store.

"She says she's ready to pitch in," Gordon said. "She says she's done it before, when we were young."

"Lyin' bitch," said Craig but softly, without heat.

"She thinks that you an' me, an' Kirsty—"

"Kirsty?"

"She knows you're married. Did you not say so in one o' the letters?"

Kirsty said, "I wouldn't be in this state, Gordon, if we weren't married, would I?"

"Suppose not," said Gordon. He was more interested in other aspects of the situation. "Anyway, Mam's got this notion you'll come home now, to Dalnavert—"

"She must be bloody daft."

"– an' we'll all live in the farmhouse, work the ground, build up the yield—"

"Dad could never make the place pay."

"We're young, though," said Gordon. "So Mam says."

"How long would we stay young, scratchin' away at yon bit o' ground?"

"Dalnavert's no' so bad, Craig."

"Cut it bloody out, Gordon," said Craig. "I know fine well what you're up to an' I'll have none o' it."

"Mr Sanderson's given her a year."

"It'll take five at least, plus capital."

"There is no money. She owes Mr Sanderson twenty quid."

"The burial never cost that, nothin' like it."

"There wasn't so much as a ha'penny in the kitty, Craig."

"She was fast off the mark findin' that out."

"It was easy to discover," said Gordon, "since there was nothin' *to* discover."

He glanced up at Kirsty as she broke an egg into the pan and the sizzle of frying filled the kitchen.

"Is that for me?" Gordon asked.

"Aye."

"I'm starved, right enough." He tilted his head and ostentatiously surveyed the kitchen, ceiling, window and floor. "No' bad. Small, though."

"This is Glasgow," said Craig.

"Some place," said Gordon. "Glasgow."

"You'll need to stay," said Kirsty. "I'll make up a bed in the front room."

"How many rooms?"

"Two," said Craig. "An' that's two more than most folk have got."

"Do ye say?" said Gordon.

"How's Lorna?"

"Fine."

"Upset?"

"Aye, very upset. It was the shock as much as anythin'."

"Did the wallin' an' the drainin' o' the high field ever get finished?"

"I did a bit."

"How much?"

"No' much."

Kirsty put down a plate of ham and egg, and returned to the stove to make tea for them all. Inside her the baby was active all of a sudden, stirring and clamouring and clouting her. The shock, she supposed, of the news had disturbed her system and the sympathy of the infant within her body.

Gordon ate hungrily. The butt of the cigarette smoked in a tin ashtray by his side. She watched him, saying nothing. Craig too was silent, lolling back in the wooden chair, lids lowered, his eyes with that dark, brooding emptiness; not emptiness but indrawnness. She wondered what was churning in his mind, what thoughts and speculations, what feelings were in his heart. His tears had all dried up and his mouth was firm. He looked fit and mature in contrast to his brother.

Craig said, "Is the new lease signed?"

Mouth full, Gordon mumbled, "Aye, but just for a year."

"Whose name?"

"Mine," said Gordon.

"Christ, so you can carry the can?"

"An' yours," said Gordon.

Craig, Kirsty noticed, did not seem unduly surprised.

"I thought as much," said Craig. "By God, but she's desperate to have me back, is she not?"

Gordon said, "We'll never do it on our own."

"What are the financial arrangements?"

"The debt an' first payment deferred until May."

"Will Mr Sanderson accept the value o' stock in the fields an' growin' crops?"

"Aye," said Gordon. "You know how kind he is. He's keen enough to lend a helpin' hand."

"But he expects me back, doesn't he?"

"I think he does."

Kirsty dumped the teapot on the mat on the table. "Craig?"

Craig said, "I get a hankerin' for the place, times, I admit."

"Craig?"

Gordon swabbed his plate with bread and popped the piece into his mouth.

"What did you think I was doin' here?" Craig said.

"Hadn't a notion," said Gordon. "Dairyman, somethin' along those lines."

"Well, like I told you, I'm a copper."

Gordon said, "How does it pay?"

"Now I'm out of probation, it pays twenty-two shillin's a week."

"An' this place, what does it cost?"

"Five pounds and ten shillings a year."

"So you're no' exactly starvin', eh?"

"Far from it," said Craig.

Gordon, without being asked, took another cigarette from the packet on the table and struck himself a match. He watched Kirsty pour tea into a cup.

"Would they take me too?" Gordon said. "To be a copper?"

Craig laughed. "You're o'er wee, Gordie."

"I'm no' wee."

"For a Glasgow policeman you are."

"Big enough t' run Dalnavert, though?"

"Are ye?" said Craig. He signalled. "Kirsty."

She poured tea for him too and then, as the brothers fell to talking once more, she went out of the kitchen and into the front room.

It was cold there, that same still clammy winter feel that the bothy at Hawkhead had had. She had not asked about Mr Clegg and Gordon had offered no information. That part of her life was over. Clegg would not pursue her now, could not harm her. Clegg was a small man tied to a handful of acres of rough hill-land and she was wife to a Glasgow policeman. She might have been in China for all Clegg knew.

She stood by the window, by the cheap curtain, and looked down into Canada Road, her hands upon her stomach. The baby had stopped kicking now. Below, a gang of young men, laughing at their own wit, slouched up from the direction of Dumbarton Road, from the pub perhaps, if they were in work and had a bob or two to spend midweek. Mr Boyle and his wife came stepping over the road, prim and solemn even in the way they walked; had been at a prayer meeting, probably, or a Bible group. They vanished below her into the close.

From the kitchen came the sound of laughter, not raucous but warm. Craig was glad to see his brother. Gordon's presence had taken the sting from the news of Mr Nicholson's death. For Gordon too, probably. They had each other, they had Lorna, and their mother still. She had nobody, and never had had anybody – except herself.

She wondered why she had not pressed Craig to marry her, and found no logical reason for her reluctance to bind herself to him. She did not know if he loved her, did not know what the word meant. It meant, she supposed, belonging – and not much more. She belonged to Craig all right. She would belong to him until he rejected her. That was it. She could not give up the faint, deep-buried fear that he would reject her, that she would lose not his love but the security he provided. The baby would not be like Craig. The baby would be her blood, her child. She would know then what love really felt like, the strange thistledown bondage of having a relative; a daughter, a son. It was, Kirsty thought, the only relationship that she could trust, the only love, perhaps, that she would ever know that wasn't demanding – aye, and in its way demeaning.

"Kirsty?"

She did not turn from the window, did not answer at first.

"Kirsty, this tea's gone cold."

"I'm comin'," she said.

"*Kirsty?*"

"I'm coming."

Craig would not stop talking. It had been months since she had heard him string so many words together. He lay by her side in the bed, hands behind his head, nose pointed at the pelmet above the window and went on and on and on about Gordon, Lorna, his dad, about Bankhead and Dalnavert and his mother.

Kirsty lay in that queer position which gave her most relief from the weight of her stomach, left arm tucked against her hip, one knee cocked, the blanket drawn up over her shoulders. She was weary but not sleepy. Even Craig's long monologue, delivered in a quiet voice, did not make her drowsy. She needed to know what was in Craig's mind, whether the prospect, the chance of going back home again had a strong appeal for him, whether or not it was that that had loosened his tongue or just the excitement of seeing his brother once more. Gordon had chosen to sleep in the kitchen. He had curled up on a mattress of old blankets in the alcove and was snoring even before Kirsty turned off the gaslight and closed the fire door on the grate.

"Nothin' to worry about from Clegg," said Craig. "He canna touch you now we're married. Anyway, he has another servant. Hired her from the McSweens. You remember yon clan from down in Galloway that come up for the harvests; well, them. She's only fourteen year old an' not quite right in the head. Mr Sanderson made a fuss about it, apparently, but Clegg had a signed paper, and that was that. Gordon says she's got a temper like a bloody wildcat so maybe old Clegg'll have to pay for his fun.

"Even if I'd been there, there was nothin' I could have done. It was a defect in the heart, the doctor said. Funny how it never showed a sign. Aye, he was fond o' the bottle, right enough, but he never lifted a hand against any o' us unless Mother forced him to it. She did most of the beltin' when we were young. I daresay we needed it, an' all.

"I wish he'd got the letters, though. It would have pleased him to learn I'd become a copper. By God, though, if he'd survived he'd have been up here at the toot when the bairn was born. He'd have been desperate to see it. He was always proud o' the Nicholson name.

"He was fond o' you, Kirsty. I think that's why he gave us the twenty pounds. If I'd known it was all he had salted away I'd have thought twice about takin' it, I'll tell you.

"It was what he wanted, though. It was his dearest wish for you an' me to—"

Craig was silent for a moment or two.

"Imagine just droppin' down dead like that. God, you never know the minute. They carried him into the bedroom in the Mains until the doctor arrived. Muddy boots, bloody head an' all. That's the Sandersons for you. They always had a soft spot for you, Kirsty; the Sandersons.

"Did I tell you I've learned to swim, by the way?"

"No. No, you didn't," Kirsty said.

"Well, I have. Near enough. Never been a Nicholson who could swim before. Dad would see bathers on the beach an' say, 'If God had intendit us t' be fish he'd have given us gills.' I don't think he'd have minded me learnin' to swim, though.

"He'd have liked my uniform. He was always keen on uniforms. He loved the kilties when the battalion camped at Sands. Remember?"

"I never got to see them," said Kirsty.

"He took Gordon an' me down to look at them. 'Would you fancy bein' a soldier, son?' he asked me."

"What did you say?"

"I never said anythin'. I was frightened, I remember, that he wanted me to be a soldier just to get rid o' me. You know what it's like when you're wee, when you don't know what they want and how you can give it."

Craig sighed and shifted position slightly.

He said, "There are worse places than Dalnavert."

Kirsty said, "Do you want to go back?"

"Do you?"

"I'll go where you go, Craig."

"Aye, you'll have to," Craig said.

It was the truth; the advent of the baby bound her to him more than the ring, more than a marriage certificate would have done. She could not send for herself, not with a baby to feed.

She said, "It's all right here."

"I'll say it is," Craig exclaimed. "Own house, good job."

"Tell Gordon—"

"She'll never manage wi'out me, though. She'll have no option but to take me back in."

"It's why she sent Gordon," Kirsty reminded him.

"I could turn Dalnavert into a payin' farm in ten years. It

would be hard, no denyin' that, but it might be worth it," Craig said. "Anyway, I should really go back wi' Gordon, just to see her."

"Can you get time off?"

"For a bereavement – och, aye."

"She'll make you stay."

"Nobody makes me do anythin' I don't want to do."

"I thought – I thought we were settled," said Kirsty.

"Gordon canna handle the farm on his own."

"Craig—"

"She'll expect me to come back with him."

Kirsty raised herself on her elbow. "Give yourself time, Craig. Don't rush into it."

"Aye, that's sense," he conceded.

"When's your next full day off?"

"A fortnight."

"Wait until then."

"She'll be mad if I don't show up," Craig said. "If I don't go back wi' Gordon my name really will be mud. She's my mother, after all."

"She's read your letters; she'll understand."

"I suppose so."

"Sleep on it, at least," Kirsty said.

"I wonder what he'd have done."

"Who?"

"Dad."

Kirsty held her tongue and, after a minute, Craig grunted, kissed her perfunctorily on the brow and turned heavily on to his side.

"Goodnight, dear," Kirsty whispered.

But he did not answer her.

The brothers left the house together. It was cloudy, not cold though, and at that early hour Canada Road had a clean and peaceful air. A midden cart ground off towards the depot and a pair of burgh council lamplighters were working their rounds, poles across their shoulders.

Kirsty stood in the front room window, her cheek against the glass and watched Craig and Gordon walk towards Dumbarton Road. There Craig would direct his brother on to a tram and, she knew, would give him money, a pound or thirty shillings; she had seen Craig in at the savings and had no need to ask the reason. She did not grudge it. She was too relieved that Craig had not committed himself, had not sent her round to Ottawa Street to say that he would not be on duty, that he had not gone home to Dalnavert.

It was not up to her to persuade him to stay in Glasgow. She had more sense than to argue with him, try to convince him that their new life was better than the old life, the city better than the country, that Canada Road offered more chance of happiness than Dalnavert.

Happiness: she was not sure now what that word meant, what images it should conjure up and what visions for the future. She was so heavy, so tired that she could not see beyond the delivery, could not imagine what it would be like to give birth.

Craig and Gordon were out of sight. From the close below came Mr Swanson and after him came John Boyle and then the Walkers, father and son. In twenty minutes or so Mr McGonigle and Andy McAlpine would come trudging in from night-shift and soon Canada Road would be bustling with children on the way to school and wives to the shops.

Kirsty felt a strange yearning to be part of it, to be quickly absorbed into the community, her and her children. There was nothing to prevent it happening, nothing except Craig, and Madge Nicholson's influence upon him.

SEVEN

The Valley of the Shadow

The cell block might have been new but the system of hard labour in use in Barlinnie Prison was as old as punishment itself. Reforms were in the government pipeline but Daniel Malone knew nothing of them and would not have cared if he had. He ground through each stage of the so-called Progressive System by which a convict's will was broken, lived only for that day when, having been 'a good lad', he would earn the privilege of exercise in the open yard and would be able to see not only the sky but the wall and the lie of the land beneath it.

In first term Malone sweated for six hours each day on the crank, cawing a long iron handle which rotated a blade sealed inside a box full of heavy gravel. One thousand revolutions was the daily requirement. He was supervised by warders to ensure that he did not slouch or slacken his pace; nor did he, not even when his palms cracked and bled and his fingers swelled up like Pollock's sausages. After stint on the crank he was obliged to sit cross-legged on a canvas mat and, without tool or implement, to pick apart twists of old rope, oakum, with what was left of his fingernails. Three pounds weight of coarse hair-like matter had to be produced per shift. Festering sores developed on his hands. They were treated by the prison surgeon who painted them with saline solution and permitted him to wear bandages for seven days. At night he slept on a plank board. He was fed on bread, gruel, tea and broth, potatoes and, every fourth day, a flake of meat. At first he craved meat, hungered for alcohol and most of all for tobacco but those appetites died in due course. To his surprise, he missed connection with women not at all. He earned no money, of course. He received no letters, no visitors and was cut off from communication with other prisoners.

Daniel Malone was too old for such a harsh regime. Dealings with 'toffs' and indulgences that his profits had bought had made him soft. From Billy and other unfortunates he had heard of the horrors of imprisonment. But he had not been able to predict the tortures of solitude and grinding monotony, had not supposed that he would be stripped of every vestige of power, that within Barlinnie's walls he would have no reputation, no edge of authority, no identity at all.

A shaven head and coarse serge seemed fitting for a man known only as No. 679, who was addressed only by number during the first interminable weeks of incarceration. How long each term was slated to last was a question to which Malone received no answer save a smirk and a shake of the head. How many 'good marks' he had accumulated was also a mystery. The first indication that he was 'getting somewhere' came on his seventh Sunday in Barlinnie.

Sunday was the worst day for a convict on hard labour. Sunday was a day of infinite monotony, passed without occupation. When the body was rested the mind churned with self-pity. By the time the leaden hours of morning had passed the prisoner longed for the crank or the oakum basket, for something, anything to do to still his thoughts.

Warder Caine unlocked the door. Malone stopped pacing the eight steps that measured the length of his cell and looked up guiltily. Was pacing a 'crime' too? Would he be docked 'good marks' just for putting one foot before another?

Warder Caine said, "Do you want a pastor, six-seven-nine?"

"What?"

"Read my lips, you idiot. Do – you – want – a – cleric?"

"Yes," Malone declared.

"What are you?"

"Number six-seven—"

"Religious bloody persuasion, you idiot."

"Protestant."

"You can have a visit of ten minutes," said Warder Caine.

"Is . . . am I . . . have I . . . earned it?"

"You also get a mattress, two nights a week."

Questions gushed into Malone's mouth. How soon would he earn the next privilege? How long before he could have a visitor? Receive a letter? Be let out into the yard? He squeezed his lips tight; he had learned to say as little as possible in case he gave offence.

The chaplain was a retired minister of the Free Church who believed in punishment and in the expiation of guilt by servitude. It was not his business to convert the pagan or offer solace to souls in torment. God alone could do that. Nonetheless as a servant of God he would not deny a man, even a convicted felon, the right to raise up his spirit and seek union with Christ Jesus, mediator and

263

saviour of all sinners. Reverend Grimmond found Malone, in
tears, on his knees.

"Are you *praying?*"

"I – I canna pray, sir. I canna make the Lord hear me. Oh,
Christ in Heaven, I need help to make my prayers rise through my
unworthiness."

"No man is irredeemable."

"It's not a man, sir; it's a woman."

Reverend Grimmond prided himself on being able to spot a
charlatan at a thousand paces. But he was taken in by Daniel
Malone, by the fact that he did not howl in mock contrition or try
to wheedle favours out of him. Malone, it seemed, was gnawed by
concern for his sister, a widow sick with 'tubercoles'. Malone did
not know if she was dead or alive. Reverend Grimmond sat on the
bed, ordered Malone to kneel before him, put a hand on his bristle
and prayed for him. He prayed for the Lord's mercy and
intervention, prayed for the Lord to lift the burden of guilt that
tormented the soul of No. 679. Malone clung to him and – without
overdoing it – thanked him profusely when the prayer was done.

The following Sunday Reverend Grimmond was again taken in
and, one week later, he brought permission for No. 679 to write a
letter – one page – under supervision and have it despatched to his
sister's address.

"What's her name?"

Warder Caine peered suspiciously over No. 679's shoulder,
admired the swiftness of his fist and the speed with which the pen
capered over the coarse brown paper.

"It's Gusset."

"Gussie?"

"Gusset, sir."

"Heh, like in drawers?"

"She's my sister, sir."

"Does she no' wear drawers, then?"

"She's my sister," said Malone again.

"Why are ye no' writin' to your wife?"

"It's my sister that's sick, sir. It's her I'm worried about."

"Got a chill in her whatnot, eh, no' wearin' drawers?"

Malone completed the letter. It was literate, properly spelled,
and contained not one word that would damage the credibility of
his story.

In due course a letter from Mrs Noreen Gusset was received at
the prison office and examined before being taken down to No.
679's cell and read aloud to the prisoner.

Malone knew that Noreen had not written the letter. In spite of her obvious attributes Noreen had never learned to read or write. He had, however, counted on her being smart enough to show the letter to somebody who would 'get the message' and was delighted to hear that the subterfuge had been sustained . Poor Noreen, said the missive, was on her last legs and might soon be summoned to meet her Maker.

Malone wept convincingly.

On a cold January day four weeks later, No. 679 was granted a fifteen-minute visit from his beloved sister.

He was escorted from his cell to the long hall where such meetings took place and had his first real chance to study the landscape of the prison.

The long table had two chairs at it. They were separated not only by the table's width but by a fence of heavy wrought-iron which reared up from the oak surface to a height of four or five feet. A warder, stranger to Malone, was already stationed at one of the hall's two doors. His arms were folded, his gaze steady and attentive. Warder Caine brought Malone to the chair, leered at Noreen, then retired to a chair by the entrance door where he sat with his sabre scabbard across his knees.

Noreen was wrapped in a ragged shawl. Apparently she was nursing a head cold. Her eyes were pink and her nose was running. She looked convincingly unwell and coughed raucously, like somebody in the last throes. As he seated himself Malone wondered what he had ever found attractive in the girl. He felt not the least regret at his enforced celibacy.

Softly, and without preamble, he said, "Who wrote the letter?"

"Jamie."

"Jamie Dobbs?"

"Aye."

"Where is he then, Noreen?"

"Who? Jamie?"

"You know who I mean."

"He joined the polis."

"Is he still in the Greenfield?"

"Aye, at Ottawa Street."

"House?"

"Canada Road, top end."

"Cough."

"What?"

"Cough, damn it. You're supposed to be dyin'."

Noreen did her bit. On the first spasm the act became reality so that she choked and barked until the echoes of her distress filled the great bleak hall. She rocked back and forth, hands clutched to her breast. It was a full two minutes before she recovered.

Malone waited patiently until she regained her breath.

"Tell Jamie I want him done," he said.

Wiping her eyes on the shawl, Noreen darted a scared glance at Warder Caine then inched the chair back from the table.

She licked her lips. "Jamie says – Jamie says he'll no' nobble a copper."

"He'll get paid double."

"Jamie says it's too bloody risky at any price."

"Tell him I said to do it."

"How'll he get paid, but? Twelve year is a long time, Danny."

"*What?*"

Fist on the hilt of his sabre, Warder Caine stiffened and his colleague by the exit door unfolded his arms.

"Vincent'll no' do it either," said Noreen. "Vincent says there's been enough trouble wi' the bloody blue boys."

"Billy's brother?" Malone hissed through clenched teeth.

Noreen shook her head. "Naw."

"Christ, after all I done for them."

"Vincent says you'll just have t' wait. Nobody'll do it, Danny."

Malone's fist closed on the wrought-iron staves. Warder Caine's voice rang out: "*Hands off.*"

Malone let go the iron and drew his hand back, closed the fingers into a fist in mid-air. Cowering, Noreen coughed again.

In a soft, soft voice Malone said, "They've wrote me off – am I right?"

"Aye."

"All o' them?"

"Aye."

"Are you livin' with Jamie?"

"Aye."

"So they think I'm finished, do they?"

"Aye, Danny."

"Well, I'm not."

"Danny, it's—"

"I'm bloody not."

"Danny—"

"You tell them, Noreen. You tell them I'm no' finished."

"Jamie says I've no' to come here again."

"I don't need the likes o' them. An' I don't need you either."

"God, Danny! Can ye not—"

"I'll do it myself."

"Do what?"

"Make certain he gets what's comin' to him, what he deserves."

"Danny, it'll be twelve year—"

"The devil it will. Stuff them. Stuff them all. I'll be out o' here soon, you mark my words."

"But how, Danny? How?" cried Noreen.

Abruptly Malone got to his feet. He wrapped his arms over his face. Shoulders heaved with emotion. He made no attempt to touch his 'sister' on the other side of the fence. Even so, Warder Caine came clattering down the stone-flagged hall with his sabre out of its scabbard.

"Oh, God! God!" howled Daniel Malone. "Noreen, my Noreen!"

Still weeping in great grating paroxysms he was led away while the girl, dry-eyed and terrified, stared after until the door slammed.

Eleven days later No. 679 received another little concession – a straw-filled bolster – which indicated that he had progressed again. Within the month he was even favoured with a half hour's exercise in the high-walled yard.

Walking round and round and round the cinder path, head hung and eyes alert, Daniel Malone searched for things that would help him to find an answer to Noreen's final question, anything that would aid the planning of his inevitable escape.

"It's the time of year as much as anything," said Doctor Godwin. "Dampness and lack of ventilation account for so many conditions; and, of course, a general absence of cheerfulness."

"I'm cheerful enough, Doctor."

"I'm sure you are. Are you getting enough nourishment, Mrs Nicholson?"

"I – I think so."

"Whole milk?"

"I buy two pints every day."

"Not from Thom's cart, I trust?"

"From the Greenfield Dairy."

"Oh, that's all right." Doctor Godwin rolled up the rubber sleeve that he had wrapped about her arm and inflated with a bulb. "I cannot find anything to suggest a problem. You're certainly quite large in the cavity."

Kirsty wished that he would keep his voice down. Only a wooden door separated the closet-like consulting-room from the crowded waiting-room. Men as well as women huddled miserably on the wooden benches out there and the thought of strangers sharing the details of her intimate condition made her cringe with embarrassment.

"I suppose," said Doctor Godwin, "that you did not mistake the date of first conception or of the first absent period?"

"I – I don't think so."

"How severe is the pain?"

"It comes an' goes."

"On stooping?"

"Sometimes."

"On pressing at stool?" Doctor Godwin seemed to roar out the question and Kirsty's cheeks glowed.

"No."

"Does your husband treat you well?"

"He's a policeman," said Kirsty.

Doctor Godwin nodded, as if he needed no more assurance than that. "Internal gases. Not uncommon." He reached for his prescription paper, uncapped a fountain pen with his teeth. "I'll give you a bottle, Mrs Nicholson."

"Is that all it is?"

"I'm sure it's nothing. However, if the pain – the discomfort, shall we call it – persists, then come back next week. I'll make no charge."

"Oh, I can pay."

"I suggest that you call upon Mrs Fernie. She's the best midwife in Greenfield and handles many of my cases. Registered, of course." He scribbled away, turned the paper. "I'll put her address on the back."

"What have I got to see her for?" said Kirsty.

"To inform her when she may expect to be called."

"I thought that you—"

"I will attend, of course, if it's necessary."

Again Kirsty said, "I can pay."

"Do you really want me at the delivery, Mrs Nicholson? If you wish, I'll come. But I do assure you that Mrs Fernie is completely reliable and experienced in home births."

Kirsty felt betrayed. The atmosphere of the Banff Street consulting-room was so different from that of the elegant house in Dowanhill. Though his examination had been thorough, as far as Kirsty could tell, she could not accept Doctor Godwin's casualness or believe that he was telling her the whole truth about her condition. He gave her the prescription and was out of his chair

and stepping to the door before she could fumble the half-crown
from her purse.

"Oh, yes, thank you, Mrs Nicholson." The silver coin dis-
appeared into a cashbox in a drawer of the desk. "Now don't
worry about a thing. You'll be in good hands."

Without more ado he ushered her out into the waiting-room. It
was lit by a smoky oil-lamp suspended from a beam, heated by a
paltry wee coal fire. Some patients paid her not the slightest
attention, absorbed in their own aches and pains. Others, though,
glowered at her as she steered her stomach between them and
pulled open the outside door.

The street glistened with the day's rain. Now that night had
come there was a snell wind off the river.

Kirsty turned up her coat collar, shivering. To add to her other
woes she had a frayed welt on her shoe and water had seeped in
and made her stocking damp. She felt thoroughly miserable and
abandoned as she waddled down Banff Street to a gas-lamp
where, holding up the paper, she squinted at the address the
doctor had given her.

It was streets away, in the opposite direction to Canada Road.
Besides, she had to have the doctor's bottle, needed relief from her
discomfort – and she still had to buy something for Craig's supper.
She would call on Mrs Fernie some other time. After all it was
thirty-five or -six days before the baby was due. All she wanted
was to be at home by the fire with Craig.

She set off towards Dumbarton Road and the hot-pie shop,
shuffling, a nagging sort of pain under her ribs and one foot wet.
Within minutes it began to rain again.

The Madagascar was the worst slum in Greenfield. It was not on
Craig's beat and he had been there only once in all his months on
the Force. He knew it by reputation, though; a delta of decaying
eighteenth-century tenements and cottage rows that protruded
out into the Clyde at the head of a timber quay where once the
Madagascar Coal Company had ferried in its wares from
Ayrshire's coastal pits. The Madagascar Coal Company had long
since gone bust but the name remained and the earth was still
black with ancient leavings and nothing but weeds grew on the
packed black mounds from which not even the coal-pickers could
sift out a harvest. The Madagascar Tavern had put up its shutters
years ago. There were two or three shebeens in operation in the
hovels and no legitimate publican could hope to compete with the
appeal of dirt-cheap alcohol, a raw and colourless distillation that

could drag a man or woman into oblivion faster than a clout with a crowbar. Now and again Sergeant Drummond would muster a team of six burly constables and make a raid on the illicit distillers but not even Mr Organ had the heart to insist on it, for drink was all that most of the denizens of that district had and oblivion their only pleasure.

It was Craig's first 'investigation'. He was handed it – an Incident Report – from the fair hand of old Drummond when he tramped in at shift's end. He had planned on going on to the gymnasium that evening. He could not abide going home early these nights, could not stand the sight of Kirsty all bloated and pale, could not put up with her uncomplaining misery. Archie Flynn was to accompany him on the investigation. Normally it would have been a more experienced constable, the night-duty man, Armour, whose beat it was, who would have picked up the report. But Armour was off with a whitlow on his foot and three other men had gone off the roster sick.

Craig was not displeased to be entrusted with an enquiry. He glanced at the slip of paper.

"What's the name?"

"Austin Galletti," said the sergeant.

"Queer handle, Sergeant Drummond," said Archie.

"Queer handle or not," said the sergeant, "Mr Galletti's entitled to call on our services."

"Theft of what?" said Craig, peering at the slip.

"The tools of the trade."

"What trade?"

"He's a professional hunchback," the sergeant said.

It took Craig and Archie the best part of half an hour to locate Mr Galletti. He lived in a dwelling that had no number in a lane that had no name. If he had been less well-known in the Madagascar the policemen might not have found him at all for the folk on the streets of the delta scurried off at first glimpse of a uniform and refused to open their doors to polite enquiry. It was only by nabbing a small bedraggled girl child, too stupid to flee, that Archie elicited the information that 'hunchie' lived in the old pig mews behind the ruin of the public house.

Even on a cold night after a day's rain the stench from the mews was overpowering. The pigs were long since gone and the sties had been taken over by families and the place glimmered with candles and dim lanterns like something out of a grim old fairy-tale. Hands on their sticks Craig and Archie walked shoulder to shoulder along the lane.

"No, muchee likee," said Archie, from the corner of his mouth. "I'm no' knockin' on any doors here."

Craig said, "There he is."

Mr Galletti lived in the last room in the mews. It was, Craig thought, like a farm bothy; a single apartment with a door that opened straight in from the cobbles. The stench here was particularly strong for the mews ran on to a slope of rank earth where a sludge pile filtered its foul wastes down through dross into the river. Austin Galletti was almost a dwarf and a small lump rose from his left shoulder. He had thick white hair, salt stubble on his rounded chin and could have been any age over sixty. Craig felt no pity for the wee chap for in his face was a fire of bitterness and hatred.

"What bloody kept ye?" Galletti demanded.

He had been loitering at the door of his home. He was not dressed for February, wore only a shirt, a ragged leather vest and a pair of breeks made out of patchwork.

Archie said, "Are you Mr Galletti?"

"Jesus an' Joseph, would there be two like me?" The man danced with rage and peered up into Archie's face. "Were ye no' told what happened?"

"Did you make the report in person?" said Craig.

"Aye. Who'd leg it t' Ottawa Street for the likes o' me? Him wi' the stripes told me you'd be here directly."

Craig said, "I believe you had some property stolen."

Archie backed away from the prancing little chap and glanced nervously down the mews. Men had slithered from shelter and slouched in shadowy doorways watching the coppers with sullen malevolence.

"Property!" Galletti said. "Jesus an' Joseph, he calls it property. It's my bloody livelihood, that's what was stole."

"What exactly?" said Craig.

"My cart, my drum, my mouth harmonium, my bloody flags," Galletti answered. "Even my guns."

"Guns?"

"What I use for firin' in my performances. Have ye no' seen me perform? Jesus an' Joseph, what kind of coppers are ye if ye haven't seen Galletti's act?"

"Tell me about the guns," said Craig.

"*Pop. Pop. Pop*," said Galletti. "Toy guns. Three o' them. He took them an' all. He took every bloody thing."

"Hold on, Mr Galletti," said Craig. "You talk as if you know the thief."

271

"Aye, I bloody know the thief."

"Did you impart this information to our sergeant?"

"What?"

"Did you tell the stripes?"

"Aye, 'course I did."

"What did he say to it?"

"Said he'd send men t' investigate my alginations. Here, all he sends is a couple o' weans."

Craig said, "How was the theft carried out?"

"I told him all that already."

"Tell us again, Mr Galletti."

"The bugger broke down my door an' took all the stuff away in my cart. He went over the stink-pit wi' it – that way."

"How do you know?"

"Saw him, so I did."

"Why didn't you try to stop him?"

"I'd just come back from up the road. I'd been for a wee refreshment. I saw him comin' out my house wi' my cart. I shouted but he ran away."

"Did ye no' give chase?" said Archie.

"Me? Look at me. Jesus an' Joseph," Galletti shouted as if poor Archie Flynn had cursed him with deformities. "It's no bloody mystery who stole my stuff. I want it back. I need it, see, if I'm t' earn my daily bread."

"Can you name the person who stole your gear?"

"Name him, aye: Sammy Reynolds."

"This person, Sammy Reynolds, is known to you?"

"Christ, he should be known to me. He's been trailin' me about for bloody years. He sits by the railin' o' the park when I'm doin' my act. He hides in a close opposite the *Palace* when I'm turnin' for the queue. He even dogs me up t' the Groveries when I go there, summer nights."

"What does he do?"

"He watches me."

"Does he annoy you in any way?"

"Naw; just watches."

"But why, Mr Galletti?"

"He's jealous."

"Jealous?"

The fierce contorted little visage thrust out of hunched shoulders. Short arms sawed the air as if beating an invisible drum. "The bastard wants t' be me."

Craig paused. "What age is Sammy Reynolds?"

"Twelve, thirteen."

"Where does he live?" said Archie.

"In Rae's tenement."

Craig nodded; he knew the building.

He said, "Let's look at your broken door, Mr Galletti."

"For what?"

"So I can put a report in my notebook," said Craig.

"An' then?" Galletti shouted.

"An' then," said Craig, "Constable Flynn an' me will walk over to Rae's tenement an' fetch your stuff back."

"All of it?"

"All of it," Craig promised.

They did not have to track him down or root him out of hiding. Sammy Reynolds did not have the wit to hide. They heard him, unmistakably, as they picked their way across waste ground that surrounded the solitary habitation. Rae's tenement was the last survivor of a clump of workers' dwellings, a century old. Once it had sheltered the Madagascar's loaders and heavers but not a breath of their labour remained. The brickwork was pitted, holed and scarred as if it had endured bombardment under siege. There was little evidence of present occupation, only a flickering candle or the wan glint of a lantern in the windows, more life among the rats that scampered over the middens that fronted the place on what had once been a cobbled street.

"Hear it?" said Archie.

"Aye, I hear it."

"Where's it comin' from?"

"Over there," said Craig. "Down there."

"God!" said Archie. "The cellar."

They skirted the big midden. The effluvia of the dump, dampened by rain, mingled with coke fumes and the low smoky reek of fried meat. Inside the building a dog snarled viciously and a voice, guttural and androgynous, barked back, made the animal yelp and be still. The constables reached a doorway in the base of an oval tower up which a staircase tottered. Gas had not been piped to this tenement and the close behind the stairs was as black as pitch. The policemen needed no light to guide them, however, for the tinny strains of a mouth harmonium and the dull thud-thump of a drum floated up from the well that led to the cellar.

"Does he live down there, do y' think?"

"I suppose he does," said Craig. "Got your stick handy?"

"Right in my fist."

"All right; down we go."

A sprinkle of light from a candle in a bottle marked the bottom of the well, for Sammy Reynolds, as if to lure an audience to his first performance, had left the cellar door ajar.

The cellar was narrow, windowless and cold. No fire smouldered in the sodden ashes in the hearth, no cooking-pot bubbled. There was no table in the room, only one wooden chair and two beds, fashioned of straw and tattered blankets. A bottle had been shattered on the hearthstone and shards of glass littered the floor. On a tin plate, smeared with gravy fat, was a heel of bread upon which fed a one-eared cat, quite undisturbed by the clack of stolen clogs or the thumping of a stolen drum. In the drab cellar Galletti's little toy cart looked anomalously gay and new.

"Sammy Reynolds?" said Craig.

It was as if he had been expecting them, had rehearsed the dance for their benefit. He pressed his knees together, splayed out his feet and bounced the painted wooden shoes hither and thither while he accompanied himself with a daft wee *yee-yee* chant upon the mouth organ. The instrument was attached to a harness of leather and soft wood that presented the harmonium to Sammy's lips and left his hands free. The drum, of no great size, was strapped against his left hip. He beat on it unrhythmically with a stick feathered in sheepskin and at the same time waved a flag, the Scottish standard, one of three that were stuck in his belt. A popgun of painted tin and stained boxwood hung from a string down his back.

"Dear God!" said Archie. "Reynolds, stop that bloody—"

"Wait, Archie," Craig said.

They watched the boy who, eyes crinkled with merriment, watched them in turn. He blew harder, beat harder and danced more furiously as if he had put his agility on trial and might earn by it not money or approval but discharge from his crime. Winded at last, he twirled the flag and stabbed it into his belt, fumbled the toy gun into his hand and with a final loud chant on the mouth harmonium fired off a salvo of one cork – and bowed.

Craig applauded. "Very good, Sammy. Very good. Did Mr Galletti teach you that?"

Sammy shook his head. He was slender and his complexion reminded Craig of Kirsty; freckles too. He looked pale but not unhealthy, though his teeth were bad. When he nodded his auburn-reddish hair bobbed with natural curls.

"How did you learn?"

274

"Watchit him," said Sammy. "Good, eh?"

Craig said, "Did Mr Galletti lend you his gear, Sammy?"

Sammy frowned. He looked down at the buckle of the drum strap and began to pick at it with a bitten thumbnail.

Archie said, "Where's your mother, Sammy?"

"Deid," said Sammy.

"Your father?"

"Oot."

"You did wrong, Sammy," said Craig.

"It was good. I done it good."

"You shouldn't have kicked down the door."

"Wouldnae talk t' me."

"Did you take any of his money?"

Surprised, then outraged, Sammy stared at them, the drum trailing on a loosened strap. "Naw. Aw naw."

The colour of his hair, the texture of his skin, and that expression of unabashed innocence – it was Kirsty, Kirsty long ago when he had first noticed her at school. Irked at the bizarre memory Craig spoke sharply. "You stole Mr Galletti's gear, didn't you?"

Sammy concentrated on another buckle, worked at it with his fingers. In his left hand the popgun's cork dangled impotently from its string.

"He's an old man," said Archie. "A hunchie-back."

"He's a dancer," Sammy shouted. "He's the best dancer in the whole toon."

"Take that stuff off," said Archie.

"You'll have to come with us to the police station," said Craig. "It's a charge, Sammy. Do you know what that means?"

"Aye," said Sammy dismissively.

"You can't steal—"

"It was good," said Sammy Reynolds. "I done it, an' it was good."

"It's theft, Sammy."

"Tell me it was good."

"You danced just fine," said Craig.

"Good."

"Yes, Sammy," Craig said. "You were very, very good."

Greenfield Police Court convened on Thursday morning with Bailie Smith on the bench. Bailie Smith was an iron merchant, a well-to-do and compassionate Christian familiar with all the ins and outs of criminal behaviour at ground level. He was a severe-looking man, however, and had that day a full bill of hearings to get through. He was not about to stand for eloquence or hair-splitting in the case of Samuel Reynolds. Craig was no longer nervous about giving evidence. Amid the unruly bustle of a court coppers were expected to be calm, concise and laconic. Mr Galletti was positioned in the public pews. He was called first before the Bailie. He would have given a performance of great flourish, dance and all, perhaps, if Bailie Smith had not curtailed it, drily remarking that he did not require the facts set to music, thank you.

Constable Nicholson came before the bench, told what he had found in Madagascar Mews and in the cellar of Rae's tenement.

"Did Reynolds deny the theft?"

"No, sir. He did not."

"Did he make a confession?"

"At the station, sir, he admitted all."

"Mr Galletti's possessions?"

"Returned to him, sir, intact an' unharmed."

"There was no attempt to resist, Constable Nicholson?"

"None, sir."

The proceeding lasted no more than six or seven minutes. Samuel Reynolds had been kept in a cell at Ottawa Street overnight. His father, Robert Reynolds, had not returned to his place of residence the previous evening.

"Has he been found now?" the Bailie asked.

It was Sergeant Drummond, who had accompanied his constables to the court, who answered. "Robert Reynolds has been found, Bailie. He was in a partially intoxicated condition and appears to have spent the best part of the night in the company of a woman of loose moral character."

"What does he do – Reynolds?"

"He is an occasional labourer," said Sergeant Drummond, consulting a notebook on his hand. "What's known as a 'tar-macadam man'."

"Where is he?"

"Not here, Bailie," said Sergeant Drummond.

"Because of work?"

"Because of refusing, sir."

"I see," said the Bailie.

He summoned Sammy to stand before him and lectured him briefly upon the seriousness of stealing away a man's source of earning.

Craig listened, for he had not been dismissed, and wondered if Sammy was taking in any of the points that the Bailie was making.

"Do you understand me, Reynolds?"

Sammy nodded, glanced round at Craig and grinned innocently. He had been well fed at Ottawa Street, had not been beaten. He had slept in a clean dry cell. He had been given breakfast and Sergeant Drummond had stood over him while he had washed his face and combed his hair. It had been an eventful morning and he had been the centre of attention. Even Mr Galletti had noticed him, had shouted at him.

"I will not have it, Reynolds," the Bailie said. "I have witnessed the penalty of leniency in young boys of your calibre. For that reason, for your own good, I sentence you to receive six strokes of the birch before release."

Sammy frowned.

"Will you see to it, Sergeant Drummond?"

"I will, sir."

"Let the usual protections be taken."

"Yes, Bailie."

"That is all for this case."

For a moment Sammy had nobody to turn to. He shuffled aimlessly in front of the bench. He had not been given an opportunity to offer explanations or reasons and Craig knew that he did not really comprehend the nature of his punishment. A beating would be nothing to Sammy Reynolds, hardly punishment at all.

Sergeant Drummond gave Craig a dig. "We take him."

"Where to?"

"Next door."

Craig took the boy's arm and drew him away. Sammy was still smiling at the Bailie who, though not disconcerted, had chosen to ignore the dealt-with offender and was signalling to the court clerk to usher in the next petty criminal.

"Come on," said Craig.

He led Sammy to the side door. Archie, who had not been called, and Sergeant Drummond followed on.

From the corner of his eye Craig sighted Galletti in the short tiled corridor. Bow-legged, crouched, Galletti beamed and winked and shouted out in a soft hoarse voice, "Gi'e him bloody licks, the bastard. Make him wriggle."

The punishment room was situated in the basement of Police Headquarters in Percy Street. That building shared the site with the court and the warren of chambers and storerooms and cells

277

below street level were all burgh property and served the ends of justice indiscriminately.

Craig had never been there before. Sergeant Drummond knew the way well enough. He went a step ahead of the constable and the delinquent, pushing doors, stepping down staircases and, somewhere en route, shed Archie who was dismissed to return to his usual duties.

Sammy did not like the basement. His step faltered and he might have shrunk back if Craig had not kept him firmly in motion, giving him a little push with the flat of his hand. The odour of disinfectant, or something more sinister, impregnated the walls here, for, Craig realised, they were in the vicinity of the morgue. They turned a corner into a long gas-lit corridor. Sammy's steps faltered again. Ahead, by a pebble-glass door, waited the police surgeon, the same elderly terrier who had attended Craig's injuries on the night of Malone's capture. He gave no sign of recognition, however, but fell into step with Drummond and marched to a dark wooden door, unlocked it with a key and pushed it open.

Craig said, "Do I—?"

"He's your prisoner, Constable Nicholson," the sergeant told him.

High on the far wall of painted brick was a slot of a window, an iron grille fixed over it. The room was not spotless by any means but had traces of dust here and there, motes swirling in gelid daylight. The floor was of unmatted stone. There was little by way of furniture in the room, only a big cabinet on the right wall and a series of devices whose purpose was immediately obvious to Craig; a wooden triangle with leather straps, man-high; a padded bench, raked to an angle, with more straps; a stool, a wooden chair and four metal pans like those used for milk in a dairy which, Craig supposed, were used to catch blood or urine. He suppressed a shudder. His mouth was dry as cotton and his stomach muscles knotted tight. He eased Sammy Reynolds forward, though the boy struggled a little and cowered back against the uniform.

"How many strokes?" said Deedes, the surgeon.

"Six," said Sergeant Drummond.

"Do you have a signature?"

The sergeant handed the surgeon the slip that he had been given by the Bailie but, Craig noticed, the surgeon hardly glanced at it.

The surgeon said, "Are you Samuel Reynolds?"

Sammy nodded.

"Speak out, lad."

"Aye, sir."

To Drummond: "Where is the parent?"

"Not present."

"The father has the right to be here, to administer the strokes if he chooses," said the surgeon. "I presume he's been informed of the privilege?"

"Let us just say that the father has waived the right."

"I see," said the surgeon. "So the constable will do it."

"What?" said Craig. "What's this?"

"No," said Sergeant Drummond. "I will be doing it myself."

Craig heard himself say. "I thought there was a——"

Softly Drummond told him, "Punishment of a juvenile is a matter for the arresting officer."

"I – I can't——"

"I'm not expecting it of you, Constable Nicholson. Nonetheless it's you who must hold the lad."

"Dear God!" said Craig.

Surgeon Deedes said, "He should have been told. Did nobody tell him?"

"He'll know next time," said Sergeant Drummond.

"Reynolds, take off your clothing," said the surgeon.

For some reason Sammy looked at Craig.

Swallowing, Craig said, "Better do it, Sammy. Get it over with."

It was so grey in the basement chamber, so still and silent. Blue serge and brass buttons, the polished belt, seemed to draw Craig on to the cruel side of the law. He tried not to look at Sammy as the boy peeled off his ragged shirt and unbuttoned his trousers. He stepped out of them, out of his soiled drawers, left them in a pool of grey on the grey floor, like shed skin.

"Boots and stockings too, please," said Deedes.

Sammy stood naked in the down-fall of light from the slotted window. He was not mature. In shame he covered his genitals with his hands. He shivered with cold and fright. His fair skin was bruised about the shoulders and Craig, staring at the boy's nakedness, could even make out the welt of a strap down the side of his slender neck. Deedes came forward with a doctor's sounder, moved Sammy this way and that. The boy was unprotesting. He appeared to be utterly malleable, vulnerable, innocent. Once again Craig experienced that strange sickening sensation of identification with Kirsty. He rubbed his palms against his

279

trouser leg and watched Sammy bend, heard him breathe to the surgeon's orders.

Sergeant Drummond removed his tunic jacket, hung it neatly on the wooden triangle, though that was not its purpose, not at all. Deedes, meanwhile, proceeded to examine the victim.

"How did you acquire these bruises?"

Sammy did not answer the surgeon.

"Did somebody do this to you?" Deedes said. "Your father, perhaps?"

"I fell," said Sammy.

"You fell," said Deedes. "You weren't struck?"

Sammy remained loyal, mute.

"As you wish," said Deedes. "Sergeant, be careful to strike the buttocks only."

"Aye, Mr Deedes, I'll be very careful."

From the cupboard Deedes brought out a tray upon which nestled three birch rods. Craig did not know what he had expected the weapons of punishment to look like but their crudity surprised him. They were just that – birch rods. They resembled the switch brooms that tinkers sold for sweeping out awkward corners, bundles of twigs thonged to a wooden handle. Deedes placed the tray on the chair and beckoned to Sergeant Drummond, who, with sleeves rolled up, examined the objects.

Deedes said, "How old is the boy?"

"Thirteen."

"Then it must be that one," said Deedes, pointing. "Forty inches in length and nine ounces in weight. Do you wish me to put it on the scales, Sergeant?"

"It will not be necessary, sir."

Drummond lifted the rod that Deedes had indicated and, turning discreetly away from Sammy, gave it a testing swish.

Sammy, making no sound, was weeping.

Deedes said, "Proceed then, Sergeant Drummond. I don't have all day, you know."

Drummond came to Craig. He held the rod discreetly by his side. He had strong forearms, thick with muscle and downed with dark hair.

He whispered, "I have a notion of what is on your mind, Constable Nicholson, and I might tell you that it is not my wish that this thing should be done – nor do I take any pleasure in doing it."

"I didn't suppose—"

"Just listen," said Sergeant Drummond. "I'm needing you to

hold him steady. Put his head between your thighs and your hands on his shoulders. Brace and support the poor lad for he will surely buck and squirm and I intend only to hurt him a wee bit and not to injure him. You must do your part and hold him still so I can strike accurately."

"How hard will you hit him?"

"Hard enough. But not as hard as I can," the sergeant said. "Now, Constable Nicholson, secure him, if you please."

However brave or daft Sammy Reynolds might be he did not surrender without a show of resistance.

Craig hated having to lay hands on the naked boy, the scuffle that ensued before he snared him and forced him into position; hated the position itself, the intimacy of it. Once Sammy's head was firmly clasped between Craig's thighs, though, the lad stopped wriggling and braced himself to receive his punishment like a man.

"Hold on," said Sergeant Drummond.

He measured the stroke and swished the spray of birch twigs downward across the boy's buttocks. Sammy yelped and jerked. Craig pressed his thighs together, hands gripping the soft cold flesh.

"Two," said the sergeant. "Hold still."

The twigs did not break the skin but left a series of thin cat-claw welts across the narrow hips and, after the third blow, a glowing flush that had Craig wincing in sympathy.

"Wait," said Deedes.

Panting, Sergeant Drummond stepped to one side and allowed the surgeon to examine the boy without having him released.

"Very well," Deedes said. "Continue."

Drummond's eye met Craig's for an instant. He shook his head slightly, frowning. A tiny bead of sweat clung to the corner of his eyelid and he brushed it away with the hand that held the rod. Taking his stance and aim he brought down the spray for a fourth time and, swiftly, for a fifth. Sammy had by now gone silent. He uttered not a whimper and did not flinch as the last blows fell. He was stiff as statuary and he did not lose rigidity even when Sergeant Drummond announced, "It is all done and over with. You may let him go now, Constable Nicholson."

Stepping back, Craig lifted Sammy up from his fixed position. Freckles were livid on the boy's ashen cheeks and his hair, damp with perspiration, clung in auburn kiss curls to his forehead.

"Sammy, it's finished," said Craig; and to the sergeant, "What happens now?"

"You escort him home," said Drummond.

"What? Right away?"

"As soon as he can walk," the surgeon said.

Sammy Reynolds limped by Craig's side along the Greenfield's pavements and said not a word no matter how Craig coaxed him to converse. Sammy had been made to wash his tear-stained face and Sergeant Drummond had seen to it that he was tidily dressed and his bootlaces tied before he was taken from the basement and released into Constable Nicholson's care to be returned to his father.

It was a long hoof to the Madagascar from Percy Street. Craig did not hurry. He made a little detour to take in Dinaro's Café and, from the back door, bought two mugs of hot tea and a couple of jam doughnuts. It was still only mid-morning. He gave Sammy one of the mugs and one of the doughnuts and the boy, though he did not speak, accepted them. Craig and the boy leaned on the wall at the back of the café, ate and drank and stared at the traffic, such as it was, that flowed along Morrison Street. All the questions that Craig asked of Sammy – did he not go to school; could he read and write; would he become a labourer like his father – remained resolutely unanswered. The act of punishment had estranged the boy from the man who had given him attention. Craig let him sulk. In ten minutes or a quarter of an hour Sammy Reynolds would be off his hands and would no longer be his concern, unless he transgressed the law again. They drank tea together and licked their sticky fingers and, leaving the mugs on the back doorstep, turned right for the Madagascar.

There was still little sign of life to the tenement, though mongrel dogs and several large cats had taken possession of the summit of the midden and a pack of very young children could be seen on the crown of the waste ground, silent and still, watching the distant figure of the copper as if they planned to swoop upon him.

The boy stopped suddenly.

"Here's where I live," he said.

"All the way home, Sammy," said Craig.

"Nobody there."

"Right to the door."

The cellar door was still ajar but there was not even the flutter of a candle to give a touch of warmth to the room. Nothing, at first, seemed to have changed, except that the cat was gone; then Craig noticed the man on the straw. He was motionless, curled up, his back to them.

"Is that your dad?" said Craig.

"Aye."

"Mr Reynolds."

The man did not respond. For a fleeting second Craig wondered if he was dead, had succumbed to drink and dissipation, if poor Sammy was free to become a ward of the state and enjoy its disciplines. He went down on one knee and shook the man's shoulder. The man rolled over but did not waken. He was drunk as a lord, a bottle without a cork clutched to his chest like a baby. He had vomited down his front and the hair on his chest and the dark stubble on his chin were matted with the stuff. The stench was foul. He opened his mouth, gave a belch and a blubbering snore, rolled on to his side once more. Craig got to his feet and stepped back.

What more could he do? He had carried out the Bailie's instructions to the letter. Sammy Reynolds had been arrested, charged, sentenced and duly punished for his crime and had now been delivered safe home and put into the custody of his parent. He, Constable Nicholson, must leave him here, turn and walk out, walk back to his regular beat, fulfil the duty, go home come evening to his loving wife, his supper, his clean warm bed. Sammy knew it too. Sammy watched him from the corners of his eyes, his face pale as fungus in the cellar's half light, his freckles plainly visible.

Craig cleared his throat. "No more pinchin' things that don't belong to you, Sammy. It'll be jail the next time or the Bad Boys' school."

"If the sun shines later," Sammy said, "he'll be up in the park wi' the drum."

"Sammy—"

"Dancin'."

It was an impulsive gesture, quite wrong, not a thing for a grown man to do. Craig could not help himself. He put an arm about the boy and hugged him. Sammy winced as if kindness hurt him like a seventh stroke of the birch, and tore himself away.

Craig turned on his heel and went out. He climbed three or four steps noisily, paused and stealthily returned to the cellar door.

Sammy was on his knees at the side of the straw bed. He had clasped a handful of the drunkard's hair and was shaking the man's head gently from side to side, trying vainly to rouse his father to sensibility.

"I was good, Paw. I tell ye, the mannie said I was good."

Without a word, Craig stole upstairs and hurried out into daylight once more.

With money that Craig had given her she had bought a comfortable loose-flowing house-robe and a pair of low-heeled slippers, and padded about the kitchen with the waddling gait of a woman three times her age.

"Were you in court this mornin', dear?"

"Aye."

"Was it that boy who stole the drum?"

"Aye."

"What did he get?"

"Ten-bob fine," said Craig without a pause.

"How did he manage to pay it?"

"His father was there. He paid it."

"I'll bet he got a lickin' when he got home."

"I'll bet he did," Craig said. "Listen, I'm thinkin' I should take a jaunt to Dalnavert."

"Oh!" said Kirsty. "When?"

"Soon," said Craig. "I'm worried because I haven't heard a word since Gordon went back."

"She'll be mad at you."

"I know," said Craig. "I want t' see how the land lies."

"The baby's due—"

"Aye, it'll be before that."

"I'll come with you."

"What for?"

"I thought—"

"It'd be better if you stayed here," said Craig. "I'll only be gone one night or two. I'm due three days' leave in early March. Before I start night duty."

"Night duty?" said Kirsty. "You didn't—"

"It pays more," said Craig. "Anyway, I've no choice. It's my turn. We'll be goin' on to three shifts in May an' that'll make a difference. Anyway, I thought I'd go to Dalnavert the first weekend in March. If you don't fancy stayin' here alone—"

"I could always go to Walbrook Street."

"If you like," Craig said.

She hesitated, hovering heavily behind his chair.

She said, "Craig, you will – I mean, you won't stay there?"

"Stay where?"

"Dalnavert. I mean, you will come home again?"

"Don't be so bloody daft," Craig said.

The Prince Consort peered blearily up at him for a final moment across the garden of Charlotte Square before swaddling North Sea haar wrapped up the city for the night. Edinburgh haar was not at all like Glasgow fog. It had no body to it, was ghostly and wet and clinging, a sea-fog that stole up from the Forth at all seasons and, that evening, swiftly consumed the statue that gave a landmark to travellers along George Street and provided David Lockhart with a focus from the window of his rooms in Albany Place.

It was a lodging of quality in one of the more salubrious parts of the capital. Uncle George had found them for him and footed the bill without a moan. Uncle George was a downy bird who knew that while a young fellow might spend his student days sleeping in a shoebox and living on ale and ambition, a Doctor of Medicine deserved better, that advances in age and station required advances in gentility and comfort. The house in Albany Place was divided into four suites and was governed by a certain Mrs Fotheringham, a woman in situation similar to Mrs Frew but in temperament far more refined. Indeed Jack had once observed that when compared to the formidable Fotheringham old Aunt Nessie seemed like a *fille de joie*.

David lowered the curtain and returned to the long table that served him as a desk. It was positioned before a cheerful fire and had upon it a double-bracket oil-lamp in green glass and polished brass. A hexagonal cabinet on castors kept his current library close to hand and a little slope-front bureau held pens, inks and sheaves of legal foolscap. Here David composed his essays on matters spiritual. Here too, once each month, he fulfilled his obligation to his father and wrung out two pages of bland facts. Tonight, however, he must write another sort of letter, set down facts that were barbed, that would wound and that would bring a volley of recrimination from far-off Fanshi.

Perhaps this letter would do what nothing else had done – induce his parents to return to Scotland on furlough from the mission. No, he thought, his father would not come. His father would not leave China for any reason, not if Noah's flood swept over Europe and left Jack and him adrift in a basket on the dreary tide, not if the seven trumpets of St John all sounded in unison. His father was tied to China not by bonds of selfless love but by an addiction to the status that he had found there, the Good White Man.

When this thought had first come to David it had seemed heretical. When he ransacked his memory, however, he discovered to his dismay that many of the episodes that had seemed innocent and amusing when he was a boy in China were not so at all, that his view had changed with knowledge, changed so radically that he felt alienated from those growing years, from the man who had spawned and raised him, who had planned his destiny so meticulously.

Jack too had doubts about their father but he refused point-blank to discuss them with his brother. David did not press. He had sought advice from Professor Landels, a moral philosopher. To his astonishment the professor did not accuse him of bad faith or betrayal, did not urge him to stand firm and do his duty as was expected of him. Old Landels had been very understanding, had explained that doubt is the core of the human condition, the inheritance of the Christian, and that a man who does not suffer doubt about his actions and beliefs is a man who does not grow. David had also written of his problem to Uncle George who had replied quickly and told him in plain terms that he must make up his own mind what to do but that he, George, would stand by him in any event.

David seated himself at the table. He lifted his father's last letter to which he must now reply. Like all the letters that had gone before, it was not a letter at all really but more of a sermon.

"*I ask you to remember,*" David read, "*that the salvation effected by our Redeemer includes infinitely more than deliverance from the guilt, power and pollution of sin.*"

David sighed. He did not know what the words meant. Sin was a 'problem' not an experience, a puzzle in morality, not a burden that he felt upon his soul day after day. In Lutheran dogmatics the whole life of a Christian was dedicated to repentance from sin. But what that sort of sin felt like, how it was expressed, David had no idea. He read on.

"*And when millions of ages shall have elapsed and millions more have run their course, His felicity shall be ever on the increase. Yes, David, though now you scarcely possess a clay-built hovel, though your garments be coarse and your fare scanty, Jesus is your Saviour and Heaven is your home.*"

To whom had his father written those words? Not to him. His rooms, thanks to Uncle George, were solid and comfortable, his garments fine and his fare anything but scanty. What had gone through his father's head when he had penned those platitudes?

Impatiently he flicked the letter aside, got up, went to the window once more and lifted the curtain. He could see only the orb of a street-lamp and the railings directly below.

It was on a night like this that he had first met the young woman, Kirsty Nicholson, in Walbrook Street. The memory of that encounter was vivid and unfading. When he thought of her it made him feel warm. He did not know why this should be. Such emotions had not been discussed with professors of divinity or explained by demonstrators in medicine. Perhaps that feeling was sin, a pollution for which he should suffer tormenting guilt. Perhaps that was the thing that had escaped him when he cut into the leathery dead flesh of the corpses in the anatomy rooms and separated veins from arteries and muscles from bone. If so it was not as he imagined sin to be, though she was wife to another man and big with another man's child. He did not want to possess her. He wanted something for which there was no exact definition. There were no girls like Kirsty Nicholson in Fanshi, girls with auburn hair and freckled noses and smiles that could warm even the coldest winter night.

The only person in the whole wide world for whom he felt love was his brother; yet he must part from Jack, sacrifice Jack to appease his longing to remain here in Scotland, to cling to the place and its people, to be part of it. Yes, that was what he wanted; all he wanted. He did not want to have strangers about him. It was after all no great enigma, no problem in faith. It was simplicity itself.

David dropped the curtain and shut out the haar. Quickly he stepped to the table and seated himself. He was sick of bland obedience, of half-truths, of holding himself at a distance. He slipped a sheet of foolscap from the drawer, uncapped the ink bottle and picked up a pen.

Dear Father,

I realise that it will come as a great surprise to you and as a disappointment but I have decided not to return to China and to Mission Work but to remain here in Scotland and seek a parish of my own.

He applied blotting paper and sat back. He read what he had written. He could hardly believe that he had done it, had been so direct, so explicit. He had nothing more to add, nothing more to say.

He laughed with sudden relief and, elated, signed his name.

Mrs Swanston and Mrs Walker came into the close together. Each carried a large wicker shopping-basket from which wafted the delicious aroma of fried fish.

"It that yoursel' up there, Mrs Nicholson?" said Mrs Walker.

"It is."

"What's that you're doin'?" said Mrs Walker.

"Cleanin' the lavatory."

"You're a night early, are you not?" said Mrs Walker.

"I had time tonight."

"My, my! But should you be doin' that at all?" said Mrs Swanston.

"I'm all right, really."

"I must say," said Mrs Walker, "that you do look a bit peaky."

"I've a wee pain, that's all."

"When's it due?" said Mrs Walker.

"Twenty-six days," said Kirsty.

"A little light exercise will do you no harm," Mrs Walker said. "Before I had Charles I papered the back room."

"Aye, but Charlie wasn't your first," said Mrs Swanston.

"I had no trouble with Jim either," said Mrs Walker.

"Well, I had trouble wi' them all," Mrs Swanston confessed. "Before birth, durin' birth, an' ever since."

"Have you been to the doctor?" said Mrs Walker.

"Aye."

"Who is your doctor?"

"Doctor Godwin."

"We go to Doctor Newfield. Up in Hillhead."

"I thought he was a chest doctor?" said Mrs Swanston.

"He's a highly-thought-of gentleman in the medical profession," said Mrs Walker. "A consultationist at the Western. He charges a considerable fee. Frank thought it was worth the expense, you know, to see me right."

"Aye," said Mrs Swanston, unimpressed.

"Doctor Godwin's all right," said Kirsty. "He gave me a bottle."

"Och, a bottle," said Mrs Walker. "I had pills."

"Pills for what?" said Mrs Swanston.

"For – something we ladies don't talk about."

"The constipation?" said Mrs Swanston.

"I'm getting this fish in before it turns cold," said Mrs Walker, and went into her apartment without another word.

"Her!" said Mrs Swanston. "She's right, though. I'd better dish up supper to my crowd before they come lookin' for me wi' knives at the ready."

"They'll be needin' a good hot meal tonight," said Kirsty, "with the weather so cold an' raw."

"Aye, no hint of an early spring." The woman patted her arm. "Are you sure you're feelin' all right, lassie?"

"I'm just tired."

"Cheer up. It'll soon be over."

"Goodnight, Mrs Swanston."

"Goodnight, Mrs Nicholson."

Breaking Warder Caine's neck proved far easier than Malone had supposed it would be. When he was younger and making his way in the world he had snapped the odd arm at the elbow and had, for a year or so, specialised in breaking folks' fingers but he had never been employed to kill a man with his bare hands.

Once, long ago, Billy had shown him how it should be done; hand over the mouth and chin, elbow locked about the windpipe, a jerking motion upwards to separate the bones at the top of the spine. Malone wondered if he had strength enough for the task but found himself charged up and more than equal to it. He had decided during his afternoon promenade that he would not have a better chance and with the plan laid out in his mind he had elected to go for it. Come what may, once he laid a finger on Warder Caine he was utterly committed to escape from Barlinnie and to stay out of the clutches of the law for evermore. If something went wrong, if luck ran against him, then he would die at a rope's end. No leniency would be shown to him. He would be topped for sure – and that would be that, the end of Daniel Malone.

Warder Caine never really knew what hit him. He had brought in the tin mug and the tin plate with No. 679's dinner on it. He had seen No. 679 only three hours before when he took him out for air. He should have been in long before dinner-time to collect the oakum pickings and give No. 679 a brush with which to sweep out the cell, but he had gotten into an argument with Warder McIntosh and had 'bent' the regular routine just a little, would do it all at the one visit, not just with No. 679 but with the four other hard labourites in the new block.

It was this irregularity in Caine's routine, plus the fact that the day had been misty, that determined Danny Malone to play his hand. The first part of it was easy, dead easy. Caine was only seconds into the cell, had just put the tin mug and the tin plate upon the bed and had turned to look at the oakum pile on the canvas rug on the floor when Malone, without any warning at all, gripped him round the jaw and, with one twist of arms and shoulders, broke his vertebrae as if they had been made of porcelain.

Danny Malone lowered the warder's body to the floor and knelt by it. He unbuttoned the uniform and unlaced the boots. Caine was a lot skinnier than he was but he got himself into the gear as best he could, strapping on the belt very tightly to draw in his girth. He put on the hat too and hastily scooped the quantity of plucked oakum into the centre of the canvas, folded up the corners and made a bundle of it. He took the keys, only three on the ring since Caine had not been an official turnkey, from Caine's fingers and hoisted the bundle up into his arms so that it hid his face. He dragged the warder to the bed and put him into it and went out of the door, which had not been closed, into the corridor.

He held the oakum bundle aloft with his left hand and arm and kept his right hand free so that he could reach quickly for the hilt of the sabre which dangled at his side in its scabbard of varnished leather. Possession of the sabre, and the satisfaction he had gained from doing for the bloody warder, heated Danny Malone's blood, imparted such a welling of encouragement that he discarded his plan to keep cool and use stealth and, when he got within twenty yards of the elderly warder who kept the block gate open at the corridor's end, flung away the bundle and ran for it.

The elderly warder was taken by surprise. He rushed at the big iron gate to slam it shut but Malone was already upon him. The man did not even have time to cry out. He was old, older than Danny, and wore a particularly high collar. Malone did not attempt to find a grip that would enable him to practise his new-found skill. He throttled the old bastard, thumbs dug deep into the windpipe. It was done quietly, very quietly. The old boy slumped without a peep, only the iron gate grating and clanging a bit when his knees pushed it on its oiled hinges. Malone unclipped the big round ring from the man's belt and also took the small ring from his fist. Now he had about a dozen keys and, if his observations had been accurate, only two doors to clear before he got into the yard. He dragged the old warder into the end corridor and locked the gate on him.

Behind him was a short corridor and a warders' cubby which, he thought, gave on to a staircase that led up to the main halls. To the right, beyond the cubby, steps went up to an exposed gallery which in turn led across to a door in the prison's inner wall and gave access to the promenade. He had been that route with Caine. Gas had not yet been installed in this part of the block and the corridors were lit by long-barrel lanterns. He took one of the lanterns from its hook.

Behind him somebody, a prisoner, shouted, "What's that? What's happenin'? Where's my bloody grub?"

Malone was tempted to tell the bugger to shut his mouth but he restrained himself and, with the lantern in his left hand, stole towards the arch of the cubby.

Inside the room were two warders. He recognised one of them as McIntosh but the other was a stranger. Luck was running his way, however, for both warders were poring over a newspaper that was spread open on a table, a racing-sheet most like. Trays with prisoners' dinner on them cooled on a dresser by the serving-churns.

Malone crept softly past the arch and turned on to the narrow flight of steps that went up to the gallery. He had counted out the steps, fourteen. Caine had always made him go up first and had kept well behind him in case of monkey business. Sometimes there was a warder on duty at the top of the steps. Not tonight, though. The main cell blocks, where ordinary prisoners were housed, were above him. He thought that he could hear them muttering, a sound like waves on a pebble shore; only imagination. He wanted to make a dash for it, to clatter along the iron gallery, but kept control of his emotions, moved casually on to the span that crossed some fifteen feet above the communal well of the block.

Never had he felt so exposed, so vulnerable. Warders walked below him. Locking up? He could not be sure of the routines here. Yes, locking up. Clash of doors, the clăck of keys, hearty voices, prisoners calling out to each other. He looked down at the pinching boots and through the fretwork of the gallery to the heads below. As a hard-labour prisoner his contact with warders had been limited. He did not know them and they would not recognise him on sight, though a close inspection would reveal him for what he was. The door in the inner wall seemed miles away. He did not hurry, though. He walked steadily along the gallery carrying the lantern, as if he had a purpose, a duty to perform.

Though made of wood the door had a vertical iron handle and a huge metal lock. Malone had no notion which of the many keys in his possession would fit the lock. He had no option but to stand at the end of the gallery and fumble, try one key after another until, at last, one dropped the tumblers with a noise, he thought, as loud as the firing of field artillery. He looked down. One young warder was staring up at him through the gridwork. Malone held his breath and then made a sign, a greeting, which the fool returned before going on about his business. Malone pushed open the wooden door, lifted the lantern and stepped into the exercise yard.

To his right, across the yard, was a big square door. It was open. Light streamed from it into the yard. He could see circular tracks on the cinder pad, the section of high wall that he intended to climb. Four hooded arc-lamps had been erected on the prison's inner gable but apparently they were not connected to the pipes yet and gave no light. He did not like that open door. It was one of only two that led into the yard. He stood in the other. He stepped into the yard, closed the wooden door behind him but did not lock it. He did not dare race for the wall, for that section where old stonework and new brick met. He stood quite still, breathing high in his chest, listening. He could hear, of all things, music. Somebody was squeezing a tune out of a concertina. Behind him and above the cells reared like a great cliff of stone. He did not look up. If any man behind those tiny barred windows spotted him and knew what he was about they would keep silent, of that he could be certain. He was so close to escape, so close. Behind that wall lay the farmlands of Riddrie and horse-tram routes into the city. Glasgow was not far away. He could almost smell the beery, smoky stink that tainted the farm mists that wreathed the prison and made the dark sky grey.

Two warders, laughing, came out of the big door. Malone put his hand on the sword hilt and drew the weapon quietly from its scabbard. He lowered the lamp, watching. The warders came no distance into the courtyard, separated and, to Malone's surprise and relief, made water against the wall. It would be 'against regulations' to do so but perhaps the lavatories were in another block. The men met again, laughed and returned through the big door, closing it behind them, shutting off light and the concertina's cranky tune.

Malone walked across the cinder, crossed to the corner where new brick met old stone. The wall seemed smoother in the darkness, higher too. At the top were bent metal staves but he did not think that the crown had been wired. He knelt and unlaced Caine's boots, sat and worked them from his feet. He tied the laces together and hung the boots about his neck. He got to his feet and glanced about him. It was uncannily quiet. He blew out the lantern and discarded it. He approached the rearing mass of the wall, sought a hand-hold, found one, found another. He scrambled for purchase with his stockinged toes and hoisted himself from prison ground.

Luck was still running with him. He could hardly believe it.

The junction had not been mortared properly and presented a ladder of hand- and foot-holds. He climbed cautiously but without difficulty and soon flung his arms over the top between two bent staves. There was no wire in place, no glass. He hauled himself up and straddled the wall.

Grasslands sloped away from the prison without impediment, open fields shaped by the mist and, not far distant, the lights of the villages that clung to the hem of the city. Malone breathed deeply, filling his lungs. He could smell Glasgow now all right, hear its pulse. The sensations excited him. He slung his legs over the wall and lowered himself. The outer facement was smoother but provided just enough friction to support him. He dropped the last ten feet to the ground.

As he rolled on to sweet wet winter turf a bell clanged within the prison and, a moment later, a steam siren screamed out. Malone did not flinch. He had left fear behind. He was clear of confinement and surged with confidence. Chuckling, he sprinted down the slope towards a thorn hedge behind which lay lights and a roadway.

He had done it. He had escaped from Barlinnie.

Now he would show the bastards.

Now he would write his name in blood.

The hue and cry that followed the brutal double murder in Barlinnie prison and the escape of felon Daniel Malone involved almost every officer and man in the City of Glasgow and the co-operation of police forces in burghs far and wide, Greenfield not least among them.

Superintendent Affleck was put in charge of a team of detectives and was also consulted by uniformed superiors on the best strategy by which the fugitive might be laid by the heels. Description of the wanted man was telephoned and telegraphed to police stations in all port areas, west and east, and City of Glasgow contract printers were roused to late-shift work to set and run off one thousand copies of a *Wanted* handbill. Before midnight senior constables and sergeants had been despatched to search the dwellings of Malone's known associates and Noreen Gusset had been dragged protesting to Partick Police Headquarters where Hugh Affleck, in person, interrogated her for over an hour.

Across the city a pair of detectives, Glover and Prentice, had traced the means by which Malone had gotten himself from the wilds of Riddrie into the city centre. The hackney cab driver had been so frightened by the man in warder's uniform, and by the sabre laid against his neck, that he had put antipathy to blue boys to one side and reported the incident at the nearest cop shop to the Saltmarket, where he had dropped his 'fare'.

Seasoned veterans of several manhunts, Glover and Prentice extracted every drop of information from the wide-eyed cab driver and had him take them to the exact spot at which the passenger had alighted; just beyond Glasgow Cross and only yards from the doors of the Central Division Police Station, one of the city's most populous areas.

"Where did he go then?"

"Vanished," said the cabbie.

"Into thin air?"

"You might say so. One minute he was standin' on the pavement, next he was gone."

As instructed, Sergeants Glover and Prentice made report by telephone to Superintendent Affleck who was on the point of leaving Partick for Greenfield. Superintendent Affleck suggested to the senior officer at Central that men be despatched to question citizens in the area in the hope, rather faint, that a man in a warder's uniform, complete with sabre, might have been spotted and remembered. Every straw had to be clutched at and progress made before Daniel Malone could strike again.

"Do you think he will," said Sergeant Drummond, "strike again?"

Hugh Affleck sipped from the cup of strong black coffee that had been brewed for him in the room behind the counter in Ottawa Street station.

"I'm damned sure he will. It's the reason he escaped. He has nothing but vengeance on his mind, scores to settle."

"Did Noreen Gusset tell you that?"

"Not in as many words. She didn't collude in his escape, not directly. She visited him once, apparently. All Malone wanted from her was information about Nicholson. The last thing that wee Noreen wants is Danny running loose. Nobody wants Danny on the streets, not even his so-called friends."

"Especially his so-called friends," said Sergeant Drummond. "Have you sent word to Maitland Moss?"

"I spoke to him on the telephone," Hugh Affleck answered. "Oh, he pretended to be totally unconcerned but it's my guess that our Mr Moss will contrive to have urgent business in some far part of the country and will not return until Danny's caught."

"Does Moss have money belonging to Malone?"

"I've no idea," the superintendent said. "What concerns me is that Malone may have cash salted away. He's always been extraordinarily clever."

"It was not very clever to butcher two prison officers."

"He felt, I suspect, that he had nothing to lose."

"Except his life."

"Have you put a watch on the Maitland Moss yard?" said Hugh Affleck.

"One man inside, one on the street."

"Enough men for a change of shift?"

"Everybody on the roster has been recalled," said Sergeant Drummond. "Except Nicholson."

"Ah, yes," said Hugh Affleck. "Nicholson."

"I went round to see the Walkers, who reside in the same building as Nicholson. They got themselves quietly together and have manned the close, front and back. If Malone is mad enough to make an attempt on Nicholson tonight he'll find a warm welcome awaiting him."

"You'll need sleep, Hector."

"Tomorrow," said Sergeant Drummond.

Hugh Affleck finished his coffee and glanced at the clock on the wall. "Time I was off to report to Mr Organ."

"At this hour?"

"The Chief Constable is deeply concerned, Hector," said Hugh Affleck. "He knows what Malone might do. What sort of man we're dealing with."

"Armed and dangerous?"

"Very dangerous," the superintendent said.

Chief Constable Organ gave no thought to the lateness of the hour or the fact that he had been dragged away from a dinner party at Bailie Smith's house between the soup and the joint and had eaten nothing since. The circumstances surrounding the arrest of Daniel Malone were still too fresh in his mind, and in the memory of the public at large, to allow him to shirk his most punctilious duty. He had, of course, already spoken with Superintendent Affleck upon the telephone but was anxious to engage the detective in a more prolonged and private conversation and, shut in his oak-panelled office in Percy Street headquarters, wasted not a moment on politeness.

"Let me ask you, Hugh," said Mr Organ, "if you believe that Malone will come back to the Greenfield?"

"I do, Mr Organ."

"Because of the statements made by the Gusset woman?"

"Partly," said Hugh Affleck. "More, perhaps, because of the nature of the man. I think he's hungry for revenge."

"Now that he's out, however, do you not think he might change his mind and simply make a sprint for it?"

"No, sir, I don't. Malone is proud, he's vicious—"

"As his slaughter of two prison warders proves, yes."

" – and it's my belief that he'll come back to the Greenfield in search of Nicholson."

"Who shopped him."

"We must protect Nicholson at all costs."

"It would certainly be a black mark against us if Malone did manage to harm one of our constables."

"Nicholson must be sent away."

Chief Constable Organ stuck his tongue into his cheek, paused, said, "Or kept on duty, perhaps."

"I beg your pardon?"

"Day-shift, of course."

"Do I understand, sir, that you—"

"Is he a brave lad?"

"As brave as the next one, I suppose. But—"

"If, as you believe, Malone is intent on revenge and single-minded in his purpose then there's no saying what sort of mischief he might get up to if his purpose is thwarted."

"Tether a goat?" said Hugh Affleck. "I'm not for that, sir."

"For it or not, Superintendent, it has value as a suggestion, do you not feel?"

"You can order Constable Nicholson to remain on duty, Mr Organ. It will not, however, be a popular decision with the sergeants."

"It's not my intention to despatch him on to his beat alone and unprotected. He'll be watched, watched like a hawk at all times."

"For how long?"

"Until Malone shows his hand."

"What if Malone does not show his hand?"

"All well and good. After a reasonable period of time has elapsed we may assume that Malone has evaded our best efforts and has slipped away out of Scotland, and our jurisdiction."

Hugh Affleck shook his head. The theory had one fatal flaw; the administration of the Force itself. While Craig Nicholson might be willing, even eager, to play the hero and set himself up as live bait, if Malone elected to remain underground for three or four weeks then the sheer cost of maintaining a roster of protectors for one young constable would scupper the watch. Besides there was always the possibility that Malone would not attack during duty hours.

Chief Constable Organ said, "Have you considered the threat to yourself, Hugh?"

"Me?"

"To your family."

"What?"

"It was at your sister's house, was it not, that the arrest was made, the 'trap', as Malone sees it, sprung? Our desperado might not be too fussy upon whom he wreaks revenge."

"Yes, I do take your point, sir."

"Can your sister be removed from harm's way?"

"If necessary."

"What about Malone's cohorts; Jamie what's-his-name?"

"Dobbs. He's livin' with Malone's mistress now, I believe."

"Reason enough for Malone to do him harm. What of Malone's legal wife?"

"She knows absolutely nothing. She's heard not a word from Danny since the day of his arrest. I think that line of enquiry would not be profitable, not if I know Malone."

"McVoy?"

"Still in prison."

"Ah, yes, of course."

Hugh Affleck rubbed his eyes with his palms. He had foreseen a long campaign of patient detective work, particularly if Malone had cash hidden away and was able to buy a safe hiding-place or – and he wouldn't put it past the man – flee from Scotland for five or six months before he returned to pay his debts in blood. He had no doubt at all that, sooner or later, Malone would make an attempt on the life of the Nicholson boy. Perhaps it would be better for all concerned, including the Nicholsons, if it was sooner.

To a degree he felt responsible for the threat now laid on Craig Nicholson's life. His zeal had led him into this nasty mess. He had underestimated Malone, had not imagined that the man would escape.

Chief Constable Organ said, "What do you say, Hugh?"

"I'll talk to the constable first thing in the morning."

"It's for the best, don't you think?"

"I hope so, sir."

Craig sensed that there was something in the wind when Constable John Boyle, looking even glummer than usual, picked him up at the close mouth. John Boyle was a Percy Street officer and had no time for those minions who served in the sub-station at Ottawa Street. He had addressed hardly a civil word to Craig in the weeks since the Nicholsons had moved into No. 154 and it was soon clear to Craig that Constable Boyle had not lingered to accompany him out of friendship.

Craig said, "What's up then, Mr Boyle?"

"I have business at Ottawa Street. I'll walk with you."

"If you like," Craig said.

He fell into step with the elder man, glancing at him curiously. Craig said, "I take it you haven't been made down?"

"I beg your pardon?"

"Sent to join us."

"I have a message, that's all."

"Uh-huh," said Craig, and increased his pace a little as he rounded the corner into Williams Lane.

Ottawa Street was buzzing like a hive of bees. Constables and sergeants, some of whom he had never clapped eyes on before, were coming and going, hither and thither. The telephone on Drummond's desk was ringing, unanswered. Boyle accompanied him into the station and then, without a word, turned on his heel and walked out again.

"Archie?" Craig called, spotting his friend at the door of the Muster Room. "What the hell's goin' on here?"

"You're wanted, Craig. Back room."

"Me?" said Craig. "Who wants me?"

"I do." Hugh Affleck beckoned from the space across the counter. "Step in here, please, Constable Nicholson."

There was an air of informality in the room that Craig had not before encountered within the precinct. Cups, a milk can and teapot littered the table and the atmosphere was thick with tobacco smoke. Sergeant Drummond, tunic unbuttoned and collar loosened, was seated cross-legged on one of the chairs. His chin and jowls glistened with beard stubble and his eyelids were heavy with fatigue.

"Sit yourself down, Craig," Hector Drummond said.

The superintendent's clothing was not untidy but he had the same sort of look as Drummond, and Craig guessed the pair of them had been up all night long.

"You may smoke if you want to," Hugh Affleck said.

It was as if they had brought him here to tell him bad news. He experienced a moment of stupid panic, thinking of Kirsty. He had left her, however, only five minutes since, waddling about the kitchen in her robe and slippers. He thought next, for no logical reason, of his mother and of Gordon and, as his panic increased, reached for the tin in his tunic pocket where he kept his cigarettes and matches.

Superintendent Affleck said, "It's Malone. He's escaped from jail. Killed two warders in the process. We have a suspicion that he may be headed for Greenfield."

"Ah!" said Craig, relieved. "Comin' for me, you mean?"

"Listen to the lad," said Sergeant Drummond. "What a conceit."

"It would be natural," said Craig carefully. "I shopped him, after all."

He lit a cigarette and listened obediently while Hugh Affleck told him what had happened and, making no bones about it, explained what the Chief Constable required of him. Craig felt no great stirring of fear of Daniel Malone and did not think that the Chief Constable had made an outrageous request. Here in the inner sanctum of Ottawa Street Police Station he was secure. Even on the streets of the Greenfield he would be within hailing distance of a fellow copper at all times. Besides, after what he had lived through this past six months Malone seemed tame.

Hugh Affleck said, "I don't want you to be careless, Constable Nicholson. Malone has deliberately burned his boats. He has nothing further to lose. If it's in his mind to make an example out of you, to try to regain his status and his power, then he will not be dissuaded by mere difficulty."

Craig said, "I'm not scared of him, Mr Affleck."

Hector Drummond said, "I would be, if I were you."

Craig said, "You want me to go on duty, as normal?"

"Yes," said the superintendent. "It's not my idea."

Craig said, "Is Malone carryin' a weapon?"

"We believe he has a sword."

"A sword?"

"Taken from one of the prison warders."

"But no firearm, no gun?" said Craig.

"Not to our knowledge, no."

"That's all right then," said Craig.

Sergeant Drummond uncrossed his legs and sat forward, resting his elbows on his knees. "What do you mean, lad – 'that's all right'?"

"He can't shoot me in the back. He'll have to catch me close before he can—"

"Good God, Nicholson!" Hugh Affleck exclaimed. "Do you think this is a game of tig? Malone'll not adhere to the rules of fair play, believe me."

"Do I go alone?"

"Yes, unaccompanied."

"Follow my usual routes?"

"Yes."

"My usual length of shift?"

"No different."

"But I'll have somebody on my tail?"

"Constables Boyle and Rogers, from Percy Street."

"Sound and experienced officers," said Sergeant Drummond.

"What happens tonight, when I go home?"

"You'll be accompanied to your door."

"I see."

"You will be required to do your part, Constable Nicholson, but nobody expects you to put your safety at risk," said Hugh Affleck. "After all, there's a distinct possibility that Malone isn't interested in you, that you're not his target."

"Oh, aye, I'm his target all right," said Craig.

"I trust you're not proud of that fact."

"Not proud, Mr Affleck. No, not proud."

He had been seasoned by the past months, by the scalded child, the naked boy wincing under the birch, the body in the river. He realised that he was proud, that it was pride in what he had already endured that made him impervious to fear of Malone. He felt a strange little prickle of excitement.

"An' after I'm home?" said Craig. "After dark, what then?"

"Stay indoors," said Sergeant Drummond. "Keep the door barred and bolted. Even Malone would not be daft enough to attack you in a building stuffed with blue uniforms."

"In addition," said Hugh Affleck, "a constable will be on permanent guard in the close."

"Who?"

"One of the Walkers, most like," said the sergeant.

"How long will you sustain the watch?"

"For two weeks at least."

"It won't take that long," said Craig.

"What makes you so sure, lad?"

"He broke from the jail to get at me," said Craig. "He's clever but he has no patience. He'll try something very soon. Do you have any idea, Mr Affleck, where he is right now?"

"None at all."

"I'll bet he's in the Greenfield. I'll bet anythin' you like he's here already," said Craig. "If that's all the word you have for me, Mr Affleck, I'll get out on my beat."

Craig got to his feet, dropped the cigarette and ground the butt under his heel. He brushed a fleck of ash from his chest and tightened his belt.

"Constable Nicholson," said Hugh Affleck.

"Yes, sir?"

"No heroics."

"Not me, sir," Craig said.

EIGHT

Voices on the Green

The Jewish burial ground had been long disused. City historians would, from time to time, sally down the length of Conger Street from Ferry Road and poke about among the headstones and fallen monuments and there were occasional 'inspections' by members of Glasgow's Hebrew community who had a mind to restore the place. But nothing came of good intentions and the plot was much the same as it had been for thirty or forty years, bristling with hog weed and willow herb, its walls shrouded in creeping ivy. In summer weather down-and-outs would congregate there to sun themselves and pass about bottles of raw spirit but that night in late February Daniel Malone had the ground to himself.

As he waited for dawn he dozed, feet propped on a wrought-iron rail, comfortably enough. He had stolen a rug from outside a villa in Markham Terrace, had made off into Bruce Lane with it, and nobody any the wiser. He had been lucky to find in the pocket of Caine's uniform a shilling and a sixpence, as well as a tin with three Gold Flake in it. He had bought coffee and a veal pie from a stall in Cranstonhill where, to his amusement, he had been mistaken for a blue boy. After supper he had walked boldly down Ferry Road and Conger Street, met hardly a soul, and was bedded in a corner of the burial ground by nine o'clock with the slap of the tide and throb of riverboats' engines to croon him to sleep.

The mist carried with it a trace of frost and Malone was up before daybreak, stiff as a board but hearty for all that. With the sabre he prised up a piece of flat slate that lay behind a gravestone marked with a distinctive little star in rusted iron. The slate clung to the turf and it took Malone a good five minutes to free it, to dig in the hard earth to a fist-sized piece of sandstone beneath which he had hidden a *Fry's Cocoa* tin. Uncapping the tin Malone took out an oilskin tobacco pouch and, squatting on the ground, unfolded it. The roll of banknotes, one hundred and fifty pounds in all, was exactly as he had left it almost three years ago, a little damp but otherwise undamaged.

He rolled up the pouch with the money inside and stuffed it into the pocket of the tunic. He replaced the tin, the rock, the slate, and warmed by activity and the successful outcome of his foresight threw the rug over the wall into the weeds and left the burial ground for Conger Street, hastening to reach his next port of call before daylight.

It was left to Jess Walker to tell Kirsty what had happened, to instruct her to stay indoors and not to answer the door. Father and son Walker had repaired to the station to be signed off night duty and to retire to bed. They would be on guard on their own doorstep again at dusk. In daylight hours, with so much pressure upon manpower, however, it was deemed prudent enough to leave Mrs Nicholson to fend for herself.

"Where are you going right now?" Jess Walker said.

"Shoppin'," said Kirsty.

"Well, I'll come with you."

"I'm only goin' to Kydd's."

"Far enough, I'd say, under the circumstances."

"Why hasn't Craig come home to tell me himself?"

"Don't you take my word for it?"

"It's not that," said Kirsty. "It's just—"

"He'll be busy. They're all busy. It's a right stramash with a convict on the loose in the district."

"Is he in the district?"

"Those in the know reckon he'll come back here to the Greenfield."

"Buy why?"

"To seek assistance from his pals."

"Assistance?"

"To further his escape. He'll need clothin' and money, won't he? Where else can he get help if it's not from his underworld pals?"

Kirsty said, "That's not the only reason, Mrs Walker, is it?"

"Only reason I know of," said the woman. "Wait right there. I'll fetch my coat an' hat an' basket an' we'll go to the shop together."

"Did somebody tell you to look after me?"

"Aye, my husband."

"Where's Craig?" said Kirsty again.

"Wait there," said Mrs Walker.

During the few minutes that it took Jess Walker to garb herself for the expedition Kirsty loitered by the close mouth of No. 154 Canada Road and let the news sink in. She did not doubt the truth of it. Mrs Walker was not the sort of woman to play a joke or contrive such a hoax. Oddly, Kirsty was not entirely surprised that Daniel Malone had escaped from prison. There was something about that earlier episode that had always seemed unfinished. She stared out at the street, a bland and undistinguished view, a still, grey, cloudy morning. A coal cart rumbled past, the coalie shouting his wares. The sound seemed threatening. She drew back into the shelter of the building as Mrs Walker came striding from her door.

"Come on then," said the woman briskly. "Let me have a wee peep outside first."

"But – but why?"

"Nothin' for you to worry about," Jess Walker said.

Nevertheless there was caution in the way Mrs Walker stepped from the shelter of the close on to the pavement, almost, Kirsty thought, as if she expected a volley of bullets to whistle about her head. Kirsty felt – how did she feel? – she felt silly. She could not take it seriously, not yet. She stepped carefully down the steps, more concerned with the baby inside her than with the threats that the empty morning might hold.

Mrs Walker took her arm and they set off down Canada Road together, heading for the grocer's shop.

Kirsty said, "They'll catch him, won't they?"

"Of course they'll catch him," Mrs Walker said.

"There's no danger he'll get away, is there?"

"Not with our lot on his trail."

Kirsty liked the sound of that phrase – 'our lot'. It incorporated her into a group, made her part of what Craig did. Even so, her apprehension was not much lessened.

"But why—"

"Better safe than sorry," Jess Walker said and, tightening her grip on Kirsty's arm, glanced over her shoulder nervously.

Joseph McGhee was not so young as he had once been and the routine of opening his pawnbroker's shop seemed to take an unconscionable time these days. He removed the padlock from the bar of the wooden gate, slid out the bar, hoisted up the gate and put it to one side of the doorway. He shuffled into the alcove, bent forward and waved the key about until he found the hole, turned it and unlocked the door. He pushed the door open with the crown of his head.

A voice behind him said, "Hullo, Joseph. Remember me?"

The old man straightened. "I thought you was inside."

304

"I was, Joseph, but I stepped out."

"Escaped from Barlinnie?"

"It'll be in your newspaper, I expect."

"What do you want wi' me, Danny?"

"A warm by your fire for a start, Joseph. And a bit o' breakfast might go down nicely too."

"Are they lookin' for you?"

"What do you think?"

"I want no trouble, Danny."

"Just do as I say, Joseph, an' there'll be no trouble at all. Now let's step inside the shop."

"I'll have to bring in the gate."

"Do it, then."

"What – what's that?"

"Never seen a sabre before, Joseph?"

"God, where did ye get it?"

"Borrowed it from a warder. How much would it fetch?"

"I canna touch it, Danny. You know that. The coppers are round here—"

"A joke, Joe, just a wee joke. Fetch in the gate then come in an' lock the door."

"Lock the – I'm supposed to be open for business."

"Get off the bloody street, Joseph. *Now*."

"Right, right."

Tiggy, the little marmalade cat that kept down mice, tiptoed from the back shop and hopped on to the counter. It squeezed between the iron grid and big silver till then stopped, back arching at the sight of the stranger. It hissed and retreated, ears back, and peered from behind the till, watching as the old man staggered in with gate, bar and padlock and put them down behind the partition.

"Now, lock the door again," said Malone.

"What if—"

"*I said lock it.*"

Joseph McGhee obeyed. He had not been in the pawnbroking business for forty-three years without learning guile. He was only too well aware that he was at Malone's mercy. In days of yore he had done enough business with Malone to realise that he was no match for the man, sword or no sword.

The cat leapt to the floor and shot into the back shop. Malone whirled round, sabre in his fist.

Joseph said, "It's only Tiggy."

"*Who?*"

"My cat."

"Nobody else here?"

"Not at this hour," Joseph said. "Come in to the back, Danny. I'll light the stove an' put on a kettle. When did you cut out?"

"Yesterday."

"Have you had any grub?"

"Not much."

"I've sausage an' bread," Joseph said. "I could nip out for some—"

"You'll nip out nowhere, Joe. We're stayin' in today. Both of us."

"In that case I've a suggestion."

"What?"

"I should put up my notice."

"What notice?"

"*Closed: Back Soon.*"

Malone thought about it and when the old man handed him a strip of cardboard read the painted print as studiously as a scholar.

"How often do you show this card?"

"Now an' again," said Joseph casually.

Outside in the street, men passed by, workers from the foundry. Joseph watched them furtively, praying that one of them might glance into the depths of the shop, might notice the man with the drawn sword.

The men clattered past unheeding.

Malone said, "If your customers see this notice they'll come back, won't they?"

Joseph said, "If they're desperate they will."

"What then?"

Joseph shrugged.

"Put it up," Malone said. "Then we'll go through back an' talk about what we're goin' to do."

"What are we goin' to do, Danny?"

"We're goin' to wait."

"Wait for what, Danny?"

"Nightfall," said Danny Malone.

It had been a strange, out-of-kilter morning and, Kirsty supposed, unaccustomed excitement had made her feel out of sorts. She was glad when at last Mrs Walker took her leave and she was left alone in the house.

Mrs Walker had not only escorted her on the shopping

'expedition' but had insisted on accompanying her upstairs and had even invited herself into the house for a cup of tea and a blether. Unused to socialising, and not much interested in close gossip, Kirsty had agreed only because she sensed that the woman, in her way, was doing her 'duty'. Mrs Walker did most of the talking. She drank three cups of Co-operative tea and ate a sticky cake, not one of Oswalds', that Kirsty had purchased from the Greenfield Bakers, and chatted away about her husband and her sons, boasting about their record of arrests which, Kirsty had already learned, was not something that constables did among themselves.

It was around eleven o'clock when Freddie, Mrs Walker's oldest, came to the door and enquired if they were all right. He was dressed in flannels and a greatcoat and wore black rubber pumps upon his feet. He was unshaven and tousled but animated in spite of a shortage of sleep. Invited into the kitchen he began at once to discourse on football, his obsession, going on and on as if Kirsty were informed about the game. Kirsty sat at the table, smiling politely, wishing that the Walkers would go away and leave her in peace.

The feeling of union that she had experienced for a few fleeting moments had been dissipated by the strain of 'entertaining' and by sharp little snips of pain that darted across her abdomen. She hid all sign of discomfort, breathing through her nose, smile fixed, her responses to the stream of chatter suitably rhythmic. "Aye, Mrs Walker. Is that so? Do you tell me now?" and so on until even the sound of her own voice became dull and boring.

She wanted to be alone. No, she wanted Craig to be with her, where she could see him, where he could watch over her. She wanted him to hold her by the hand, assure her that everything would be all right, that Malone would be caught and incarcerated in a prison from which he could not escape, that the pains meant nothing at all, that she would carry to full term and be swiftly delivered of a fine healthy baby, a boy if that's what Craig wanted, and would be up on her feet in two or three days; that he would not feel impelled to travel down to Dalnavert, that she would hear no more from Dalnavert or about Dalnavert or Madge Nicholson, and would have him and her baby all to herself for many years to come.

At long last Jess Walker took Freddie away.

Kirsty washed saucers, cups and plates and put them away. She felt so pinched and cramped, though, that she brought out a chair to stand on to reach the shelf. She did not risk a high stretch.

She wandered into the bare front room and stood by the window and looked down into Canada Road.

There was a breeze now and it would be cold out. At least the cloud had not brought rain. She watched a message-boy on a bicycle, heard his cheery whistle, watched three old men hobble back from the pub, puffing on their pipes. She saw one of them laugh and wondered what amusement was to be found at such an age, and if she would ever be old, old and idle and content.

Mrs Boyle came back from 'the steamie', the public wash-house, with her week's laundry squatting in a great moist bundle in an old perambulator within which, once, poor down-in-the-mouth Graham must have goo-ed and gaa-ed and blown bubbles to delight his mother.

The pain was lower. It did not race across Kirsty's abdomen but clenched her so that she gasped and clung to the window sash for support. Perhaps her time had come early. Perhaps she had mistaken the dates. She waited for the pain to establish a pattern but it did not. It disconnected and went away again.

She returned to the kitchen and sat by the fire for ten minutes to recover. She had not spared a thought for Malone or for Craig for at least a quarter of an hour. She found that when she thought of Malone now it did not induce anxiety. She had more to concern her than some convict on the run, however dangerous. 'Our lot' would take care of Malone.

In a minute or two she would boil an egg for her dinner, take it beaten in a cup with a knob of butter. In the meantime she had better make sure that the midwife's address was to hand, in case of emergency.

She took her purse from the dresser drawer and searched its compartments but could not find the slip that Dr Godwin had given her. She poked about in the drawer, on the shelf above the stove, even looked in the bottom of her shopping-basket. She could not find the address.

She was not unduly concerned.

It would do tomorrow.

Yes, Kirsty told herself, tomorrow would be time enough.

Boyle and Rogers had changed into plain clothes taken from lockers in Percy Street. Constable Boyle wore a baggy suit of Harris tweed and a hat with a grouse feather in the band. Constable Rogers had squeezed his bulk into a pair of blue cotton overalls. From a distance nobody could have identified either man as a copper, though a glance at their black boots would give the game away. Craig grinned when he caught sight of one or other of the watchers. If he had not known who they were he would have challenged them and questioned them, been suspicious of their intentions, particularly in the quiet back streets of the beat, down by the riverside.

He was surprised at how calm he felt now that he was clear of Ottawa Street. The routine round was soothing and he did nothing out of the ordinary. Only occasional glimpses of Rogers and Boyle reminded him that there was danger in the streets today. At least he could put a face, a name to it. Tonight, on his way home, he would buy an evening newspaper and read all about Malone's daring escape from Barlinnie, about the murder of two warders. He would not show the newspaper to Kirsty, not in her condition. She would have been told by now that Malone was on the warpath and would be on her guard. He did not seriously believe that Danny Malone would attack a pregnant woman. It would not be a brave or manly thing to do and Malone was all pride.

Craig trudged along the edge of the embankment. Rogers was on the pavement below, some two hundred yards behind, hands in the pockets of his overalls. Craig did not turn to look at Rogers but kept his eyes skinned for Boyle, who had taken up position near a lamp-maker's shop a quarter of a mile ahead, leaning against the wall like an idler, arms folded. Malone would spot the watchers a mile off. Malone would not dare pounce while he was protected. He would have to be patient, would have to wait.

He went down by the bridge. Boyle pushed himself away from the wall and cut diagonally across the street to loll in a close mouth at the bottom of Wolfe Road. Wolfe Road! There was a name for newspaper johnnies. Craig could see it in black print, visualise the column headlines – *Murderer Arrested in Wolfe Road*. He composed the report in his imagination and wondered, if the battle were bloody enough, if he might receive a letter of commendation from the Chief Constable. That would be something to paste into the album, to show to his son in years to come.

Out of devilment Craig did not cross the bottom of Canada Road at all, and did not carry on up the short length of Wolfe Road. He could imagine Boyle's bewilderment and temporary confusion and how he would have to stir his sanctimonious stumps to catch up again. Constable Rogers would still be with him, so he would be safe enough. He trudged off on a swing out to the pawnbroker's, towards old Joe McGhee's. It would soon be dinner-time and he would drop into the back of the café as usual for a bowl of soup or a hot pie. What would Boyle and Rogers do about dinner, he wondered.

There were three of them, two women and an elderly man. He knew them by sight and by their nicknames. One of the women, Biddy, was Irish and all three lived hand to mouth – bottle to mouth might be more accurate – by hawking the middens and picking up here and there an item that could be pawned. They were 'professional poppers', enjoyed scavenging for its own sake, the thrill of making a find that would earn them two or three pence. They eschewed contact with proper dealers in junk and were known not only to old Joseph but to three or four other pawnbrokers in the Greenfield. The old man's name was Clash. The second woman, who seldom opened her mouth, was known as Bloomy, though nobody seemed to know why, not even Hector Drummond.

Today, though, Bloomy was nattering away, weather-brown features fierce, one hand clutching the canvas sack that was their receptacle for stock-in-trade, the other fist locked round Clash's forearm.

By God, Craig thought, *she's doing her dinger!* He stopped, let the three come on towards him, though only Biddy even seemed to see him and gave him a surly nod.

Craig said, "What's bitin' you, Bloomy?"

Bloomy's mouth closed. She pursed her lips. She had few teeth left and her lips extended outwards in a grotesque pout, exaggerated by hollow cheeks. She wore a huge flowing shawl and a clean blouse and had a cameo brooch pinned at the throat. She scowled at Craig as if he were the cause of all her woes.

"Naethin'," Clash answered.

He was a thin, creased man, ten or fifteen years older than the women but still spry and quick of tongue.

"What's in the bag?" said Craig, pointing.

"Stuff."

"What sort o' stuff?"

Biddy said, "It's a chamber-pot wi' flowers, if ye must be knowin'."

"Stolen?" said Craig.

"Retrieved," said Clash.

"Worth six pennies," said Biddy.

She must have been handsome once, Craig thought. She had blue eyes and flaxen hair, though all streaked with grey and tousled and bristling with pins. She too was clean, however. Only the old man was dirty.

"What's wrong, then?" Craig said. "Won't Joseph give you a ticket for it"

"Joe's no' there," said Clash.

"Ga'n out," said Biddy.

"Gone where"

"Gotten his notice up," said Clash. "He never cam' back but."

"Wait," Craig said. "What notice?"

"Ye've seen it, surely," said Clash. "*Back Soon.*"

"Bloody liar," said Biddy. "Bin hangin' round all the mornin' long. He niver cam' back."

"Perhaps he's sick," said Craig.

"Gates's down," said Clash.

"Padlock's off," said Biddy.

"Are you sure he's not inside?"

"Christ, if he is he must be deef."

"Or deid," said Biddy.

"Takin' it up tae Stein's," said Clash. "He'll get oor business this day, so he wull."

Craig was hardly listening now. He had a strange tight sensation in his midriff. Pawnbroking was a strictly regulated profession and, as far as Craig knew, Joseph McGhee was both honest and efficient in the governing of his business. He could not remember old Joe's shop ever being closed during stipulated hours, except for a few minutes when the old man hobbled down to the corner shop for milk or tobacco or to buy a newspaper. It was obvious from the testimony of the experts that Joseph had been gone much longer than minutes.

"Stein'll no' gie us sixpence, but," said Bloomy, confessing at last the source of her annoyance in a rusty Ayrshire accent.

Clash and Biddy glanced at her as if, in finding voice in a stranger's presence, she might now go on to reveal all sorts of dark trade secrets. Craig did not notice. He had sneaked a look over his shoulders and saw that Boyle and Rogers had met and were conversing, still with mannered casualness, at the corner of a lane some hundred yards away.

Craig said, "Why don't you go back an' give Joe one more chance?"

"Joseph McGhee's had his bloody chance," said Clash.

"Bugger him," said Biddy.

If the gate had been taken down and carried out of sight, if the padlock had been removed, Craig realised that the pawnbroker's shop was secured only by a single lock on the front door. Common sense told him that he should hop round there immediately to make sure that old Joe was not lying sick or injured within, or that thieves or desperate clients could not easily force an entry in the owner's absence. Old Joseph was probably back by now, sitting in his chair with the cat on his lap and his pipe pouring out smoke. On the other hand it *was* unusual for the old man to abandon the shop for more than a few minutes. The hair on the nape of Craig's neck prickled slightly. Something told him that he should tread cautiously, not confide his unsubstantiated suspicions to anyone, least of all to Rogers and John Boyle.

Without a word of farewell the three disreputables trudged off along the broken pavement. Bloomy was silent again, the sack cradled in her arms like a baby. Craig watched them go. He waited in alarm for Boyle and Rogers to stop them, engage them in conversation, find out what he already knew – that there was something fishy going on at Joseph McGhee's establishment and that, just possibly, Malone was behind it.

Biddy, Clash and Bloomy brushed past the plain-clothed constables without a word and shuffled out of sight into Mill Lane.

Craig turned and, without sign or signal to his guardian angels, set off for Brunswick Street at a normal, unhurried pace to see what was what at old Joe McGhee's.

Daniel Malone wiped his mouth on his sleeve and pushed away the empty plate.

"Is that all there is t' eat?"

"Aye, that's it," Joseph said. "I could always pop out for groceries, if y' like."

Malone laughed. "Naw, naw, old man. D'ye take me for daft? You'll sit right there where I can keep an eye on you."

The cane chair had been moved into the rear portion of the shop, a long room, crammed with unredeemed pledges, in which there was a small barrel stove and not much else by way of domestic amenities. Every inch of space seemed to be given over to the collection of ornaments and utensils that Joseph had collected over the months, each with a sticky label attached to it. Racks of clothes muffled the sounds in the back room, deadened the vibrations of heavy horse-lorries that ground past the front door from time to time.

Malone walked by the racks, inspecting the items that hung there, one looped over another in matted confusion that only the broker could untangle.

"Does no bugger ever reclaim anythin'?" said Malone.

"Hardly ever," said Joseph. "What are ye lookin' for, Danny?"

"Somethin' to wear."

"Frock coat? Got a nice one over there."

"Are you pullin' my leg, old man?"

"I'm serious," Joseph said. "If it's a disguise you're after what better than a frock coat"

"How about a kilt?" said Malone.

"Kilt? Aye, there's several on that table."

"What table?"

"Under the coats. You could pass for a soldier no bother, Danny."

"Keep your sarcasm t' yourself, Joe."

Nonetheless Malone rummaged under a fall of overcoats, summer- and winter-weight garments for women and men, found the edge of the table and, using strength, swung away the rack and inspected the kilts that were laid out there along with other items of military apparel.

"Where did ye get these?"

"Wounded veterans, mostly," said Joseph.

"Deserters from the ranks, more like."

"Maybe," said Joseph.

"What do you do wi' them?"

"Sell them to an outfitters for cleanin', repair and resale."

"Make a good skin on it?"

"Enough t' buy my bread."

"Got a wife?"

"She's been dead these eleven years."

Malone held a kilt to his waist and measured its length against his knees. "Family?"

"Daughter. Married. Lives in Aberdeen. Son in merchant service. A stoker," Joseph said. "Look I could find a sporran t' match that tartan, Danny, an' a blouse too."

"A fine sight I'd look gallivantin' about the Greenfield in that lot."

"Danny, *did* you do for that warder?"

Malone lifted back the overcoats and stared long and hard at the pawnbroker who had not stirred from the cane chair in half an hour.

"What if I did?"

"They'll be huntin' you high an' low."

"What if they are?"

"I can give you some money; no' much, but—"

"I've got money, pots o' money."

"Is it – is it your intention t' run for it?"

"When the time comes," Malone said

"Is that why ye need a disguise?"

"I've somethin' to do in Greenfield first."

"How will ye get out – when the time does come?"

"What the hell're you jawin' on about, McGhee?"

"I can do you up t' look like a toff, Danny."

"Wi' this haircut?"

"I've a wig, lots o' wigs."

"A toff?" said Malone. "I suppose I could."

"Shave off the whiskers, hide the crop, dress the part, an' no copper'll look twice at you," Joseph said.

"Why are you doin' this?"

"Eh?"

"Helpin' me?"

"I don't want my throat cut," Joseph said.

"I might cut your throat anyway."

"I heard you were always decent to your pals."

"What's goin' on here?" said Malone.

"I'll dress ye up so your own grannie wouldn't know you," said Joseph. "Hand-luggage, leather boots, silk cravat, top hat, glasses, false hair, the lot."

"And?"

"Tie me up an' leave me when ye go."

"What if nobody finds you?" said Malone. "You'll bloody starve t' death."

"Somebody'll find me."

Malone said, "I'd suit the part of a gentleman, eh?"

"Down to the ground," Joseph agreed.

Malone leaned against the rack of overcoats. They smelled of mothballs and damp, smelled too of the homes from which they had descended. He could see frock coats and silk-faced topcoats, lum hats, the things that Joseph had promised him. It had been his intention to leave no witness but a corpse. Now that he was out of prison, however, a little of the cold fury that had fuelled him had leaked away.

"I'll think about it," Malone said.

The outer door rattled. Malone sank back into the cover of the racks, pressing the garments about him, enveloped in odorous fabrics.

"What's that?" he hissed.

Joseph made no attempt to rise from the cane chair.

"Customers," he said. "Clients."

"Are they breakin' in?"

"Just anxious."

"What'll they do when they find—"

"They'll go away, go elsewhere."

"Christ in Heaven, McGhee! If you're—"

The din ceased.

Calmly Joseph said, "See, they've gone already."

Malone crouched and ducked to the partition that hid the storeroom from the front shop. There was a long deal counter protected by an arch of iron gridwork, a door in the counter to the left. Scales, the till, a ticket spike and other tools of the trade made a battlement along the counter-top. Malone hoisted himself cautiously until he could look over it. Daylight patched the dusty floor, made a wedge out of the glass-fronted door itself. He could see shapes against the glass. He crouched lower, eyes above the level of the counter-top. He watched the shapes swim away and saw, through the window, two old women crabbing off towards Partick.

Still seated, still calm, Joseph said, "It'll happen on an' off all day, Danny. There's nothin' we can do about it."

"When, at night, do you close your doors?"

"Nine o'clock."

"An' when does the beat copper make his round?"

"Seven or half past," Joseph replied.

"Not before?"

"Seldom."

It was the question that Joseph McGhee had been dreading all morning long. He knew perfectly well why Malone had returned to Greenfield and why he needed to hide until evening, why he did not seek to make contact with his former cronies.

"What's the bloody copper's name?" Malone said.

"Jock Rogers," the pawnbroker lied.

"Not Nicholson?"

"No, Danny. Nicholson you'll have to find for yourself."

To his knowledge Craig had not met the women before and they knew him only as the young copper who patrolled a beat near their houses in the top side of Brunswick Street. He cornered them outside the pork butcher's in New Scotland Street and told them he would give them sixpence each if they would do something for him. It was quite against regulations to bribe a member of the great public to serve as an accomplice in police matters but it was the only way that Craig could think of to gain their attention.

He had no means of knowing that one of the women had once made a tidy living 'doing things' for men of all shapes, sizes and professions and that, in her day, she had entertained more than one bored young constable.

"Where?" she said. "Up a close?"

"It's not bloody that," Craig told her and, glancing apprehensively over his shoulder, explained what he wanted them to do.

As requested the women went round to old Joe's pop-shop – the route being familiar – read the notice, shook the door handle, peered in through the whorled glass then returned to the lane's end where the daft young copper waited and held out their hands. Craig put six pennies into one feminine mitt, a sixpence into the other. "Well?"

"*Closed*, it says, *back soon*."

"Is the door locked?"

"Aye."

"Right. Tell me, do you think there's anybody inside?"

"Sure there is."

"How can you be certain?" said Craig.

"Saw the smoke."

"Smoke? Is there a fire?"

"Pipe smoke. Joseph's pipe smoke. He's in the back shop, lyin' doggo."

"Did you see anybody else inside?"

"Somethin' in the glass mirror."

"What?"

"Somebody movin'. You told us no' t' loiter."

"So I did," said Craig.

"It's an easy tanner," said one of the women. "Are ye certain ye don't want t' go up a close?"

"No thanks," Craig said. "Not a word to a soul about this. Keep it secret."

"Cross m' heart," one woman said.

"That's no' your heart, Sadie; that's your—"

"Thank you, ladies," Craig said.

"Come back an' see us again, son."

"Aye, when you're no' so busy."

He heard them laughing, without malice, as he hurried off down the lane.

At the first corner he almost collided with Constable Rogers. Rogers hissed, "What the hell're you playin' at, Nicholson?"

"Just keepin' on the move," said Craig.

"I think you're deliberately keepin' us on the hop."

"Think what you like, Jock," Craig said. "I'm goin' to Dizaro's for my dinner in a quarter of an hour or so."

"What about the pubs?"

"I do them after," Craig said.

"Be careful." Rogers wagged a stern finger.

Craig nodded and moved on.

Boyle was far off, lounging at the corner of New Scotland Street to the discomfiture of a gang of youths who had been planning some mischief or other and thought that the copper, whom they recognised at once, had been sent to put paid to it.

Craig adjusted his pace. He felt a strange compulsion to leg it to Ottawa Street, to blurt out his suspicions to Sergeant Drummond or Mr Affleck. They would, without doubt, take him seriously, would bring down a squad and surround the pawnshop, back and front, would send in a couple of burly Highlanders experts in raids of this nature. But if he was wrong, if he had mistaken the signs, then he would be a laughing-stock, a joke – and if he was right he would only have a marginal share in the glory of Malone's capture.

Craig dabbed his brow under the brim of his helmet. He was sweating slightly.

Boyle had faded away from the New Scotland Street corner. The man would be trying to get ahead of him, to out-guess him. At any time he could give the pair the slip, be off on his own. Before they could report back to Percy Street or to Hector Drummond, he, Craig Nicholson, could make the nab, could take the dangerous fugitive single-handed. His name would be in the newspapers. He would be famous again, properly famous this time.

It was not logical to make decisions in such a manner. Nonetheless Craig did not turn his steps towards Ottawa Street. He slowed his pace, let Rogers come in sight behind him and, leading both watchers, strolled along the back of Brunswick Street, scrupulously avoiding the proximity of Joseph's shop, and headed for the café.

Craig gave a little nod to himself.

If Danny Malone was hidden inside the pop-shop then he had nothing to fear until nightfall; and when Danny emerged from his hiding-place at or after dusk, when Danny came out to search for him, Danny would be in for a shock.

She had fallen asleep upon the bed. When she awakened the pain had started up again and it was raining. A wind had sprung up and raindrops pattered against the glass and the sky seemed greyer than she had ever seen it before.

She sat up.

It must be near nightfall. She had slept for hours. She did not feel refreshed. She felt sick. She put her hands to her breasts. She could feel them throbbing, or so she thought, to match the throbbing in her loins. When she swung her legs from the bed she was seized by pain again and, without hesitation, dragged herself to the kitchen and took her coat and hat from the peg on the door.

It did not occur to her to cross the landing and summon help from the Pipers, though she could hear the strains of a chanter and the *rub-a-dub-dub* of drumsticks on a practice board from behind their door. She had forgotten that the Walkers would be on guard at the close entrances, did not notice that they had not yet come out for their evening stint. She got herself downstairs and into the fresh air. She stood uncertainly at the pavement's edge, looking this way and that.

Canada Road was busy. The growl of traffic from Dumbarton Road sounded heavy and threatening. Rain peeled out of invisible cloud and gas-lamps hissed on their poles. She fumbled in her purse, searching again for the address of the midwife. Somehow the concentrated effort seemed to push the pain away for a minute or two, allow nausea to recede. She was better, felt better. She sucked air into her lungs and blew it out. Her breath made a cloud, raindrops flickeringly visible in it.

Graham Boyle loped past her, head down, without a word. He vanished into the close of No. 154.

Kirsty whirled. "Graham, tell—"

The boy had gone.

She looked up. Drops splashed against her cheeks. There were lights in all the windows, even bedrooms. She felt as if the tenement would fall on her. She put her hand on the lamp-post to steady herself. She did not feel sick any more but she did not feel at all herself. She wanted Craig. She felt angry that he was not with her, would not be home for hours. How many hours? She could not tell. He was out chasing a bad man with 'our lot'. She could not hold that against him, could not demand an unfair share of his attention. Baby-making might be a man's business but bearing through to labour was a woman's job.

She remembered that she had not found the slip of paper with the midwife's address on it. She remembered that she had been warned not to leave the sanctuary of her house. She frowned. She experienced a startled fear of the pedestrians that thronged

Canada Road, girls and boys, men and women all coming and going like ants about a nest. Hurry-scurry, pell-mell. She sucked in another deep breath. She was out now. Nobody had even noticed. She was in the high end of Canada Road within sight and earshot of a hundred good folk. Surely she would be safe enough among them if Daniel Malone threatened her.

She pushed herself away from the lamp-post and took a few tentative steps. When she walked it did not hurt so much. She had a vague fevered notion that she might find the midwife's house even without an address to guide her; yet she turned away from Greenfield west and headed instead along familiar roads that would take her to St Anne's, to Walbrook Street and Mrs Frew.

When she realised where she was going Kirsty paused and sighed. She felt sudden relief that she had escaped from No. 154, from the strain of waiting for Craig, for wanting what she could not have from him, his time and attention. Common sense, revived by the cold wet air, was guiding her towards the one place where she would be sure to find comfort, consolation, perhaps even love.

Hands pressed to her side, she quickened her step.

Behind her, unseen, a man slipped from the shadows, a large man, clearly a gentleman, in frock coat, tile hat and patent leather boots.

In his left hand he carried an American travelling-bag of nut-brown hide; in his right, hidden in the folds of his sleeve, a carving-knife with a slender ten-inch blade.

The pawnbroker began his arduous journey only seconds after Malone left the shop. Old Joseph did not suppose that Malone would return. He had no reason to return. With luck he would never see the evil devil again, except perhaps if he was summoned to appear in a witness-box and give testimony against him. He would do that cheerfully, would help send the bastard to the gallows if he possibly could. For tonight, however, Danny Malone was on the streets and he, Joseph McGhee, was alone once more in his darkened shop.

The ropes were made of mock silk, ties stripped from dressing-robes that Malone had found on the racks. He had knotted them expertly and very tightly and had bound not only Joseph's wrists but his arms to the chair-back. Ankles and knees were strapped to the chair's legs with luggage belts and a ball of crepe paper had been stuffed into his mouth and fastened there with a lady's scarf. Joseph did not dare utter more than a gurgle in case he swallowed the sodden paper ball and choked to death on it. That possibility worried him more than the loss of blood to his fingers and toes, a constriction that would do permanent damage if he had to endure it all night long. Even so, if Danny Malone had told him a lie, had said that he was simply 'on the run' and intended to bolt across the border in disguise then he, Joseph, might have sat it out. Danny, however, had told him the truth – and the truth sent a cold shiver down Joseph's back.

"How do I look?"

"You look fine, Danny, just like a toff."

"Think they'll know me?"

"Your own mother wouldn't know you."

"It'll have to do for a while. All I need is to get to Canada Road without bein' recognised."

"Canada Road?"

"Where he lives."

"Who?"

"Nicholson; the bastard who sent me up."

"I – I heard he was in the police now."

"Aye, he's a bloody copper."

"Won't it be difficult to find—"

"I know where he lives. Besides, if I can't get him, I'll take his wife. She'll do instead."

"Danny, she's got nothin'—"

"Shut your mouth, McGhee."

"I only said—"

"Want your throat slit?"

"Is that – Danny, is that my carvin'-knife?"

"Aye. Do ye want a taste o' it?"

"I think I'd rather not, thanks."

"Then shut your bloody mouth an' keep it shut."

It was at that point, with rage simmering in Malone again, that Joseph decided on his own particular plan. He had lied to Malone about the copper; Nicholson would be around to check the Pledge Book without fail. Danny had locked the front door behind him – what had he done with the key? – but had not been patient enough to put up the gate and bar.

Aye, Danny was not half so clever as he thought himself to be. Either that or he had lost some of his brains in Barlinnie. If he had been really smart he would have put up the gate and taken down the notice and would have made sure that the chair itself was roped to something heavy, that he, Joseph, could not, by a racking contortion, inch it forward towards the counter.

By God, but it was tiring; a long, long journey across the back shop towards the counter and the grille.

He arched his back, using muscles that had been inactive for years, thrust out his chest like a pouter pigeon, and did a little dance with his feet. He gained an inch at a time, and rested. He performed the movement again. He rested.

There was the usual clamour outside, voices, cart wheels, the clatter of hoofs. Some of the factories and the foundry day-shift disgorged at six o'clock. Others would not pour out until seven; sounds he had heard for thirty years and had never really listened to before. He listened tonight, though, straining his ears for the rattle of the door-handle, his eyes inquisitive for sight of some figure outlined against the faint yellowish light that seeped in from the street.

New-wakened from a long day's nap in her nest in a crib behind the racks, Tiggy gave a tiny mew. He could see her squatting on the counter-top, splinters of light in her green eyes.

He had rested enough. He surged his body forward, lifting and dragging the chair. He surged once more. He must make the counter before Nicholson arrived at the door. He could not entirely count on Nicholson's intelligence, on the constable's curiosity. In fact, now that he thought of it, if there was a hue and cry out for Malone Nicholson might not be on duty at all.

He stopped. He gagged on the paper ball. He got it with his tongue and managed to push it forward in his mouth to free his breathing. In lulls in the growl of traffic he could hear the clock ticking away the minutes. He closed his eyes for a moment. It had been a very wearing day. He resisted the temptation to rest. He did not have far to go, really, ten or twelve feet at most.

Joseph was still some three feet short of the counter when somebody rattled the door-handle and, seconds later, called out his name.

"*McGhee, are you in there?*"

It was not a man's voice, not the constable.

"*I've a bloody nice vase here but you're no' gettin' it 'less ye open up right now.*"

At that point the pawnbroker's patience snapped. He ached in every muscle and had lost faith in the exactness of his original plan. Somebody was at the door now and he felt impelled to take a chance that they would hear him. He craned forward, rocked, pulled the rear legs of the chair clear of the floor and, as intended, brought his forehead crashing down on to the big metal keys of the till.

The cash-drawer shot out and struck him on the mouth and the till bell *spanged* loudly. Caught by surprise poor Tiggy leapt from the counter and whisked away into hiding with a wail like a banshee.

Unable to protect himself, and still tied to the chair, old Joseph toppled and fell to the floor.

For a moment there was silence, then a man's voice shouted, "*Malone, I'm comin' in*," and the front door flew open before Constable Nicholson's furious charge.

Archie Flynn had been assigned to a short safe beat on the borderline of Greenfield and Partick, a square acre of docile dwellings and timber warehouses where very little ever happened to disturb the peace. Like all other members of the Force he had been instructed to keep a weather-eye open for Daniel Malone and had in his pocket a printed bill which gave a detailed description of the felon. The language of the handbill made Malone sound like a fiend out of hell and Archie was damned glad he would not be abroad in the Greenfield much after dark for he doubted that he had the guts to deal with a desperate dangerous criminal armed with a military sabre.

Now that dusk had fallen Archie was skulking. There was no other word for it. He did not suppose that there would be any inspectors or sergeants sufficiently 'loose-endish' to come checking up on a mere third-grade constable and crabbed from one safe niche to another, his back always to a wall.

He was surprised when he saw Mrs Nicholson and, forgetting his apprehension, stepped out to greet her.

"I thought you were ordered t' stay indoors?" Archie said.

"I'm goin' to spend the night with a friend."

"Who's that then?"

"Mrs Frew, in Walbrook Street, where we used to live."

"Is Craig stayin' there too?"

"No, but if you see him please tell him where I've gone."

"Aye, I will." Archie peered at Kirsty. "Are you feelin' all right, Mrs Nicholson?"

"I'm – I'm fine."

"I'd walk down to Walbrook Street wi' you," said Archie, "but it's out o' the burgh an' I'm no' supposed to leave the beat durin' duty hours."

"I understand," said Kirsty. "I'm really all right. I can walk there myself."

"I don't think you should be—"

"Constable Flynn, I'm not a prisoner nor an invalid," Kirsty snapped. "If you see Craig—"

"I'll tell him," Archie promised.

The young woman gave him a nod and, apparently disinclined to linger, sidled round him and went on her way.

Archie put his fists on his hips and stared after her.

It was almost full dark now and the section that led down to Highland Street which led in turn to the end of Walbrook Street looked bleak and almost deserted. The big timber sheds, pulled back from the docks, employed only a handful of men and the 'change shift' had taken place at six o'clock. There was something about the young woman's gait, not just her pregnancy, that touched Archie, made him shelve his concern for duty and correctness and neglect his own nervousness.

"Mrs Nicholson," he called out. "Wait."

She stopped and turned round, holding a hand against the wall of one of the larger sheds.

Archie caught up with her. "I'll walk wi' you."

"I can manage, I tell you."

"Just to the end o' Walbrook Street," said Archie, compromising with her independence and challenging her irascibility.

The young woman sighed, a sucking breath that seemed to come from her stomach and not her lungs.

"Thank you, Constable Flynn."

"Call me Archie. I'm a pal o' Craig's after all. An' while we're bein' so friendly I think you should take my arm."

She put up no further argument but held on to him tightly through the quarter of a mile of dockland fringe that brought Archie to the very limit of his authority and Kirsty within sight of Walbrook Street.

"Well, there y'are," said Archie. "You'll be all right now, Mrs Nicholson. No' far to your friend's house, is it?"

"No, not far," said Kirsty.

She disengaged her arm from his and nodded her thanks but she did not linger. She seemed, Archie thought, driven by some urgency to get on into the broad gaslit street.

He watched her go, waddling, heavy and vulnerable, down the pavement by the railings of the posh terrace that curved away into a rain-wet infinity. He continued to watch her for two or three minutes and then he became aware that it would soon be time for the ending of his duty and that he had better make his way back to the Greenfield proper.

By God, he would be bloody glad to get off the streets and into barracks tonight for there something other than rain to bring a little shiver to the skin, though for the life of him Archie Flynn could not put a name to it, unless it was Malone.

Craig held the heavy stick in two hands as he had been taught to do when going in against a man armed with an edged weapon. He had kicked in the door of the pawnshop with two stabbing blows of his boot and a short surging attack with his shoulder. His heart clenched in his chest as he plunged over the threshold. Something small and fierce darted at him and he would have kicked at it if he had not heard its yowling and, not a moment too soon, realised that it was the little marmalade cat.

The beast scooted between his legs and out into the street. He heard the woman whose help he had purchased with his last sixpence scream as Tiggy went past her like a rocket.

"*Malone?*"

Craig gripped the stick in his fists and held it at a level with his throat. It would deflect a downward blow and could be raised or lowered in response to any angle of attack.

No attack came.

He peered into the gloom, into the jumble. He had been prepared to meet Malone head on, had expected a sudden violent encounter with the man and felt now a resurgence of that fear which had been deadened by excitement.

"*Come out here, y' bastard.*"

From behind the counter came a groan. Still cautious and alert Craig let himself through the door in the counter and almost tripped over old Joseph McGhee strapped to the cane chair.

Craig looked about him then swiftly knelt and untied the scarf from about the old man's mouth. He probed with his forefinger and scooped out the wad of paper that formed the gag.

"Was he here, Joseph? Was it him; Malone?"

"Yis."

"Has he gone?"

"Yis."

Craig took a grip on the chair and hoisted the old man up. There was blood on the side of his face and Craig's fingers were slippery with it. He wiped his hands on his lapels and fumbled with the old man's bonds.

"How long since he left?"

"Hour. Gone for—"

"Gone where, Joe?"

"For you."

"But how did he know where—"

"Or – or your – your wife."

"Christ!"

"Stole – stole a frocked coat, tall hat, bag."

"Are you wounded?"

"Mouth." Joseph, arms free, wiped his cheek, wincing, then caught at Craig's sleeve. "Leave me, son. You'd best be gettin' after him. He has a knife."

"The sword he stole?"

"Knife," said Joseph.

Kirsty saw the figure behind her when she was still two hundred yards from No. 19. She thought nothing of the appearance of a man dressed so elegantly, in such an old-fashioned style. The fact that he carried an American bag suggested that he was a gentleman making his way to visit friends or to seek shelter in a comfortable and respectable lodging. Perhaps he was a minister headed for Mrs Frew's.

Kirsty turned to face the street and then, for no valid reason, glanced again over her shoulder.

Adjacent to her was the bowling-green fence, that quiet stretch of Walbrook Street with the tall windows of drawing-rooms heavily curtained against the sting of wintry rain and the wind that whistled up from the river. The houses looked implacable and remote. There were no other pedestrians in her immediate vicinity, only two indistinct figures at the faraway corner.

The pain across her diaphragm burrowed downward. She pressed her hands to her stomach as if to contain it, to hold it to her for a little while longer. She looked back once more.

The gentleman was running. He was running straight at her with a long loping ungainly stride, the tile hat tipped back from his brow so that she could see his face.

She stumbled as she swung round, went down on one knee and thrust herself up again. She could hear no sound but the clashing of his boots on the pavement. She ran, ran as fast as she possibly could, ignoring the sudden flooding emptiness in her belly that seemed to have replaced pain.

If the child in her body had not been heavy she would have run like the wind, would have outstripped the man and reached the doorway of No. 19 long before he overtook her but she was not a girl now but a woman wrapped in motherhood, and would be killed because of it.

She did not turn again. She ran on, waiting for hands about her

325

neck or a cudgel to strike her skull. She was reconciled to the hopelessness of her situation. She opened her mouth to scream for help but the air in her lungs pumped so fast through her open lips that only a squeak came out. To cry for help she would have to stop and she did not dare stop. If she stopped she would collapse and he would have her. Deep in her mind was the terror that had lain dormant since that night at Hawkhead, a black fear that she would be penetrated against her will and now, with a baby grown in her body, that it too would be damaged by the savage indifference that was bred in men whether farmer or fugitive.

She found herself at the step of No. 19 and swung herself on to it, shouting in a pitiful, almost inaudible squeak.

By her left side the shape was like a gigantic crow flapping black wings. The knife tore down her shoulder and the upper part of her arm. The blow was cutting not direct and her clothing smothered the worst of it. She was at the door and beating on it with both fists before she realised that she was bleeding at all. It all seemed liquid and warm. She wondered if dying was like drowning. She fell, rolled stomach up, saw him above her, the long knife pointed down at her belly, at her child.

She gave a kick, caught him on the shins. He stepped back to the side and, stooping, pinned her to the stone, his left hand rammed like a stake into her breast.

Softly Malone said, "So I've got his cow, have I, an' his bloody calf? Next time I'm back here I'll get him too."

She waited for the knife to bury itself in her body. But it did not happen. She detected blurred movement, light spill over the step and, twisting, saw David in the doorway above her.

"David, help me," she cried.

Pressure lifted from her breast. Malone reared back. She heard the whack of David's fist upon Malone's flesh, saw more indistinct movements as the young man struck out again.

Malone toppled down the steps to the pavement, the carving-knife flying from his grasp.

David leapt after him but Malone was quick to find his feet and ran off down Walbrook Street towards Greenfield. David did not give chase. He knelt by Kirsty, touched her gently and then, without a word, lifted her into his arms and carried her into the house out of the rain.

"David, is she dead, is the poor girl dead?"

"Out of my way, Aunt Nessie, please."

"Where are you taking her?"

"To your bedroom."

"Is she not dead?"

"No, she's in labour," David said.

Frantically Kirsty clung to him, sure that if he was with her she would be safe from harm.

"I'll – I'll run out and fetch a doctor," Mrs Frew said.

"No time, I'm afraid," said David. "It's started."

Kirsty glimpsed the painting of gloomy old Saint Andrew glimmering on the stairs and then she was in bright light in the bedroom at the rear of the house.

"Oh, God, David!" said Mrs Frew. "What can you do?"

"Deliver her myself," David Lockhart said.

The force of the rain increased suddenly and dramatically. It came in great ferocious spirals over the cranes and gantries of the river reach, swept into the city from the west driving folk hastily into shelter or chasing them, with newspapers over their heads, in a gallop for home.

For five or ten minutes the deluge was so intense that the horse-trams ground to a halt, lines turned to rushing rivers and horses blinded by the tails of rain that lashed over the rooftops and scourged the cobbled roads. Men and women huddled in shop doorways, scanning the sky above the sizzling arc-lamps for sign of let or halt. In closes the street children crouched, grinning and stimulated, and watched the drops bounce outside and heard, with shivers of delight, the tearing sound of the downpour in the backcourts and thought of the big brown lakes that would lie like jelly in the hollows and how they would paddle and cavort in them and, the more inventive, make rafts to sail from shore to shore.

Archie was caught within sight of the *Vancouver Vaults*. He did not have the temerity to make a dash from the warehouse door to the public house and would not have been surprised to find some officious sergeant in there already waiting to take names. He turned up his collar and shrank back against the dripping woodwork and listened to the funny noise the rain made on the slatted wooden roof, like a million wee creatures in coppers' boots doing a dance on the tar-macadam cladding. He had just managed to light a cigarette and take a sook on it, holding it cupped in his palm, when a constable came charging across the end of the street.

Guiltily Archie dropped the cigarette and put his heel on it. At first he was inclined to sing dumb and stay hidden, then he recognised the figure and, disregarding the rain, ran out, shouting, "Craig, for God's sake, man. Come in here."

Craig skidded to a halt, swung round and came at Archie as if he intended to assault him.

Archie raised an arm defensively.

"What the hell's wrong wi' you?"

"Have you seen Malone?" Craig demanded.

"What? Naw. Naw."

"He's here, he's gone after Kirsty, he's wearin' a frock coat an' a tile hat."

"Christ!"

"You have seen him?"

"Frock coat—"

"*Archie?*"

"I saw her, your wife. She was goin' down to Walbrook Street. I walked part o' the way wi' her."

"Kirsty? She's supposed to stay at home."

"She said she was fine but she didn't look too grand to me," said Archie.

Craig laid a hand behind his neck and pinched it to make him tell the truth. "You bloody did see him, didn't you?"

"Aye, I'm thinkin' maybe I did."

"When?"

"A quarter-hour ago."

"Why didn't you challenge him?"

"I didn't know it *was* him, did I? In a bloody frock coat like a bloody toff."

"Where did you see him?"

Archie hesitated. "Goin' towards Walbrook Street."

Craig released his grip on Archie's neck and stepped back. He drew in a lungful of wet night air and expelled it.

"All right," he said. "Now, Archie, I want you to run to Ottawa Street—"

"Where are the coppers that are supposed to be with you?"

"Lost," said Craig curtly. "Listen, up to the station. Rouse them out, every man that's there. Malone's in the Walbrook Street area, dressed like I told you. He has a knife now, not a sword."

"How do you—"

"*Shift it, Archie.*"

"Where will you be, Craig?"

"Lookin' for my wife."

Wringing her hands, Mrs Frew said, "I cannot allow you to do this, David. It isn't – isn't decent."

"Decent or not, Aunt Nessie, I've no choice."

"Wait until I fetch a proper doctor."

"She is, I believe, close to expulsion. Do you want to risk her life and the baby's because of modesty?"

"How many babies have you delivered?"

"Twelve," David said. "Now, Aunt, I haven't time to argue the point. Will you please take off her garments then fetch clean linen and towels."

"Take off her—"

Angrily David said, "Will I have to do it myself, Aunt, when I've so many other things to get ready?"

"I still think—"

"There isn't any time," David told her again. "If it makes you fell better by all means leave on an upper garment, a nightgown, or put a sheet across her."

"But you've no – no instruments."

"I've these." He held up his hands.

Leaving his aunt to ponder and act upon his instructions he hurried out of the bedroom into the kitchen. He had not spoken to Kirsty yet, had not asked the questions that would confirm his opinion that birth was imminent. He was frightened of what he might find when he made an examination, what complications might present themselves, situations with which he could not cope. He had told his aunt the truth; he *had* delivered twelve babies, ten of them alive and kicking. He had not told her, however, what a harum-scarum thing the course in obstetrics was for youthful and exuberant students of the medical faculty, how the cynicism that marked the breed was never more manifest than when confronted with the mystery of birth, that messy entry into the world.

He recalled one night in particular when he had attended a woman in Maryhill in company with a fellow student, Binks. Binks had been half-seas over when the call had come and the woman had been mad with pain and restless. He had walked her round and round the tiny stinking kitchen, observed for most of the labour by four other children huddled under the table. Father had kept out of sight, drinking in some shebeen or other until the great mysterious event was over. Binks had fallen asleep on the woman's bed and when he had finally roused Binks to let the woman lie down, Binks had been sick all over the tousled clothes. Binks laughed about it later, boasted of it in fact, but he, David, had borne the brunt of it.

It would not be like that tonight, David told himself as he stripped off his jacket, rolled up his sleeves and laved his hands in soap and warm water. Aunt Nessie's bedroom was clean and warm and he would bully the woman into assisting him. He would need help. Kirsty Nicholson was in distress and, since the baby was premature, he might be faced with a transverse lie or a shoulder presentation or some other foetal abnormality. As he trimmed his fingernails with a pocket clipper, he ran over the procedures in his mind, rehearsing them.

He had, he suspected, only minutes to make ready and, now that he had committed himself, wasted no more time on self-doubt. If, after preliminary examination, he found a severe trauma or abnormality he would send at once for expert assistance or for an ambulance from the Western Infirmary. Somewhere in the vicinity there must be a doctor or midwife. Indeed if Walbrook Street had been less genteel there would have been a gang of spectators gathered about the door to offer help and advice. He went back into the bedroom.

Aunt Nessie had dressed Kirsty in a pretty floral-patterned nightgown and had draped a large Irish linen sheet about her lower limbs. Kirsty had assumed the position of 'naturalness'. He saw at once that his guess had been correct. She had entered commencement of the second stage. The membrane had ruptured and the sheet was stained with forewaters. The left shoulder and arm of her nightgown was bloody but Aunt Nessie, as an emergency measure, had padded it with a towel. He had quite forgotten that Kirsty had been wounded by the devil with the knife. He ignored the wound for a moment and got down on one knee by the bedside.

"When did the pains begin, Kirsty?"

"David?"

"Yes, it's only me, I'm afraid."

In spite of it all she tried to smile. She looked less than pretty, quite ravaged, in fact, but he felt towards her a greater weight of responsibility than he had ever felt in his life before. He brushed back her hair and touched his hand to her brow. She was perspiring but was not much fevered, not more than a degree or two. He must, of course, take the effect of shock into his calculations.

"The pains, Kirsty?"

"All – all day."

It was possible that she had gone through first stage labour without realising what it was, especially as the child was three weeks in advance of its term. Why had the blasted doctor not given her fuller instruction or put her in touch with a midwife who would have explained what to expect?

"I'm going to look, Kirsty," David said. "Hold tightly to my hand. Squeeze if the pain becomes too great to bear. Don't be afraid to cry out."

Aunt Nessie left the room. Had the whole thing become too much for her delicate sensibilities? Had she gone for help? To his relief the old lady soon returned with a canvas apron pinned over her frock, a big enamel basin full of hot water in her arms.

Kirsty panted. The vigour and frequency of abdominal contractions were considerable. Involuntarily she stretched her legs and feet and sought for the bedboard. He assisted her, helped her slide downwards. He adjusted the bolster beneath her head. Her face had become congested and she could not find breath to speak to him.

Observing the distention of the oval, David counted out the minutes. Thank God, it seemed that he would not have to interfere, that presentation would be normal.

The infant's scalp, dusted with dark hair, was visible.

As soon as the contraction eased he would begin the process of delivery, would guide the head to ensure that its smallest diameters passed through the outlet.

Kirsty gripped his hand fiercely and let out a cry.

Aunt Nessie touched his shoulder and passed him a napkin with which to cleanse the discharge.

Unbidden he heard again the voice of his obstetrics professor, James McKinnon, as he boomed out rudimentary instruction.

The core of that lecture, the language of it, had affected him oddly but the romance of the words had vanished when he had finally confronted the reality of a woman in the throes of labour. But with Kirsty's hand clutching his and the child's soft crown visible between her thighs David experienced once more, just before he began his work, a little of the wonder that some men find in woman's obligation.

"Factors in labour are," McKinnon had declared, "the Passages, the Powers, and the Passenger."

David glanced over his shoulder. Aunt Nessie had placed the basin on the rosewood table which she had swept clear of its clutter of dainty ornaments. She was watching with interest now.

"Bring me a reel of strong cotton thread, Aunt, if you will."

"Certainly," the widow said and went out.

David studied Kirsty for a moment and then put his hand upon her body, the sheet discarded.

Pain appeared to recede. She gasped and sought his arm. He could not give it to her. No further recession of the infant's head had occurred. It had engaged much more rapidly than he had thought possible.

With the fingers of his left hand he touched the crown and pressed it very gently.

"Kirsty," he said. "Bear down."

The Passenger was due to arrive.

Craig did not reach Walbrook Street or learn what had happened to his wife. At first, fear for Kirsty's safety churned within him but what really drove him on was hatred of Malone's cleverness. Malone did not have an excuse of poverty or ignorance or that miserable lack of will which induced most law-breakers to commit crimes. Malone was selfish, greedy and mendacious. To murder for revenge was evil. He had no heart at all. What was more, he coaxed from Craig a similarly heartless response. As he raced towards Walbrook Street through sheeting rain Craig felt as cold and hard as the pavement beneath his feet. Red anger contracted and his one real fear was that bloody Malone had slipped away, clever enough at the last to trade vengeance for freedom.

It was ironic that torrential downpour had brought the traffic of the district and its citizens to a temporary halt, that the only movement in the night was the scuttle of a train along the embankment, its funnel spouting sparks. Far, far off in the distance Craig caught the sound of a police whistle. He checked his dash for Walbrook Street and paused, chest heaving, cocked his head and listened intently for that 'chain' of shrill urgent whistles that would indicate that an officer had sighted quarry and required assistance. He heard nothing after that first faint blast and soon swung to the left and found his stride again – and saw not Malone but Sammy Reynolds, quite unmistakably Sammy, seated on a kipper box by a blank brick wall, with a torn black umbrella held over his head.

"Sammy?"

"Aye."

"Remember me?"

"Aye."

"I'm chasin' a man, a tall man in a black coat, with a lum hat on his head."

"Aye."

"Did he come this way? Did you see him?"

It was like crying into a close mouth and hoping for an echo. Craig could hardly believe his luck when Sammy nodded.

"When did you see him?"

"Just now."

"Please, Sammy, tell me where."

"He went up there."

"Up the embankment?"

"Aye."

"Are you sure?"

"Saw him, so I did."

Sammy gave the brolly a twirl, spinning droplets from protruding spokes, and looked, Craig thought, quite smug and manly for a moment.

He had to be certain, however. "Lum hat, frock coat?"

"Up there, t' the trains."

Craig gave the boy a gentle pat on the shoulder.

"You're a good lad, Sammy," he said, then ran.

Splashing, he crossed the road and threw himself at the barricade of heavy wooden sleepers that braced the ramp of earth, ash and charred grass, hauled himself over it and dropped to the base of the embankment proper. Instinct told him that Sammy had been right. It was exactly the sort of thing that Malone would do, make for the railway, claw on to a passing truck or wagon to ride along the edge of the Greenfield, through police cordons and away to Bowling or Dumbarton, any place that did not buzz with blue boys agog to nail him and see him topped.

Rain had turned the slope into mud. Craig slipped and slithered as he clambered towards the skyline. He did not feel winded or blown, did not notice that he was wet to the skin. He climbed swiftly, using his hands. Rain reflected every scrap of light and made a strange pale curtain across the sky. Craig could discern the plane of the railway and its curves, the bridge to his right and the small squat shape of a plate-layer's hut.

Crouched, cautious, he came out on to the stone-fill and checked the lines, up and down. A thousand yards away, towards Greenfield West, the local track linked at the junction. There was a signal-box, lit like a watchtower against the sky, tiny but distinct. He had no clue as to which direction Malone had taken, whether he had gone towards the city and the welter of lines that fanned out from the goods and mineral yards at Stobcross or had headed towards the West box.

Rain pocked the cinders and splintered the lines. Craig lay chest and belly against the ramp and wondered what the devil to do.

The engine loomed out of darkness, straight from the shed at Kelvinhaugh perhaps, a single tank-engine, sturdy pistons beating purposeful rhythm, two lamps like eyes, a streamer of smoke flaring from its flat funnel. Warily Craig watched its approach and then, glancing to his right, glimpsed the man by the plate-layer's hut just as he stepped from shelter to peer along at the advancing tank-engine.

Craig's heart skipped a beat. He held his breath and pressed himself against the cinders. It seemed ridiculous that Malone should still sport the tile hat, an obvious mark of identity, all that Craig needed to be certain that he had located the fugitive. He lowered himself down the slope, rolled on to his feet and ran across the mud towards the hut, screened by rising ground. Below, the lights of Greenfield looked like boats moored in a river delta. The cobbled lane that led through the tunnel under the bridge glinted like a flowing stream. Craig felt as if he was engaged in a race with a tank-engine. It chugged along the line above and behind and he darted glances over his shoulder to check on its position. At length he changed angle, scrambled up the ramp and came on to the shoulder thirty yards or so from the hut, crouched low.

Clearly Malone was considering the possibility of hoisting a ride on the engine. He had come to the edge of the down line and stood between the sleepers, poised and intent. He did not see Craig at first and Craig was able to narrow the distance between them. To his left, over the ridge of the railway, he was aware of warehouses, quays and moorings that flanked St John Street, of river traffic nosing through the falling rain. He tugged his truncheon from its holster and held it by his side.

Malone saw him, started, straightened.

For a split second Craig thought that Malone intended to hurl himself across the track in front of the engine but Malone was not so much of a fool as all that. He stood his ground and let the tank-engine thunder past.

"Is that you, Nicholson?" Malone said.

"Aye, it is."

"What are you doin' out here in this weather?"

"Lookin' for you."

"It seems you've found me."

"It seems I have."

"Now I suppose you'll want to take me in?"

"That's my job, Danny," Craig said.

"A hard job it'll be."

"I don't doubt it."

"The Dumbarton express train will be comin' through in a minute or two," Malone said. "Does it still slow at the signal at the bridge?"

"Usually it does, aye."

"I could be on it."

"It would be a rough ride, Danny."

"How much will the fare cost?"

"What?"

"How much will it cost for me to be on it an' for you to walk away?"

"No sum o' money will buy you that ticket."

"Forty pounds?"

"Where did you get—"

"Oh, I've got it," said Malone. "Right here in my pocket. Fifty pounds?"

Craig said, "Did you see my wife, Danny?"

"Your wife? What way would I see your wife?"

"You followed her into Walbrook Street."

"Not me, Craig. I wouldn't know your wife from a piece o' cheese."

"Same as you wouldn't know Joseph McGhee?" Craig said.

"Come on, damn it, how much will my last chance cost me?"

"I told you, Danny," Craig said. "I'll not be bought."

"You're goin' to try to take me in?"

"That's it."

"Christ, Nicholson, I had you pegged wrong right from the start."

"Will you come quietly, Danny?"

Malone laughed. "I did see your wife, as it happens. Not only did I see her, I stuck a knife right into her fat belly."

Craig said, "I'm not fallin' for your lies any more, Danny."

"It's no lie, sonny. It's the God's truth."

The passenger train from Glasgow emitted a shrill whistle as it cleared the tunnel at Stobhill. On the down line Craig saw a fire-smudge of a shunter halted in obedience to the signal at the single-track's end. In two or three minutes the express and the shunter would pass on to this section.

Craig plucked the silver whistle from his pocket, stuck it into his mouth and blew as hard as he could.

The sound seemed puny in the wide wet night.

He blew again, and again.

The shunter moved through the signal, over the bridge and into the section, rolling a host of empty wagons behind it.

Malone did not turn round.

"Arrest me, then," Malone said. "Take me in."

"Put your hands above your head, Danny. Step away from the track."

"Aw, naw. If you want me, sonny, you'll have to take me where I stand."

"The engines—"

"Don't tell me you're afraid o' the engines?"

Raising his baton Craig rushed forward.

It was a rash move, the wrong move, the move that Malone had been waiting for. Malone carried no knife but had found and concealed a length of rusty chain. He lashed out at Craig with it and caught the young man across the side of the head. Only the brim of his helmet prevented him being knocked insensible. He was, however, thrown off balance. He fell to one knee. Before Craig could rise again he was struck violently across his shoulders. On all fours he straddled the line. Out of the tops of his eyes he could see the shunter as it sped over the bridge. He lifted his baton and thrust it upward into Malone's groin, bored it in and lifted himself up as if he were sticking a pig. Malone roared and backed away and Craig, still dazed, hurled himself on to the man. They fell together, tangled, on the track. There they struggled, rolling on to the stone-fill between the sleepers, each trying to smother the other's blows and obtain the upper hand while the Dumbarton express rounded into the straight in a billow of smoke and steam.

Craig buried his fingers in the material of the frock coat, heavy with rain. Malone had lost his hat in the first assault and Craig could find no hold on the bristling scalp. He was not dominated by the larger man. He was strong too now. He wedged his knee under Malone's belly and drove up. Malone did not release his grasp of Craig's tunic and the young man was yanked to his feet. Leverage, force, balance were the elements of the struggle. Craig's fear grew as, over Malone's shoulder, he saw the shunting engine loom up, heard its piercing whistle.

The fireman, leaning from the cab, had spotted them but Craig doubted if there would be line enough left to brake the engine to a halt. He had a horror of being ground beneath the metal wheels and he shouted his fear into Malone's face.

He did not, however, let go.

The express reached them first.

Noise enveloped him, flickering lights flayed at his senses and numbed his reason. With effort he kept his eyes open, wide open, as the locomotive and its carriages swayed and thundered only inches from his head. He had secured a good firm grip on Malone's collar and held fast by it, the baton cocked in his fist.

The wide night, the quays, the river, the Greenfield's little streets were all blotted out by the roar of the Dumbarton express and the shriek of the braking shunter.

Craig no longer knew who was clinging to whom and felt not shock but consternation when the buffer knocked him down.

The sponge, filled with warm soapy water, soothed her and she lay light and lethargic as it brushed her limbs. She did not know who it was that held the sponge or why she felt so contented in the midst of exhaustion. She had never been bathed before, never been given that close attention, had never been nursed.

Whirling, whirling, her mind roved about the problem without settling upon it. She could not concentrate upon the thing that troubled her, that would rouse her from the soft luxurious state of semi-sleep. Lazily she floated in a moist innocence, like a baby in the warm dark womb.

She opened her eyes.

"Where is it?" she demanded.

"Easy, Kirsty, be easy," a man's voice said. "Don't excite yourself."

"Where's my baby?"

"He's here."

"I want to see—"

"Aunt Nessie's washing him. She'll only be a moment. Please, Kirsty, lie back."

"Is it – is it—"

"It's a boy."

"A boy. I want to—"

"In due course, Kirsty. You've lost a lot of blood, you know."

"Where *is* he?"

She was desperate now but so weak that she could not even pull herself into a sitting position. She could find no purchase on the slippery surface of the bed. She gave a little cry of frustration and shook her head to clear away the clouds and bring her eyes into focus.

"See, dear, here he is."

"Hold him closer, Aunt."

Kirsty felt pillows being drawn behind her and leaned on them gratefully. Somebody pulled a sheet over her breast. She sought to free her arms. A towel stroked her brow. She blinked and at last saw that it was David by her side and that Mrs Frew was stooping over her, smiling.

In the widow's arms was a cocoon of towels, fresh and white. In the towels was a tiny red creature, so scarlet and angry that Kirsty felt, for a moment only, an unexpected twinge of revulsion.

"Is that—?

"Yes, that's him, Kirsty; that's your son."

"What's wrong wi' him?"

"Nothing. He's perfectly sound," David said.

She could not take her astonished gaze from the tiny red thing. David went on, "He's exceedingly small, however, and will need to be nurtured with great care for a month or two."

"I want to hold—"

"Oh, isn't he lovely," said Mrs Frew.

Upside-down her friend's features seemed predatory. She was beginning to recall all kinds of ugly things. She could see Mrs Frew's teeth, tongue, nostrils, and a wickedly-pointed brooch at the throat of her dress. The dress itself was stained.

Struggling again, Kirsty stretched out her arms.

"He's mine."

David put a hand upon her arm. "Kirsty, listen to me—"

"*Mine.*"

"Kirsty, you're in no fit condition to nurse him yet. I've sent a messenger, a neighbour, to fetch an ambulance to take you to the Samaritan Hospital where you'll receive expert care."

"He's not sick, is he?"

"Not exactly," said David. "Just – early."

Mrs Frew put the cocoon against Kirsty's breast. Instinctively Kirsty folded her elbow to receive it. She let her head sink and touch the folds of the towel and looked at the tiny red face with its imperfect features and dusting of dark hair. His eyes were closed but, when she touched him, he pursed his lips and uttered a thin sound, a long *eeeeeeeee*, and she knew that he was alive and breathing; and she began to cry. David put an arm about her.

"You've had a dreadful time, Kirsty. But it's all over now."

"Did you—?"

"I had to," he said. "There was nobody else and the wee chap was reluctant to wait. I hope you don't mind."

David was in shirt-sleeves, had no tie, no collar. He looked weary, dishevelled and flushed. Now that she had her baby close to her she felt quite lucid.

She said, "I'm grateful to you, David. I would have died, perhaps, and him with me if it hadn't been for you."

"Nothing to it," David said, flustered. "Nothing to it at all."

Kirsty said, "The baby will be all right, won't he?"

"Of course he will."

"Why are you sendin' us to hospital?"

"As a precautionary measure," David told her. "It's absolutely normal in premature births."

"Was he hurt?"

"Don't you remember what happened?" Mrs Frew asked.

"I remember Malone. What happened to Malone?"

"He's gone," David told her. "He'll be caught and brought to book, never fear."

"He tried to kill me, didn't he?" Kirsty glanced at the neatly bound padding that protected her arm. "I see. I see."

"Yes, he got you with a knife," said David. "It's a clean wound but a deep one. That's why you've lost so much blood."

"I thought—"

"The baby will go with you," David told her. "You'll both ride in state in a nice comfortable ambulance. It isn't far."

For a minute Kirsty was quiet, her eyes on her child, then she said, "Could I not stay here?"

"You can come back here," said Mrs Frew. "To convalesce, to regain your strength."

The baby whimpered. Kirsty hugged him and said, "I'll need to see him fed."

"In a while," said David. "You really must rest until the ambulance arrives."

"I am tired, aye, but I want to keep him by me."

David said, "I'll hold him, if you like."

"Don't take him away."

"I'd never do that. See, I'll sit right here." He leaned carefully over her. "May I?"

"Aye," Kirsty said.

She watched him lift her baby, heard the sweet little girning sounds and, as she sank back against the pillow, saw David settle beside her on the bed with the wee one tucked safe in the crook of his arm.

She did not know whether she had slept for minutes or hours. All sense of time's passage had ceased. The whole of that day and evening had furled into a skein of moods and sensations and, in her present sleepy state, she could not separate one from the other. The mutter of voices in the room brought her awake. Once more she forced her eyes to open, saw not David and her baby beside her but only the rough texture of an ulster and the sombre plane of a police uniform at the bed's end.

She had a raging thirst, her mouth so dry and sticky that she could hardly croak let alone cry out. She had a sly instinct, though, a moment in which she was convinced that they had lied to her, had conspired to deceive her, that she had not given birth at all, that the thing wrapped in towels was not her baby, that it was a monster deformed beyond hope and that David had put it away. She lay quite still, enduring the torment of thirst, lids fluttering, and listened to learn the truth.

To her surprise they were not talking of her or her child. They were arguing. Hearing the see-saw of familiar voices, male and female, she found that she could put a name to the speakers and identify the owner of the overcoat.

Hugh Affleck said, "I got here as fast as I could, Nessie."

"We could all have been murdered. Indeed, if it hadn't been for David—"

"Yes, yes. I admit it was fortuitous—"

"Fortuitous is not the word for it. If it hadn't been for him that brute would have slain us all. David acted like a hero, I'll have you know. I think he was sent by Divine Providence."

"Be that as it may, Nessie, I'll need to talk to the girl."

"Tell her, do you mean?"

"Of course, tell her."

A third voice, accented and distinct; Sergeant Drummond said, "Has she not been asking for him already, Mrs Frew?"

"As a matter of fact, no, she hasn't mentioned his name."

"Is she in delirium?"

"What *do* you want, Hughie? Another 'statement'? Can you not give her peace?"

Sergeant Drummond said, "Nicholson is her husband, Mrs Frew, and the father of the infant—"

"Oh, you always stick together, you men. If Craig Nicholson's concerned about his wife and child why is he not here with her?"

"He can't be," said Hugh Affleck.

"*Shhh!* I think Kirsty's awake."

They turned, all three, and she saw their faces, pale and solemn, looking down at her, that strange upside-down ugliness in each of them. Mr Affleck loomed towards her, huge and menacing in the unbuttoned coat, his hair plastered flat, the deerstalker hat held in both hands, his fingers twisting the material.

Kirsty licked her parched lips.

"I can hear you," she said.

Behind the man, out of sight, a door opened.

David said, "The ambulance is here at last. I've the baby all wrapped and ready. I would prefer not to delay, Aunt Nessie."

"Do you hear that, Hughie?" Mrs Frew said. "No delay."

Hugh Affleck said, "I'll only be a moment."

"Ambulances cost money."

"Nessie, hold your damned tongue."

Kirsty said, "Did you catch him?"

"Yes, lass. Yes, we caught him."

"Craig?"

"The man who hurt you has been caught."

"Craig?"

"Daniel Malone will not trouble you again."

"Oh, tell her if you must, Hughie."

"Your husband – Craig – he caught Malone for us. Single-handed."

"Where is he?"

"There was an accident."

"Where is he?"

"Injuries sustained in the course of duty."

"David," Kirsty said. "Where's the baby?"

He came immediately and knelt beside her. His face did not look at all ugly or warped. He took one of her hands in both of his hands. "The baby's fine, Kirsty, all ready for his first journey. Your husband is fine too, really he is."

"You're only sayin'—"

"He can't be here with you because he has a lot of cuts and a fracture – not serious, I'm told – of the wrist. I think he'll be able to visit you tomorrow, once he's properly patched up."

"Craig performed his duty with great courage and fortitude, lass," said Sergeant Drummond. "You should be proud of him."

Her relief at the news was mild, almost casual.

"We must go," David said.

The sheets were fresh and dry, the blanket as soft as moss, the big quilt silky as a cocoon. When David lifted her she felt light and weightless in his arms.

The faces receded, voices too.

"Will you come with me, David?" she whispered.

David answered, "Yes."

The sun came up a little after four and all the signs were that it would be another beautiful day. The river lay flat as varnish and the only indication that the tide had turned came from the gulls that, for some reason nobody could explain, abandoned the Govan shore and flocked to the roofs of timber warehouses along the end of St John Street. Their cries were raucous and fretful, at odds with the tranquillity of the summer morning but, Craig thought, they made a fitting sort of chorus for dawn in the city.

He liked the night-shift best of all, though he longed for the time, not far hence, when he would be allocated a more lively beat and a more amiable companion than dour Peter Stewart. Even so, with the long cold months of spring behind him and the sun in the sky and hawthorn in bloom and laburnum and lilac colourful in the park, he felt that he had little to complain about, even although nothing seemed quite as satisfactory as he had expected it to be; not his marriage, not fatherhood, and certainly not the aftermath of his capture of Daniel Malone.

The fractured wrist and twisted knee joint healed quickly but he was left for a week or two with the nightmare in his mind, that dream of steam and steel and blackness, Danny Malone's face, streaming blood, at the centre of it like the head on an old coin. It still seemed a miracle that the shunter and all its wagons had raggled over him, that it was Malone who had had his skull cracked by the link of the shunting-chain and had lain in his arms for what seemed an eternity while the wagons rolled and chuckled over them and the brakes squealed and finally brought the load to a halt. And bloody Daniel Malone had managed to escape justice after all, had not collected his just deserts by stepping on to the gallows with a hood over his head and a rope around his neck. Danny was still alive, after a fashion, locked away for ever in the depths of the Judgehead Asylum for the Criminally Insane. The big shunting-chain had done what society could not, had reformed him instantly, knocking all cunning and wickedness away even as it cracked his skull and addled his brains.

Malone would never be fit to stand trial for his crimes, Superintendent Affleck said; it was not in the nature of Scottish law to top a fellow who had lost not only his wits but even the power to stand unaided. Craig regretted it, would have preferred to have had Danny Malone go up those wooden steps like Satan's bosom pal, unrepentant, unrecondite, puffing on a last cigar and tipping his hat to all his chums and the adoring females that would gather at the gallows' foot to bid him farewell, to bow out in the grand manner as he would have been allowed to do in days of yore.

It was daft to think in such a manner. Malone had been evil, had tried to kill Kirsty, among his crimes, and Craig said not a word about his regrets or his nightmares to a living soul. He pondered them from time to time, however, as the weeks stole past and the new shift system came into operation and he trudged the quiet night streets with Peter Stewart one week in three; and slept better in daylight with bairns rampaging outside the window and his own child girning in the kitchen, though Kirsty did her best, now that she was well again, to keep the wee beggar quiet.

342

No great lasting fame had accrued from his 'arrest' of Daniel Malone. He had been summoned to the drill hall in Percy Street, marched out before the ranks of the Burgh Police Force and had a letter of commendation read over his head by Mr Organ who had then shaken his hand and had presented him with the letter, a sort of scroll with the Burgh Seal on it, in a cardboard tube. He had been promoted a full grade as reward, which meant more money in his pocket and a little more status in Ottawa Street. He found too, oddly, that many folk who had thought him a nark and a traitor now regarded him with no more than natural antipathy and would even give him a grudging nod when they passed him in the street. All the newspapers reported the incident but Danny had not been at large long enough to stir public imagination, had been nailed before he could become a menace to public safety, a bogeyman to haunt the Greenfield after dark.

Craig had had his name in print several times over, had been labelled 'brave' and duly praised for what he had done but there had been no outcome from all of that either, except that he clipped the pieces from the papers and sent them to Gordon in the care of Mr Sanderson at Bankhead Mains. Gordon had even managed to write a reply, a short, stilted, jocular note which had told him very little of what was happening at home and had contained no postscript from their mother.

Night-shift duty, even back-shift, suited Craig just fine. He had the bed in the front room and Kirsty had moved into a new bed in the hole-in-the-wall in the kitchen where she could be near the baby for feeding and changing, let Craig sleep undisturbed. She had her own routine, shaped around his shifts, of course, and seemed happy enough to tend the skinny wee thing and give him all the special attention that such an early arrival demanded for survival and growth and in which she had been instructed at the Samaritan before her discharge; bathing, changing, feeding, a whole smelly, skittery rigmarole that rapidly thinned Craig's paternal feelings and drove him out of No. 154 to swim in the pond of the Cranstonhill Baths or exercise in the police gymnasium. Sometimes he would take a tram into the city centre and stroll the populous main streets or slip into *The Heritage*, a cosy public house at the western end of Argyle Street where off-duty coppers from several burghs congregated to drink and talk shop.

He had insisted on choosing his first-born's name, however, had been adamant about it. It was his name and his father's name: Robert Craig Nicholson. Kirsty shortened it immediately to Bobby and Craig was happy enough with the contraction which seemed well suited to such a spindly wee creature.

It was Kirsty who stamped her feet about kirk baptism, though the birth had been registered at once.

"I thought you'd want him christened quick," Craig had said, "just in case – you know – anythin' happens to him."

"Baptism's not an insurance policy," Kirsty had said. "Besides, we have to join the church first."

"Both of us?"

"Aye."

"Well, I suppose it's not somethin' to rush into."

"I have to find out somethin' first," Kirsty had said.

"Find out what?"

"Whether or not you an' me have to be church married."

"Church married? We're not married at all."

"I don't think we have to show marriage lines or anythin' like that."

"Better find out," said Craig. "Look, if it comes to it, we can slip quietly off to the registry."

"I'll enquire," Kirsty had said, "about baptism."

"Aye, you do that."

It rankled him that she showed no eagerness to legitimise their 'marriage' but he was too stubborn to go down on one knee and beg her to do it. If it did not affect the baby and she was happy then it suited him well enough to let matters stand as they were.

She had not yet allowed him to sleep with her.

"I'm not right yet," she would tell him.

He did not understand what 'right' meant but did not ask for an explanation which, he suspected, would involve a catalogue of messy disorders since that's what birth and motherhood seemed to be all about. He did not understand much about Kirsty Barnes, really, and concerned himself less with surrender than with a gradual and subtle retreat.

Nothing much happened in the course of the summer night duty, no break-ins, no fires, no 'suspicious characters' to question and move along, no lost weans to be found, no 'disturbances' to be quieted. Routine inspections had unfolded step by step until the sun had come up in dabs of saffron and pink and the gulls made their mysterious migration from Govan to the Greenfield. Peter and he made a last circle of warehouses and, about five-thirty, started back for the corner of Banff Street where, under the optician's sign, they would be met and relieved.

Peter said, "Aye, there he is again."

"Who?" Craig glanced up from his beat book.

"Your shadow."

"God Almighty, does the wee bugger never sleep?"

"Will I chase him away?" said Peter.

"Naw, let him be. He's doin' no harm, I suppose."

"What does he want, though?"

"I don't know."

"Will I ask him?"

"He'll just run away an' then come back again?"

"Must drive ye daft, Craig, havin' a shadow."

Craig shrugged. "You get used to it."

"Is he starved, is that it?"

"He never asks for anythin'."

Peter stopped, turned and stared at Sammy Reynolds who made no attempt to 'vanish' but stopped too and stood, hands in trouser pockets, looking back at the coppers. He wore a filthy shirt and had abandoned shoes and stockings for the summer months. His hair, tousled and unwashed, made a sticky sort of halo round his head.

Craig called out, "Hey, Sammy, can ye no' sleep?"

Sammy answered, "I've got somethin'."

"What's that then?" said Craig.

"Got somethin' good."

"Come on over, Sammy, an' let's have a swatch at whatever it is."

"What about him, but?"

"Constable Stewart'll no' bite you, not if you've done nothin' wrong," said Craig. "Hurry up, though. I'm off shift in ten minutes."

Sammy hesitated and then came forward.

Peter whispered, "Does he not go to school?"

"Only when the truant officer catches him."

Sammy was shy in the presence of a stranger, though he had been observing Peter Stewart for most of the week and had dogged Craig's tracks on back-shift and day-shift and must know by now all the routines and systems of the burgh force.

"What's this you've got then, Sammy?" Craig said.

The boy fumbled in the breast pocket of the torn shirt and brought out a whistle on a chain.

"See," he said proudly, holding it up.

"Where did you get that?" said Craig.

"Found it."

"Don't lie, son," said Peter Stewart.

"I did. I found it."

"It's a nice one," Craig said. "Can I see it for a minute?"

Sammy extracted the chain from his pocket and dangled the whistle out for Craig's scrutiny.

Peter Stewart said, "Is it real?"

"Aye, it's real. It's old an' rusty but it's got a number on it," Craig said. "Where did you find it, Sammy?"

"On the midden."

"Where?"

"Our midden."

"At the Madagascar?"

"Aye. Buried down deep," Sammy said. "It's good."

"He shouldn't have that," said Peter Stewart. "It's official issue."

"I wonder who it belonged to an' why he threw it away."

"Mine now," said Sammy and swung the whistle back into his possession on the short length of chain. "See, I can blaw it."

"No, Sammy, don't—"

Too late; the boy stuck the whistle into his mouth, puffed out his cheeks and gave a great blast that, to the constables' relief, resulted in no more than a hiss from the rusted barrel.

"It's broken," Peter Stewart said.

"Naw, it's no'," Sammy cried. "Hear this."

He thrust the whistle into his mouth once more and blew again, reddening with effort, but managed no sound but a lisping hiss.

Peter glanced questioningly at Craig.

Sammy wet-lipped and panting, said, "Is that no' awful good?"

"First class, Sammy. Just like the real thing."

"Like you do it."

"Aye, just the same."

"Be like you, eh?"

"When you grow up, perhaps."

"Got ma whistle already."

"Give it another go, Sammy."

Still no sound of any volume came from the pitted barrel. Only Sammy could hear the good strong ardent blast that would make dogs sit up and take notice, would make bad men cower and bring coppers running to his side.

"Good, eh?"

"Craig, we should report—" said Peter Stewart.

"Marvellous, Sammy," said Craig. "Now you keep that whistle polished an' in tune until we're ready for you; right?"

"Right, Mr Nicholson."

346

"Say goodbye to Constable Stewart."

Sammy snapped his right hand to his brow, saluted smartly. Peter Stewart did not return the mark of respect but turned and walked off towards 'the spectacles' that overhung the corner of Banff Street and Brooks' Loan. Craig fell into step with him.

"That whistle had an official number on it," Peter said.

"An old number."

"The lad's crazy anyway."

"Look behind, Peter."

At a respectful distance Sammy marched along bootless, bare feet matching the constables' gait, an unmistakable mimicry. He still had his hand to his brow and the whistle in his lips, cheeks huge with the force of the blasts he blew.

"Cheeky young devil!"

"Harmless," Craig said. "Anyway, can you not hear it?"

"What?"

"The whistle."

"What?"

"I can – when I listen hard enough."

"You're as daft as he is, then."

"I wish I was," said Craig. "By God, I wish I was."

The Greenfield had but one park, a modest fifteen acres of lawns, flowerbeds, trees and shrubs. It had been presented to the burgh in the year of 1871 by the family of Sir James Forrester who had been born to a pig-farmer's wife in a hovel near the Madagascar and, by dint of hard work and imagination, had risen to become a magnate in shipping and had made a vast fortune in trading with Canada. For its size the Forrester Park was excellently well equipped. It had a bandstand, a boating-pond, a playground for children and an imposing statue of Sir James in the centre of a cartwheel of gravel pathways. Towards the river there were groves of willow and great dark banks of evergreens and two great chestnut trees and quiet arbours where lovers, if they were quick, might kiss and touch unseen. Its walks were broad and could accommodate two perambulators riding abreast and there were many sheltered benches along their lengths. While the Forrester did not have the 'tone' of the West End or the Botanical Gardens it attracted a fair share of nursemaids and nannies as well as street arabs and old folk and it was to the Forrester that Kirsty wheeled her son to take the air each afternoon when the weather was fine.

She had a need to be out of the house, to be on the move, and she needed time with her baby when she did not have to creep about and remember that Craig was asleep in the front bedroom and wonder if he was being disturbed by kitchen sounds or by Bobby's occasional wails.

It was Mrs Frew who had presented her with the perambulator, a magnificent carriage-style Cornwall with a joined hood, brass handles and a clip brake. It was quite the handsomest pram in the park, Kirsty felt, and the envy of all the other mothers and nannies. With her strength resumed after the ordeal of that terrible night in March she walked briskly, bowling along the outer walk before she cut down the long avenue that divided the park and linked its two gates. Sometimes, quite often in fact, Nessie Frew would catch a tram up from Walbrook Street and would wait for Kirsty on a bench near the main gate and would walk with her and have a shot with the pram; and sometimes Mrs Frew would bring a picnic in a basket and they would spread a blanket on the grass under the trees and drink tea from a flask or fizzy lemonade and eat seedcake and Nessie Frew would talk and talk and talk and reveal to Kirsty aspects of her character that she had shown to nobody else, not even Hughie, and exchange confidences with the young woman in the assurance that her 'secrets' would be safe with her friend; and Bobby, this past week or two, would seem to be listening too as if he found his 'Aunt Nessie's' confessions fascinating, until he was distracted by trembling leaves overhead or the glitter of sunlight on the pond or the sudden whirring flight of a fat pigeon as it swooped down to scrounge for crumbs.

Afternoons in the park meant a lot to Kirsty whether Nessie Frew was with her or not, and she felt restored and strengthened by her jaunts out of the shadow of the tenements, freed for a time from the thin but perceptible tensions of her odd, uncertain 'marriage' to Craig. She had come so far since that bitter blue evening when she had led the horse up to Hawkhead, when Clegg had terrified her, and Craig had stood by her. But since then she had glimpsed a world of possibilities, had seen things that she could not have imagined twenty months ago, had met people of a different stamp from the villagers of the Carrick. Perhaps if she had married Craig in Bankhead kirk, all neat and legal, had become his wife in that narrow and familiar landscape she would not have had in her a faint, inconstant yearning, a restlessness that she could not properly define, a need to taste the adventure of romance.

Stern with herself, and loyal, however, she put no names and no faces to that misty feeling, and told herself, sometimes out loud, that Craig loved her as best he could and showed it as best he could and had kept his end of the bargain by providing security and a home.

Craig had been in a jovial mood that morning. He had kissed her, had held Bobby on his knee for three or four minutes while she had fried bacon for breakfast. But Craig had gone off to bed straight after the meal and had been snoring before the Burgh Hall clock had struck seven. She had sat on the low chair by the grate and had uncovered her breasts and had fed Bobby the first of the six small feeds that the senior female nurse at the Samaritan had recommended. Kirsty had no notion of what a 'small feed' meant or how to measure one and she let the infant suck until he seemed satisfied. She had no lack of milk, had not, as had at first been feared, become dry in the wake of her ordeal and from loss of blood. Her arm and shoulder had healed rapidly, leaving only slender white scars and an itching that did not seem to want to go away. She felt that she was in good health again and had certainly found energy enough to care for Bobby-Come-Early who needed a great deal of attention in those first months of life.

Kirsty was utterly devoted to her son, possessive but not foolishly so. She did not fly off the handle when Craig lifted him awkwardly from his cot, when Mrs Frew planted scores of moist kisses all over his brow, when Mrs Swanston prodded him critically and declared that he was not very sturdy and would be lucky to survive a winter, not even when young Calum Piper tried to lull him to sleep by playing a reel on the chanter right into the hood of the pram. Even so, she preferred to have him all to herself, to revel in the unique intimacy of their relationship and did not have to divide her attention with Craig or anyone else.

On that beautiful summer's afternoon there seemed to be no threat at all to Bobby's comfort; no wind, no trace of rain, no acrid drift of smoke from the tannery, not even the anvil clang of the foundry or the pounding of its massive steam hammer to make him blink. She had him peacefully to herself and experienced a touch of contentment which some fortunate women substituted for happiness without ever knowing the difference.

She scudded along the pavement to the park at a speed that, in six months or so, would have Bobby sitting up and prattling with delight. Now, though, he lay on his side, snug under lace and protected from the sun by a canopy of pale brown holland. His eyes were open, that dark little glint in them, and there was no sound of protest on his lips. Perhaps Bobby too was content, Kirsty told herself, though she could no more tell with him than she could with Craig what it was that swung his little moods about, that made him girn at one minute and lie quiet and good as gold the next.

She bowled through the gates of the Forrester and glanced at once towards the bench where Mrs Frew sometimes sat.

Nessie Frew was not there today.

David Lockhart was. He had his aunt's wicker basket on his knee and a book in his hand. He wore a jacket of cool grey linen and black shoes. He did not seem to need to see Kirsty to know that she had arrived and he turned at once and got to his feet, put the book into the basket and, smiling, came forward to greet her.

Kirsty flushed. It had been three months now since she had last seen David. He had come to call on her during her stay in the Samaritan but she had been too groggy to do more than thank him for saving her life, and saving her baby too. He had been modest, had protested the importance of his role in the events of that night, had left a bunch of Dutch daffodils by the side of her bed and had gone back, she supposed, to his own sort of life.

He had written to her once, through Aunt Nessie Frew, and Kirsty had written back to him, a short note of gratitude. Since then she had heard news of him only through Mrs Frew, and not much of that. For a moment, though, when she saw him there in the sunlight she felt that she had known him all her life long, that she had never been without him in her heart. She knew instantly that there was no sin and no deception in her feelings for him, only that their lives were out of kilter and all that she was and all that she supposed David to be would keep them in this innocent state, meeting and parting, yet never being quite separate again.

She stared at him, then dropped the brake on the pram.

David put his fingers self-consciously to his collar.

"Don't you like it?" he asked.

"I didn't realise that you'd become a minister."

"Well, not quite the genuine article, not yet."

"But the dog-collar – ?"

"Brand new. I bought it off the shelf this morning."

"Then you're ordained?" Kirsty said.

"I'm licensed to preach the Gospel but I won't be inducted and ordained until I have a parish of my own."

"A parish in China?" Kirsty said.

"I've decided not to go back to China."

"But, I thought – your father an' mother—?"

"They'll have to contain themselves until Jack gets there."

"You're not leaving after all?"

He shook his head. "No."

"After all that hard work, all that training?"

"Don't tell me you disapprove, Kirsty," he said. "Don't you want me to stay in Scotland?"

"Yes, oh dear, yes."

"Good," David said.

She felt, however, a strange panic in her. She had reconciled herself to being apart from him, not separate but safely distanced. She felt that she could best love him in her thoughts and in her memory. Now he had told her that it was not to be, that she must learn a deeper truth, find out by practice what loyalty and fidelity meant. He was not, and never would be, the sort of man who would force a choice upon her, who would challenge her and destroy what there was between them. She did not need him to explain it to her.

She did not know David Lockhart well, though never again, she felt, would any man know her so well. She wanted to ask him outright why he had changed the direction of his vocation, what reason he had found to stay here. But she was afraid that he would tell her the truth.

"In the meantime I've been taken on as an assistant at St Anne's," David said. "And I'll lodge with Aunt Nessie in Walbrook Street for a while."

"That's – that's convenient."

"It's what I want, Kirsty, what I really want," David said, without gravity. "Besides, I'd like to be in the vicinity, shall we say, while this little chap's growing up."

"Will you christen him? Can you?" she heard herself say.

"Now, now, don't rush me." David laughed. "No, alas, I can't administer the Sacraments until I'm inducted."

"Will you be there, though?"

"Of course, if you want me to."

"Yes."

"Are you sure that your husband won't object."

"How can he? After what you did," Kirsty said and then, sensing that she was touching on a dangerous subject, asked, "What else can you do, as well as preach the Word?"

"Funerals and weddings. The really serious stuff, that will have to wait."

"Are funerals and weddings not serious?"

"Kirsty, are you teasing me?"

"Yes."

"Thought so," he said. "Very well, to make up for it you'll have to let me have a shot of the pram."

"Are you licensed for prams?"

"Oh, I see. Taking charge of Master Nicholson is very serious stuff indeed. How is he? Is he thriving?"

"You're the doctor. See for yourself."

Gently David lifted the fringe of the canopy. He held his hand aslant to prevent the sun's rays falling directly on to the baby's face. He leaned to inspect the child that he had brought into the world.

Kirsty watched. As she watched she saw tenderness and love in David's expression. Her hesitations waned away. She could not deny what she felt for him, though she understood even then how the emotion must be expressed. There was too much honour in him for there ever to be more between them than friendship. But love without loving had a quality all its own and would perhaps survive long after passion and desire had burned away. She put her head under the canopy and the tip of her ear touched his shiny collar, her hair brushed softly against his neck.

"Well?" she whispered. "What do you think, David?"

"He's filling out nicely. Look, I think he realises that we're talking about him."

She gave her attention to her child, to the dark, alert eyes that would soon find focus and survey the world that she would make for him. It was so warm, so still under the canopy and the sounds from the park were filtered and soft-edged, the motion of air in the trees like a murmur, faint and far off.

"David?" she said.

"Hush, Kirsty," he told her.

Together they emerged from the stillness under the brown holland, close together but not quite touching.

"Walk with me, David, if you have the time."

"How far, Kirsty?"

"Twice around the park."

"What then?" he said.

"Then I must go home."

"You'll always go home to him, won't you?"

"Yes, always," Kirsty said. "But I wish—"

"Hush," he told her again, then stooped and picked up the picnic basket, unclipped the brake, grasped the handle and pushed the perambulator forward. "We'll walk together, though."

"Why not?" said Kirsty and fell into step by his side.